WITHOUT YOU HERE

A novel by
Jody Hobbs Hesler

Flexible Press
Minneapolis, Minnesota, 2024

Print ISBN: 979-8-9887213-8-3
eBook ISBN: 979-8-9887213-9-0

Flexible Press LLC
Editors William E Burleson
Vicki Adang, Mark My Words Editorial Services, LLC
Cover William E Burleson

"An event occurs in a child's life that sears into her body and brain. She loses the one she loves most, who is also the person she fears she'll become. Jody Hobbs Hesler shuffles the past and present to mimic the fluidity of memory in this heartfelt, redemptive, and compassionate novel."
—Sharon Harrigan, author of the novel *Half* and the memoir *Playing with Dynamite*

"Can a niece inherit the mental illness of her adored aunt, along with her passions and gloriously unruly hair? Like a double helix tracing the lives and shared struggles of Noreen and Nonie, *Without You Here* is as intricately composed as it is deeply moving."
—Jane Alison author of *Meander, Spiral, Explode; The Sisters Antipodes*

"Jody Hobbs Hesler's heartbreaking and compelling novel *Without You Here* excavates the years that lead up to a tragic event and that follow from it, asking key questions: Can we escape the fate that others imagine for us? What happens when attempts to save ourselves from the past entrap us in the present? Hesler writes with nuance and beauty about mental illness and resilience, family and friendship and love, about characters who are so much more than a diagnosis. She is a masterful storyteller, both honest and hopeful."—Lori Ostlund, author of *After the Parade* and *The Bigness of the World,* and editor for the Flannery O'Connor Award for Short Fiction

Bear the weight of my voice and don't forget—
things haunt. Things exist long after they are killed.

–J. Jennifer Espinoza, "Things Haunt"

Resources

Although this novel is a work of fiction, the problems its
characters struggle with are very real.

If you or anyone you know is contemplating suicide,
please call 988 or the National Alliance on Mental Illness
(NAMI) hotline by phone 1-800-273-TALK (8255)
or text TALK to 741741.

Support is also available for family members and friends of
those lost to suicide at the American Society for Suicide Prevention (afsp.org) or at the Alliance of Hope (allianceofhope.org).

For anyone in an abusive relationship, please contact the
National Domestic Violence hotline for confidential support at
1-800-799-7233.

Without You Here

Jody Hobbs Hesler

Twenty Years Before.

NONIE'S PLAYING TIGHTROPE on the floor while her mother pays bills at the table beyond the counter. The kitchen smells like the fried chicken her mother made for her bridge ladies the day before. If Nonie squints her eyes right, the floor tiles line up, and the seam between them becomes the rope. She feels herself aloft, senses a city street below, with its different smells of bus exhaust and restaurants, plus crowds milling, beginning to gather, craning to see the little girl so far above. They jostle, whistle, and cheer for her, hoping she won't fall.

"Nonie, why don't you go play outside?"

Her mother's voice startles her, and she almost slips. The crowd gasps, jumps apart, as if making room for her to crash.

And then they're gone. Nonie can't see them anymore.

"I'm being very quiet," she says. Her mother always wants her outside, but right now the tightrope beckons. She concentrates to get it back, to recall the people, the height, the distant sound of traffic.

Nonie has heard talk of people who run away to join the circus. She doesn't know how they know where to go. Do they have to wait until a circus comes to their town? Is there an office somewhere? She pictures a tall, round man, balding with a black fringe of hair at his ears, sitting behind a desk in a crisp, clean suit with a flash of red at the breast pocket. He's a circus man, so it could be a magic handkerchief, one that pulls and pulls and pulls and changes color, makes people laugh, but his face is serious. He isn't used to girls no taller than his waistline presenting themselves for work.

"I'm very good at the tightrope," she tells him.

"A girl so small as you?" His face crinkles in doubt.

"I'm not so small anymore. I can wash my hands at the kitchen sink without a stool. I can see over this countertop right here." Though the man probably can't see the counter, since he's not in the kitchen but in the circus office, so she pictures drab brown walls pinned with flyers featuring clowns juggling, horses wearing feathered bridles, and ballerinas pirouetting on elephants' backs.

"I can walk across any rope," she says. "No matter how high."

At mention of the word, the seam between the floor tiles transforms back into a tightrope, and she and the circus man now stand near the ledge of a tall building from which the rope extends, connecting to the ledge of another equally tall building across the street. People gather once more, shuffling and clamoring below. Their noise reaches Nonie as a muffled hum.

"I'm not sure I should let you do this," the man says, rubbing his chin and shaking his head, keeping his distance from the edge.

"I can do it, sir," Nonie says. "I'm not afraid."

"Nonie!" Her mother's voice is sharp. "I can't think with you muttering away in there."

Nonie ignores her. The circus man's face pinches. He holds both her hands in his and levels her with an important look. "You must be very careful."

"I'm always careful," she says. "I'm very good at this."

She drops the man's hands and makes a T with her arms, gently places one foot on the wire. It wobbles, wobbles. She places her other foot. The crowd whoops. The rope swoops, then steadies. She places one foot forward. Then the next. Repeats.

"You're doing it!" the man calls from what seems very far away. She knows better than to look back or to look down. She must look only straight ahead, at the end of the rope where the last step will deliver her to a group of excited reporters. They jump up and down waiting for her. Cameras flash.

"Nonie. Enough!"

Her mother's words let loose a surge of unease. The crowd below has lost its faith. Now they wish for her to fall. Clouds shift outside, and sunlight knifes across the kitchen floor, carving a whole new line that slices the kitchen tile pattern in half. Splitting her rope in half.

She sees and can't look away. She can't fix her eyes on her destination anymore, and she knows a great height stretches below. Ahead of her, the floor, one half bright, one half dark, and her broken rope dangling. There is no choice but to fall. Wind seems to rush as if Nonie is plummeting. She wraps her arms around herself. *Mommy,* she wants to say, *help me,* but she is falling already, the way she always falls, time after time.

The tightrope is long gone, along with the circus man, the crowds, the reporters. Out of her mouth comes a wordless growl, and the shivers hit full force. She calls the feeling "the shivers" because they make her feel cold deep inside. They start in her toes, then creep upward and erase one piece of her at a time. An emptiness that fills her up, from her toes to her shins, her rib cage, the heart beating inside, until none of it belongs to her anymore.

Objects around her lose definition, as if she's dropping slowly down a well, but her body remains still, and her mother's face remains clear. Her face saying how taking care of Nonie is too much work. That her other children never taxed her this way. Ruth with her tennis, Brynne with her track, and both with their good grades and teachers who say how wonderful they are. Nonie's the one who ran the full half-mile home the only time her mother dropped her at a Brownie troop meeting. The one to hold her breath so long at swim team tryouts that her lips were blue when she surfaced again. The one whose body loses itself with no warning.

She screws her eyes tight. Squeezes her fists against her head, trying to squash the shivers out of her. Something pries at her arms, and she holds herself tighter, afraid whatever it is that barrels up inside her now also towers over her from outside. But it's her mother, clamping her hands around Nonie's wrists, trying to pry her to standing. The sunlight splits her face in half, too. Half fear, half anger. She won't let Nonie turn away.

"Do I need to send you across the street again?" she says. "Or can you settle on your own?"

Her mother thinks she's stubborn when she doesn't answer, but Nonie can't speak until the feeling lets go of her. She wants to say, *No! Don't send me away! Just hold me!* But the words don't come. They can't right now, and anyway, her mother wouldn't understand such a plain request. If she scrapes her knee, her mother props her up, brushes her off, swats her bottom, and says, "Right as rain," as if that phrase soothed scratches, wiped blood, eased pain. Nonie stomps her feet. Her mother thinks she's angry. She just wants her feet back. Wants her body back.

"Go, then," her mother says, wadding a five-dollar bill and sinking it into Nonie's fist. "Go sit with Mrs. Mackey until you calm down. I don't know how she can stand you when you're like this, but thank God she can. Go on now."

If only telling her to go could make her body work again. Nonie tells herself to move all the time. To calm down. Scolds herself from inside about what a worthless child she is so her mother doesn't have to, but she can't cross the room, walk out the door, take herself to Mrs. Mackey on her own. She never could.

"Can't you quit this by yourself, one time?" Her mother huffs a disgusted sound, then turns toward the stairway and shouts, "Ruth!" A few beats later she shouts again, then a rainfall of footsteps patters down the stairs. "Take her."

Ruth knows where, but she kneels on the kitchen floor beside Nonie first.

"Don't coddle the child, Ruth. Just get her out of here."

"You okay?" Ruth whispers in Nonie's ear, lifting a twist of curls out of her eyes and winding them around her finger. When she does this, the curl tightens and behaves. Ruth stands again but keeps hold of one of Nonie's hands. "She's scared, Mother. Can't you see?" Nine years older at fifteen, Ruth spurted to nearly their mother's height within the past few summer months. Her new tallness fits her like oversized pants, and she always seems to be pulling herself upward to fill it.

"Scared of what? She has to learn to get a grip on herself. You can't reward her for falling apart."

"She just needs to collect herself."

"Hogwash. My parents were forever warming milk for my baby brother when he got upset. Closing curtains in the middle of the day. Telling the rest of us to hush when we were playing. A lot of good that did. The world can't adjust to you, you have to adjust to it." Their mother crouches behind Nonie, nudging her shoulders forward. "Hup, two, hup, two," she says like a drill sergeant. "Get this show on the road. Collect yourself at Mrs. Mackey's."

Ruth slips her hand underneath her mother's to unlatch her from Nonie's shoulders. "Stop it, Mother."

Their mother spins toward Ruth. "What did you say?"

"I said stop it. She's just a kid. A scared little kid."

Their mother's arm flies backward, then lashes forward across Ruth's cheek. She's often distant, often fierce, but never physical. Ruth claps her hand against the spot and holds it there, staring at her mother in disbelief.

"Two things I will not abide are weakness and insolence."

Ruth stands rigid as a wall, but Nonie feels her fear. She feels her mother's anger, too. She feels every feeling present in a room. It's exhausting.

"Now take your sister to Mrs. Mackey's and don't ever talk back to me again." Their mother's words are short, sharp blasts, but, from her face and a shift in the air, Nonie can tell the slap surprised her, too.

Still, their mother's impatience electrifies the air, and Nonie would give anything to move away from it, but the shivers plunge her farther into their dark farawayness. No matter how hard she struggles to come back to herself, they suck her away from whatever room she's actually in, keep her from doing what's expected of her.

Somehow Ruth manages to drag her across the threshold into the front yard. "Here," she says and points to the edge of the row of azaleas by the front porch, bright with coral blossoms. She lets Nonie rest there, beyond the vantage of the front window.

The grass soft beneath her, Nonie curls into a ball and hugs herself as tight as she can, waiting for the shivers to swallow her. Swallow her whole and be done with her forever. She always thinks she'll die this way, never thinks the feeling will ebb, but slowly it does.

She doesn't know how much time has passed, but when she comes back to herself, Ruth waits beside her. A cool breeze laps Nonie's hair, and the sun that was too bright moments before warms her face.

"Do you have the money?" Ruth asks, taking up her hand again. Ruth is always patient and gentle with her, but she also sticks to business.

Nonie uncurls her other fist to show the now-sweaty ball of a five-dollar bill. One day she'll be so bold that she'll manage to leave by herself when her mother tells her to, and instead of walking to Mrs. Mackey's, she'll march the extra few blocks down to the newsstand. At the store she'll unwrinkle the money onto the counter and ask for as many fireballs as it will buy. There'll be so many she won't be able to stuff them into her pockets. She'll have to make a cradle of her hands to hold the rest. She never imagines a bag. Tidiness would ruin it.

Today, though, Ruth takes a first step toward Mrs. Mackey's

house, and Nonie follows, one foot in front of the other. One, two, one, two. Just like on the tightrope. Ruth waits for Nonie to ring the doorbell, then nods and turns away, goes back to doing whatever she was doing before.

When Mrs. Mackey answers, her face is neither kind nor unkind. Her shoulders crouch forward, and a gnarled gray cardigan hugs her shoulders. She opens the creaky screen door for Nonie, and the smell of her house escapes, close and cabbagey. She accepts the sweat-wrecked five-dollar bill. The metallic scream of the door closing behind them scrapes at Nonie's nerves, threatening to set off another round of shivers. From the shadows, Mrs. Mackey's evil Chihuahua snarls, and the scar on Nonie's thumb throbs with memory. She knows better than to try to make friends with the dog now.

The tail end of Mrs. Mackey's soap opera fills the TV screen. Nurses, doctors, a patient lying prone and dead looking. Smoke from endless cigarettes fogs the edges of the room. Nonie sits straight with her hands folded neatly in her lap on the soft chair where she always waits for her mother. She eats the stale vanilla wafers Mrs. Mackey offers her on a plate. She's always so very tired after the shivers come and go. She would like to lie down to sleep, but she's sure that would break some kind of rule, and she doesn't want to embarrass her mother any more than she already has.

Nineteen Years After.

NOREEN LOUNGES WITH Evie under the giant oak tree in the front yard on an old purple bedspread that belonged to her aunt years ago. Chubby clouds inch overhead, and a warm breeze flutters bright green leaves above them, tossing Evie's curls, her hair not the white blond of Noreen's childhood but yellower, like George's from the few toddler pictures she's seen of him. Bluebells droop along the sidewalk. The ridges of Church, Hogback, and Knob Mountain ripple like wavelets against the horizon, and the sunshine is warmer than usual for April.

A sliver of gravel road peeks back at Noreen through a break in the overgrown boxwood hedge. It's five more miles before you hit pavement. Evie's tug at her elbow makes her realize she's been lost in a phantom image of the two of them driving those five miles, then turning left toward Harrisonburg. Or right toward Route 64 and beyond? Either way is good enough, just getting them the hell out of here.

There's nowhere to go without a car though, so she scoops Evie into her lap, tickles her belly, and coos, "Wiggly fingers! Wiggly fingers!" Evie laughs on cue, but Noreen feels like an imposter.

The house's remoteness hadn't bothered her right away. Singer's Glen, the name for this loose scattering of homes and farms, sounded as peaceful and idyllic as it looked, and she fell as hard as George had for the foothills and the sunshine and the trickle of stream down the hill. The old farmhouse sits on about ten acres, a solid twenty minutes from Harrisonburg and James Madison University where George now teaches. At first, the drive felt luxurious. Twenty scenic minutes of Virginia trees and hills, the Blue Ridge casting its sheen along the horizon every time it dipped into view.

Back then, the never-ending home improvement projects felt wistful and clever—replacing doorknobs, repairing and repainting cabinets, stripping and restaining old hardwood. The work let them put their own imprint on the place and kept them busy until Evie came. Noreen remembers calling it the perfect place to raise a family. That was a long time ago now, and remembering is different from feeling the same way.

Her gaze drifts back toward the road she thinks of as The Road Out of Here, and she wonders if she'd leave George if he didn't drive their only car twenty miles to work every day. An adamant yes would be as helpful as a decisive no, but no answer comes.

"Wiggy finger!" Evie says now, poking her grass-stained fingers into Noreen's chin.

With Evie, Noreen's love is certain. The first time Evie opened her own pale green eyes and met her mother's looking down at her, the biggest love Noreen has ever known gawped its mouth and swallowed her. She could tell Evie recognized her at once as the person whose heartbeat and voice she already knew from the inside. So, days like today—days Noreen calls her cloud days, when she loses traction on the present—she has no patience for herself. Evie is in *this* world, not some ghost world down the way, she reminds herself. She knows too well how exhausting it is to coax someone back from that place and hopes never to put Evie in that position. Two now, she talks in spurts of words and phrases, making the kind of sense toddlers make, and Noreen assumes she's savvier than she can say.

"Wiggly fingers," Noreen says back, but this time even Evie looks doubtful.

A second car would help, would give them other places to be and other things to do, but doing without was one way to economize while Noreen stayed home and cared for Evie. They'd made the choice together, their first real family decision, and most days it still feels like the right thing, but she wishes their move here hadn't interrupted the last requirements of her teacher certification. Doing without a car is harder than she expected, and whenever she lobbies to reconsider, George ticks off their latest mortgage balance, plus the number of years until he might be granted tenure and the raise that comes along with it, hefty enough to cover new debt. When she offers to finish certifying so she could return to work earlier than planned, George chuckles and reminds her that putting her back in school and Evie into preschool at the same time, *and* buying a new car to make all that possible, costs yet more money. Then he might say, "We could always ask my father"—the human checkbook whose expensive gifts come with invisible strings and unfulfillable expectations. George's shiny new midnight blue Volvo sedan was his PhD graduation gift, replacing the used Volvo he'd gotten for his high school graduation, both gifts payment for years of weekends his father lured him home, stealing him away from his studies, time and again, to look after him if he was feeling poorly or to help him move offices at work or to hang pictures at home or whatever other handful of uses he might put his son to.

How about a visit this weekend? At least one of the cars I bought you should get you here, she can imagine him saying with his usual teasing bluster that somehow brooks no disagreement. His fatherly love is a yo-yo, spooling George out only to whir him back in again, and George hasn't figured out how to untie himself from it yet.

The same sort of family knot she's still untying herself, so she can't blame him. Not completely. Her family's yo-yo is the old worry that she'll turn out like her aunt who died from suicide almost twenty years ago. It's hard not to be bound by things families believe about who you are and what you owe them.

Evie squirms from her mother's lap and lumbers toward the edge of the purple blanket, turning back toward Noreen with the widest smile on her face when she reaches the grass. Noreen loves how Evie always smiles when she sees her, even when Noreen can't muster the energy to smile back.

The phone rings, snapping her back to the moment yet again. She takes Evie's hands and puppet-walks her up the front porch steps, swaying her side to side and humming a made-up tune, "Here we go, up the stairs, up the stairs." Evie bounces along with her mother's rhythms and parrots the song back to her, as if it were real.

Inside is dark after the sunniness out front, and the old house holds onto the chill of winter like a deep inhale. Spring will hurry forward, and soon enough summer's heat and humidity and throngs of insects will bear down on them again, making Noreen long for this drafty coolness, making her forget how empty and unwelcoming it actually feels.

On the phone, her mother says, "Have I caught you at a good time?"

A good time feels laughably inept to describe the heaviness she carries with her today, so she says, "I can talk." It's Wednesday, her mother's half-day at Charlottesville's central library downtown for as long Noreen can remember.

Charlottesville's only an hour away, and Noreen and Ruth speak by phone often, but Noreen would visit more if she had that blasted second car. On a day like today, Evie could play in the sunny front room of Ruth and Hugh's new-to-them home on Lexington Avenue while Noreen and Ruth sipped tea. Or Noreen could slip away to read her book for a few minutes without waiting for Evie's nap. Or walk by herself down the streets of her childhood. She wishes she could like George's dad more, interpret his gifts more as kindness than burden.

Easy to blame him. If Noreen really snuck off for time alone during a visit with her mother, she'd risk triggering the next round of Nonie comparisons or thinly veiled assessments of her mental stability. No matter where she goes, or stays, the afternoon will feel the same.

Nearby, Evie churns her tub of blocks, eventually upturning the whole bin. One more thing to clean up. Noreen's to-do lists self-generate all day, and George wants her sole attention once he walks through the door. She clenches the phone against her ear and rubs her forehead with her free hand.

"The dryer was making the strangest noise earlier," her mother says. "Not like fingers on a chalkboard because that's only a quick screech, then it's over. This kept going. Unnerving really."

"Unnerving. Sure." Noreen's attention unmoors, flits between Evie and the specks of dust sparkling in shafts of afternoon sunlight.

"It was after I read the paper this morning. I wonder if yours ran the same article. Have you read today's paper yet?"

Noreen glances from the living room into the dining room at the mound of the week's papers, still bound, in the center of the table. The news bubbles over with stories about people she'll never meet in places she doesn't go. Horrible things happen to them, or they accomplish feats Noreen hardly has energy to imagine. George insists they take the paper and spends an hour each Sunday clipping coupons she doesn't use. He chooses things that must seem useful to him but bear little relation to food they eat or cleaning products Noreen prefers.

"No, I haven't read it yet."

"There was a story about this man who charged at a police station, swinging a handgun in front of him, the paper said. Shouting nonsense."

Evie adds a half circle to the top of a precarious tower, then chops into the middle of it, cracking the tower in half and clattering the blocks to the wood floor.

"Are you sure you can talk?" her mother says. "I don't want

to keep you if Evie needs you."

"She's okay. Just building, you know the way she does."

"She's a regular little destroyer, isn't she?" Noreen can picture the proud look on her mother's face.

"She is that."

Her mother picks up with the story of the man in the police station, how he had tinnitus from flying corporate jets for twenty years, and the sound never left him. He couldn't sleep, couldn't think. "When I heard that noise in my dryer, it made me think of him. Probably it was a zipper, scraping around as it spun." She explains how she went in to listen, up close. First, she laid her head against the machine. The warmth made the scratching noise more bearable, but being so close made it louder too. So she tried lying down, closer, on the cold floor.

"You were lying on the floor? To listen to a zipper?" When Noreen feels bleary on the inside, any conversation can be a challenge, but she suspects her mother's anecdote would confuse her on the best of days. She doesn't sound upset exactly, but there's a hint of emotion Noreen can't place yet, something not quite right.

"Hugh must have thought I'd gone crazy, finding me like that." Her mother chuckles into the phone while Noreen imagines her mother's husband double-taking at his wife, prone on the utility room floor. "But I was just testing it out."

Another tower succumbs to Evie's marauding fist. One of the blocks bounces into her chin on its way to the floor, and she looks at Noreen to share the injustice of it, tears threatening. Noreen makes a funny face and shakes a scolding finger at the offending block, which sends Evie into a trill of giggles instead.

"What do you mean you were testing it out?" Noreen says.

"You know, seeing what it was like up close."

"The noise in your dryer?"

"Yes, the noise in the dryer reminded me of the man." Her mother articulates each word as if Noreen were having trouble hearing. Then she self-corrects. "This must not be a good time. I'm sorry, Noreen. We can try again later."

"It's okay." Noreen kneads her forehead again. When Evie naps, she savors those few hours of not having to think of anything to say to anyone. She'll tidy the blocks, clear away dirty dishes from breakfast and lunch, then maybe relax on the sofa and melt into a book. Live someplace else for an hour or two. No, she doesn't want her mother to call back later. "So, this sound in the dryer made you think of the man from the paper?"

"Yes, because of the tinnitus. When he stormed the police station, Noreen, they shot him down. Right there in front of everyone."

"Lord," Noreen says. "Did this happen nearby?" Proximity might explain her mother's fascination, but sensational news stories don't usually grab her interest, no matter how shocking.

"No, no. Hampton Roads, maybe? I'm not sure, but later, they found a note. It said he couldn't take it anymore, the ringing in his ears. He actually left a note. They're calling it suicide by police."

The word *suicide* zeroes Noreen's attention. Her mother's baby sister, Nonie, was twenty-seven when she died from suicide. Noreen's age now. The purple velvet bedspread she'd been sitting on in the yard? It was hers when she died. One of many things Noreen has learned unwittingly. Snippets overheard as a child when relatives forgot she might be listening nearby. Imagined scenes to answer questions she didn't know how to ask. Things no one would have told an eight-year-old that she's never had the courage or prurience to resurrect through conversation since. When she was still very young, it felt like Nonie whispered some of the stories straight into her dreams. Dreams so vivid, she woke with the flowery fragrance of Nonie's shampoo fresh in her nostrils. There's a sound that goes along with the stories, too, a heaving rhythm that a pendulum of body and cord might grind out against a pipe. She'd heard it earlier today, in fact, when a strong gust rollicked across the yard and set something, some-where, swinging. Eerily familiar, it always chills her with the cold of a soul passing.

"I wanted to know if that's what it was like for Nonie," her mother says. "A feeling so constant and annoying she couldn't ignore it, no matter how hard she tried."

Noreen wishes no one else would ever kill themselves again. Not from some noble desire for global well-being but simply be-cause Nonie was enough. Enough suicide to count for the whole world. For every generation of all people for all time.

"What do you think?" Ruth says. "Her feelings, do you think they were like a constant scraping? Something that drowned out everything around her? So she couldn't even think of how much it would hurt us to lose her?"

Noreen draws a breath. No wonder she's felt the shadow of Nonie all morning. "Oh, Mom," she says. Evie turns to her, her glossy eyes so much like her own, like Nonie's. "I forgot. Today's her birthday, isn't it?"

Evie sits back from her ruined towers and digs her fist into her ear, a signal that she's ready for her nap.

"She would've been forty-six," Ruth says.

The number seems impossible. Forever twenty-seven in Noreen's mind, and a fey twenty-seven at that, Nonie hopped into Noreen's imaginary play as if she were a child herself, tiptoe-ing barefoot in the grass, searching for fairies or butterflies. Transforming at Noreen's request into a spy or an old man or a broken-legged patient for Noreen to tend. If she hadn't died, Noreen might have grown away from her, might have matured to a point where Nonie even seemed silly, or as reckless as the rest of the family insists she was. As it is, Noreen's Nonie never has to exist as anything but that magical, whimsical person who loved her best in the world. Even if she also hurt her most. The space she'd filled had been so vast, Noreen's never managed to fill it back up.

Evie starts to cry, but Noreen covers the mouthpiece so her mother won't hear. Her mother hears anyway. "Sounds like Evie's naptime."

"That's all right, Mom. She can wait a few minutes." Noreen gathers Evie from the floor and sways to keep her quiet.

A gust as strong as the one earlier whips through the screen door, rattles the doorframe, and sprawls a pile of Evie's scribbled drawings to the floor. It might as well have been Nonie trying to tell her something, though it's always hard to guess what. Noreen favors the word "visit" over "haunt" because the sense of Nonie's presence surprises more than frightens her, whether it's the flash of her reflection looking out from a mirror or, like now, a breath of wind, more like a restless companionship. After a moment's startled recognition, an inkling of comfort always follows.

"I'm sure you're right," Noreen says. "About what it must have felt like for Nonie. A constant scraping. That makes sense."

"There's just no way she would've done it if she'd realized how much it would hurt us."

A hint of pleading underscores her mother's words. Too often, her talk of Nonie swerves into worrying about Noreen instead. In photos of them at the same ages, Nonie and Noreen are almost indistinguishable, but for Nonie's slightly darker hair. Mannerisms, too, seemed to follow the DNA so that when Noreen is deep in concentration, she bites her lower lip. When she laughs, she tilts her chin up ever so slightly. When she gets angry, she closes her eyes for a moment before speaking. All things Nonie did. Nonie had panic attacks and severe depression, too, conditions only slightly better understood now than when she died. Any evidence that Noreen might suffer even a pale shadow of these same things she hides from her mother and always has.

"She loved us as much as she could," Noreen says. "She tried her hardest to stay with us."

"Yes, I think you're right," her mother says. "Anyway, here it is her birthday again."

As soon as Noreen hangs up, Evie cranks up her fussing. Plenty of children cry without tears, especially when they're tired or hungry, but for Evie, the tears are always real. They seem oversized for her tiny face, as if they drag the world's suffering along with them.

Noreen hugs her against her chest and shushes softly in her ear. "I'm right here, little angel," she says, Nonie's nickname for her. "I'm not going anywhere." If Evie turns out like both of them, Noreen wants to celebrate it instead of fear it. Nothing good comes from teaching someone to fear themselves.

During.

IT'S SATURDAY, SO Nonie should be here, sashaying into the den with a tray full of the sugar cereals she brings each week for cartoon watching with Noreen and Mark while their parents sleep late. Sometimes she buys Fruity Pebbles or Kaboom or those variety packs of tiny boxes whose sides you bend back like wings and pour milk straight into. Nonie nestles between her and Mark and *beep-beeps* with the Road Runner until Noreen laughs so hard her sides hurt.

But Nonie isn't here today, and instead, her mom's other sister, Brynne, is visiting from Richmond to babysit. Of course she brought her boys along. Noreen thinks of Henry and Luke as noisy engines in the background, swooping and droning around the den like the fighter planes Luke's always imagining into the air.

"Try to be good for your aunt today, okay, Noreen?" her mother says in a voice that wants her to feel good about something that isn't good. Like spending this whole day with her unfavorite aunt, who folds napkins into swan shapes, then punishes you when you float them in the kitchen sink to see if they can swim. Or, what kid eats anything that looks like the snacks she's making across the kitchen right now? Rolled-up bologna slices pierced with toothpicks and topped with olives.

The rest of the grownups will drive the orange rent-a-van over to Nonie's apartment and move her stuff out of there and into the dark, squished little room under Grammy and Grampy's basement stairs. Noreen's mother explained how they only have the moving truck for half a day, and how she'll scrub the apartment clean while her dad and uncle move the furniture, and how some of the furniture won't fit in Grammy and Grampy's basement, so they'll have to find somewhere to donate it, but no one will explain why they're moving Nonie out of her apartment in the first place, with its kooky green kitchen sink and the welcome mat Noreen picked out herself.

Her father glides into the kitchen for a second, skimming his keys from the counter and into the pocket of his cutoff jeans. Both her parents wear cutoffs and old T-shirts. Her father's has the shape of an iron burned into the belly of it, and her mother's has a hole along the neckline. Her father finger-flicks one of Noreen's stray curls, the way he always does, and says, "Morning, little skiddoo."

Next to him, her mother pours cups of coffee for him and for herself from the silver percolator plugged into the wall beside the stove. "We'll only be gone a few hours." She slides a mug to Noreen's father.

"Where's Nonie though?" Noreen asks. The only Saturday Nonie missed cartoons was right after Noreen broke her arm falling off Grammy and Grampy's tire swing about a month ago. Nonie had spun the rope extra tight for her, then let her unwind with it, so fast. When Noreen fell, her bone broke through the skin, and Nonie lost her breath or breathed too fast. Noreen couldn't understand it very well, especially from where she landed, on her back in the dirt with her arm splayed funny behind her. Whatever happened to Nonie made the ambulance rush both of them away together. Even after all that, Nonie only missed that one Saturday.

"Don't you worry about Nonie," her father says at the same time her mother says, "At Grammy and Grampy's."

"But *why* is she there instead of here?" Noreen says.

"You're only eight," her father says. "You don't need to know everything in the world quite yet." When he smiles, his lips hardly budge at the corners, then he strides out of the room toward the den, rumbling with the thuds and pows of the boys' imaginary war.

After Noreen's father is out of sight, Brynne twists toward her sister from across the kitchen and says, "Honestly, Ruth, I was wondering where Nonie was, too." Her bright blue polo collar stands stiff at her neck, and two tortoise shell combs hold her long straight hair in place behind her ears. Noreen can smell her Emeraude perfume from across the room. "How can she let everybody move her things for her? Wouldn't you be embarrassed?"

"You didn't see her the other day, Brynne. She's not up to it."

"But how do you know?" Noreen says. Sometimes Nonie gets moods when her whole body seems to lose its air like an old balloon and her eyes don't focus on anything. Not even her, Noreen, her favorite niece. Her favorite person in the world. Days like that Noreen calls cloud days. You never know when they'll happen, yet today her mother seems to know ahead of time.

"It's all right, Noreen." Her mother holds her coffee mug to her lips with both hands and blows across its surface.

Noreen's arm begins to itch inside her cast, and she wants to jam a fork down there to scratch it out of spite. She's the one who rode to the hospital next to Nonie while she gasped for air, moving her bluish lips trying to tell Noreen something before the paramedics in their crisp white shirts strapped that clear plastic mask over her mouth and asked a thousand questions. She deserves to know some of those answers now, even if the grownups are afraid to tell her.

"Don't you need some breakfast?" her mother says, then reaches up to the high shelf to get Noreen's favorite bowl for her, the one with the squirrel and acorn pattern around the rim. Noreen reaches into the cabinet under the counter and grabs the Froot Loops, left over from last Saturday's Nonie visit. She scoots the box up onto the yellow countertop with her free hand. Everything is awkward one-handed.

"So what if she hyperventilated?" Brynne says. She lifts her arms in the air for emphasis, and a fork with an olive stuck to its end pokes out of her hand like a torch. "So what if she didn't tell anybody she lost her university job and she's stuck waiting tables again at that same old dive downtown. She didn't self-destruct. How can moving her back in with our parents be the best answer?"

Noreen's mother angles herself between her and Brynne, as if she could shield Noreen from hearing more by blocking her view. "There's more to it than that, and you know it, Brynne."

Plenty more, Noreen guesses, but her mother will make sure they don't say it in front of her. Because she's only eight and doesn't need to know everything in the world.

In the hallway, her father calls a ten-minute warning up the stairs to Uncle Emmett. More noise surges from the den, coffee cups are everywhere, and her cousin Luke's security blanket coils at the foot of the refrigerator in everybody's way. It's a mess and nothing like things should be.

Noreen tiptoes over Luke's blanket and opens the refrigerator for the jug of milk. Her mother hoists it out of her hand and sets it beside her bowl for her. "Want me to pour today?" She doesn't wait for an answer. With her cast, Noreen can't even bathe herself. Her mother knots a garbage bag around her arm to protect the plaster and sponges soapy water down her back like when she was a toddler. At least she can hobble onto the kitchen stool by herself.

Across the room, Brynne turns her back again and peels off the next bologna slice, then rolls it into a tidy meat scroll.

Last week when Nonie came for cartoons, she made a game out of eating cereal left-handed so Noreen wouldn't feel so bad about her arm. Mark did it. Nonie, too. Milk splattered everywhere, and they had to catch their breath from laughing. It's not as funny without the game. Milk dribbles down her chin the same way but just feels messy. She rubs her chin against her shoulder to sop it up.

"Does she even want to move out?" Noreen asks. She remembers back to the very first day Nonie moved in. She was so excited she invited Noreen over for a tea party. Upturned moving boxes stood in for a table and chairs, and Nonie unpacked Great-Grammy Noreen's fancy dishes to serve tea to her and her half-hairless doll, Harriet. Plus, Nonie spread slices of white bread with margarine and sprinkled them with cinnamon and sugar, then cut them into strips on her plate. The teacups were feather light, the tea warm and sweet. Her first cup ever.

Anyone could tell Nonie wanted that place, not Grammy and Grampy's junk room. Last time Noreen was in there, it was full of broken record players and bikes with flat tires, and it stunk like the inside of an old car.

Her mother gives a flat-lipped smile. "That's enough questions, love," she says, her voice thin and tired, same as when she scolds Noreen and Mark for fighting on long car trips.

The phone rings as Noreen wobbles the next spoonful to her mouth. Her mother answers at the wall phone beside her, the same yellow as the countertop. "Hello?" then hangs up a second later. It rings again while her mother rummages in the hall closet for shoes. This time Brynne steps away from her bologna treats to reach around Noreen to answer. Her gold bangles clank against each other in Noreen's ear.

"Hello?" The long cord wraps around Brynne, so she twirls the opposite direction to free herself. "Hello?" she says again, louder, then waits before slamming down the receiver. "Nobody." The cord slackens again and slides along the counter beside Noreen's bowl, then twines back around itself. "Some people have nothing better to do than waste other people's time."

Ruth pads back into the room in her navy blue Keds. "Play nice with Luke today, okay?" she says, her voice back to normal.

Noreen nods but wishes her mother would tell Luke instead. The only toys of hers he plays with are Barbies, which she hardly bothers with anymore, but that doesn't mean she likes when he make-believes them into airplane bombers, flying them around the house, trumpeting blowing-up sounds through his lips, and dropping them into pretend explosions on the floor.

The games the boys play are boring, and her cast means today will be extra boring. Mark, Henry, and Luke can run around, inside, outside. They could even run through the sprinkler if Brynne would set it up. But Noreen has to stay cool, dry, and careful. If Nonie were here, she'd make things interesting. Put a blanket on her head and pretend she's invisible. Talk with a British accent so they can act like royalty. The boys with their chaos and energy always seem to use Brynne up. She's not very good at fun.

The phone rings again after Brynne follows her mother through the swinging door to the utility room next to the kitchen for last babysitting details, like where Ruth keeps things and what time she expects them to get home. "Just ignore it," Brynne calls through the door. Noreen swallows her mouthful of cereal and grabs it anyway.

"Hey, little angel," comes Nonie's voice. Noreen's favorite nickname, and only Nonie uses it. Hope rises in her throat. Maybe Nonie'll come over and rescue her from this boring day after all. Mark and the cousins can wrangle each other in the den and torpedo her Barbies as much as they want, swing from trees, or somersault down every hill, and she and Nonie can take off for the library or go get ice cream at Mayberry's.

On all the days that aren't cloud days, and most aren't, the world is a carnival with Nonie around. She hides surprise candy bars in her purse for Noreen. Once she wound a butterfly necklace around one of them, too. Noreen touches the charm where it rests at her neck.

"I'm so glad you answered. You're exactly who I wanted to talk to," Nonie says.

The hope in Noreen's throat dries up. Nonie's voice, thick

and dull, proves that her mother guessed right about the cloud day. Noreen's stuck with Brynne for sure. Nobody tells her where all Nonie's sadness comes from, but probably that's because nobody knows.

"You wanted me? Really?" Pressing the phone to her ear with her right shoulder, she brings a wavering left-handed spoon of cereal to her mouth, then has second thoughts and lowers it back into the bowl.

"Yup. Just you. I wanted to say I'm sorry," Nonie says.

Her uncle Emmett thumps down the steps at last. Her father jangles his keys at the front door the way he does when he's ready to go, and her mother's voice has that winding-down sound to it, so Noreen's pretty sure they're all about to leave.

"What for?" Noreen figures she's apologizing about missing cartoons, but her mother makes you tell what you're sorry for. Otherwise, it doesn't count.

"I'm just sorry." That wouldn't have been good enough for her mother, but maybe Nonie doesn't know the sorry rule. "I'm sorry, and I love you very much, Noreen."

"I love you, too."

Noreen wants to say she wishes Nonie would come over, but her aunt hangs up too fast. It probably wouldn't have worked anyway. Noreen catches sight of Brynne peeking around the corner into the kitchen as she's swiping milk droplets from her chin with her shoulder again. Brynne whisks across the room with a tiny square napkin, the kind her parents use when they throw parties.

"This is for your mouth," she says. "And this," she peels a banana from a fruit bowl on the counter and lays it beside Noreen, "this is for your health. You really shouldn't eat that garbage for breakfast."

The instant Brynne looks away, Noreen plops the banana into the trash.

The day unrolls as expected. The boys wage tiny wars in the den. They build forts out of sheets and chairs, then charge into them, destroying them. They ignore Brynne's "No roughhousing" warnings one after the other, stomping up and down stairs, wrestling on the floor. When they beg Brynne to take them to the neighborhood pool, she says no. When they beg her to let them play in the backyard, the same. They build more forts, run up and down the stairs shrieking at each other, and break a glass Noreen's father forgot about on his desk.

In the far corner of the den, Noreen holes up at a card table, fitting shards of blue and orange shapes into what will become an ocean teeming with brightly colored fish. By now she's already pieced it together a dozen times. Cartoons are long over. The boys' ruckus made them impossible to watch anyway.

At snack time Brynne carries in her weird olive-topped rollups, fanned out like decorations on a plate. Mark calls them bologna eyeballs, which makes Brynne huff right back out of the room. Mark and Henry stuff the sandwich meat into their mouths and bean each other with olives. Little Luke steps on one and runs crying to his mother.

If they'd been at Brynne's house in Richmond, she would've let them run around the yard because they have a fence. Here there's no fence, and Brynne worries about the pond because Luke only just learned to swim. Brynne always worries about something. The pond isn't even that deep, and the boys are restless and annoying, impossible to please.

"You can see the whole backyard from the sunroom," Noreen tells her, "if you want to keep an eye on them." She has to pull her aunt all the way to the back window to convince her. Then, finally, Brynne says yes, and the boys shoot out the back door like wild animals.

Her cast makes it tricky, but Noreen hauls a stack of books

her mother brought home from a recent shift at the library, balancing them against her chest, all the way to the sofa in the sunroom. Brynne takes the seat opposite, a wicker chair with white cushions and a perfect view of the pond. She flips through magazines from the coffee table and peeks out the window at the boys every paragraph or so. Noreen likes reading with her aunt, even if the boys claim half her attention. It's the only thing she can remember doing with just the two of them.

After a while, Brynne peers over her magazine pages. "You know what's funny? Some days I dream about quiet like this." She laughs and tosses the magazine onto the table. "But this is too quiet. Let's have some music." She crosses the room to Noreen's parents' albums and slides one onto the record player, places the needle, and John Denver's reedy voice pipes into the room. Whenever Noreen hears one of his songs, she pictures his round face and his circle glasses, his hay-straight hair flat against his ears.

The music isn't very loud, and they go back to their reading. Until "Grandma's Feather Bed." Noreen thumps her foot against the sofa cushion in time, and Brynne stands up again, reaches a hand for Noreen. Brynne stomps one foot and claps her hands to the rhythm. Noreen follows along, slapping her hand against her knee instead of clapping, her broken arm like a chicken wing at her side. Soon they're belting out the words. Brynne takes Noreen's hand in hers, and they spin around the room that way.

When the song ends, they start it over. They fly in circles, and their hair swirls outward. Brynne's is long, straight, and silky, like her mother's, except she wears hers shorter, even with her jawline. When the boys march in, mad because someone kicked a ball onto the roof, Brynne sends them back outside.

✿

Noreen is nearly asleep when she hears the front door open downstairs, spilling sounds into the house of night bugs chattering and frogs chirping by the pond. Then shoes clap against the foyer's slate floor. She must have been all the way asleep because her eyes were closed, and when she opens them, she has to squint against the brightness edging her doorway.

Something draws her out of her bed and into the hallway. Her parents, her uncle, they must all be home now, but after the coming-inside noises, no one's drumming up the stairs. No one turned on the TV news. No one says a word. What comes upstairs is the opposite of sound, an absence of something, a thickness to the air that doesn't make sense.

Noreen stands in the hallway a long time. Even with nothing happening and nothing to run away from, she feels like she's standing in the middle of a nightmare. There's so much nothing it seems to breathe down her neck. The cast arm grows heavy. Her whole body feels heavy there in the dark, waiting for something, but she has no idea what. When she finally hears her mother's step on the carpeted stairs, slower and heavier than usual but still familiar, the nightmare feeling tightens around her.

Her mother crests the top of the steps without seeing her at first. She's looking at her own hands, ghostly in the hallway's dim light. She flips them over and over, as if she's staring questions into them that they don't seem capable of answering. At the sight of Noreen, she gasps and stutters backward half a step like she's in a nightmare, too.

"Noreen?" Her mother's voice is flat and exhausted.

Noreen takes a backward step, too, aware of the gaping holes behind her of her own bedroom doorway and her brother's. Mark and the cousins unzipped sleeping bags into one giant sleeping carpet on the floor of the den, with layers of bedsheets on top. When they'd asked if they could, Noreen had been sure Brynne would say no, but she said yes to everything after that phone call right before suppertime. Brynne's businesslike "Jamison residence" had carried all the way from the kitchen into the den, but Noreen hadn't overheard another syllable.

Afterward, Brynne let them eat hot dogs with melted Velveeta for dinner over newspapers on the floor in front of the TV. The *Fantasy Island* theme song snapped her back to herself enough to hurry them to bed, but she hadn't as much as mentioned tooth-brushing.

Silence continues to pump up the stairs like smoke, and Noreen backs herself against the wall between the bedroom doorways. Fingertips from her unbroken arm graze the wall for the solid feeling of it. Her mother's face sags along with her whole body. Her shoulders list forward while her expression re-mains wrung out and plain.

"Are you sleepwalking?" Noreen asks with a flush of hope-fulness, thinking of a book she'd read about a little girl who sleepwalked to her barn and rode her favorite horse at night after a bad fall had made her too afraid to ride. The frightening free-dom of waking up on horseback, thundering across the moonlit pasture, fingers threaded tight into her horse's mane.

"You should be in bed, love," her mother says, the words seeming heavy in her mouth. She reaches toward Noreen, and Noreen lets her mother herd her back to bed that way, lets her sit beside her and pull the sheets up to her chin. Her mother smells of dust and sweat and something thicker and unfamiliar, and she smooths Noreen's hair, one patient stroke after another, until Noreen slips back into sleep.

When she opens her eyes in the morning, she half-expects her mother to be there still. In place of her, there's a murky feeling that brings Noreen back to the moments before she fell asleep. How had she let herself do that? Fall asleep like any other night, when, obviously, something awful happened when they were moving Nonie's things.

Noreen throws her covers back with one hand and stumbles out of bed, barrels into the hall, practically bulldozing into her mother with a stack of bright yellow guest towels in her arms. Ruth trips backward a step.

"You have to tell me what happened," Noreen says, "I know something happened."

"Oh, love." Ruth hugs the towels to her chest and kneels in front of Noreen, their faces level.

So close, Noreen sees red tracks on the whites of her mother's eyes, pouches of gray beneath them. She's not wearing lipstick and hasn't showered since the night before because her hair is dry, but it isn't curled or brushed and still smells faintly of yesterday's hairspray. Her mother kneels there, eye to eye, but doesn't say anything.

"What happened?"

Her mother piles the towels beside them on the floor. Bright as marigolds. "It's Nonie," she says.

"What about her?"

Her mother shudders out a stale breath. "She died, Noreen. Nonie died last night."

A thousand sirens shriek in Noreen's head. Plus a constant rush of water. She shakes her head, trying to stop the noises. Her free hand flies up to cover her ear, but her mother blocks it from landing and pulls her close, though the cast interferes and Noreen wriggles free.

Noreen's great-grandmother, the woman she and Nonie were both named for, was ninety-one when she fell down the stairs and died. "Old people die."

"Sometimes young people die, too," Ruth says.

"I don't believe you."

"I'm so sorry, Noreen."

"How?"

Slowly her mother scrapes her hands down her face, balls them into little fists under her chin, then reaches to wipe a tear from Noreen's cheek with her pinky. "She was very sad, I think. For a long time. I don't know what made her think of it yesterday. But she decided she didn't want to be alive anymore."

"That's a lie." Nonie wouldn't make herself die. Not on

purpose. She wouldn't leave Noreen behind. Her favorite person, her kindred little niece. Who looks like her, acts like her, has the same name. Noreen hadn't known Great-Grammy Noreen well enough to belong to her, with her pin cushion face, puffy and tight at the same time, smelling like Spam mixed with baby powder. No, the name was hers and Nonie's alone. They were two halves of the same heart. How could one die without the other?

Tears stream down her mother's face with no sobs to bring them out. Water flowing like a spigot turned low. She doesn't brush them away. "She couldn't help it, love."

When her mother lays a comforting hand on Noreen's face, Noreen hunches away from it. "No no no no no no no." She stomps her feet and finally covers one ear, a useless effort thanks to the stupid cast.

If she could block out every sound. If it could still be Friday night with the promise of Nonie coming in the morning, like usual. If it could be yesterday morning and they could be eating breakfast and joking about how Mark's bedhead stiffens his hair into horns. If Noreen hadn't danced with Brynne like nothing was wrong. Most of all, if Noreen ever thought you could undo time, from now on she knows for certain that you can't.

She clenches her eyes shut and hums a dull, erasing sound and imagines herself backward into the world before her mother started talking. Last memories before the event that the rest of her life will come after.

Lying in the grass in the backyard with Nonie weeks ago. Moments before she broke her arm. Maple branches dicing the sunlight overhead. Clouds sliding through the sky. Taking the shape of a fluffy dog. A parasol. Hot summer earth cupping their backs. The warmth of Nonie beside her. The scent of cigarettes on her breath. Her own head rising and falling with Nonie's breathing. She can't be dead.

"What do you think you'll be doing in the year 2000?"

Noreen can almost smell the wild horses she invented for

herself. Horses she alone could ride. Can almost feel ropy strands of mane clutched in her hands. "What about you, Nonie? Where will you be?"

"I'll be one of your horses, and we'll gallop away together, wherever you want to go." Her voice a promise, and Noreen almost hears a secret warning in it: *Remember this forever, little angel. Remember this instead of what comes next.*

*Weeks
Before.*

IN THE HARDBACK chair beside the hospital bed, Nonie's mother practices perfect posture. Sometimes she reads the latest issue of *Newsweek*, folding it back on itself. Other times she smooths it shut in her lap, and a montage of Ronald Reagan faces peeks back at Nonie from the cover while her mother, her lips two flat lines, fixes her eyes on the green rise of Brown's Mountain out the window or massages the put-upon expression from her brow. Nonie wants to tell her that sitting there looking bothered only makes things worse, gnaws the dark hole inside her wider, but when she tries to speak, her mouth feels full of cotton, and her lips won't move.

Sedation hazes her eyes, too, so the hospital room itself feels blurry, as if its actual edges are smudged and glowy. She fades in and out of the room with no idea how long gaps between awareness last. The room smells of antiseptic with faint undertones of summer grass. Her parents' backyard. Where Noreen fell from the tire swing, her arm bone jackknifing through the skin. Nonie fought as hard as she could to stay clearheaded, to do what Noreen needed, but her shivers took her anyway. Made her useless. She's always useless. Her breath dropped out of her and didn't come back.

The medicine holds her, dulls her, elongates her breaths so they come slow and heavy. Her thoughts bounce softly in her mind, reminding her of lightning bugs dancing in darkness. Her eyes flutter shut.

Once when she opens her eyes, a doctor peers down at her, a penlight in one hand, the other stretching her eyelids open. So, in fact, *he* has opened her eyes, unaware that she is aware of him. It's the strangest feeling of the day. Swimming, swimming up and out of the medicines in her veins. An animal in a zoo. Everyone watching.

The medicine muffles the doctor's words and serves them to her in a senseless chain: hyperventilating, panic disorder, Dr. Yang, appointments skipped, prescriptions unused. Her mother from her chair, sounding tired and old, says, yes, she'll remind Nonie. She'll urge her to make another appointment.

It must be much later when Nonie feels gentle pressure on her head and surfaces to meet it. Her sister Ruth stands beside her, stroking her forehead. Worry knits her face into premature wrinkles, and this time Nonie knows she's the cause for only some of it, with Noreen recovering from surgery somewhere else in the hospital. Nonie manages to gargle out the word, "Noreen," and Ruth's distant expression focuses on her with surprise. She tells her not to worry, that accidents happen and Noreen will be okay, but the lines on Ruth's face give away the secret that she doesn't know this for sure, that she's saying so to make Nonie feel better. She mentions that Ted is with Noreen, that they're staying as late as the hospital will let them before leaving her overnight, which is when Nonie realizes her own mother has gone. She pictures her mother eyeing the schoolroom-style clock on the wall across the room, willing its hands to reach the end of visiting hours, deciding that fifteen minutes earlier more than fulfills her duty. From the corner of her vision, the array of Ronald Reagans still gaze back at Nonie from the chair where her mother was sitting, holding her absence like a bookmark.

Ruth's words fade, then the light fades, sleep joining sedation, plunging her deeper into darkness she can't seem to rise through. Her memory merges with dreams, and visions come to her of childhood things. Forgotten dolls she cradled in her arms, singing lullabies. Who had taught her lullabies? Her grandmother, maybe, or Ruth, who must have tended her the way Nonie tended her pretend charges with their painted plastic faces. Then a puppy with a crinkled ear that followed her home from the neighborhood playground one day. His quick steps and warm marble eyes that looked up at her as if she in all the world were the best, most wonderful thing. The way Noreen sometimes looks at her now, only so much more knowingly and sometimes edged with fear.

The puppy only lasted a week. Her mother says it was because Nonie left the back gate unlatched, but she hadn't gone through the backyard that day. She and the puppy had come in from their walk through the front door. If anyone let the dog out back, it hadn't been her, but her mother insisted. *It doesn't matter when you forgot to latch the gate. It's always supposed to be latched, and you're the only one who forgets.* This, while tears coursed down Nonie's face, minutes after a driver had knocked on their front door with news that he had swerved, he had done his best, but the dog came out of nowhere. He was so, so sorry.

And a bird she found, half-mangled under a tree. A neighborhood cat must have gotten to it, chewed at its wing. Nonie found an old shoebox in the basement, lined it with pine needles and twigs, thinking it might feel like a nest, and settled that makeshift infirmary onto the dining room table. She slathered it with mercurochrome and murmured soft things, but she could see from its slowly glazing eyes, could feel from its heartbeat threading out and losing rhythm that there was no hope, long before her mother stormed in and shamed her for bringing such a mess into the house, for being hopeless, hopeless and never doing anything right. She feels like that bird as she slips in and out of the hospital room, in and out of knowing, in and out of feeling all the way alive. The bird had gone, like the puppy, like her grandmother would after that. Everything goes, eventually. Flame, flicker, gutter, then nothing. Nothing at all.

Immediately After.

NOREEN THINKS THE big room looks like a church, with its deep red carpeting, dark brown pews. It sounds like a church, too, with people whispering and the heavy carpet swallowing noises their feet make, but it's not a church, only a funeral home. One from a bundle of secrets she's overheard in the past few days is that Grammy and Grampy's church refused to host a funeral for a suicide. The man running the service isn't even a minister. That's what Noreen's mother told her when she asked who he was. His whole job is talking at funerals. Noreen pictures him traveling town to town, from one stranger's funeral to the next, reading special books to learn how to talk about people you've never met.

Noreen sits with her family in the front row wearing the black-checkered dress she borrowed from her friend Claudia. The pendant from the butterfly necklace Nonie gave her keeps slipping under the neckline, and Noreen keeps plucking it back into view. Her family only goes to services at Christmas and Easter, when they go with Grammy and Grampy to their church, and Noreen already grew out of her Easter dress, which is why she had to borrow this one. Her mother said her Easter dress was the wrong color anyway. As if there could be a right color for a day like today. Her cast caused a whole other set of problems, which is why her mother chose this dress, with its halter top, from the stack of hand-me-downs Claudia's mother brought over yesterday. It's too big, even after Noreen's mother tied it extra tight to keep the front from sagging outward and showing her chest. The halter ribbon chafes at her neck.

It feels weird to sit in a pew that's only for funerals. Noreen dangles her feet over the edge, numbly aware that in actual pews at actual churches she swings her feet during services and risks curt side-eyes from her mother. Today she doesn't want to fidget. She also doesn't want to look at the feeble, dusty Jesus hanging from a cross behind the funeral man. Before the service, Brynne whispered to Uncle Emmett and pointed at the little cart the Jesus stands on, guessing that they wheel it in and out depending on which religion goes with each funeral. So even the Jesus doesn't really belong. On the other side of the funeral man is Nonie's coffin, and Noreen doesn't want to look at that either, so she fixes her eyes on the man himself, staring so hard she thinks he must feel her eyes drilling into him. That might explain why he coughs in the middle of his sentences and jerks at his shirt collar.

Grammy's sister Ida from Manassas sits in the row behind them. Her powdery scent drifts up to Noreen and itches her nose. Ida's two daughters and their husbands are there, too, though their children aren't. People Noreen sees every few Thanksgivings. Their hushed words to each other alternate with the funeral man's choppy words.

"Poor Martha," one of the daughters says, referring to Grammy, who's seated only a few people away and as likely to overhear as Noreen. "She's so withered."

One of the husbands says, "And Jack? He must have taken a wallop with that bandage and the bruising," referring to Grampy, seated next to Grammy. Gauze stretches across his entire forehead, secured into place with thick strips of hospital tape. Bruises under his eyes. Of course Noreen had noticed, you couldn't help but notice, but no one explained it to her directly.

The funeral man says, "Tragedy always takes us *ahem* unawares."

"Must have been awful to find her like that." One of the women this time. Noreen's mother cranes around in the pew and serves them a stern glare while their words twist in Noreen's stomach. What she's been able to piece together chills her like the worst ghost story. That Grampy "found" Nonie somewhere he had to get her down from. That Nonie fell on top of him when he did. That he slammed his head into the basement stairway on his way down.

The funeral man says, "Anyone who knew Nonie knew her *ahem* passion for life, her *ahem* quest for originality." Someone must have told him about Nonie then, but still he doesn't know her. Not what she looked like, what her laugh sounded like, how the air got lighter when she sat down beside you. Sweat dots his forehead, and Noreen can tell he wants to rush to finish and dismiss everybody. What Noreen wants is for the whole world to know Nonie's gone. For the newsman to talk about her tonight. Not the way he talks about those hostages in Iran, far away and unknowable, and not the way this boring nervous man is talking, but with real sorrow. Surely the news could spare five minutes to talk about Nonie? A few photos of her smiling face in the corner of the screen. Because something horrible and permanent has happened. Something beautiful, lost forever. It should matter to everyone.

Each *ahem* makes Noreen angrier. She yanks her mother's sleeve. Ruth bends to listen. "When will he stop talking?"

Ruth pokes a finger to her lips and razors her eyes at Noreen. A whole set of rules for funeral behavior. They have to sit in the first row. They're supposed to look sad but not make noise. What's the point of sitting still and being good? What's it for?

Behind her, somebody else says, "So like Percy, isn't it? Such a heartbreak." The framed picture by Grammy's front door is the only reason Noreen knows who Percy is, Grammy's youngest brother. He died long before Noreen was born, maybe even before her mother was born. No one talks about him, though

Grammy passes his picture every time she walks through her own door. Why would anyone think of him now? In the grainy gray-and-white photo, Percy and a much younger Grammy sit next to each other in the front seat of an old-timey convertible, both their faces wide open with laughter. If her mother hadn't told her, Noreen would never have guessed that happy young woman was Grammy.

"Wasn't there a great-uncle, too, after the first World War? I've heard it runs in families, like hair and dimples."

Noreen and Nonie have the same hair, the same pale green eyes, the same laugh, the way it fizzes up to the surface like foam when you shake a soda bottle. At Grammy's house, anytime Nonie gets caught acting a certain way—like herself, as far as Noreen can tell—Grammy scolds Nonie, then turns on Noreen and scowls at her, too, as if she existed solely to remake her aunt's every mistake, a human version of déjà vu. Noreen rounds toward the last voice and casts a narrow-eyed glare. *Shut up shut up shut up*, she wants to say. *You don't know what you're talking about.*

The funeral man says a prayer about everlasting peace, for Nonie and *ahem* for all of us gathered here, and he gestures toward the reception in the next room. The red carpet gives way to white linoleum spidered with brown veins. Scents of roast beef and lilies replace the odors of carpet dust and pine cleanser from the room with the pews. A recording of organ music plays in the background, slow tunes Noreen almost recognizes.

The walls are white and bright, but there are no windows, no sunlight. One long table heads the room, swathed in maroon tablecloths and spread with food and flowers. Small tables with white tablecloths dot the rest of the room with little vases of lilies and rosebuds in their centers. In a far corner, an arrangement of lounge chairs and overstuffed sofas reminds Noreen of living room displays in the Miller & Rhoads furniture department downtown.

It's enough people to make a crowd. A mixture of seldom-seen distant family members, neighbors, people Nonie knew from college, work, and elsewhere. Everyone wants to touch Noreen's head or shake her mother's hand or hug them. So many stiff hugs. Like holding cardboard boxes. No one really expecting you to rest your head on their shoulder and cry.

"Make them stop touching me," Noreen says to her mother. Too loud again, judging by the look her mother gives her. Instead of scolding her though, Ruth searches the room, catches Noreen's father's eye, and waves him over.

"Ted, can you get Noreen a plate of food and set her up at the table with Mark and the cousins? She doesn't need to be greeting everybody with me."

With a palm on her head, her father pilots Noreen toward the table where Mark and Henry and Luke are already seated, picking at plates heaped with food. A hank of her father's tree-bark brown hair slides across his eyes as he kneels beside her chair. He tosses it aside with a flick of his chin. "How's my little skidoo?"

In her other ear, Noreen can almost feel the warmth Nonie's whisper would make, renaming her. "Little angel." Who wants to be a skidoo? She wants to kick her father away from her, kick the whole room away from her.

"I'll bring you some food," her father says, then taps one of her curls the way he does and slips back into the crowd.

Next, Claudia shows up with her usual pin-straight braids and a sunburnt nose, smelling of chlorine. The uniform of regular summer. "My mom said I should come over here."

Noreen doesn't know what to say to that, but Claudia doesn't wait for her to answer.

"I'm sorry about your aunt. I liked her."

It's nowhere near enough to say, so Noreen swallows back a *Me, too.*

"My mom says you can come over later. Spend the night. Ask your mom." More command than invitation. Claudia is used to getting her way.

"I don't want to," Noreen says. Last year in the middle of second grade, Claudia moved to town and landed in Noreen's class out of nowhere. Back then, her mother fretted about Noreen's shyness, and her teacher made things worse by forcing her to sit in the front row and requesting conferences with her parents. Noreen made friends with Claudia to stop people from worrying, which meant she would have done anything Claudia asked her to.

Like steal one of her mother's tubes of lipstick. Persimmon Frost. She still has it, buried deep in her sock drawer. Whenever her fingers brush into it, her stomach tickles the same as when the car goes too fast over the hump of a hill. Right now Noreen wouldn't care if a door blew open and the wind sucked Claudia straight up into the clouds.

"That's okay," Claudia says, giving in to Noreen. A first. She pulls herself onto the chair beside her and laces their fingers together, the way Nonie had sometimes.

At Noreen's other side, her cousin Henry draws a tic-tac-toe board for Luke on a napkin. Someone left a pack of crayons on the table. They're some off-brand, the kind that's too waxy and smells wrong. Mark draws monsters on his napkin. Claudia sits beside Noreen, holding her hand, until her mother arrives at the table to collect her.

"Don't you look pretty," Mrs. Mays says, as if that could matter. Noreen feels anything but pretty in Claudia's too tightly tied dress, her cast seeming to paperclip it in place. Only Claudia, her brother, and his best friend, Donny, have signed it in thick black marker strokes. The rest glows white as bone. Probably she's supposed to thank Mrs. Mays for the compliment, for lending her the dress, for coming today, but Noreen doesn't say anything. Her father delivers her plate of food in time to speak for her. He pumps Mrs. Mays' hand two or three times, braces his other hand on her shoulder. "It means a lot to Noreen that you came."

What it means that anybody came, the whole reason they're

gathered here, is that Nonie is dead, and Noreen will never see her again.

Mrs. Mays, her father, and Claudia dissolve back into the other milling guests, and Noreen is left with her brother and cousins again. Mark folds slices of roast beef into his mouth, and Henry copies him. They compete for who can fit the most in their mouths at one time. Their cheeks bulge, and they point at each other and laugh. Their full mouths muffle the sound. Henry chews with his mouth open and belches after he finally swallows. Their laughter amps louder.

"Cut it out," Noreen says.

"What?" Henry says. "We're never allowed to laugh again?"

"You're acting like babies."

Mark is ten to Henry's nine, but Henry carries himself as if he's older. Mark always sides with him. "You can't be sad forever," he says.

What if you can? No one told Noreen that sadness could ache, but she aches all over, as if she's been hammered with bricks. Maybe even that could last forever. She rests her free arm on the table in front of her and lays her head against it. The boys never crept into Nonie's lap after a bath and let her finger-brush their hair, patient around every tangle. They never lay back on the dirt to close their eyes and breathe slow with her so they could hear every sound in the world. Each individual bird. An airplane in the distance. The hum of bees on the azaleas in Grammy and Grampy's side yard. The whiz of tires along a rain-damp road. Silent, listening, Noreen could feel the earth slipping away beneath her shoulder blades. The world turning, Nonie explained. She made Noreen notice things, feel things, belong to things in a way nobody else does, and she never worried about her or made her feel like she should be different from how she is.

"You're getting mustard in your hair," Luke says.

Noreen ignores him and lets tears fall privately in the tent her face and hair make against her arm. She hears the plate beside her slide farther away and feels Luke gently daubing mustard out of her hair, hears the papery rustle of the napkin.

"My mom says she's an angel in heaven now," he says into her ear. "That's not so sad, is it?"

Noreen peeks at him through a curtain of her curls. She wants to say something nasty, but Luke faces her with his little pink smile and big brown eyes, and the will to make him feel bad just because she does evaporates.

Are angels and ghosts different? She searches past Luke, gazing up to the ceiling as if she might see through it, out to where Nonie's ghost-angel eyes might be looking back at her. Yearning for any hint, any fragment of her presence. For a moment the whole room shimmers with—angels? dead people? Or is this what happened to Nonie? That feeling she talked about, of slipping away from herself with no trace of how to return. Like a shadow falling across her on the inside. She'd disappear into it, empty herself from her eyes. Hug her knees as if bombs were falling on her head. Watching it happen to her aunt, Noreen would try anything she could think of to stop it. Now, she wants to connect to it, the strange promise of finding Nonie inside it, but all she feels is a zing of energy, like a flurry of tiny angels darting around inside her. Then everything unshimmers, turns back into the regular room, with its forks squeaking against plates, the low chatter of people talking, and that organ music piping through unseen speakers.

No Nonie. Not anywhere.

Her brother tosses grapes in the air, trying to catch one in his mouth, laughing when they miss and bounce onto the table or floor. Henry copies him. When she frowns their way, Mark beans his grape into her chin instead. She scrapes her chair backwards and stomps away. Halfway across the room, she stops, realizing she's been searching for Nonie. Remembers she'll never find her anywhere again.

In the far corner, her grandfather slumps forward in one of

the living room chairs, resting his forehead on a bag of something in his hand. Ice, probably, for whatever happened to his head. However he hurt himself finding Nonie. Whatever *finding Nonie* means. Grammy stares ahead of herself, a plate of food on her lap, her hands holding its sides. Her mother and Brynne, finally finished shaking everybody's hands at the entrance, lean toward each other at the far end of the sofa.

In the opposite direction, fancily dressed people poke at offerings along the food table. A chunk of bright pink sherbet eddies in a huge punch bowl. White icing and pink rosettes decorate a giant sheet cake. Like a backwards birthday party.

"Twins," says a man standing nearby. She'd been so disoriented she hadn't noticed him before. He's a tall Black man with a big afro wearing a bright yellow dress shirt and a tie with a green army jacket and one sleeve pinned at the elbow. He uses his eyebrows and a tilt of his chin to gesture between that and Noreen's cast. She nods, tries to smile at the similarity.

"Nonie lived downstairs from me."

"She was my aunt."

"You must be the famous Noreen? I thought I recognized you from the pictures she showed me. She talks about you all the time." He coughs. "Talked."

Despite herself, for the first time that day, she smiles. "What did she say?"

"Just that the sun and stars shined out of you," he says. "That you made her happy."

It was hard right then to think of Nonie being happy. "She made me happy, too."

With his one hand, the man rolls and unrolls the hem of his jacket cuff. "She had a happy spirit. Gave it to everybody around her."

Spirit. Another ghost word. Can ghosts be happy? Her cast feels suddenly heavier.

The man talks for a little while longer, about how he and

Nonie looked out for each other, how she was the only civilian who understood him. Civilian is a word Noreen has only ever heard on TV news. She isn't sure what it has to do with Nonie.

"I don't want to keep you," the man says, meaning he probably caught her stealing glances toward the end of the room where her family bides their time on the fake living room furniture. The man tilts his head to look at her. She can feel how sad he is through the air. "I just wanted to tell you I'm sorry and to let you know how much your aunt thought of you. But I bet you already knew." He winks. The saddest wink she's ever seen, but it makes her smile again. She thanks him and nods the way she's seen so many adults doing today, then aims for her mother.

A cluster of white-haired women approaches Grammy at about the same time. Relatives whose names Noreen has either forgotten or never knew. First and second cousins of Grammy's, smelling of flowers and wearing shoes that clack on the tile floor.

When she reaches the living room set, Noreen scoots onto the sofa beside her mother, flopping onto her back as gracefully as her cast allows and laying her head in her lap. Her mother strokes her hair. Words muffle and unmuffle in time with the sweep of her hand. "I keep thinking we were supposed to figure out how to stop her," she whispers to Brynne. "There must have been signals. Something we could've said or done."

"Nonie was never easy to help," Brynne says. "You could always tell she needed something, but who knew what?"

Down at the other end of the sofa, the white-haired cousins are saying their sorrys to Grammy. One holds a handkerchief to her mouth like a veil for her words. "It must've brought back sad memories of Percy."

"Nonsense," Grammy says, sitting straighter than before. A carrot stick rolls out of place on her untouched plate. "Nonie was selfish. Percy, too. Selfish and self-pitying. They should've pulled themselves together the way the rest of us have to. Every day."

The cousins bob their heads like birds at breadcrumbs, then

trade meaningful looks before excusing themselves to the food table. Grammy swats the air behind them, as if trying to wipe them away. A handkerchief tucked between her palm and thumb flashes a surprise of white that catches Noreen's eye. When Grammy notices Noreen looking her way, she purses her lips yet tighter. "Don't you go and turn out the same, little Miss Head in the Clouds," she says in a voice directed only at her.

Over her head, Brynne and her mother trade a few more whispers about what they might have done if they'd known, so they miss Grammy's warning. Noreen covers her eyes with her free hand to block Grammy's face, taut with anger.

Ice shifts in the bag in Grampy's hand, and he boosts forward on his chair, closer to Grammy, brushes his hand against hers. Noreen peeks between splayed fingers and watches her grandmother's face soften briefly, then she squints and sits rigid as a soldier again, hands stiff beside the plate in her lap. Brynne flicks a thread from her dress and crosses her arms over her chest, seeming to study something far across the room. Her mother drapes a hand across Noreen's shoulder and lets out a long breath. For a moment, all the grownups sit silent and still, staring into separate pockets of the enormous room.

Noreen rolls her head to look up into her mother's face, then asks quietly, so only Ruth can hear, "Are you mad at Nonie, too?"

"Mad?" She keeps her voice between the two of them, too, but tightens her gaze on her own mother, as if she'd overheard everything after all, before shaking her head and looking at Noreen. "No, I'm not mad. I do wish she would've taken her medicines though. That she would've called and asked for help when things got to be too much for her."

Noreen scrambles to sit up. "She did call." She hunches deeper into the sofa beside her mother, trying to fend off a sudden chill. "She called me. That morning."

"You talked to Nonie that day?"

The look on her mother's face reminds Noreen of ghosts

again. She checks over her shoulder, just in case. Nothing but men in suits and women in dark dresses eating little sandwiches.

"What did she say?" Ruth asks.

"She said she was sorry."

Her mother closes her eyes and presses her hand to her lips. "Yes, I'm sure she was."

At the other end of the sofa, Grammy lights a cigarette. Its smoke trail wavers up the side of her body, like a skinny ghost of something. Ghosts and ideas of ghosts everywhere, but none of them are Nonie.

Six Weeks After.

NOREEN WANTS TO go straight home from school. Her throat hurts. That's why the nurse called her mom in the first place, but her mother wants to stop at the Kroger. They need lettuce and bananas and a few other things. It'll only take a minute, she says.

Inside, the colors of the produce feel too bright. Her mother selects a head of iceberg lettuce, places it in the grocery cart. Mrs. Perwitz, a classmate's mother, approaches the radishes nearby. Close enough for speaking, she slices her glance toward the floor and swings her cart toward the case of refrigerated salad dressings instead.

Right after Nonie died, people rushed to speak to them. First they came to the house in droves, offering casseroles and Bundt cakes. Then they hurried toward them wherever they went. Shopping for underwear at the Miller & Rhoads, waiting in line at the post office, walking through the neighborhood to go to Greenleaf Park, even swinging on the swing set there. Everyone wanted to tell them how they'd been praying for them or how awful the tragedy was. They would gaze on them with sad puppy eyes, clamp onto their hands, tsk and shake their heads. Some seemed truly sorry, and others seemed curious in a way that made Noreen's stomach hurt.

Now, not quite two months later, when people see them, most can't even manage to say hello. Like Mrs. Perwitz, they resist eye contact and pretend you're not there.

The iceberg lettuce rolls in the seat meant for children smaller than Noreen. Rolls around like a separated head. As if her mother overheard her thought, she plucks it out of the cart and puts it back among the other icebergs. She fingers heads of red and green leaf lettuces instead. Handles some romaine. She doesn't fix on any of them.

"Mom? Are we almost done?" Noreen's voice is quiet as a breath, each word a flame on her throat. The school nurse said strep throat was going around. Noreen's never had strep throat, so she doesn't know if that's what's making her legs feel noodley.

"I'm sorry, love." Maybe her mother's voice seems off because Noreen feels so woozy, but more and more lately her mother's words drift away from their meanings, run into other words, forget where they're going. Here among the vegetables, she looks like a lost child. Like Nonie the day Noreen broke her arm. All at once Nonie had run out of breath, like someone dropped her puppet strings. She fell forward and clutched at her throat as her cheeks reddened, lips purpled. If her arm hadn't broken and the ambulance hadn't come, would Nonie have died that day instead?

Some nights Noreen shouts herself awake from bad dreams that play out different ways she might have killed Nonie from not knowing what to do. Over and over, Ruth reminds her that grownups take care of children, not the other way around. What happened to Nonie had nothing to do with Noreen, no matter what her nightmares tell her. That day in the yard, and of course later, Nonie needed help, but not from Noreen. She had attacks that frightened her. That's why she went to a special doctor who could help with things like that. Her mother explains and re-explains that Nonie had hyperventilated that day, which is when you take in too much air at once. Too much air suffocates you. Even though that doesn't make sense, that having too much air is exactly the same as having no air at all. It knocked Nonie out. Ambulance or no ambulance, alone with Nonie or with all of them there together, no matter what, hyperventilating would have done the same thing and no more. It never would have killed her.

Hearing this explanation for the ninth or tenth time, Noreen braved asking, "Did I make her do that? Run out of air?"

"How could you make her do that?" Ruth had been standing at her bedside, but then settled beside Noreen on the edge of the bed.

"Because of my arm. Did my arm scare all the air out of her?" She'd been wondering since the first moment Nonie glimpsed it, twisted behind Noreen's back. The doctor told her later that the bone was sticking through the skin, which would've terrified her if she could've seen it.

Noreen's mother fidgeted with her curls, brushing them out of her face the way she did when she couldn't think what to say. Outside the open window, crickets kept up a steady hum. "I'm sure she was afraid," she said. "But that's not your fault."

"Whose fault was it then?"

Her mother reeled back at the question, dropping Noreen's curls and letting them bounce against her temples again. "No one's. It's no one's fault."

Here in the supermarket, with her mother acting so strangely, Noreen reminds herself that it's not her job to know what to do. It's hard, though, because her mother doesn't seem to know either. She plods along behind her, away from the produce aisle. They hover over tiers of blue-edged pasta boxes. Jars of sauce in ranks just beyond. One spaghetti box goes into the cart, two. One goes back out. For weeks they've eaten spaghetti and salads or takeout pizzas from Anna's #9 over by UVA.

"Could we please have something besides spaghetti?" Noreen asks.

Ruth laughs lightly, as if Noreen were waking her from an unexpected dream. "We have had a lot of spaghetti," she says and puts the rest of the pasta back on the shelf. They roll to the frozen foods. Ruth scans the packages of vegetables behind the glass doors, her head batting from one to the next and back again.

"How about peas?" Noreen says. She knows they eat a lot of peas, but she doesn't know if they're out of them. She only wants her mother to do something, anything that seems right to do at a store. Her mother nods distractedly and lowers a big bag of peas into the cart. Then they're back in the produce section. Bananas, carrots, radishes. One after the other. The spurt of decisiveness encourages Noreen.

The produce section ends in a corner of shelves of bread. Her mother chooses their usual brand, but something catches her eye, and she drops the loaf to the floor. Her mother appears to be staring at a Black man farther down the aisle. A small basket hangs from his wrist with a loaf of bread and some apples in it. He's wearing a green army jacket and shoes that make a shush noise against the store's tile floor. Noreen wants to stop her mother from staring, but she doesn't know how. She tugs at her sleeve, trying at least to bring her attention back to her.

In a loud whisper Ruth says, "I think I know him. I think he was a friend of Nonie's, from the funeral."

Noreen looks at the man again. Most of the funeral guests blend together for Noreen. So few had said anything personal or specific, but Noreen does remember the one-armed man. How he knew who she was because Nonie had talked about her and how he called Nonie a "civilian." This man in the store is about the same age and height as the man from the funeral, but he has two arms and in every other way looks different from Nonie's quiet, lanky friend. Maybe this man had been at the funeral, too, and Noreen hadn't seen him, but she's pretty sure her mother is wrong and that this man is a stranger.

"He stopped by her apartment, too, when we were packing her things," Ruth says. "He asked after her there. She meant something to him. She was kind to him, I think." Her mother looks proud that Nonie meant something to other people.

Noreen had felt the same when the one-armed man had spoken to her at the funeral. The man who most certainly is not this man.

He spins around to face them. Either he overheard or was simply changing direction to find the next item on his list, but his swift motion surprises her mother. The cart scoots out of her grip, and when she brings a foot backward to steady herself, she slips instead and clatters to her knees.

Noreen's throat feels like fire, and the lights are still too bright. There must be something she's supposed to do. All she wants is to lie down.

The man bends toward Ruth. "Are you okay?"

"I think you knew my sister." Even as the words come out, any sign of recognition fades from her mother's face to be replaced by red blemishes of embarrassment.

"Your sister?" the man asks, puzzled.

He helps Ruth to her feet. Noreen clings against her. The shelves feel too tall around them, and exhaustion turns to static in her ears. She needs to lie down, but they can't seem to get out of the grocery store. It's like one of those dreams when a monster is chasing you and you can't move your legs or make any noise to scream.

"Maybe you should sit down?" The man looks around for a seat of some kind, then returns moments later with a manager.

"Ma'am, you're bleeding," the manager says, startled. Ruth's pantyhose ripped at her knees when she fell, opening a hole around each kneecap. Both are scraped, but only one is bleeding. The mess and blood make Noreen want to cover her mother's knees somehow, to keep people from seeing.

"Let me help you," he says. "We'll get you cleaned up in my office."

The manager wears a red plastic badge that says *Al Harris* and John Denver-style glasses. On him, the glasses make his eyes seem bigger than normal and give him a look of fear. Maybe he is afraid. Noreen is.

The manager's office is at the back of the store, through the swinging doors that say *Staff Only*. They turn left. Turning right would have landed them behind the butcher's counter. They hear the nearby hacking of meat.

With one hand, the manager slides a stack of papers from the red plastic chair beside his desk and gestures for Ruth to sit. Noreen remains standing at her side, but she leans as much of her weight as possible against the chair's plastic armrest.

The manager calls in a clerk to help. The clerk, the same age as her mother with short curly hair like Carol Burnett, lifts a first-aid kit from the bottom drawer of the gray metal desk and kneels in front of Ruth. She rips an antiseptic cloth from a tiny packet and cleans each knee, even though only one is bleeding. Next, she fixes Band-Aids into place, finessing the sticky edges under the flaps of torn pantyhose. Behind them, the manager fishes a purple lollipop from a drawer. Noreen tears away the wrapper and sucks, letting the syrup coat her throat.

"Who could I call to pick you up?" the manager says.

"That won't be necessary," Ruth says. "I just slipped. I'm fine."

"I'd really rather call someone." Even he can tell Ruth needs something extra today, but his voice is gruff, like figuring out what to do with them isn't worth his time. Ever since Nonie died, Noreen notices gruffness everywhere. "You can't let it ruin you," her mother tells her sometimes, "the roughness of the world." It's probably what ruined Nonie though, which is why it upsets Noreen.

Despite Ruth's arguments—about the car she drove here and how much trouble it will be to leave it behind and come back for it later, about how she has to get home in time to meet her son off the bus—the manager insists that someone come to pick them up.

"I don't have energy to keep arguing with you," Ruth says, giving up the way she sometimes does with Noreen's father. She reels off Ted's office phone number.

The manager clacks a pen against his metal desk while he waits. "Mr. Jamison?" he finally says. "I'm calling from the Kroger. I have your wife here. She's all right, but she fell down and seems a little rattled."

"Oh, for God's sake," Ruth says, then a little louder, "Ted, really, I'm all right. The man just doesn't want to be sued." The manager ignores Ruth and explains to Noreen's father where his office is and how he can park at the loading dock so Ruth won't have far to walk.

It's quiet in the manager's messy little office. White-painted cinderblock walls. A bulletin board covered in papers. Shiny binders in slipshod stacks splay across the desktop, and the heat seems to be working overtime.

"How's that lollipop?" the manager asks Noreen. "How do you like school?" Each time she talks her throat hurts a little more. She sucks the lollipop until its soggy paper stick unravels.

When Noreen's father arrives, he bustles in, frazzled and an-noyed. Noreen wants to explain how her mother seemed lost today, and she wants him to gather them quickly and usher them away to keep her mother from spinning aimlessly through the store again and embarrassing herself in front of strangers. But she doesn't want him to make her feel bad about it, so she doesn't say anything.

"I'm all right, Ted," Ruth says.

"We just want to be careful." The manager speaks over her. "Anytime there's a fall."

"Like I said, he's afraid of a lawsuit." Ruth aims her snide tone at the manager. "It was nothing, really."

Ted registers Noreen's presence now as something unex-pected. "Why isn't Noreen in school?" He flicks a glance at his watch.

"A sore throat. I was just picking up a few things on the way home."

"When Noreen's sick?" Her father lifts Noreen into his arms, presses his cheek against her forehead. "She's a little hot." Still, he looks at her mother and not at Noreen.

Ruth's face pinches into worry lines. "Have I dragged you all around the store with a fever, Noreen? You didn't have one when we left." She holds her wrist against Noreen's forehead to test the temperature. "Oh no, you are hot. I'm so sorry."

Balancing Noreen on his hip, Ted reaches his other hand to help his wife stand. Ruth's shoes skid against the slick tiles, and she almost falls back into the chair. "It's nothing," she says and swats Ted's hand away. Ted and the manager both look at her with doubt on their faces.

"Anyway, we still need supper," Ruth says, recovering her footing at last. "I had groceries."

"Leave us your list," the manager says. "And your address. I'll have someone deliver. We can bill you."

"You deliver?" Ruth says, handing over her ratty list, the first Noreen has seen of it.

"Not normally," the manager says.

Ted scrawls their home address on the back of one of his business cards and hands it to the manager. "I can't thank you enough."

Still carrying Noreen, Ted leads Ruth from the manager's office and down the hall behind the butcher's station, which reeks of raw meat. The back door opens onto the loading dock, where her father's car waits.

Her father can't see the keys jangling in his hand because Noreen's blocking his view, so he switches her to his other hip and braces her there while he clambers to unlock the door. He's impatient, so it takes two tries. He slides Noreen from his hip and into the back seat. "We'll have to figure out how to get your car later," he says to Ruth.

"That's silly," her mother says. She slips into the passenger seat and clicks her seat belt into place. "My car's around front.

I'll show you. You can drop us off there."

"No time," her father says. He reverses around an eighteen-wheeler backed up to a loading bay, then brakes for a man wheeling a dolly of collapsed boxes toward a dumpster. "We have to get home before Mark's bus."

Ruth turns away from him. "I don't know what happened. I thought I saw a friend of Nonie's. I was going to say hello, and I slipped. That's all."

In the back seat, Noreen rubs her hands and shivers. Everything takes on watery edges. Green, silver, black cars, streaks of color in the sunshine. Beyond them, trees in a kaleidoscope of greens, golds, and oranges melt into cool lines of blue mountains.

Her father curses a red light. "Mark is going to beat us home, and I have to get back to my meeting."

"I'm sorry, Ted," Ruth says. "I should've refused when the manager insisted on calling you. I was fine, really."

Noreen doesn't think her mother was fine, but she doesn't want to argue. She surrenders to her closing eyes. Her parents' words sound swimmy from the back seat.

"You were disoriented. And bleeding. Of course he had to call. I would have."

"I said I'm sorry." Her mother's voice is brittle. "What more can I do?"

The car switches between lurching and staying still. The chuff of the engine and the buzz in her ears smother some of her parents' conversation.

"There was a piano teacher," Ruth says after a while, in the nighttime voice she uses on long car rides when she assumes Noreen and Mark are sleeping. "Nonie went to him when she was little. One time she told me she found dirty magazines in his bathroom."

"And?" Ted says. The next light turns green.

"You know how people have those repressed memories? Something bad happens when they're little, but they forget for years and years? I read an article about it, waiting in the hair salon the other day."

"Yeah, I've heard of it, but, what? Are you saying Nonie had repressed memories? Of porn in a bathroom?"

"Ted, you don't have to get angry."

"I'm not angry."

He does sound angry though. Noreen wishes they would talk about something else.

"I'm just saying, what if her piano teacher was a really horrible guy, and we didn't know it?"

Noreen parts her eyes open. Another traffic light. It blurs red as her eyes drop shut again.

"Shit," Ted mutters. Noreen's spine stiffens at the bad word. "You've got to stop it, Ruth."

"Stop what?" Noreen hears the crush of the seat as her mother leans forward. The turn signal's ticking sounds like a clock.

"You worried about Nonie all her life," her father says. "You can't explain what happened to her. And you couldn't stop it. Nobody could."

"We should've brought her to our house instead of Mother and Dad's. Like I wanted."

Noreen's father strikes the steering wheel with a loud crack. "Then what? Have her hang herself in *our* basement?" He whispered *hang herself*, but Noreen heard.

"Ted!"

"You couldn't fix her when she was alive, and you have to stop trying to fix her now that she's gone. You have to let it go, Ruth."

Noreen's throat burns hotter. She peeks through the slits of her eyes, and everything fogs pink from the brake lights of the cars ahead of them.

"You think scolding me will help?" Ruth says.

"I have no idea what will help."

At home, Noreen's father pulls the car into the drive. "Can you do this?" he asks, looking toward the house, sounding fed up. Noreen sits up as noisily as possible, to remind them she's here, that she can hear every word.

"Do what?"

"Go inside, like a regular day, and take care of Mark and Noreen?"

Ruth reaches a hand to his chin and turns him gently to face her. "This is hard for me," she says. "I'm doing the best I can."

Her father lets his chin droop into her mother's hand. His features relax a little. "I know, Ruth. I know you are."

Her mother unlatches her door just as Mark comes into view at the top of the street. A batch of school papers for her to sign wags in his hand. Ted toots the horn and waves at Mark, then drives away, leaving them there on the sidewalk.

Before Mark reaches their yard, Ruth crouches to Noreen's eye level. Her nylons gape at the knees and show tidy Band-Aid squares. "I'm sorry I scared you today," she says. "From now on, I promise to do better."

Then Mark lunges into the yard, and her mother twirls toward him with a day-bright face. "Look who skinned her knees today, Mark. Like a toddler. In the middle of the grocery store!" They both giggle, like it was all a joke. Then Ruth scoops Noreen into her arms and, finally, carries her inside.

Nineteen Years After.

IT'S NOREEN'S FIRST overnight trip anywhere for months. Her first visit with anyone other than George, Evie, and her Saturday playgroup's fellow moms and toddlers since her last visit with Grammy O'Malley in the ICU, nearly a month earlier.

"It's a terrible reason for a road trip, I know," Noreen says, but she feels oddly cheerful piling the duffel bag for her and George, plus the extra little one for Evie, into the back seat of the Volvo to head to Charlottesville for Grammy's funeral. "I know it's weird under the circumstances." Noreen buckles Evie into place, taps the tip of her nose, then waits until Evie taps hers in return before ducking out of the back seat. "But I can't help being excited to have the family together. Most of them have only met Evie a few times." Evie turns three this spring, and Noreen can hardly believe it. She slips into her seat, shuts the door, swivels around, and flashes three fingers at Evie. "Such a big girl!" Facing forward again, she says to George, "I love how happy my mother looks with Evie around."

"I know," George says. He waits while she clicks her seatbelt, then follows their half-circle driveway to the gravel road.

"And my dad's coming down from Boston," Noreen says. The only reason he would make the trip for his ex-mother-in-law's funeral is to be there for her and Mark, which is more effort than he usually makes. Her father left when Mark was already away at college, so she navigated the fallout alone at home—her mother's metastasizing sorrow, her own burgeoning anger, plus acne and PSAT prep. It took her a few years to soften toward him, and by then he'd remarried and moved to Boston.

Over the years since, he's fallen in rank from family to more like family friend. They trade polite conversation over the phone every month or so. When he travels anywhere near Virginia, he lets Noreen know where he'll be, and on these occasions they've met up at highway diners and posh restaurants, whatever happens to fall at the midpoint between them. Noreen knows the names and ages of her half-brother and -sister, has met them a couple of times, but her father hasn't rolled them into a more formal sense of family. "If he wants to try harder with me, I'm open."

"You've said."

"All of it?"

"A few times."

"Sorry." She double-checks Evie in the back seat, makes a puffer fish face. Evie chuffs a laugh, half-mast because they've timed the drive for her naptime. "But people light up when Evie's around. You can't blame me for looking forward to that, can you?"

"No, of course not," George says.

In her bed in the ICU, days after her second and final stroke, Grammy had sat up straight against a bulwark of pillows, her gray hair trimmed in its usual flat line, lips their usual shade of pearly pink. She looked almost like herself, if you ignored the apparatuses spidering between her and the array of bedside machines, the downslope of her mouth, and the vacancy of her expression, as if she had begun to leave her body behind already. Noreen had combed her wispy hair, and her grandmother had thanked her, drily, then asked for water. They both seemed to know they wouldn't see each other again.

Only one visitor was allowed at a time, so Ruth had entertained Evie in the waiting room with a tiny quilted house Evie could carry like a purse. Noreen wishes she and Evie could've stayed overnight then, too. Her mother could have used the break in her caretaking routine. Grammy's last stroke marked the end of a long downward spiral in her health, and with Brynne and her family in Richmond, Ruth had been alone in her daily visits to the hospital for some time already. Between George's regular teaching schedule, though, and a Saturday commitment for a department committee he'd joined to bolster his tenure portfolio, the soonest the car was available was the Sunday a few days after the stroke.

So the visit offered no break for her mother. Instead it deputized her to look after Evie during Noreen's time with Grammy, all while every hospital waiting room TV ran seemingly nonstop montages of Columbine High School footage, showing survivors being marched out of the school after the massacre, then chains of the same students clinging to each other later at funerals and memorials, parents weeping. Ruth had to stand on a chair to turn the TV off so she could play with Evie in peace, and, still, rather than seeming overwhelmed by the babysitting or the extra onus of protecting Evie from the latest scourge of the world she'd been born into, her mother brightened at the prospect of time with her granddaughter and the excuse it gave her to crack into the storehouse of toys she keeps on hand for their visits.

Which are rarer than Noreen would like. If only talk of a second car didn't drag George's father's money between them. She sneaks a glance at George now, wanting to blame him, but his sure expression fixes on the road ahead the way it always does. He means to be looking out for both of them, for all three of them, even when she thinks there are better ways to go about it. At least her short time with Grammy had felt like an almost-proper goodbye.

When they reach the blacktop road, Noreen powers down the window and lets the wind riffle her fingers the way she had sometimes as a kid. All the way to the highway, her stomach dips with relief. She wishes she could love that old house as much as she did when they'd bought it. Instead she's come to resent its seclusion along with its never-ending needs. Wind damages rooftops, faucets leak, old furnaces get fussy. Outside, she can ignore the nagging presence of unfixed things inside, and Evie loves romping around in the grass or tossing pebbles into the creek. Or mostly watching Noreen toss them. Evie drops hers too soon or rolls them instead of winging them through the air. Either way, Evie claps her hands at the splashes and begs, "More, more, more!" Same as when Noreen clasps her by the wrists and spins her in the air. Over and over until they both fall over in the grass from dizziness, laughing and laughing, with Evie scrambling back to standing first, then lifting her arms toward Noreen again. "More, more, more!" The sorts of things she and Nonie had done together, she's sure. Nonie, who taught her what joy feels like. *Little Miss Head in the Clouds*. Her grandmother's bitterness, like acid in the mouth.

"I wish I had fonder memories of Grammy," Noreen says, sealing the window again and settling her hands in her lap. "My cousins visited from Richmond once or twice a month when we were small, and we'd run wild in Grammy and Grampy's yard." At first, only the boys ran wild. When Nonie was alive, so much younger than Ruth that she'd felt more like a big sister than an aunt, Mark and the cousins would hurly-burly around the yard with each other, and Nonie would belong to Noreen alone. After Nonie died, no one tried to take her place or ease her absence during family gatherings. Grampy even cut down the tire swing that had been a sort of haven for Noreen and Nonie. It had hung from the best old maple tree in all of Grammy and Grampy's yard. Springtimes, Noreen and Nonie would collect handfuls of maple seedpods and toss them into the wind to watch them helicopter to the ground. Summertimes, they'd lie flat under it for the shade and the advantage of the slight rise of hillock there that seemed always to face into a breeze. Not a trace of the swing or its rope remained once Grampy got finished with it. Noreen imagined he blamed it somehow for Nonie's death, or possibly afterward he could no longer bear the sight of any hanging thing. The bald spot beneath the tree was the only sign the swing had ever been there.

Before weeds and grass finally covered it over, Noreen would often rest there against the earth and read a book in the quiet or close her eyes and concentrate until she could feel the earth spin, the way she had with Nonie beside her. The boys teased her when she wandered off alone that way. She knew they'd never understand what that patch of ground meant to her, so she'd hop up to join them when they found her, and she'd hurl footballs across the lawn or chase Frisbees or play war, because she felt like she was supposed to and there was nothing else to do. It might have made a difference if Grammy or Grampy had fished her from the pool of rowdy boys and asked her if she was okay. "We were at their house a lot, but they were never so much a *part* of things."

George doesn't say anything, but he often doesn't. He says he likes to listen, and she hopes he means it. As soon as he comes home from work at night, she finds herself throwing a barrage of words at him, scatterings of ideas and impressions that pile up during the day with no one but Evie to tell them to.

"Even when I broke my arm in their backyard, Grammy and Grampy didn't come see what happened." Five years married, she feels like she and George know everything about each other, but then something like this comes up. "Have I ever told you about breaking my arm?"

"I think I remember you'd broken a bone before."

"That's what the scar on my arm is from."

"I'm sure you've mentioned it," he says.

Now she studies the mark over his eyebrow, recalling it from early on when they'd cataloged each other's scars on their way to mapping each other's bodies. He'd run into a sliding glass door as a little boy, not realizing it was closed. Her fingertip warms with the memory of that first time she'd touched those flesh-sutured ridges, and even now she feels a surge of pity for how much the broken glass must have hurt and frightened him.

"It was a bad break." Not for the first time, she tries to describe the feeling Nonie brought with her, how she made Noreen feel special, important. Also, the spinning of the tire, the rope unwinding and burning her palms, then the clarity, that moment before she fell, when she knew she would but hadn't yet. Then the unrealness of the fall. Watching what happened as if from a distance, as if it had happened to someone else. "My parents shot out of the house, but Grammy and Grampy only came as far as their front porch."

Noreen stops describing but keeps remembering. The sound of the siren from inside the ambulance. The way it seemed to belly up from her own gut. Nonie there beside her, a plastic mask pumping her full of the air she'd run out of as soon as she'd glimpsed the wreck of Noreen's arm. Almost real, Nonie's face comes clear, as if broadcast onto the passenger window, with that same drawn look she'd had the moment before she called for help for Noreen. The moment before she needed help herself, and the one moment when it was unquestionably clear that Nonie would never, ever do anything to hurt her. Not on purpose. She never meant to hurt anyone else.

The story's urgency has drained away, flattening the tone of Noreen's voice. "My grandparents watched the ambulance drive off with their arms folded, like it was nothing. Like they expected disasters to happen."

"You get so sad when you talk about your aunt," George says. "I wish you wouldn't."

She doesn't know if he means he wishes talking about Nonie didn't hurt her or that she wouldn't talk about her. "I was talking about my grandmother," Noreen says. She inches closer to the passenger door and farther from him.

Tractor trailers hem them in on all sides, cutting off sunlight from the faded sky. In the backseat, Evie's head tips sideways, her mouth pursed open, eyelids purplish and misty with sleep. Noreen hopes Evie never knows the kind of sorrow a death like Nonie's brings, a wound that never finishes scarring over but stays forever raw and new.

Strange, though, how joy rides on the back of sorrow. You have to feel both to feel either. And no amount of best intentions can keep you from hurting what you love.

Without looking away from the road, George rests a hand on her knee and traces his fingers along her thigh. Her neck tightens, as if he could be privy to her thought sequence, his touch an omen.

In the next lane a truck speeds up, passes, and opens her view to a flash of mountain ridges zipping past until more traffic comes along and obscures them again. She focuses on the strip of dirt at the edge of the road sliding past.

Everyone at the funeral will tweak Evie's cheek and say how much she's grown, how much she looks like Noreen. They'll think it, but they won't say how much she looks like Nonie, because of course she does, and no one wants to think about that. Nonie, the only one who'll never meet her.

Weeks Before.

WITH THE SUN beating down on it, little Noreen's hair is so blond it makes your eyes hurt. At least it makes Nonie's eyes hurt. That could be one of her migraines, though, or one of her hangovers. Each makes the other worse. This feels better. Closing her eyes against the brightness. Sprawling head-to-head in the summer grass of her parents' backyard with her niece and namesake. The only person who makes her feel necessary. The steaming Virginia earth beneath them. If Nonie could hold this feeling in her hand like a stone, she would never let it go.

Dr. Yang calls them intruders, the thoughts that make her feel like a speck of dirt on the ground of the earth, the shadow of a dust mite, the still of the air that comes after a big wind and no one knows is there. She will not give way to them today. Not here. Not now, in the sunshine with Noreen.

"Watch this," Noreen says. She holds her hands above her own eyes, opening and closing her fingers like birds' beaks. "It's like a light show. Try it."

Nonie tries it, squinting against the light. Spokes of maple branches already splice the sky into shards. Her fingers scissor them into yet more pieces.

"Now blink, like this," Noreen says, rolling her head toward her and blinking in rapid succession, her mouth gapped open in a lazy smile. Nonie laughs at the sight of her, starts blinking just as fast, wincing whenever the light comes too strong and bangs into her headache.

Inside the house, her sisters and their husbands lounge in the air-conditioned living room with their parents, Noreen's grandparents, talking about who-knows-what. Will it be the Hollywood actor for president, or will the peanut farmer gain a second term? How many more days for the hostages in Iran? Subjects that tire Nonie for being so far out of reach. Out front, Noreen's brother and her other nephews shout, run, toss footballs, climb trees. Like the hum of distant flies.

Lying beside Noreen in the grass, blinking the sky into a wonder of lights, feels like home, but the rest of them feel like strangers, even though she grew up right here with her sisters, in this same house their parents have lived in for close to forty years. That awful Mrs. Mackey's house across the street, its porch sagging now. Fry's Spring Beach Club and Wayside Chicken a few streets away. Her father's office in UVA Hospital's accounting department a mile up the train tracks at the bottom of the yard. Familiar and not familiar. Real and not real.

Growing up, Nonie would rush to the tracks, day or night, at the sound of passing cargo trains. Wind, grit spiking against her. The promise of other places and other lives spooling out of view. Her mother yelling at her from the front porch not to stand so close.

"Nonie? Are you sleeping?" Noreen pokes her shoulder.

"No way," she says. "And miss hanging out with you?"

Above them, clouds shift in and out of shapes. "What do you see?" Nonie asks.

Nestling her sweaty head into the crook of Nonie's arm, Noreen points out an elephant, a fluffy dog. Nonie finds a dragon, a parasol, a cake. "Do you see it?" she asks. "That one, there. The one that's pulling apart like crumbs?"

Noreen sees it. She sees everything. Yet Ruth only worries about her. One minute Noreen is too shy at school, the next she reads too much, the next she doesn't have enough friends. Nonie wants to tell her sister not to worry, that when Noreen's with her, she's always happy.

That could be half the problem though, that Noreen is happiest with her, the family fuck-up. The nervous kid who fell out of bed with nightmares until she left for college. Cut class to smoke dope with the shop teacher. Set fire to the trash can in the girls' room when her prom date danced with someone else.

"Without you here, I'd think this was someone else's family," Nonie says, tapping Noreen's nose.

Noreen wriggles away from the touch. "Not my nose," she says. "And whose family would it be then?"

Nonie puts a finger to her lip and studies the sky for a moment. "Dracula's," she says in a vampire voice, and they both laugh until a breath of air rearranges leaf shadows and spikes a white-hot shaft of sun into Nonie's eyes. She blinks hard against it and rolls toward her niece. "Clouds always make me think of time going by. The way they rush across the sky like they're late for an appointment."

Noreen giggles. "Clouds don't have anywhere to go."

"Yet they're always leaving."

She and Noreen rest the backs of their heads on the nests of their clasped hands and witness the scattering of several more cloud shapes.

"What do you think you'll be doing in the year 2000?" Nonie asks.

"That's a million years away." Noreen's tone is playful, as if she's expecting a punch line any second.

"Not a million, only twenty. You'll be twenty-eight."

"A year older than you!"

"Except I'll be older, too, silly." She blows a spurt of air onto Noreen's forehead, something that normally spins a spray of curls upward. Today, sweat pastes her niece's hair in place, and the burst of breath hardly moves a strand. "So, what do you think? What's your big plan?"

Noreen closes her eyes so tight her forehead crinkles. She

takes everything seriously. Yet another thing Ruth worries about.

"It's not a test," Nonie chides. "We're pretending."

Her forehead smooths, and an idea seems to lock immediately into place. "Then I'll have a herd of wild horses, and I'll be the only person on earth who can ride them. They'll run faster than Mark on his bike! They'll take me anyplace I want." With each new detail, her voice rises a notch.

"It's always good to have your own way out," Nonie says.

"Out of what?"

"Whatever you need to get away from."

A clumsy June bug zips a line above their heads. Noreen hunches her shoulders away from it and covers her face until it's gone. "So, what about you, Nonie? Where will you be in the year 2000?"

It's Nonie's turn to hesitate. The pressure of the future unlooses some of the feelings she tries to keep at bay when she's with Noreen. How will she tell her parents, or keep them from finding out, that she quit the proper job they'd strong-armed her into getting? That she's waiting tables again. That she stopped taking the medicines Dr. Yang prescribed because they muddied her thoughts and haunted her with nightmares that still felt real after she opened her eyes. That she stopped going to see Dr. Yang at all so she wouldn't have to lie about it.

She rocks upward so she's sitting cross-legged, and Noreen collapses across her lap. The migraine rebounds, and her mind fuzzes with that woozy feeling she gets, like something's about to happen. Something's always about to happen to her.

But it won't. Not today. She won't let it. She forces her eyes open wider, touches Noreen to make her real again, smears her sweaty hair from her forehead again.

"Well?" Noreen says. "You have to answer."

"Oh, I'll be far, far away from here by then," Nonie says.

"That's not a real answer." Noreen swats her arm.

Nonie recovers herself enough to chuckle and rub the spot,

pretending Noreen's little slap had smarted. "I'll be a horse then. One of yours. We can run away together. Anyplace you want. Anytime you need."

Nonie scoops Noreen from her lap and pulls herself to all fours, snorts, paws the ground, and pretends to buck.

"Whoa, girl," Noreen coos and reaches out a steadying hand.

Tamed, Nonie lets Noreen grab hold of her shoulder and swing herself up onto her back. Then Nonie circles the tree in a loose, slouchy gait before rolling to her side and tumbling them back to the ground next to where her purse gapes open, its leather fringes tangling in the grass. Noreen scrambles to sitting and drags it toward herself to root around for the candy bar Nonie always brings her.

The purse is cluttered with things Nonie doesn't remember stashing there. Key rings one-time lovers forgot at her place, with keys to cars she's never seen, doors she's never opened. Her own wallet and hairbrush. A half-empty bottle of aspirin. A sticky bottle of Pepto-Bismol. Hairspray belonging to a university colleague who practically shellacs her hair each morning. Nonie must have collected it for her from the employee bathroom on her last day. Before she knew she wouldn't be going back.

"Hand me my cigarettes while you're in there," she says to Noreen.

Noreen coughs whenever Nonie lights up and looks nervous when Grampy calls cigarettes coffin nails, but she does whatever Nonie asks. She tosses Nonie the new pack of Camels. Seconds later, she finds today's candy bar. A Chunky. Waves it over her head like a prize.

Nonie rips open the cellophane wrapping, palms her lighter from her jeans pocket, lights up, and lobs the pack back onto her purse. She takes a long pull off the cigarette, letting smoke fill the empty places inside herself before spouting haloes into the air.

Humidity traps the heat even in the shade. Nonie could use a breeze, so she stands and brushes dried grass clippings from her arms. Cigarette clamped between two fingers, she latches onto the tire swing's rope and spins the tire quickly, batting it with her empty hand to wind the rope as tightly as possible, then hops on. One hand holds the rope as it unwinds, the other extends with the cigarette wavering its wispy smokestack into the air. She tilts backward to watch everything spin by upside down. A repeating pattern of wrong-side-up tree trunks and stretches of grassy hill leading to her parents' house flash past. The twirling aches in her head, but the wind and speed make her laugh. That and Noreen's upside-down face laughing with her.

Melted streaks of chocolate paint a moustache over Noreen's lips. Having fished out her gift, she's forgotten the purse in the grass. Now she throws herself onto her hands, kicks her feet skyward, in efforts toward handstands. Each attempt topples her sideways, ends in giggles.

Nonie doesn't remember a time she felt as carefree as Noreen seems. Who ever brought Nonie a candy bar? Who ever lolled about with her on a sunny summer day? When Nonie was little, homework and boyfriends and sports teams kept her much older sisters from her. Their mother sipped gin and tonics and spaded weeds from the garden, gossiping with friends. If Nonie tried cartwheels on her mother's watch, she'd tell Nonie to quiet down, concoct any number of excuses to send her on an errand, out of sight. Or she'd pack Nonie off to the cranky neighbor with the nippy dog. Which she did so often that the memory of the grating sound of Mrs. Mackey's screen door scraping shut sneaks into any sound the least bit like it and swells Nonie with shame.

The only one in the family who always makes time for Nonie is Noreen. Whenever the family gathers, Ruth and Brynne sock themselves away in the house, taking advantage of the quiet to talk to their parents while everyone else runs loose. Her sisters always have things to say to their parents. Nonie always runs loose.

The tire spins its last, and Nonie hooks her feet in the bottom, enjoying the aimless sway. She flicks ash from her cigarette, bobs her head back to blow smoke straight up. Clouds of her own.

"My turn," Noreen says, rushing toward the swing.

Nonie drops to the ground, grinds her cigarette butt into the dirt, and helps Noreen clamber into position, the swing too high for her to pull herself into place on her own. Situated, Noreen grins up at her, and Nonie twirls the rope until it's wound its tightest. Then she lets go. The rope whap-whap-whaps, unwinding. Noreen clutches it and tilts her head back, the same way Nonie had, and screams with thrill. Her pale face a pearl in the fan of her curls. Its expression more familiar than her earlier simple happiness. Delight bordering on terror.

Something jounces the swing mid-spin and lurches Noreen out of place. Her ankle catches the lip of the tire as she falls past it. Her small body thuds into the earth. The sound clenches Nonie's stomach. That, plus another sound. Not a twig snapping, not something she's heard before.

What made the tire bounce that way? Had Nonie turned away without realizing it? Kept her eyes closed too long between blinks?

Sweaty hair gloms to Noreen's forehead, and Nonie wipes it aside. "Little angel?" Eyes glazed and dull, Noreen doesn't seem to hear at first, even though Nonie kneels in the dirt beside where she landed. She waves a hand frantically in front of her eyes. Taps her cheeks.

She can't do anything right. She can't even stand beside a tire swing right.

"Noreen? Are you okay? Please say something."

Had she shut her eyes? For a second? The air buzzes in her ears. All you ever want in the world is to keep from hurting the people you love. "Noreen, please?" This would be the wrong timing for one of her shiver fits. She must hold herself together. Must not let herself unravel.

"Oops," Noreen finally says. The word bursts from her

mouth. The fall must have knocked the breath out of her. The return of her voice brings other sounds back with it. A low chug-chug-chugging—Mr. Baxter mowing his grass a few lawns up the hill. A blue jay squawking from the tree above. Mark shouting about the football, Brynne's oldest, Henry, shouting back. Loud shrieks of *Throw it here! Me, me, me!* from four-year-old Luke, and the yips of a dog a few houses away.

"Everything's okay," Nonie says. "You're okay." She rocks back onto her heels, aftershocks of adrenaline still coursing through her.

She closes her eyes. On purpose this time. She'll be more careful. Her life a broken chain of such promises. But children fall down, don't they? For no reason at all. They fall down all the time, even with perfectly capable grownups standing beside them. Hasn't Ruth said that very thing herself? Nonie can picture her, holding a martini by the pond at her own backyard barbecue, talking to the neighbors while children run around. Someone skins a knee, gets a splinter, knocks somebody down. Every time. "That's the way a story always starts when someone gets hurt. 'I was standing right there…'" The other parents, holding matching martinis, laugh. Ruth sounds exactly like them. She fits in, wears the same hairstyles, the same colors of Avon lipstick. Nonie doesn't match anyone.

"Noreen, I was so scared." She kisses Noreen's face, sees it more clearly now.

"I'm okay," Noreen says, trying hard to smile. As if Nonie's the one who needs comfort.

"Oh, don't cry, little angel."

"I didn't mean to let go. The rope burned my hands. I'm sorry."

"Sorry? You didn't do anything wrong."

Still flat on the ground, Noreen moves the arm she landed on, but it splays backward from her and looks wrong. The motion makes her flinch, and her face turns to ash. Nothing's okay after all.

"Ruth!" Nonie shouts toward the house. "Mark! Henry! Luke! Get Ruth!" Up to now, she's been ignoring the boys and their chaos, but they zoom into her peripheral vision, popcorns of action, until one of them finally pounds on the front screen door and shouts into the house.

For now, she stays beside Noreen on the ground, deep breathing like Dr. Yang taught her. *Avoid imagining things to be worse than they are. Be where you are.* She clasps Noreen's free hand, utters what are meant to be soothing words but come out garbled, strangled instead.

A broken arm hurts. Noreen hurts. Nonie swoons with it, as if the hurt swims out at her through the humid air. *Be where you are.* Noreen will be okay. She knows this as sure as breathing. That Noreen will always be okay. If only Noreen could know it, too, if she could feel it deep down, that no matter what people around her do or say about her, she will always be the one true thing on this earth. Her mother will pass her own bundles of worry off to Noreen when she means to pass love. Accept it as love, whenever you can, Nonie wants to say, because at this moment it's clear to her. Love is a broken thing. We pass it back and forth and sometimes knit it back together, sometimes break it more. Always knit it together, she wants to say.

She can't say any of it, though, because of the buzz in her ears, and that hovering feeling, that clammy unease that coats her, mingles with her sweat. A spreading chill vies against the burning sun. Panic disorder. Panic attacks. More terms from Dr. Yang. At least the shivers have a real name. Her toes tingle. It always starts in her toes, and she hates its inexorability, how the cold climbs from deep inside her, clamping one cell at a time, it seems, until her whole body is consumed.

But she will not. Noreen needs her.

Feet and faces drum toward them. At last, at last.

There will be a cast, yes. A quick trip to the emergency room.

Nothing tragic. Children fall down. No one can stop them.

Mr. Baxter's lawn mower chokes and wheezes to a halt. The scrape-slam of Mrs. Mackey's door across the street. Though she died years ago now. Nonie's toes prickle, hot and cold, but she will not. She will not let go.

Dr. Yang, with her liquid voice. *When all else fails, count to twenty. Over and over. As many times as it takes.* As if Nonie had never tried that on her own.

One. Two.

But sometimes it works. And that woman who pulled over, the time the shivers took her in the middle of a road late at night?

Three. Four. Five.

That woman and her cigarette, an orange bouncing ball in the dark. She waited while Nonie rocked and moaned and thought she would die. The way it always goes.

It will not.

Six. Seven.

The woman told her about stars. A maiden saved. Cassiopeia. The most beautiful word. Cassiopeia.

Nine. Ten.

She will not leave Noreen.

Cassiopeia. Cassiopeia.

Faces swirl over hers. Ruth's, pinched. Always pinched. "Nonie? Can you hear me?"

She can, but she can't say so, can't say, *Not me! Not me!* Can't point them to Noreen, prone beside her. She tries to take a breath. Light drains away. Her toes, her feet, her knees, the shivering reaching up up up.

Noreen, shouting "Nonie! Nonie!" and tugging at her with her free hand from what feels like miles away.

She tried as hard as she could, with the medicines and doctor visits. But the dry mouth, the nightmares, waking up halfway down her apartment stairs in her sleep T-shirt and bare feet, apartment door yawning open. That daylong sense of someone shouldering a door closed in her mind. Anytime they might step aside and let it open. Anytime.

It's opening now.

No air.

Seven? Six? Cassio…

No breath.

Nonie braces her arms around herself, but nothing stops the shivers once they take hold. She folds herself in half. Locks her arms tight around her knees. Hopes she won't start screaming before the feeling passes. Hopes she'll still be alive if it does.

Noreen's arm, cracked. Breathless voices calling her name, worried about her instead of Noreen.

You can't die from this. Doctor promised. But it feels like death. Death feels exactly like this.

Continued.

NOREEN'S MOTHER'S EYES are puffy from crying when she and George arrive. Evie squirms in Noreen's arms, cranky from waking before she meant to, but Noreen pulls her mother close anyway. "Mom, I'm so sorry," she mumbles into Ruth's silky, silvering hair.

"I'm an orphan now. Just Brynne and me left."

She hadn't considered it during the ride here, the tally of dead her mother has buried. Her baby sister, her father a few years after that, now her mother. Somewhere in there the divorce from Noreen's dad, which she grieved like a death. Thinking Evie might ease the pain of loss set up a false equation. Joy doesn't cancel grief as much as it complicates it.

Her mother's husband steps in for a hug next. Mid-embrace, he presses his face up to Evie's, cajoling her to turn toward him and away from Noreen's collarbone. As soon as she does, her post-nap grumpiness winks away. She grabs onto his ears like handles and holds his face in place that way, a game they play.

Her mother married Hugh not long before Noreen married George, which might explain why she can't resist comparing the two. Behind them, George hovers in the doorway laden with luggage. Hugh thrusts a hand toward him, and George meets it, awkwardly balancing a duffel bag under his arm. Hugh's handshakes are warm and mighty. His stature and bushy white eyebrows suggest a personality ten times larger than the calm, gentle reality of him. Beside him, George appears small, half-drawn. Each visit home, Noreen hopes he'll soften, but he continues to speak to her mother and Hugh in formal phrases, waits to be invited before walking all the way through a doorway, to be reminded to make himself at home before as much as shrugging off his jacket.

Ruth nods at George, dodging a more personal greeting by slipping Evie gently into her own arms. Despite the weight of sorrow on her face, she manages to blow horsey lips at Evie, who rubs the last of her nap from her eyes and sputters her own lips back at her grammy.

"Your brother won't be here until tomorrow," she says. One more spurt of horsey lips, and Evie closes her eyes, leans into the wind of it, and laughs. Ruth seems almost happy for a moment, too, before her face clouds over again. "And Brynne and Emmett made excuses about not coming tonight. Not wanting to put us out, they said. How would it put us out to be together?" Her mother's eyes sparkle with more tears. Noreen gathers her close for another hug, sandwiching Evie between them. "I'm sorry to blabber on, Noreen. I'm glad you're here."

Hugh steps in and relieves George of the bags, then leads them upstairs. Noreen thinks of this house as her mother and Hugh's "new old house," a 1920s Cape Cod they bought together after each sold the houses they lived in before they married. Selling off her children's childhood home, Ruth felt compelled to compensate by appointing one spare bedroom for Noreen and another for Mark. She and George have only visited a handful of times, so the house still feels unfamiliar. If Hugh hadn't been guiding them, Noreen might've forgotten to turn right instead of left at the top of the stairs.

He sets their bags on the floor inside the door and offers the room with a wide gesture of his arm. "So you can settle in and freshen up," he says.

The new bedrooms are nothing like the old ones, and Noreen hadn't expected to miss her childhood furniture—her white iron-frame bed with all its squeaks and her old bedspread of blowsy purple flowers—but the new flat wooden frame with a futon mattress and a sage coverlet with scalloped edges set off a tinge of nostalgia. Furniture from the rest of their old colonial, its shag carpeting, dark kitchen, and kitschy greens and golds have been upgraded in this house with a mix of antiques and spare, modern furniture, refurbished hardwood floors, modernized kitchen, and earthy tones of paint and throw rugs.

"It feels like a hotel," Noreen says, bouncing at the edge of the mattress, testing it out. "I know it's silly, but I can't get used to it." A ceramic figurine of a basket of flowers—the one item salvaged from her original bedroom—comforts her a little from the top of the new dresser across the room.

"He said we should freshen up," George says. "I can think of something fresh." His attempts at allure often strand him at this signature expression, mixing pleading with sexy. He stands in front of the bed where Noreen sits and loosens his belt, unzips his fly.

Times like this, she ignores the queasy feeling she gets. She doesn't want him to know she doesn't like oral sex as much as he does. She doesn't even like the terms for it, which is one small part of why she doesn't talk about it, but the larger reason is that when she talks about what she does like, George inevitably asks about other men she's slept with and what kinds of things she did with them. No matter how strongly he insists that he only wants to learn to please her better, he can never seem to handle what she tells him. For one thing, she feels like he expects epic love stories when all she had were scattered, random experiments in high school and short-lived mismatches in college. No regrets exactly, but the sex always fell inside the learning curve of not quite knowing each other's bodies yet and fizzled from there. Still, the scanty details trouble him. It's easier to say less.

Besides, they've tried plenty of other positions she didn't like at first but got used to. She figures she'll get used to most of it over time.

George braces his hands on her shoulders, positioning her. Ever since Evie was born—with how often Noreen falls asleep in the spare bed next to the crib, giving in to her exhaustion from entertaining a mostly preverbal child day in, day out—she's been turning George down a lot. At least here Evie is taken care of, so they won't be interrupted.

George does plenty of things for her he doesn't feel like doing. Regardless of how busy he gets at work, he fills the gas tank in their car because he knows Noreen hates the smell on her hands. He takes out the garbage when it's full. Rakes the leaves, kills or sets free the nastiest bugs and the one or two mice that have made their way into their house. She can do this one thing for him. Even if she's sad and thinking a thousand other thoughts. George lowers his hands to cup her breasts, his breath throaty and fast.

Afterward, she's queasier than ever. George hikes his pants back into place and rebuckles. "I feel at home already," he says in that voice that's just for her.

He doesn't offer to reciprocate. She's pretty sure she doesn't want him to anyway. At least he seems relaxed now. The stress of his job works knots into his muscles—tenure track pressure, committees, papers to publish, students to advise, exams to grade—but when she suggests a trip or an evening out, thinking of his need for release, sometimes his temper shortens.

"It's good for you to take a break now and then," Noreen tells him now. "We should do this more often."

"*This* we can do anytime," he says, and his meant-to-be-sexy expression misfires into that pleading look again.

"I mean taking little trips," Noreen says, correcting him, possibly a beat too quickly.

George threads his fingers into Noreen's hair, strokes her ear. "I never need to go anywhere," he says, "as long as I'm with you."

Thirteen Years After.

THERE'S EUPHORIA IN it. Jumping a train with your best friend. Holding on for your life. Wind rips Noreen's hair behind her, slaps it into her face or pokes it into her eyes at every shift of her weight. The train was trundling slowly past when, without thought or warning, she and Lizbeth surrendered to the same impulse and grappled onto the ladder at the near end of the closest car, then held fast to the same rung with their hands, landed on the same rung with their feet, and levered themselves to stand seam-tight against the side of the car, where they still cling as the train clatters down night-darkened tracks, faster and faster and faster. Only a fat, blinding moon to light the dead-kudzu-covered lands flying past.

These moments, train-flung, or dangling their feet from the top of Slusher Hall dorm their first weeks at Virginia Tech, or times they've drunk too much and lay flat on their backs in the graveyard closest to the Harrel Street brick ranch whose upstairs half they've rented since sophomore year, staring up into the swirl of the Milky Way, giving themselves to the stars streaking across the heavens, or the swim of sounds in their heads, the dew of cemetery grasses seeping in through their clothes like the dampness of death itself. These moments knit them into a cocoon feeling of being parts of the same person while time ticks away in the background. This, their last year at Tech, their last days together before life cleaves them apart.

Noreen lets go of the train in her best imitation of every TV or movie scene she's watched of someone leaping from a speeding car. They always manage a full-speed roll, but she wrenches her ankle with such force it calls to mind breaking her arm as a child, bringing the familiar whiplash speed of that tire swing unwinding, her aunt laughing one second, turning into Munch's *Scream* the next, elongated and desperate. That's when a blitz of nerves ratchets through her body. Like she's come loose from Earth's gravitational force, liable at any moment to fling wildly into space.

"How far do you think we got?" Lizbeth says, giddy. "Christiansburg, maybe? Radford? Which way do the tracks even go?" She swings her head, panning a look up and down the tracks, as if she might be able to conjure a cardinal direction from the air.

Maybe she can. Noreen can't. Noreen has no idea where they are. No idea how they'll get home. With pain radiating a slow burn from her ankle up her shin, the need to know feels urgent and frightening. She wants to know how to get home, how she got here, how she can stop getting places like here. She leans over her ankle, breathing a little fast. She doesn't realize she hasn't answered Lizbeth until she speaks again.

"Noreen? Are you okay?"

Jitters dance along her nerve endings, threatening to overtake her the way they sometimes do, especially moments like these, when feeling vividly alive gives way to some nameless abyss, but this time they drain away. The ground beneath her becomes the ground again. Cold, winter hard. Noreen's ass hurts, her ankle worse. "I'm not sure."

The jitters, the shivers, the shudders are a secret Noreen keeps for herself. They come with sparkling lights behind her eyelids, her heart beating like a hummingbird, the smell of rust. The feel of Nonie's presence shimmering in the air beside her. It's impossible to separate the nervous tremors from the physical pull of connection. She keeps them secret because she can't imagine explaining them, but also because if she admitted them to Lizbeth or anyone else, they'd want to help her figure out how to make them go away, and she's not sure she wants them gone. Dusty filaments linking her to her long dead aunt. Break them, and she doesn't know who she'd be.

One shoe is lost in the ditch somewhere, and the moonlight allows only minimal searching. Lizbeth tugs her to standing, ducks her head under Noreen's arm to secure it around her shoulder. Even to go for help, Lizbeth wouldn't abandon her—half-shoeless, hurt, and tangled in brown ropes of kudzu in the middle of they-have-no-idea where. The lights of the town they aimed to land in lie farther off than they realized.

Noreen limps and leans into Lizbeth as they slowly close in on the brightest of the lights, a gas station and convenience store with a sad old sign saying "Ray's." Fluorescent lights throw an eerie halo around two gas pumps and a dusty plane of cracked asphalt. Lizbeth eases Noreen to the curb in front of the shop. "I'll get you some ice," she says. Hard to imagine needing anything icier than the ground beneath her bare foot, but Noreen smiles her thanks and waits, hoping the shudders won't come back, that one of her headaches won't take hold.

The train's racket left her ears muffled at first, like after a loud concert, but now she hears wind rattling the last unfallen brown leaves of nearby trees. The air is cold enough to send its own shiver that rinses her last nervy tingles away. Noreen and Lizbeth had wandered down the street for a better view of the moon. The train chuffing into view brought with it the very notion of jumping aboard. They hadn't meant to be gone more than a few minutes, hadn't brought a penny. Now they can't even make a call from the phone booth at the corner of the lot.

The lot faces two intersecting country roads with acres of trees on one side, farmland on the other. Quiet lonesomeness stretches out into the darkness. She'd never admit it to Lizbeth, but sometimes their adventures leave her feeling as wrenched out of her socket as her ankle feels. Not because of the shivers, but because of the inevitable aftermath. Lizbeth hops on a train, hops off again, whistles her way into a shop in the middle of nowhere, enjoying each second. It's Noreen, always Noreen, who twists an ankle, breaks an arm, or attracts the least stable person in the room, like she had after Lizbeth's surprise Halloween party.

Halloween night, Lizbeth stationed a handful of their friends around the graveyard off Roanoke Street, about as far from campus as it was from their house, in one of the many residential areas around Blacksburg slowly losing ground to student rentals. When she and Lizbeth walked by, supposedly on their way to some other Halloween party, Lizbeth hacked a weirdly loud cough, and a half-dozen of their friends popped up from behind gravestones, cheering to surprise Noreen. "If it was your birthday, you might've suspected something," she'd said.

One of their friends flipped on a boombox. All of them carried beer or liquor, and they danced and drank for hours. Neighbors shouted at them from nearby houses until cops showed up, locked them in the drunk tank for the night along with a slew of other drunk kids from a busted frat party, finally releasing them at dawn to stagger back to their various apartments and dorms. In the cramped jail cell, Lizbeth managed to connect with a fellow party-goer, a philosophy student who later wooed her with ukulele serenades and lengthy foot massages. They dated until winter break and broke up only because the guy graduated midyear.

Meanwhile, in that same jail cell, Noreen attracted a completely unrequited admirer. Tall, stoop-shouldered Lars, who'd happened upon the party on his way someplace else. No matter how she positioned herself in the cramped cell, protecting the space between them, he kept saying he felt like they'd met in another life and scooted closer on the crowded metal bench. The room smelled like liquor-sweat and piss, and Lars's breath smelled worse. In such tight quarters, with everyone still at least tipsy, it felt too risky to tell him off, and, truth is, she felt sorry for him. Noreen always feels sorry for the awkward brand of loneliness that drifted off him along with his various odors. No one should feel like nobody likes them.

"Why do they need to feel like *you* like them, though?" Lizbeth has asked her more than once. The upshot being that, while Lizbeth swooned through a few months of surprise post-drunk-tank romance, Noreen fielded a series of Lars's messages on their answering machine, grimaced at a pile of badly written poems, and turned him away, as politely as she could muster, day after day. When he knocked on her door or tossed pebbles or twigs at her bedroom window, Lizbeth shook her head in the background and prodded Noreen to, "Seek joy over pity, Nor. Joy over pity." A perfect illustration of how luck likes Lizbeth better than Noreen.

The discrepancy used to be a joke between them, but Noreen doesn't find it funny anymore. After they graduate, she'll be on her own. Without Lizbeth, what's to stop her from falling off trains and getting stranded in ditches in the dark alone? Or finding herself stuck with the least likable people as her only friends in the world? At what point did Nonie find herself alone? With her panics, her demons, her doubts. What's to keep Noreen from finding out what that kind of loneliness does to a person?

Noreen bends her head into her knees and taps her forehead with her fingers. A headache brewing and a shimmer beneath her skin.

Breathe, breathe, breathe.

Right now, her ankle hurts, but Lizbeth is with her, so she's going to be okay. When Lizbeth comes back out, she'll carry the ice Noreen needs, and the pressure to solve every problem at once will dissolve, along with the dreadful pang of this moment, reminding her of every failure of her nature, sucking her breath away, leaving her emptier than before, telling her, *You are alone in the world. You are alone in the universe.*

A navy blue Volvo sedan rolls up from the road, coasts into

place at the pump in front of her. The man who steps out seems to glow in the light. He's Noreen's age or a few years older. His hair thick and lustrous in the strange gas-station-plus-full-moon shine of the night. He flicks a smile her way, an impersonal acknowledgment that he's seen her. Noreen hugs her knees to hide her one bare foot, to pull herself to a more respectable posture, to get warm. Until he smiles a second time, this time curious, she doesn't realize she's trailing the man with her eyes.

Light seems to frost the tips of his golden-brown curls. Now he seems to see her clearly for the first time. The way she is, stranded, pathetic. He leans slightly forward, concerned. Not pitying, at least. He emanates a sense of control, of calm, like he never feels the way she's feeling. Like feeling this way might not be required of her.

"Did your car break down or something?" he says.

"Definitely 'or something.'"

He cranes a look over both shoulders. "Are you by yourself? Are you all right?"

She's about to say no, she's not all right, to admit her fear of losing traction on the earth, but Lizbeth bursts from the shop, a Ziploc baggie of ice swaying in her hand.

"Who have we here?" she says, looking from Noreen to this new person, unsure suddenly, in a way Lizbeth rarely is.

"George," he says and extends his hand—to Noreen, who had not asked his name. Unlike so many other men she's met in college, he doesn't look past her to see Lizbeth better. "And it looks like you need a ride?"

It turns out he's headed back to Blacksburg himself. A chemical engineering grad student at Tech, on his way to a PhD—information he spurts before Lizbeth has made it all the way into the back seat, before he's even asked their names. A pet peeve of hers is when men tell more about themselves than they ask of you, so she darts a raised-brow look Noreen's way.

He does ask Noreen's name, though, as soon as she's safely

buckled in. She tells him, then offers their part of town, their address. He asks more questions. Her major. Her favorite writer. Her headache fades away. The car's front seats are heated, and warmth and calm so soon after thrill and buzz lull Noreen halfway to sleep. Her answers come dreamily. She stays awake enough to appreciate his smile, though, and the probing attentiveness of his gaze.

George is attractive in a script-ready college boy way, with carefully trimmed hair except for one wavy shock that flops over his forehead. His windbreaker fits loosely around his arms, but in the dim light from the dashboard, she can sense the firm outline of his body underneath. She fantasizes for one moment that he drove into that gas station on purpose to meet her, that he will visit her again, and more than once. She imagines his voice saying her name in a midnight whisper, then coughs and sits up straighter when she realizes she's let herself imagine the feel of his beard stubble against her cheek, the moist pressure of his tongue in her mouth.

Her track record with men is scattered, so she trains her eyes toward the road again, answering his questions politely, expecting nothing. First came college boys from when she was bored in high school and Claudia dragged her party hopping. Later came overzealous, quasi-stalker types like Lars or handsome lover boys who charmed her into their beds after parties, most promising but failing to call again. She's never managed a middle ground, a man who was worth more than the thrill of a short adventure, a person she actually wanted to see again.

When George pulls the car in front of their house, Lizbeth puffs gentle snores from the back seat. In the moments before Noreen registers that the car has come to a stop, George tears the corner off a map from his glove box, scribbles his name and number on it, and folds it into her hand. She clenches it tight in her fist when Lizbeth stirs again. George clearly isn't Lizbeth's favorite type of guy. His one gaffe of unasked-for self-disclosure enough to mark him in her book. Noreen slides the paper into her pocket before Lizbeth can see it. Could George really mean for her to call when the most he knows of her is that she does stupid things and does them badly? The most she knows of him is that he's handsome and helped her when she needed it. A scenario much more like one that typically befalls Lizbeth. But maybe this is her luck changing.

She almost forgets her twisted ankle until it hits the pavement, and she gasps in pain. Lizbeth waves away George's offer to help and circles Noreen's arm around her shoulder again to help her into the house.

※

Her ankle wakes her in the night. It feels like someone poured boiling water into the middle of it. Jumping a train—what did she think would happen? Did she think? She doesn't realize how loud she's moaning until Lizbeth's shape emerges through the blue darkness of her doorway.

"Shit, Nor," she says. "Is it your foot?"

"I think I need a doctor."

Lizbeth's Chevette, the only car between them, sits at the curb outside, but a stretch of below-zero nights at the very start of the semester knocked its battery out, and Lizbeth hasn't replaced it yet. For the past couple of weeks, they've managed on groceries from Mecham's Necessaries around the corner. Cheap wine, ramen, Pop-Tarts. It had seemed a fine arrangement until now.

"Should we call an ambulance?" Lizbeth says.

"Is it that bad? Do you think it's that bad?"

Lizbeth sits on the bed next to her and takes her hand. "You tell me, Nor. Is it? We'll do whatever it takes."

Whatever it takes, she'll need a ride. She can't think past Phineas in *A Separate Peace*, dying in surgery for his broken leg. That whole idea of marrow going rogue feels all too possible at the moment. On the crowded scarf-swathed milk crate that serves as Noreen's bedside table, a crumpled slip of paper catches the blue glow of her clock. George's number.

"I could call that guy," she says. "The one who drove us home tonight."

"What, Serious George gave you his number? And now you want a tax consultation?"

"No, silly, a ride," Noreen says. "And he wasn't that bad. I thought he was sweet."

"We need to get you out more."

"I've been out plenty," Noreen says. A slideshow of recent evenings whips through her mind. Too much alcohol. Too many handsy men. Too many mornings when she wasn't quite sure what happened the night before. This is her senior year, the year she's supposed to figure out what the rest of her life will look like, and for the first time since they'd become inseparable freshman year, Noreen wonders if she and Lizbeth want the same things. What happens to their friendship if Noreen wants something different from their usual breakneck escapades?

She reaches for the phone.

"You're not calling him now?"

"The only other choice is an ambulance, right? I don't think I should put this off until morning."

Waiting for the phone to ring, her ankle throbs, which distracts her from the oddity of calling a near-stranger in the middle of the night. When he answers, his voice is thick with sleep and sounds nakedly private. He says hello a second time before she can speak.

When he arrives, he knocks softly at her door. She's rousted him from bed, a strange, wild girl he hardly knows, but he greets her with a half-warm, half-cynical smile, as though they already have a lifetime of private jokes between them. "My chariot awaits," he says, formal and playful at the same time. He bends his knees to bring his shoulders within reach, and she laces her arm behind his neck, as if they've done this before, as if they already know exactly how their bodies fit together.

Lizbeth steps away to make room for them to shamble out the door, then scrounges for her shoes and coat to come along. Noreen tells her not to worry. "At least one of us should get some sleep."

"I don't mind, Nor." She holds a shoe in one hand, looking at her curiously. At a party one of them might leave with a boy they hadn't known beforehand, after a quick private signal to assure the other all was well, but phoning up this man and going off with him alone into the night clearly seems out of protocol to Lizbeth.

Noreen smiles at her from the nook she's made of George's body. "Really, it's okay."

The after-midnight musk of him makes Noreen forget her pain until they start limping toward his car. When she releases her grip on his wrist and sees the dents her fingernails left, she realizes how tightly she'd squeezed onto him. Lizbeth stands silhouetted in the open doorway and watches them drive away.

✻

He didn't have to answer his phone when she called or drive to her rescue, and he definitely doesn't have to stay with her, chatting like they're at a party and lending her his jacket against the draft in the waiting area. The fact that he does any of this makes Noreen feel grateful and undeserving at the same time.

One half of the waiting room opens onto a nurse's station, the other wedges into a corner. Noreen and George sit in the corner with a table of well-worn magazines between them. A man reeking of liquor snores in a nearby chair, his hand bandaged roughly with blood leaking through. A few seats away from him, a frightened-looking woman clutches a baby to her chest. Noreen can't tell which of them might be ill, but at least the baby is asleep with an angelic look on its face.

Half an hour in, a nurse asks Noreen the first few questions and brings an ice pack. After an hour, no doctor has looked at her yet, but George has searched out a refill for the melted ice pack and offered his knee as a roost to prop up her foot.

Hospitals have their own kind of quiet, built up from a thousand small sounds. The odd TV. The scuffing of sensible shoes across floor tiles. Low rumbling intercoms issuing orders for doctors and nurses. Phones ringing. Papers shuffling. The drunk man's snores. The baby's snuffling breath. The sounds blend calm and dread, wrapping Noreen and George into the same private bubble. She finds herself wanting him to like her.

"I'm not some wild child." Her tone rings of confession.

"What are you then?" He'd been eyeing a sports magazine absently and tilts it into his lap now to look at her again.

"I just mean, I don't end up in the ER every weekend."

"What *do* you do then?"

She decides not to tell him about those hazy nights or handsy men or the surprise Halloween party at the cemetery. Or how jumping the train had been her idea, or hers and Lizbeth's at the same time, she couldn't tell anymore. There are plenty of other stories she keeps to herself, too.

"Every weekend? What everybody does, I guess," she says. "Get together with friends. Go to a party or two. What about you?"

"No such thing as free time in grad school. I spend most of my weekends in my lab. Running simulations."

"Ooh. Simulations. Sounds sexy," Noreen teases. "But you went somewhere this weekend. Otherwise you wouldn't have been all that way out of town, right where we needed you to be."

"I went home." He winces at the word *home*.

"Is it rough at home?"

He cuts her a sharp look. "Not rough. Not exactly."

"What then?"

"I don't usually talk about my family."

"Do you usually give girls rides to ERs in the middle of the night?"

He pushes the magazine toward the edge of his lap. Thumps his knee. Measures how much he wants to say. "My dad's a good guy, in his way, but he's a lot." He tosses the magazine back onto the table between them.

"You really don't talk about family. You look like you're about to be sick."

George laughs. "It's just personal, I guess?"

Noreen gestures to her leg in his lap. "We've gotten pretty personal."

He drops his arm onto his chair's narrow plastic armrest and lets his hand slide into his lap, his fingers brushing her leg near the ice pack. His soft touch next to her hot pain. "I just can't believe you want to hear all my trivia."

"You're an interesting guy," Noreen says, her voice soft, coaxing. "If it makes it easier, I'll trade you a secret for a secret."

He stares into his lap first, seeming to study the splay of his fingers against her leg, trains his eyes there as he talks. "I was ten when my father crashed his car. I was in the back seat." He lists a string of details. A pickup T-boned the driver's side. The impact buckled the car, crumpling it to within inches of where George sat, pinned between the wreckage and the embankment the collision had shoved them into. Most of the wreck is a collage of images to him, but he tells her how he remembers calling to his dad and getting no answer. A long wait and not knowing for sure if help was on the way. Counting and recounting the stripes on his shorts. First the dark ones, then the light ones, then starting over. His fingers along her leg seem to parse out the same exercise now, though she's not wearing any stripes. His father hasn't been able to walk since.

She studies his face, cast in fluorescent garishness of hospital light, and pictures him in the back seat of that smashed car counting the stripes on his shorts, wondering if his father was alive beside him. "What about your mother?" she asks.

"She didn't stick around," he says. "Couldn't stomach the logistics, I guess." He lets out a breath from the bottom of his belly and sits straight again, half-smiles at her.

"That's hard."

"Everybody's got something."

"Yeah, but you were just a boy."

"That's not the secret though. Everybody at home knows that part," George says. "And he's not helpless. He's the Roanoke personal injury lawyer nobody wants to go up against. Billboards around town with his face as big as a house." He shakes his head. Noreen's not sure he realizes he's still stroking her leg. She holds still so as not to stop him.

"The thing is, he makes a lot of money. Pays for stuff, then pulls a string and I jump."

"How so?" Noreen's family has always had enough money, but not enough to pull strings with. She can't imagine what that's like.

"He asks for stuff." George leans his head into his hand, his elbow on the armrest, so she can't see his face while he explains how his father calls on him to do projects around their house, their yard. Work George has done ever since the accident. A few years ago, his father moved office buildings right before George's midterms and expected him to come home and drive a rental van to haul his furniture and files across town.

Noreen wants to thread her fingers into his, ease some of his discomfort, but the reach across her leg is awkward.

"He pays my rent, and he bought me my car, so I do owe him," George says. "Not just for being my dad. But I don't know how much my saying yes comes from wanting to make sure he signs the next check." Now he peeks up at her, afraid she'll be disgusted with him. "Or how much his asking comes from expecting the other half of a transaction."

Something open in his body closes. Her legs still stretch across his lap, but his hand falls away.

"Thing is, I'd like to say no when I need to without feeling like an asshole. It's all stuff he could hire someone to do, but—I don't know. If I do it for him, it's like he feels like he's still doing it for himself? So, for now, he calls, and I go."

She scoots forward on her seat so she can reach his hand. "I'm so sorry, George," she says.

He double-takes, looks almost betrayed when he meets her gaze. "That makes me sound pathetic."

"No, I mean, I did the same thing, didn't I? Called you in the middle of the night, and you came?"

He squeezes her hand. "It's not the same. I promise," he says.

She releases his hand and rests back in her chair again. "Good."

"This wasn't what I'd pictured, but I wanted to see you again."

"You did? The wacky girl with one shoe?"

"You said it yourself. You're no wild child. I saw through to the other part of you. Wanted to get to know her better."

Her cheeks flash hot. Is there really another part of her? She's glad she called him tonight, but, for his sake, she wishes she knew for sure that she would've called even if she hadn't needed his help. Yes, he's handsome, but in some perfect, unreachable way, she'd thought, and he was nice to her when she needed it, but she usually skims away from nice, conventional things.

"Jamison, Noreen?" A nurse with a clipboard peers around the groggy scattering of halt and lame. George helps her to her feet.

"You don't have to wait for me, you know, if you need to go. I've already asked too much."

"I'm not going anywhere," he says, plopping back into the chair, palming the sports magazine again. "You owe me a secret."

At least now she knows she *should* have called him. That was half as good as knowing she would have.

❧

Much later, with her ankle wrapped, badly sprained but not broken, plus a handful of instructions and crutches under her arms, Noreen hobbles back out to the waiting room. George's head tips sideways, and his breaths come out heavy, sometimes bursting through his sealed lips with a tiny pop. For the moment, she's glad he's asleep. Her sudden happiness at the sight of him waiting for her scares her. Feelings for him came too fast, and she's usually expert at keeping them at bay. She understands now what Lizbeth's been talking about for so long, how she gets in her own way with men. As afraid of being left behind as of being the one to leave. As afraid of getting hurt as of hurting someone else. Fears that tie her up so tight inside she runs the opposite direction.

What if she doesn't this time? What happens if she tries to stay?

She nudges his foot with her crutch. "I'd let you sleep, but you'll hurt yourself with your neck like that."

George blinks twice, getting used to the light again, stretches his arms above him, then shifts forward and levers himself to standing. "Let's get you home," he says, the way her father might have. Before he divorced her mother and moved so far away. Back when they were close.

"Did they prescribe anything for the pain?" George asks after she's belted into his front seat again.

"They said ibuprofen would be fine."

"Do you have any?"

"She gave me a couple while I was there, and I'll just send Lizbeth to Meacham's when they open."

"I can stop at the 24-hour place. Pick some up for you."

"You don't have to do that. We need bread and stuff from Meacham's anyway."

But he pulls into the drugstore parking lot. Asks if she needs anything else. Comes back with ibuprofen and a bag of Hershey's Kisses. "I would've gotten bread, too, but they didn't have any."

He rips the candy bag open and places one in her hand, takes another for himself, then settles the bag in her lap.

Maybe it's the pain or the exhaustion after such a long day or a rebound of adrenaline from earlier, but the surprise of the candy landing in her hand brings tears to her eyes and makes her voice choke a little when she says, "That's too nice."

He looks over his shoulder to back the car out of the parking space. "Aren't you used to people being nice to you?"

The first thing she thinks of is her grandmother leering toward her after Nonie's funeral. *Don't you go and turn out the same, little Miss Head in the Clouds.* Imprinting her with a family's worth of fear when what she'd needed was months and months of hugs and hot chocolate and new stuffed animals to chase her nightmares away. "The world can be a spiteful place, you know? Niceness shouldn't come as a surprise, but it does."

George nods and signals to turn onto the road. Dawn is beginning to leach darkness from the sky.

"You don't even know me, and you've spent a whole night taking care of me. That kind of niceness is always a surprise. I don't know how I'll make it up to you." She pries the foil from the chocolate and lets the candy melt in her mouth.

"Well," he says, shooting her a half-smile, his eyes narrowed and teasing. His effort at flirting, she guesses. An engineering student mired in equations and experiments might not get a lot of flirting practice. "Someone did promise me a secret."

If her secret's meant to pay him back for anything, she has to choose one that makes her as uneasy as his made him. "I lost an aunt to suicide when I was eight. I was her favorite person in the world." That's not the secret part, but in the stillness of the car, she can feel its weight. "She used to get these panic attacks? She described them like trains rushing through her. Some other relatives got them, too, I think, a long time ago."

A feeling in her gut reminds her of the moment before she'd grabbed onto the train, that one second before it would be too late to change her mind. "Anyway, Nonie and I were a lot alike. Same hair, same eyes. Same off-kilter way of looking at things. My whole life my mom's been convinced I'd turn out like her that way, too, like I'm a bomb and she can hear me ticking." Noreen stretches her leg in front of her, aching to prop it up again. "Thing is, I never told her. I never told anyone. The same thing does happen to me. The first time was right after her funeral."

The next clack of the turn signal fills the car in place of words.

"Mine can't be as bad as hers were. Hers made her miserable, made her lose jobs. Mine? They don't happen that often, and when they do, they make me think of her. There's a horrible bit, right in the center, when I'm not any place or any time, and that's about the worst feeling in the world, but until then, I think, 'These belonged to Nonie once.' It's almost like being close to her again."

After she's said it, her body feels wrung out. If her mother knew, she'd freak out. Maybe empty the house of sharp objects preemptively. But suicide isn't hereditary, Noreen always wants to tell her. Though she's read articles that suggest otherwise. She's sure her mother has read them, too.

Without knowing it, Lizbeth saw one of the fits happen once. She watched Noreen try to comfort herself, rocking in place on the floor. Lizbeth tapping her, calling her name, Noreen not answering, until the feeling released her, let air move in and out of her lungs again. Let words come. "It was nothing, no, really. I was nauseous for a quick second there. Afraid I'd throw up if I said anything." Lizbeth fixed her a plate of saltines, brought her a glass of water, crouched beside her on the floor, but believed her when she said she was feeling perfectly back to herself. That she had no idea what had happened.

She doesn't mention to George now, and hadn't mentioned to Lizbeth then, that sometimes, in the middle of jumping a train, say, or swinging her feet off the edge of Slusher's dorm's rooftop, she gets a feeling dangerously similar, without the freezing in place or shuddering of nerves, but a glimmer of it, a fleeting sense that the world's orbit is about to hiccup and hurl her into nothingness to fall and fall and fall and never land again.

"I'm fine, though," she tells George. "It's not the same." As if he could hear the conversation waging in her head. As if he'd ever call her again anyway, this train-jumping weirdo with a secret nervous condition.

At the curb in front of her apartment, he opens the door for her, unpacks her from the car, makes sure she has her medicine, her purse, the refreezable ice pack they sent her home with. The sky is white with almost-morning by now. He makes ready to walk her to her door, but she leans onto her crutches instead.

"I can do it," she says. "I need the practice anyway."

"How will you get to class on Monday?"

She sags into the crutches. She'd only psyched herself up enough to make it up the four steps of her front stoop. "I'll figure it out," she says, trying for brightness in her tone. She doesn't want him to worry.

"How about I give you a ride?"

"But I couldn't ask you to drive me to class."

"You didn't. I offered."

A thousand reasons to tell him no sprout up in her mind. *How could he possibly have time? He doesn't even know me. How could I let him do such a thing?* But his face is so pure. She doesn't know how else to think of it. Uncluttered. Sincere. He's told her his deepest secrets already, and she's told him hers, and he looks unfazed. It seems silly to feel so magnetized so quickly, but she is. They both are. She lets him.

By the time Lizbeth finally replaces her car battery, letting George drive her around has become a habit she doesn't want to break. Letting him open her car door for her, slide her crutches into the back seat, ask her where to go next. When he kisses her the first time, her ankle's still too weak for tiptoes, so he crouches to her height. They laugh into each other's mouths at the shape they make.

Thirteen Years After.

"YOU'RE GOING OUT with Serious George again?" Lizbeth asks. "Already?" She stands in Noreen's bedroom doorway, one hand hanging from the doorframe, the other holding this morning's third cup of coffee.

"He's making me supper at his place." Noreen is tying her shoes. Her left ankle is still swollen, so she ties that one more loosely than the other. She doesn't need the crutches anymore, but she's nowhere close to back to normal either. George will be here to pick her up and ride her to class in a few minutes.

Lizbeth bounces her eyebrows. "So serious. You'd tell me if you slept with him already, right?"

Noreen shrugs a shoulder. She's always dished on dates with Lizbeth. Other men she's been with felt like strangers to her though, so talking through how they touched her or what they said had more to do with what Noreen had felt or hoped for, less to do with the men. With George, even though they haven't done much beyond kissing yet, what they have done feels like it belongs to them alone. Telling Lizbeth would betray that.

"Because making someone dinner? That's a total sex move, you know," Lizbeth says. "Are you ready for that with him?"

"Why wouldn't I be?" Noreen heaves her zipped backpack into her lap and glances at her watch.

"He seems like a guy who fucks and stays, that's all. Not your specialty exactly."

"Thanks a lot."

"Not a criticism, Nor. Just an observation " More than once, Lizbeth has answered Noreen's laments about the latest guy who hadn't called her back with a catalog of signals Noreen had given off to make sure he didn't and a perennial accusation that she must, in fact, intend to stay alone. "George seems like a guy who's been waiting on the edge of everything for the right girl to come along for his happily ever after."

"He's making me dinner, not asking me to marry him." At her mirror, Noreen flicks a fallen eyelash and double-checks her eye makeup.

"Not yet," Lizbeth says.

"What would be so wrong with somebody asking me to marry him? I imagine someday I'll want that." This being one of many potential forks in the road of their friendship's future. Noreen peeks at her watch again.

"I didn't say it was wrong."

"You've never said anything nice about him." Noreen fluffs her hair one last time, then turns her back on the mirror.

"You've only known him two weeks."

"You don't have to pucker up your face like you ate something sour every time he walks up though. If you have something to say about him, just say it."

Lizbeth swings her arm down from the doorframe and braces it across her chest. "It's only been two weeks, and this is, what? Your fifth date? On top of taking you to all your classes? It's a lot, really fast."

"He's nice to me, Lizbeth." Noreen squeezes past her toward their front room where she'll be able to see George's car when he pulls up. "Whenever he drops me off, he waits to be sure I get where I'm going before he drives away. In the mornings, he brings me coffee and little pastries from Our Daily Bread and mix tapes with his favorite songs. Maybe you're used to boyfriends being so good to you, but it's new for me. Let me enjoy it."

Lizbeth follows Noreen toward the front window and pretends not to notice Noreen's compulsive head turns at every car that passes. "You're right," Lizbeth says. "You should enjoy that."

More than wanting Lizbeth to let her enjoy this, she wants her to enjoy it with her. To greet Noreen's excitement at George's arrivals with some kind of answering excitement. To refer to him as something besides Serious George. To recognize this for what it is for Noreen. Calm in place of chaos. Certainty in place of doubt.

"Why don't you sound convinced then?" Noreen says.

"Everyone should be nice to you, Nor. It shouldn't be the exception."

"I can't help that it is."

Lizbeth's face has a question on it, but she doesn't ask it. At the pop of the toaster, she nods and backs toward the kitchen, leaving Noreen alone at the window.

✦

George throws steaks on his balcony grill, bakes potatoes, pours glasses of dark red wine. Noreen's still getting used to the modern starkness of his place, the stylish, if colorless, shades of beige and gray, accents of chrome and glass. Proof of the father he'd talked about in the hospital waiting room, everything expensive and up to the minute. Fitting, too, that the décor is cold and utilitarian, favoring precision over warmth. White plates, simple stainless steel cutlery with knobby weighted ends, white linen placemats. Spread out on the glass tabletop after they've eaten, even their post-dinner mess looks staged for a photo shoot.

Lizbeth is right about the dinner. After George clears the table, he stacks the dishes in the sink but doesn't pause to rinse them before turning back toward Noreen, lifting her hand and leading her toward his bedroom. For her first few visits, they'd snuggled on the sofa, kissed and touched and lost themselves a little, but stayed aware of the clock, of times they needed to be other places. Now he touches her slowly, tentatively, undoing each button and zipper with tender care, hesitating at her sore ankle until she nods her okay.

He smooths his hands across her flesh as if no one has touched her before. Underneath the gray duvet, silvery sheets. Silk, they glide across their bodies and slide away, cool, slippery, decadent. In the background XTC sings "Senses Working Overtime" while George gazes along the length of her body, appreciating her with his eyes in a way that feels more than sexual. Her first taste of mango comes back to her, how Nonie had made her close her eyes for it, then the fruit's juicy meat zinged sudden, unimagined flavor against her tongue. With George, sex is as new, her whole body as new as that taste had been.

Finished, he breathes hot next to her while a herd of feelings gallops through her. Sex before this was work. More effort than pleasure. She'd convinced herself that intimacy was a prelude to departure, fixating on keeping herself from getting hurt by what she expected was inevitable, and so fulfilling the very prophecy she wanted to subvert. Leaving before they could leave her. Lizbeth was right to wonder if she'd wanted to be alone, but Noreen hadn't been able to see it until this moment, when she doesn't want to leave George but doesn't trust that she knows how to stay either.

As if he can read her thoughts, he whispers "Shh" and curls his head into the nook between her underarm and chest, places a warm palm against her stomach, and whirls the sheet up to their necks with his free hand. What if staying could be as easy as letting him fall asleep against her, the soft huff of his breath tickling her neck? As easy as closing her own eyes and letting herself fall asleep, too. Nowhere else to be but here.

❧

And she does fall asleep, but lurches upright in the darkest hour of night, hands clutching her throat. Air won't come. Every cell in her body fizzes, and she doesn't know where she is. The only sliver of light she can find comes from the wrong direction. All she knows is that she's naked, in a dark place, and not at home. Screams form and form and form but will not rise from her throat. Her lungs hurt from being unable to gulp air.

A hot hand lands on her shoulder, and a squirt of scream slips out. She twitches away from the touch as if it burns.

"Noreen?"

Her name in the darkness. Her name, and that hand, that makes its way back to her shoulder, hesitant now, but familiar. Her eyes adjust, and the place is familiar, too. George's place. George's warm hand. Her shoulders bow forward with an exhale of too-long-held breath.

"Hey," he says, squeezing her shoulder now. "What happened?"

This time panic started in her dream and wrenched her awake. Did Nonie's panics get worse as she got older, too? Noreen always assumed they'd been worse her whole life. That she and Nonie were alike in a host of good ways, but fundamentally different in how they fell apart.

"Did you have one of those things?" George rubs his face, maybe trying to wake himself up enough to help her. "Those things you told me about? I'm sorry. I can't think of the word."

He's the only person on earth who knows. Knows how terror comes to her in flashes so bright and sharp the world seems about to end. That she's more like Nonie than anyone guessed, even if he knows next to nothing about Nonie herself. For a second, Noreen regrets having told him. A feeling of peeling a layer away of her innermost self. To be this naked. In front of anyone.

"Is it over? Do you need a glass of water or something?"

She can see his eyes now, full and round, and he's not afraid or troubled. This is something that happens to her, and he's ready to help her figure it out. A rush of relief floods out the regret.

"I think so," she says. "I think it's over."

"Do you want to talk about it?"

"It started as a dream." He lies flat beside her now, his arms out in a T. She leans backward onto one of his arms, and he rolls toward her, enclosing her in the other as well.

"A nightmare, I guess?"

She nods, her head rocking into his shoulder so he can tell despite the dark. Disconnected fragments of dream replay themselves. Nothing intelligible, except that Nonie was there. Nonie populated her dreams for years when Noreen was younger, but she's a rarer visitor these days. A deep breath drags the scent of her shampoo from the dregs of time. A spare shudder wracks her. George hugs her more tightly. As if the extra pressure might wring the feeling away. Maybe it will.

Her heart rate slowly ticks back to normal. His body cups hers, and the weight of it comforts her, anchors her. For the first time in her life, it's finally safe to be exactly who she is. Their breaths synchronize, then his slow, deepen, then spurt in sleeping puffs that filter through her hair and warm her ear. Her body slowly lets go of the last energy of panic, and her eyes flutter, flutter—then spring wide once more.

One clear shard of lost dream. Nonie shouting: *Run, little angel. Run for your life.*

Under her hand, Noreen can feel her heart trotting again. Nonie would take this away from her, too, then. First, her own love, now George's.

Love. She thinks that's what this is.

Her fists clench around a tuft of silk sheet. She measures each breath with bitter caution, determined to soothe herself.

No. This time, she won't run.

❦

A few weeks later, her limp is improving, but George's apartment is half a mile closer to campus. Rather than have him drive her to class, she could stay over, walk from his place.

A handful of objects at a time, she disappears from the house she shares with Lizbeth, from the life she's known up to now. George is her safe haven, and she wants to be safe. Has always wanted it, without knowing what to name the want.

Fourteen Years After.

HER BEDROOM SMELLS the same. Jergens hand lotion plus shag carpet dust with woody undertones from the dresser set she's had as long as she can remember. Which she'll leave behind forever after today. She inhales, imprints the scent somewhere to keep, then the flutter of Lizbeth's hands at her shoulders brings her back to the moment. Getting ready for her wedding in her childhood bedroom, at the same vanity where she'd applied her first makeup back in middle school.

Back then and throughout high school, hairbrushes, gels, eye shadows, nail polish, and mascara had cluttered its surface, along with folded notes with scrawled confessions of first crushes she'd traded with her friend Claudia long before their falling out the summer after their freshman year of college. The fight was over something stupid, a T-shirt Claudia borrowed without asking, but it cannonballed into a fight about everything that neither of them had seen coming. Or both had. Her mind tosses Claudia's last angry line back to her: "I only made friends with you because I felt sorry for you." In the moment, it scalded her with shame. As a child she'd felt set apart, on the outside, especially after Nonie died and left her behind. Add to that how her mother fussed over her, worrying about everything that made her different, that made her herself. Claudia's words underlined some truth about herself she tried to keep secret—that she didn't really fit anywhere. If Claudia had stopped short of saying it, maybe she'd be among the guests milling about in the yard now.

What Claudia had said, though, Noreen could as easily have said to her because she didn't fit anywhere either, forever pretending to be someone besides herself and roping Noreen in to doing the same. They spent a decade putting up with each other instead of caring about each other. Surely, both had deserved caring. Both failed as friends. Making Noreen that much more grateful for Lizbeth, whose zippered bag of makeup pooches open on the old vanity next to a small pile of bobby pins she draws from every few moments, fixing Noreen's nest of curls into place.

"We're almost there," Lizbeth says, meeting her eyes cheerfully in the mirror. She's the maid of honor, her only attendant. Through the mirror, Noreen watches her hands styling her unruly hair, Lizbeth's green satin dress shimmering in the background. Soon they'll walk downstairs together, into the backyard, and a minister friend of her mother's will marry her to George.

A knock at the door and her brother leans into the room, his hand across his eyes, whispering, "Are you decent?" After he drops the hand, she can see how exhausted he is. Every time she's seen him since he started med school, he's looked tired. It's a visible reminder of the busyness he blames for his terrible track record as a correspondent. He lands a kiss on her cheek and crouches next to where she sits. "You look beautiful." He sends a grin through the mirror, which she answers in kind. They haven't spent much time together since he started college and their parents divorced. His attention feels unnatural now, makes her feel conspicuous, shy.

"Are you nervous?" he asks.

"Taking notes for yourself?" Noreen hopes teasing might at least lighten his intensity. His own wedding is only half a year away, right before the last med school spring break, which he and his fiancée finagled as a last shot at time off before their fellowships begin. Betty couldn't make it today but sent the delicate pearl drop earrings Noreen's wearing to match the necklace her mother loaned her for something borrowed. Betty's already a better correspondent than Mark. She'd checked in with Ruth about what gift to send and mailed the earrings weeks ago, along with a card and a long letter wishing her well.

Mark turns to Lizbeth next. "You know better than I could," he says. "Is this George person good enough for our Noreen?"

Lizbeth squeezes Noreen's shoulder ever so slightly at his use of "our," a gesture showing she registers the awkwardness Mark is trying to smooth over, his near total absence from her life for the span of her friendship with Lizbeth, apart from occasional postcards from state and national parks where he and Betty hiked on precious days off.

"Noreen says he is," Lizbeth says, "and that's good enough for me." Another gesture, smoothing over her own reservations about George. Noreen clasps her hand over Lizbeth's where it rests on her shoulder, a thank you.

"It's a big day," Noreen says to her brother.

Mark echoes the words, nods, jingles change in the pockets of his light gray tux, rented to match George's. He's the best man, though they only met last night at the rehearsal dinner George's father hosted in a rented hall at a nearby country club. His milieu, not her family's. Far more formal than the backyard wedding about to begin. "I better get back to the man I'm besting for." He winks, then hovers a moment, both of them unsure how to cross the distance that's spread between them, then he's gone again.

Her father arrived a couple days earlier, took her out to lunch and shopping at a new upscale kitchen shop on the downtown mall for a pile of kitchen gadgets as her wedding present. Skillets, spatulas, mixing bowls. He met George for the first time over dinner that night, a few days before Mark did. Meeting her father out in public spaces instead of in the home where she grew up feels strange, but he doesn't belong here anymore. Hugh and her mother have merged their belongings into this house while Hugh rents out his place. Both are readying their houses to sell so they can settle into a new one together one day. For now, Hugh's framed ancient maps hang in the den in place of her father's old framed museum prints. His medical journals splay across the coffee table in place of her father's legal files. Today her father will be relegated to visitor in his old house and yard, guest as opposed to host. She knows she shouldn't, but she hopes her mother's new happiness will sting him, if only a little. After their divorce it took her mother a lot longer to find her feet again than it did him, and Noreen blames him for that.

Downstairs a flurry of noises reminds her that time is short. The guest list totals about fifty. Family, neighbors, friends, parents' work colleagues. Modest or not, it's a lot to organize. Caterers clank pans and platters in the kitchen. The phone rings with last-minute calls. The doorbell signals flower deliveries and early guests who missed the welcome sign outside, pointing them toward the backyard. Her mother's voice every so often rises up the stairs, murmuring directions to caterers and guests alike. Calm, pleasant, efficient, if not enthusiastic.

"You just took me by surprise," Ruth had said to explain her tears at news of the engagement. Not champagne-cork-popping surprise but *Let me find words that won't hurt your feelings* surprise. "I didn't realize you were so serious so quickly….I feel like I'm still only getting to know him….You're so young. So very young."

Hairstyle complete, Lizbeth says, "Ta-da!" and holds a hand mirror so Noreen can see the entirety of her shapely chignon with tendrils framing her face. "What do you think?"

"It's exactly how I pictured." Noreen examines herself, touching the edges of her hair, too lightly to disturb it, but enough to feel its shape.

Lizbeth digs into the old-fashioned toiletries suitcase she brought, stocked full of zippered bags of creams and makeup, which are now mostly scattered across the vanity in front of them, and she withdraws a bottle of amber liquor and two paper cups. She fills each, then holds them up for a toast. "May your marriage be exactly how you picture it, too." They knock their cups together and throw back a swallow.

Whiskey, so sharp it makes Noreen cough and laugh at the same time. Her eyes water, so she waves her hands. "Tissue! Tissue!" Lizbeth hands her one, and she dabs her eyes to keep from smearing the makeup Lizbeth so carefully applied. Real tears sneak up behind the droplets, but she dabs them away, too. How she wishes at least one of the people she loves could see George the way she does. Whenever she's with him, he fills her with utter confidence. Holding her hand, sitting beside her, just the sound of his voice. It's when he's not beside her that she wonders.

Nerves. Ordinary nerves.

Her mother ducks her head through the door. "How're you coming along?" She steps halfway into the room, keeps a hand on the door.

Noreen wants her to come all the way in, kneel beside her and tell her how perfect she looks, how perfect this is, but her usual worry glazes her face instead.

"You look lovely," Ruth says. "How are you feeling?"

"Nervous, of course. Everyone's nervous on their wedding day. You were nervous, weren't you?"

Her mother gives an inscrutable smile. An apology? A warning? "Not with Hugh." As if to say, *Not when I got it right. Those dozen-plus years with your dad were just a mistake....* "I better get back. Everything's nearly ready." Halfway out the door, she halts and swings back toward them. Maybe now she'll say something comforting. Something motherly. "Lizbeth, thank you. What a good friend you are."

Noreen second-guesses leaving Claudia off the guest list. She'd been a bulldozer, bossy and self-involved, but she would've liked George. She liked handsome men and the spoils of attachment. Once high school started, you'd hardly see her without a relic from one of her admirers, a chunky high school ring bobbing from a necklace or an oversized college sweatshirt after she began masquerading as a college student herself, studying in the university library to make her next conquest. She'd thumbs-up the idea of a wedding as much as the match itself. Little comfort, though, coming hypothetically from an absent former friend.

"Maybe you should let me finish," Lizbeth says, gently spinning Noreen to face her again. She is a good friend, so much more compatible and enjoyable than Claudia had been. There's plenty of time for her to grow to like George.

A light touch-up of mascara. A smudge more blush. Eyeliner, "To make your eyes pop," she says.

Noreen cuts her eyes toward Lizbeth in the mirror. "Are you happy for me?"

"I'm happy when you're happy," Lizbeth says, applying careful strokes of lipstick now, her own lips stretched against her teeth in sympathy for the motion. Then she meets Noreen's gaze in the mirror. Lizbeth, fully herself. "Are you happy?"

"Yes," Noreen says. "I am."

"Then I am, too." And, at least for this moment, she means it. "You're my heart, you know that, Nor?"

"And you're mine."

"We might not get to see each other so much, with the marriage and all." Lizbeth replaces the lipstick cap and fiddles with the other wands and tubes and compacts, tidying them back into her toiletries case.

"I'm not moving to Mars."

"I know, but George doesn't love me the way you do. It might be hard to stay in touch sometimes." She gives a neat smile, zippers the last of the makeup into place.

"Why would you say that?"

"I'm saying that no matter what, I'm on your side. I'll be here. Anytime."

Trouble works a seam into Noreen's forehead. "That sounds

more like a warning than a blessing."

"It's not meant to, Nor. I just want you to know you'll always be right here." She thumps her fist to her heart. "Even if months go by. Years. No matter what."

"This sounds like goodbye?"

"It's just, I love you, Nor. You're the best friend I've ever had. Marriage makes life different."

"I know you don't like him, but I hope you will one day. I hope you'll both learn to…"

"This isn't about him," Lizbeth says. "Not exactly. Whether we want it to or not, our friendship will change now."

Noreen knows this, has known it for some time, but still she shakes her head no, holds a wedge of tissue up against her eyes to stem off more tears.

"We're in the real world, Nor. I have an actual office. In a few minutes, you'll have an actual husband. We're changing, sweet friend. We're supposed to, you know? I'm just saying, no matter how much changes, this…" Fist to heart again. "This won't change, okay?"

Noreen nods, can't speak, but thumps a fist to her heart, too.

"I'm going to check if they're ready for us, okay?"

The door closes behind her with a soft click. Her footsteps pad down the hall and away. "Ruth?" Lizbeth calls from the top of the steps, then a drumroll of footfalls down the stairs, a more distant, "Ruth?"

Her question will take only a minute, then it will be time to go.

Noreen stands from her seat at the vanity. She swivels her head back and forth to loosen her neck after staring at herself in the mirror so long. Thinking too much. At the window, she parts closed curtains, careful to stay hidden in case George is already out there, and takes stock of the crowd.

There are the McKenzies from down the street, even Lorna, who's the same age as Noreen but never paid attention to her at school. Probably because Noreen was a troublemaker and Lorna was studious, cautious. Noreen would say hello to her, careening past in the high school hallways with Claudia, in the throes of some drama or another, and Lorna would sidestep, eyes wide, and whisper hello back to her, as if she carried disease. Their parents had played cards together years ago and took turns hosting cocktail parties, which must be why they're here today.

Brynne must be helping with setup, driving her mother half nuts, but Uncle Emmett and their sons, Henry and Luke, grown now, claim front-row seats, next to Grammy O'Malley, who looks faded and brittle without Grampy to bolster her anymore. Luke sits closest to her, a high school senior still growing into his very recent height, looking spindly and nervous in his lightweight summer suit. The off-centered tie proves his mother hasn't glimpsed him there in the yard yet. He bends toward Grammy to ask her a question, and Noreen watches her mouth a one-word reply. Disappointed, Luke casts a look around the yard for anything else to pass the time.

Behind the seats arrayed for the ceremony, long white-cloaked tables are bedecked with food and flowers. At the edge of one table, a huge tin, a few makeshift plates of crackers someone had to run out to purchase. Without warning, George's dad had brought a mother lode of caviar and a few magnums of Dom Perignon for the reception. If it hadn't been for Lizbeth, she wouldn't know about it, but she'd been down in the kitchen when Mr. Putnam arrived, blustering into the room with the reluctant assistance of his sister who navigated his wheelchair through the mudroom. He pretended, or really believed, that her mother's only hesitation about incorporating his offerings into the carefully planned spread of other refreshments was her disbelief at the expense, not the last-minute inconvenience of it, the obvious clash with the simplicity of the rest of the buffet, or the fact that he'd overstepped. "Don't worry," he said. "It's a gift. A gift from me."

Her mother wouldn't have repeated a story that made George's father seem so crass, but Lizbeth doesn't share her scruples. The way people were tiptoeing around him amused her. "Everyone trying so hard to pretend he's not a dick." Her idea was to laugh with Noreen about this eavesdropped morsel, but she softened at Noreen's reaction. "Oh, Nor. I'm an asshole. He's your family after today. I shouldn't have said anything."

His glitzy gifts look as haphazard and unnecessary as they are, crowded at the end of the table that way. Her mother, and especially Brynne, will cringe throughout the reception about the messy showiness of it, but the guests won't care. Twenty years from now, no one will remember. Noreen takes comfort in this and hopes she can keep George from feeling embarrassed.

Noreen discovered George's father had helped him buy her engagement ring a week after the proposal, when she met him for the first time. He kissed her hand at their introduction, then held onto it too long. "She's a pretty one, George," he kept saying. "Worth the price."

Afterward they'd fought about the ring. "It should have been something you could afford," she'd said, but "affording" meant something different to him since spending his dad's money was his normal. Eventually he pled with her to accept the ring anyway, and she did, though it feels too heavy and reminds her of costume jewelry. She's not sure he understood how queasy-making his father's attitude was then, so his father's foisted gifts might not embarrass George, even if he knows about them.

Only, she wishes they would.

She knifes her hand to her side again, dropping the curtains at the sight of George's profile walking onto the scene. When he's out of sight, sometimes she imagines packing a suitcase jammed with necessary things—books, underwear, soap—and stowing herself away on a train. Any train. Riding the rails day and night, maybe jumping off at some random Canadian town and starting a brand-new life from nothing. Leaving everyone and everything behind without looking back. When she sees George, though, she remembers why she means to stay.

It's bad luck to see him on their wedding day though, even if he does look so handsome in his light gray tux, the sun brightening his brown hair. Even if seeing him makes her feel certain again. She presses her hands together at her heart, resting her chin on her fingertips. Whatever it is inside her that sometimes makes her feel about to whirl apart, or disappear, George settles. No one else can.

Back at the vanity, she inspects her hair to make sure her quick walk around the room hasn't disturbed it. Of course it hasn't. Lizbeth's work was perfect. In the mirror, she scans from her hair to her face, then gasps. Her aunt Nonie looks out of the glass at her.

Noreen looks more and more like her aunt the closer she gets to the age she was when she died, the age Noreen remembers her best. Swap her white muslin cocktail gown for corded bellbottoms and ponchos, her mother's something-borrowed pearls for a chain of hand-picked daisies, and the transformation would be complete.

Today's reflection feels different though. Paler. Stern. Noreen reaches to touch the cheek in the glass, cold against her fingers.

He doesn't love you enough.

She gulps for air. Pats the dresser top in search of a glass of water that was here a moment ago, knocks lipstick and mascara-stained tissues to the floor. Careful of her makeup, she takes one small sip. Swallows around her heart beating in her throat, then bends toward the mirror one more time. "Who are you to talk? You're the one who left me behind."

Bent close now, she sees only her own face. Cheeks, rosy and fresh. Bright green eyes, shiny and clear. The chignon perfectly turned, two corkscrew curls still frizzless and symmetrical on either side of her face.

Another knock at the door. "They're ready for us, my girl."

Fourteen Years After.

NOREEN READS WHILE waiting, laying aside her Fay Weldon from time to time to peer out the window for signs of Lizbeth's beat-up silver Chevette. Lizbeth took a half-day at her graphic design job in Richmond and is scheduled to roll into town by six. Their first overnight visitor. A damp chill hangs in the air, and Noreen hopes that doesn't mean snow. The sky fades from wintry white into the orange of twilight.

February. Noreen has been married six months.

Despite all her checking, she hears the familiar rumble of the old Chevette before she sees it. She races out her storm door and down the front stoop. Lizbeth's car door yawns open behind her, pinging a warning, and she and Noreen fly together in the middle of the sidewalk. Next come bursts of laughter and chatting as they drag Lizbeth's overnight bag from her car.

Lizbeth asks for a tour of the place. A brick ranch much like the one she and Noreen had rented for most of college, but farther from Virginia Tech on a street with fewer students, an office in place of a second bedroom, and no basement neighbor. Noreen had talked George out of his fancier apartment so they could afford rent themselves, rather than start out beholden to his dad. Artifacts of his father's influence inhabit every room though. Stark chrome-edged, glass-topped coffee table and side tables in the living room. Espresso maker that they hardly ever use on the counter. Boxy side chairs. Noreen had found a nearly new sofa bed at a neighborhood yard sale, excited because it made room for visitors in their tiny house, but its tweedy ordinariness stands out against George's father's trendier acquisitions.

"You're such a grownup," Lizbeth says in the bathroom where fluffy white towels trimmed in navy blue hang beside a matching shower curtain, neat as a catalog photo.

"No more grown up than you," Noreen says. "Just married."

Lizbeth lifts a lemon-shaped soap from the ceramic dish beside the sink. "I'm not *this* grown up." They laugh.

"I don't know if anybody is," Noreen says. "They're wedding presents, all the fancy soaps and towels." Their haul of gifts was as modest as their backyard wedding, but she gets what Lizbeth sees in them and in George's expensive trove of belongings, how they define the space and scream *Married people live here!*

A passing train whistles not far away. Lizbeth twirls toward her, her face radiant with memory. "Don't you think of it every time you hear a train?"

"Yeah, I do," Noreen says, but for her, that joyride of hanging on for their lives is just one of many wild times with Lizbeth, but the one and only time she met George.

They round back to the kitchen where Noreen digs cheese from the fridge, makes a plate of it with crackers and grapes, and hands Lizbeth two glasses and a bottle of wine. In the living room, they drop side by side onto the pullout sofa, Lizbeth's intended bed for the evening, and set the snacks and wine on the coffee table.

"Looks like you and George have settled into much quieter times then." Lizbeth spreads her arms wide to indicate the whole place. "Is that hard?" Her nose squinches with the question.

Noreen works the cork free. Hardly nine months apart and it's like Lizbeth has lost her whole sense of what Noreen's life is like. "I think I was ready for a little less craziness, you know?" She pours them each a glass of wine, and they click rims and take first sips.

"I guess we were crazy sometimes," Lizbeth says.

"Can you believe we're the same people?" Nothing in her own life is so spontaneous as it was in college, which feels like yesterday and ten years ago at the same time. Lizbeth's life is different now, too. Full-time graphic designer at a big ad firm. Living on her own in an apartment in the Fan. Responsibilities, commitments—even planning this simple get-together took them months of failed efforts. Once Lizbeth got sick. Another time Noreen's professor assigned a last-minute paper. Twice George's father called, demanding some kind of service. She doesn't like him to go on his own. If it hadn't been for the visiting bigwigs from CalTech who George and his lab-mates have to show around this weekend, her father-in-law would've foiled this latest plan, too.

At George's refusal last night, Noreen heard his father shouting through the phone from across room. Afterward, George told her, "I can't be everywhere," with a hint of malice, as if speaking sharply to her could compensate for how small his father makes him feel. A defensive reflex she understands but doesn't like. Often she reminds herself that he can't help what he needs, and over time she'll train him to be more thoughtful about it. George's father could learn some self-restraint, too. They help him when they can, but the visits tax George's patience and make him fall behind with his research, forcing him to stay in his lab past midnight for nights in a row afterward. Last night she ignored George's tone after the call and hugged him close. His muscles rippled with the effort of letting himself be held, and he hardly slept. She felt sorry for him, but relieved, too. Finally, a visit with Lizbeth.

"It's been so long since I've had a night like this." Noreen relaxes into the cushions. "So comfy. Nothing to do but chat."

"You must have friends?" Lizbeth says.

"Sure." She layers some cheese onto a cracker and takes a bite, then brushes a spray of crumbs from her knee onto the floor to worry about later. "I'm friendly with some people in my classes, but it's busy, you know?" She explains some logistical hurdles she'd created for herself by mixing a master's in education with a master's in English. Lesson plans and practicums a couple of days a week, then massive reading and intense critical analysis papers the rest of the time, balancing all of that with her twenty-hour-a-week job at the writing center. "I can hardly rub one minute against another most of the time, and George is no better with his teaching assistantship and all his lab time. We hardly see each other, let alone anybody else."

Lizbeth looks skeptical.

"What? This is what grad school's like."

"Fun-less?"

Noreen balances her wine glass and reaches for a book on the coffee table. Her favorite class this semester is on the journals of literary women. "This is fun," she says, waving *Linotte* in the air. "Nin started keeping this journal when she was eleven years old on the ship that brought her from Europe to America. It's like her brain bleeds straight into her pen and details flow out, exactly what she's seeing and feeling. It's like being right beside her and inside her mind at the same time." She rests the book in her lap and her hand with the wine glass on top of that. "So I'm busy, and mostly solitary, but I love what I'm studying."

"That's good, loving what you're studying, but, I mean, you have to go on living, too. You can't just hole up here forever, you and George and no one else."

"We're newlyweds, Lizbeth. It's not like we're tired of each other."

"It just sounds confining."

"Maybe it would be for you." Noreen leans into the armrest and away from Lizbeth, scoots the book back onto the table. She's always loved reading. Lizbeth knows this. It feels like she's in third grade again with her mother and teacher in a flutter about her reading too much, as if they could know better than Noreen what she wanted for herself. If it hadn't been for everybody pushing her to be more social, she might not have spent so much time with Claudia. She might've saved herself a few regrets.

"What about you, then? Your friends? What's your life like these days?" Noreen asks, fussing with the hem of her T-shirt rather than making eye contact.

Lizbeth starts with a woman in her office. "Madeline, you should see her. She's a wreck. I mean, she comes late to meetings, her shirt half-untucked, her hair a mess, but she has the best ideas, and her drawings are amazing. The non-work ones, because what we draw for the job is pretty standard most of the time. Anything from logo design to full-color ads." Lizbeth pulls another swing of wine. Talking about herself switched on a light inside her that her worries about Noreen had dimmed. "Some of the campaigns about kill me. Like the catalog we had to do for some company that sells hygiene products to prisons. That one was grim. Anyway, Madeline's a hoot. She keeps me from getting *Deliverance*-level down on what we do." Noreen had forgotten those characters started off as disaffected ad men. When she and Lizbeth rented the movie, they'd watched the worst of it between finger slits, their hands covering their eyes.

From there, Lizbeth narrates the latest carnival ride of her love life. The man at her office who looks normal but sends her passionate notes written onto violently pornographic magazine centerfolds. Another man at the health food co-op who waits for her Saturday mornings, then pretends it's a happy accident they're shopping at exactly the same time. A man she hooked up with who turned out to be a married police officer with a cocaine habit. A life full of variety, risk, and room for mistakes.

"You must think my life is so boring," Noreen says.

Lizbeth leans over her glass, swirls the wine. "I don't worry about you getting bored so much as I worry about you getting lonely."

"You shouldn't worry about me at all." Not everything about

loneliness is bad, she wants to say. Something about it suits her nature, though surely Lizbeth would object to the notion. She suspects Lizbeth wouldn't mind picturing her holed up with someone if that someone weren't George. If only she could see him the way Noreen does, those moments when he knows her better than anyone, when he drowns out old echoes, *Don't you turn out the same,* by simply saying her name. This weekend she wants Lizbeth to finally meet that side of George and for the two of them to learn to like each other.

"I'm in love, Lizbeth. These are good days."

The Smiths warble from the stereo in the background, and Lizbeth and Noreen nestle together, letting their eyes go glassy, muscles slack from wine and comfort. Noreen unfolds a blanket from the back of the sofa and billows it in the air, settling it onto their legs. "I know it's not what you meant, about how I should be more social than I am, but I've always liked meeting people in books. You shouldn't worry about me for that. There's something beautifully tragic, especially about Nin, that keeps me company."

Lizbeth sweeps a veil of bangs from her eyes to get a clearer view of Noreen. "Is that how you feel? Beautifully tragic?"

She hadn't meant it that way, and odd images come to her at the question. The tire swing in the hot air. A sky full of clouds and the ground against her back. The ride in the ambulance with an oxygen mask scrunching Nonie's hair in weird tufts. That extension cord she never actually saw, dangling from a pipe in a dark basement.

"No, not me." Noreen's voice comes out quiet. Lizbeth touches her hand.

Long after they reduce the cheese and crackers to a plate of crumbs, the grapes to a stem skeleton, Noreen fixes pasta with lemon and garlic, tosses everything with olive oil, and serves the result in a dish that was Lizbeth's wedding gift. After supper, they polish off their bottle of wine at the kitchen table. They're on the verge of calling it a night when George stumbles through the front door. He shrieks an unfamiliar laugh and collapses face first into the sofa. The kitchen connects to the small living room, so they form a distorted half-circle.

"Went out with the boys," he says to the floor. "After the big important dinner."

"What boys?" Noreen asks. Lizbeth couldn't know it, but George is normally all work and almost no play. This behavior is so out of character for him, it's funny, and after last night's call with his dad, she's relieved to see him silly instead of somber.

"Buncha guys from the lab. Harry, Minh, and some guy from Nebraska." He drags himself into a more normal position on the sofa. "Ne-*bras*-ka," George says again, drawing out each syllable, then snickers.

Lizbeth trains her eyes toward the farthest corner of the room. George natters about ridiculous things for another half-hour or so with no sign of letting up, and Lizbeth excuses herself to get dressed for bed. While she's out of the room, George falls asleep right there on the unopened pullout sofa, his snore like a drill. So when Lizbeth returns—wearing the same favorite penguin print pajamas from the years she and Noreen roomed together—there's nowhere for her to lie down. It's almost 2 a.m.

"Listen," Noreen says. "He doesn't wake up easily." Truer is that he complains and acts grumpy for a long time if you wake him from a deep sleep, like a little kid from naptime. Plus, he slept so badly last night, she'd rather let him rest. "You can share the bed with me, if you don't mind. He looks like he's out for the night."

She walks Lizbeth to the bed, tidies some things on the bookshelf on George's side, picks up a dirty sock he'd forgotten. Then she goes back to cover George with the blanket she and Lizbeth used earlier. She adjusts his head against a throw pillow and removes his shoes. Kisses his sleep-warm cheek.

When she finally crawls into bed, Lizbeth holds up an edge of the silk sheet, rubs it suggestively, and teases, "Sexy, huh?"

"Serious George has serious sheets," Noreen says. They giggle at the sheets and the nickname that's only theirs. "Look at us now, with jobs and grad school and a marriage." She rolls onto her back and gazes up as if she could find lost time on the ceiling.

"Yeah, the pod people got us."

They lie that way for a while, talking about little things, laughing hushed nighttime laughs. For the first time in a long time, Noreen feels filled up. She breathes deep, savors the feeling. "I'm so glad you came," she says.

"Me too, Nor."

❧

Shuffling and thumping startle Noreen awake. A shape hovers over Lizbeth's side of the bed. Noreen's first thoughts are of burglars and rapists. She stretches toward Lizbeth in a desperate motion of protection, then stifles a scream as soon as she realizes the shape is actually George, half-wrapped in the blanket she threw over him after he fell asleep. The sky outside is dark gray rather than black, so it must be approaching dawn.

"George?"

He laughs, high-pitched and thready, but quiet. "Somebody's in my bed. My side of the bed."

"George? Are you even awake?" Noreen heaves herself to standing and rushes to where he looms over the sleeping Lizbeth, reaches behind him to shepherd him away from her.

"What're you doing?" he says and yanks out of her grasp. "I want to go to bed now." She can smell alcohol, somehow still strong on his breath.

"You were asleep," Noreen says. "I didn't want to bother you."

"Aww," George says, patting her head, swaying. "Sweet little wife."

She tries to direct him back toward the living room with a

hand on his shoulder, but he swoons again, grabs for the sheet. "I want my bed."

By now Lizbeth is stirring. "I'm so sorry," Noreen says. "I've never seen him quite like this."

"Do I look different?" George laughs his new weird laugh again.

"It's okay. I'll move." Lizbeth rises, avoiding George's clumsy stance.

Noreen lowers George onto the bed, then follows Lizbeth to the living room. "The sofa bed's already made." She jerks the pullout from under the sofa cushions. She had made it before Lizbeth got here and stored it, along with a folded empty pillowcase, for her arrival. George collapsed onto it before she got the chance to pull it into service.

"We don't have extra pillows yet," Noreen explains, shimmying a throw pillow into a pillowcase. "You're our first guest."

Lizbeth smiles at her, half-asleep, and curls into the makeshift pillow.

Back in the bedroom, George is standing again, ripping at the sheets. "Smells like her."

Noreen shushes him, but he doesn't pay attention. She hopes Lizbeth is already asleep again, not hearing any of this.

"I can't smell that all night. It itches my nose." As if to prove this, he sneezes. Then he staggers, can't steady himself, and retches onto the worn-out wood floor. "Oh God." And he does it again.

"Smells worse now," Noreen mutters on her way to get some rags and cleanser from the bathroom closet.

"What'd you say?" George is standing behind the vomit, still wobbly on his feet. "What did you say to me?"

"Nothing." Noreen snaps on rubber gloves. "But, Jesus, George, you fucked up."

He might've slipped in the vomit or just lost his balance, but she can't believe he means to fall into her, even though his hands are braced in front of himself in a gesture of pushing. Whatever he meant to happen, he winds up falling forward into the mess he made, his upper body glancing into Noreen's, causing her to trip a step, fumble backwards into the doorknob of the closet she'd left open behind her. "What the fuck, George?" A knob-shaped pain throbs at her hip. She rubs it with one hand and stares at him in disbelief.

"I don't like when you talk trashy," George grumbles, sliding as he tries to steady himself again.

"You're on your own." Noreen peels the gloves off, tosses them onto the floor next to the bucket, and stalks out of the room. She climbs into the sofa bed next to Lizbeth and uses her hands as a pillow, curling onto the side the knob hadn't smashed into. The spot on her hip seems to radiate heat into the blankets on top of her. Her breath catches when she inhales, not letting her take a full breath. The way it happens with one of her episodes, a slow sputter threatening to skitter out of control. She grips the edge of the couch mattress to keep from falling into the feeling. Holding onto something often anchors her. Holding onto George works best, but that's not an option tonight.

Lizbeth rolls toward her. Dawn isn't far off, so Noreen can see her face in the fading dark. She lays a hand against Noreen's cheek. What she needed, but not for the reason Lizbeth thinks. "You could come home with me, you know. Make a life for yourself in the big city."

Finally, a full breath and she eases her grasp on the mattress. "Richmond's not that big a city," Noreen says, a joke to play off Lizbeth's concern.

"Bigger than here."

"I really am okay. You don't need to worry about me so much."

"You're the worrier, Nor. You worried this whole night what I'd think of George. You always worry what I'll think of George."

"I want you to like him."

"It doesn't bother you that you have to try so hard?"

"He was stupid tonight. He'll be sorry tomorrow. This isn't how our life is."

Lizbeth nods, her hand still resting on Noreen's cheek. "If it ever is, you know where to find me."

Noreen smiles, but what she feels is sadness. Lizbeth rolls over again, and her breath slows almost instantly. For a long while, Noreen lies there, rigid and sore.

By the time she and Lizbeth wake up, George is gone. He left a full pot of coffee for them and a note in the middle of the table. "Embarrassed. Out of your hair." For Lizbeth, it's just one more failed interaction. Even if it could help Lizbeth see him differently, Noreen won't spill his secrets, about his dad's call the night before she came and all the pressure he feels. Everything that makes a person unique and breakable is private. She rubs her hip one more time. In the light of day, she's certain he hadn't meant to push her. Why would he?

In the bedroom, a vague odor of throw-up lingers, but there's no sign of the mess. The rags and cleanser and gloves remain exactly where she left them, and the bed is stripped bare. While Lizbeth showers, Noreen scrubs the floor and opens the windows, letting cold air stir through the room. Taking out the trash later, she finds the silk sheets and the shirt George had been wearing knotted in a wet snarl of vomit and stuffed into the trash can behind the house.

*Five Months
Before.*

SOMETHING RATTLES NONIE awake. For a bleary middle-of-the-night second, she's back in her childhood bedroom in her parents' house, the ghost of a train pattering down the tracks nearby. Streetlight haze slants through her window at the wrong angle for that though. Her bare feet hit the worn hardwood floor and replant her across town in her Little High Street apartment. One of six carved out of a once grand old home a few worn-out blocks from the new downtown pedestrian mall that's meant to reclaim business from the not-as-new Fashion Square Mall in the county just north of town. Familiar sounds of crickets and other night bugs, plus the occasional car passing by the street below, whisper through her cracked window and settle her more into place. Then the soft drumroll of Doug's fingers on his floor, her ceiling, clears any last doubt and calls her to attention. The warning signal for one of his episodes.

When it happens to her, it starts in her toes and immobilizes her. When it happens to Doug, it starts in the air around him, he says. If he screams or strikes out, he's just trying to protect himself. If she thought she could swat or hurl the shivers away, she'd do it, too.

She ties her ratty bathrobe over her yellow nylon nightgown. In her kitchen, she forages the junk drawer for his key, pockets it. Searches her shelf for the whiskey she usually brings, but they must have emptied it last week. She grabs her percolator instead, a bag of coffee, and an apple, just in case.

Hardly midnight, it's on the early side for Doug. She would've missed this one back in her days waiting tables when 2 a.m., any night of any week, was the earliest she might make it home. Even now she would've missed it on a normal Friday, the only night she's ever busy. Drinks with friends from work. Becky was out sick today though, so Nonie wound up following her same routine from the rest of the week, starting with a cup of ramen at her bare kitchen table for supper and ending curled on her sofa spooning Heavenly Hash ice cream from the half-gallon carton while she watched the Friday Night movie alone.

It took months of feeling disguised and invisible behind her standard issue desk at her standard issue cubicle drafting letters to beg money off rich alumni before Cooper invited her to join them for drinks after work at the Virginian, the bar catty-corner to UVA's Rotunda, as famous for attracting students as the local best, worst, and weirdest. Nonie thinks of it as the good old bar for the good old boys, because no matter how eclectic the crowd may be, it still skews preppy and overeducated, but their drinks are decent, and she likes feeling included. For six months since that first invitation, she's spent most Friday nights there with Cooper and Becky, but she still thinks of them as new friends, or even people she's getting to know. Their personalities match their business wear—Cooper as straitlaced as his UVA preppy-chic bowties and crisply ironed oxford shirts, Becky as perky as her vibrant madras plaid skirts and Peter Pan collars—while Nonie feels like an imposter stepping into her plain white blouses and khaki skirts, pinning the life out of her bouncy hair, cramming her Day-Glo painted toenails into tight, closed-toe pumps in accordance with the university dress code.

She'd blended in better waiting tables at El Mercado, but she'd mistaken her coworkers' lazy acceptance for friendship. While she worked there, they'd stay after closing sometimes and drink beer from the taps or get high on Marco's homegrown stash. Maybe Marco would strum his guitar, and they'd dance or sing songs from the radio. When they could scrape enough cash together, they'd slip over to the C&O Restaurant by the train tracks and see who was playing at the bar. Once they'd squeezed in at the back and caught Townes van Zandt singing "To Live Is to Fly" and "Pancho and Lefty." She has to remind herself that they did all these things, that they'd had good times together and acted like real friends, because they'd quit calling almost as soon as she clocked out the last time.

With Doug, unlike with Cooper and Becky and anyone else at her no-longer-new job, she feels like her actual self. She goes as she is to visit him, her hair loose and wild, padding barefoot up the apartment steps to his door, not caring that her old terrycloth robe is torn at the hem or that her nightgown is misshapen from too many washings. With him, she's enough exactly the way she is. Her throat gets tight thinking about it.

At his door, she knocks softly and leans in to listen for the low uttering that usually follows his drumming, a sound like he's in pain. Whenever she's around for one of his episodes, she rushes to get to him before one of their neighbors calls the cops. Seventy years old and in a forgotten part of the city, the place is run down, but it's solid. Noise doesn't travel that easily, so anyone could choose to ignore Doug on his bad nights. People don't have to be mean, but often they choose to be, and Doug has spent some nights in jail. Disturbing the peace. Which is ironic. It's his peace that's disturbed. He likes to say he never made it all the way back from 'Nam, and not just because he left half an arm there. Anyone calling the cops on Doug must be the kind of asshole who thinks being Black turns you automatically scary, no matter that he's the least scary person Nonie knows. The person she feels most at home with, besides Noreen.

"Doug?" she calls when he doesn't answer her knock. She likes to warn him before she barges in. She balances her awkward armload, withdraws his key from her pocket, turns it in the lock. His noises surge into the hallway, louder through the open door, so she jerks it closed behind her. The apartment is dark except for the fog of streetlights spilling through uncurtained windows.

"Doug?"

Trailing a hand along the wall, she feels her way toward the kitchen, drops her armload onto the counter, and hits the light switch. Huddled on the floor beside his couch, Doug winces, covers his eyes, and moans again at the shock of brightness.

"Just me." She fills the percolator with water, scoops grounds into the basket, and plugs it in. A few days' worth of dishes molder in his sink. Crumbs litter the green Formica countertop. Nonie seldom meets men who look after themselves properly.

While the coffee brews, she kneels beside him, giving him a chance to realize she's there, then rests a hand on his shoulder. He wears nothing but his dog tags and boxer shorts, faded beyond color. Normally he won't leave his bedroom without sleeves long enough to cover the stump of his lost arm. Scars seam the nub, purple against his brown skin. He's several days unshaven, and his bare feet show his gnarled-up toes. More scarring, something else to do with 'Nam. He saw some shit over there. Still sees it, apparently, pretty often, eight years later. If the new medicines Dr. Yang put her on work as promised, she'll tell Doug about them, see if he can get the same treatment at the VA Hospital in Richmond.

Dr. Yang says plenty of things can trigger an attack. You don't have to have a war to blame. The best Nonie can figure is that hers come from feeling unwanted, plus a much-harder-to-explain sense of coming loose in the hugeness of the universe. Dr. Yang says you don't have to have a reason to feel what you feel.

Doug's windows are open, and a cool breeze breathes through the space. "I'm still here," she says.

His eyes are closed, head bent toward his lap, and his one hand clenches a fistful of hair, but she can tell he's surfacing from wherever he goes. Wherever she goes.

"You can let it go now," Nonie says.

His muttering downshifts into throat clearing, and his eyes flutter open, find hers. "It don't let go of me."

"I know it." She rubs his shoulder, then fetches him a cup of coffee and the apple she brought. He takes both, looking like he's still partway somewhere else.

"It's just us now," Nonie says. "Nobody but us."

"It's never gone."

"Just us."

He lifts the coffee and takes a first sip. The apple rests on the floor beside him.

"Just us two," Nonie says again.

Lifting the mug to his face, he closes his eyes and breathes in the steam, lets his breath out again. Steadier now. "You're a good one," he says.

"You'd do the same." If her fits came on as noisily as his, she's sure he would come to her, but hers are usually too stealthy for anybody else to notice. The few times someone has kept her company have helped more than she can explain.

"Maybe," he says with a jagged smile, as if his lips didn't all the way remember how to make the shape. "Will you stay?"

She hides a yawn, tries to check the clock without his noticing. No matter what she does Friday nights, Saturday mornings she catches cartoons with her niece and nephew. "I have to be somewhere in the morning. Do you have an alarm?"

Cool spring air puffs into his bedroom through the window that doesn't open all the way, promising rain and leaving the sheets damp and clingy. Nonie shakes wrinkles from the top sheet, straightens the bottom one, retucks the edges around the mattress. Doug punches his pillow twice before dropping into it and reaches his arm around Nonie, clasping her in place in front of him.

It's not sexual, or if it is, he doesn't say and doesn't act like it. Maybe another war thing. But his grip is tight. She laces her fingers with his and spoons against him until their breathing comes matched, measured, and slow.

The calm lasts a while, but, nights like these, Doug never settles all the way into rest, even in sleep. Nonie spends much of the night perched at the edge of the bed while he thrashes or utters low, agitated sounds. By the time the alarm blares, the sun has already brightened the room, and Nonie's pretty sure most of the sleeping she did came in the last hour.

Gently, she clicks off the alarm and slides from between the sheets, plants a soft kiss on Doug's forehead, then quietly gathers her coffee pot and tiptoes back down the flight of stairs to her apartment. Saturday morning cartoon watching with Noreen and Mark is a pajamas-only event once she walks through her sister's door, so she steps back into her after-work jeans and tucks her nightgown into them like a shirt. On her way out again, she collects her purse and shoes and scrunches a pair of slippers into her purse for later.

At Reid's Super Saver, Nonie chooses boxes of Kaboom, Quisp, and Fruity Pebbles and cradles them in her arms—all cereals her sister crinkles her nose at, but the super sugar extravaganza is an essential part of the Saturday tradition. "They can be healthy every other day of the week," Nonie told Ruth early on. Ruth lets her have her way, probably because Nonie's cartoon pajama party lets her and Ted sleep late Saturdays.

Sleeplessness left Nonie's skin clammy. Her hair is a wreck. She swipes at hanging fronds of it and yawns. The box of Fruity Pebbles tumbles to the floor. A Reid's clerk in a red apron and matching ruddy complexion fixes Nonie with a glare.

"You'll have to pick that up, ma'am," she says. Her hairnet sags below her hairline, making her look angrier.

"What else would I do?" Nonie balances the other cereals to stoop down for the Fruity Pebbles.

"How would I know?" the clerk snaps. Her attitude seems to point less toward Nonie's clumsiness and more toward her ratty hair and thin yellow nightgown-shirt and whatever those details insinuate to this woman about where she's been or what she's like.

Everybody thinks they know you.

Anger and a wish for a shower collide inside, but it's time to go. Her mouth feels septic. She'll have to buy a pack of gum so peppermint overtones might kill the odor and keep Ruth from asking questions right away. She doesn't like to tell her sister how she spends her evenings, even when she spends them innocently, like last night. Ruth has a way of misunderstanding, forever turning Nonie into an object of worry, much as she does with Noreen for being like her.

Nonie hefts the cereals and a yellow pack of Carefree gum onto the checkout counter and waits while the clerk there—this time a young man with helpless acne and thick-lensed squarish glasses—clacks prices into the register.

Ruth's house is a newer colonial on a street of mostly older homes not far from Rugby Avenue. Nonie parks on the street and skims down the driveway toward the side of the house where the plastic rock with the slide panel opening waits underneath the rose of Sharon bush, not yet in bloom. She upturns the rock and dumps the secret key into her palm. Back when they'd started this tradition, Noreen was a wisp of a toddler, Mark was five, and Nonie was freshly out of college and prone to losing keys.

Inside, her feet sink into the mustardy shag carpet. The whole house seems to swallow sound, except for the distant patter of cartoons from the den. She trades her shoes for the slippers stuffed in her bag, then detours to the bathroom where she stows her jeans. She wraps her gum in a square of toilet paper, tosses it into the white wicker trash basket, then lathers up with one of Ruth's tiny rose-shaped soaps. She washes her hands and face in cold water, dries off on smoky pink towels, runs rose-scented hands through her tousled hair, and scoops handfuls of water to drink.

Every week she looks forward to the cool cleanness of Ruth's house and Noreen and Mark's excitement at the treats she's brought. She loves how they make space for her between them, like a fellow sardine, on the floor in front of the TV. She loves the Road Runner's beep-beep because of the way it makes Noreen laugh, and she loves the certainty of belonging beside them, of trusting that, in this moment at least, same as with Doug, she knows exactly what to do.

At least until her sister wakes up.

Concluded.

ON THE MORNING of Grammy's funeral, Noreen's mother zips from room to room tidying and dusting things that are already tidy and dustless. Hugh brews coffee in a rented urn and mixes pitchers of lemonade in the kitchen. Noreen scours ancient card tables that had been moved from the old house and stored in the shed here. They were standards from back when her mother and father hosted card parties after she and Mark had gone to bed. Ruth asks her to cloak them in white tablecloths and line them up along the front windows in the living room as a serving area. George stays out of the way, grading last exams in their bedroom.

A Foods of All Nations delivery truck arrives with plastic-lidded trays, and Noreen helps her mother spread them across the tables. All Ruth wanted were Grammy's simple Southern favorites—ham biscuits, potato salad, green salad, pasta salad, coconut cake—which she could've ordered anywhere or made herself, but she trusted Foods of All Nations to upscale it and prettify it enough to fend off Brynne's hypercritical judgment. Another van delivers flowers, and they arrange them as bookends for the food and around the room, then leave for the short service at Dunlop House, Grammy's assisted living center.

She had moved into a condo with Dunlop's lowest level of care about five years earlier, then notched up a tier after her first stroke. If she had pulled through her second one, she would have returned to a new room in the wing that offered the complex's highest level of care, a looming brick living mausoleum of a place Noreen is secretly grateful she'll never need to visit.

After the service, she and Ruth hurry out of the Dunlop House chapel to arrive home ahead of the small crowd they expect. Bouquets of gladiolas and lilies now perfume the house with sweet reminders of death, the faint scent of Ruth's Shalimar almost undetectable beneath it. People arrive one by one and in small clusters—family, Ruth's neighbors and friends, a dozen or so primped and powdered older women from Dunlop House.

The leisurely, personal visits Noreen had imagined having with her father and brother, one at a time in her mother's living room, prove to be ludicrously out of reach amid the reality of the event. People coming and going. The incessant patter of polite condolences. She and Brynne and her mother in a state of constant vigilance over refreshments.

Her father and brother share the wide, squat ottoman in the middle of the room, balancing plates of food in their laps. Noreen stands in front of them, hands clasped at her chest, eyes still scanning for incipient messes. True to form, dark rings underline her brother's eyes, plus tufty bedheadedness left over from his redeye the night before. Still, he could offer to help rather than lounge groggily, picking at his plate of food like any other guest.

Useless to blame him for being himself though, so she sneaks a carrot stick from his plate and tousles his messy hair.

Their father has a better excuse for ducking responsibility, having ducked out of the family altogether more than a decade earlier. So much time and love lost between them over the years, there's nothing leisurely or personal about their time together now, and his presence next to her brother relegates conversation with both of them to small talk.

With Mark, she talks spouses. "How's Betty?"

"Good. Busy. George?"

"He's around here somewhere. Blending with the floor lamp over there. See him? He's on baby monitor duty."

"We spoke before Evie's nap. She looks just like you."

With her dad, she's more comfortable asking after his sailboat than his children, a boy and a girl, closer to Evie's generation than her own. Luckily Ted loves his boat, and he swallows a quick mouthful of food to tell her about its latest round of embellishments, plans for Nantucket in the summer, earnest invitations for her to bring Evie and George along for a visit and, as he puts it, "a spin on the water."

She can tell her mother appreciates the gesture of his presence, but it exhausts Noreen. She escapes to the kitchen where her mother also seems to be hiding. After only thirty minutes, she suspects Ruth is already ready for everyone to leave. She busies herself organizing trays of extra food, checking supplies of paper napkins and beverages, chores Brynne commandeered the instant she breezed into the house, rendering her actions redundant now.

Noreen's hand on her mother's arm startles her. A little lemonade from the pitcher she's refilling splashes onto the counter.

"Sorry, Mom." Noreen reaches for the cloth hung from the kitchen faucet and sponges the spill. "I just wanted to see how you were." Finished with the rag, she pours a lemonade for her mother and herself.

"Where was she the rest of the time?" her mother grumbles, glancing through the doorway at Brynne in the room beyond, comforting one of Grammy's friends near the fireplace with such magisterial posture that, if you didn't know better, you might assume the house belonged to her. "It might be simple, but I planned it all. Bought plates and cups in funeral-appropriate colors. Ordered the food." Ruth tilts her face into her hands to fend off a rush of tears. Blinks them away with a shake of her head.

"You did good, Mom."

"It's not that. I don't really care about this one thing, the reception. It's everything. I answered the middle-of-the-night calls from Dunlop House whenever anything went wrong, rushed to the ER when she had her strokes. I moved her out of her house in the first place. I'd talk to Brynne when things happened, but I did everything. And she waltzes in here and takes charge?"

"That's just her way, isn't it? This is what she's good at."

Ruth laughs, watching Brynne weave through people and tables to deliver a load of trash to a garbage can she'd hidden discreetly under the flaps of one of the tablecloths. "Everyone has their gifts, I suppose." She sips from her lemonade. "She's the most like our mother. Efficient. Task-oriented. Focused on appearances."

"So, are you doing okay?"

"Tired," her mother says. "Thanks for checking on me. What about you?"

"I was so excited for everyone to see Evie again," Noreen says, gesturing in a vague way toward Ruth and Hugh's upstairs bedroom where Evie lies sleeping, tucked into their enormous bed. "But that seems so silly now, and everyone—"

"Everyone is a handful," Ruth says.

"They are that," Noreen agrees. She drains her glass of lemonade and sets it on the counter in a stack of dirties. "I haven't seen you take a bite of anything. You need something." A memory of Nonie's funeral reception inevitably flashes to mind, the tiny uneaten foods arranged on a plate in Grammy's lap. The bandage across Grampy's forehead. Her childhood self adrift in a sea of wounded adults, alone in a way she'd never been before.

Her mother asks how George's job is, how the improvements on their house are coming along.

"Things are mostly in place, but you know how old houses are," Noreen says.

"Always waiting for the next thing to break."

Clearly her mother is talking about the house, but an old reflex makes Noreen recoil. Her mother always seems to be on the lookout for when Noreen herself will break. Her clipped inquiries about George just one of many ways she probes Noreen's life for weaknesses. She isn't sure her mother is aware that she treats Noreen's marriage like an hourglass she's continually measuring, but occasional comments strike Noreen as part of an invisible countdown. Last crystals drizzling away.

A recent windstorm ripped the door off their shed, so Noreen answers her mother's literal question, ignores potential subtext, retracing how she tracked the door down, marooned on the creek bank, then dragged it back up the hill to screw back into place. Something broken but fixable.

"You work so hard out there," her mother says, her facial expression awash with outsized, if sincere, concern.

Another recoil, and again Noreen restrains herself from correction, so *We both work hard* remains unspoken.

In the other room, Uncle Emmett chats with some Dunlop House women and munches from a hearty plateful of snacks, checks his watch every few minutes. Henry and Luke were too busy, apparently, to come to their grandmother's funeral, which strikes Noreen as typical and absurd at the same time. Henry, with his brand-new wife and some kind of computer job, spends most weekends coaching track at his old middle school. Luke's excuse is a banking conference in Delaware. George stands at the edge of the crowd as if the room is a train station and he's standing among strangers, waiting to go somewhere else. Not only because she's deputized him to keep an ear out for Evie, but because this stilted manner is what George brings to family gatherings. He's only slightly less formal with his own father and then only at his father's initiative. Less fixable fissures.

Her mother scrubs a serving spoon, rinses it, then towels it dry and claps it onto the counter with a loud clank. She touches her hand to her mouth in surprise at her own clatter. "I guess I'm angry," she says. "A little bit angry."

"Well, you should be. That was a lot for you to shoulder alone, and it's not like Brynne couldn't have—"

"Angry at Nonie." Ruth casts a look down into the sink and shakes her head. "She should be here for this, you know? Her own mother's funeral." She turns around and leans against the counter, facing Noreen. "She'd make a mess of things. Forget whatever it was she was supposed to pick up, come in late. But it feels wrong without her."

Noreen scoots nearer and leans beside her. "Do you know what Nonie would do if she were here right now?" she asks, then whispers into her mother's ear, "She'd blow this popsicle stand for a cold beer somewhere."

Ruth uses the corner of a silver napkin to dab her eyes. "She would," she says with a short laugh, then scans the kitchen, the layers of mess, Evie's abandoned blue rabbit waiting on the counter for her to wake up. The sounds of people from the other room wash over them like waves.

Noreen takes her mother's hand and pulls her gently toward the mudroom door. "If we leave through here, only the washer and dryer will see us go."

Ruth tugs her hand away. "We couldn't do that." She shakes her head, makes half-hearted gestures toward the objects around her again, the obvious obligations they entail.

"Your mother isn't here to mind, and no one needs our help eating biscuits and mumbling useless phrases. George is on Evie duty, and Brynne can make excuses and see everyone out, if it comes to that."

"Then we should tell her, at least. We can't just go."

"She'll figure it out." Noreen pulls again, and Ruth doesn't resist. They pick up their coats by the mudroom door. "Brynne will gloat about this for years, being the Person Who Took Care of Everything. We'll be doing her a favor."

"What will Hugh say?" Ruth says. "He'll think I've gone crazy. And your father and brother? George?"

"They can take care of themselves for a little while," Noreen says, though the idea of George gives her a twinge of second thoughts.

The downtown pedestrian mall is several blocks away. Their black pumps snag in sidewalk cracks and slide across slicks of fallen crabapple blossoms. Noreen leads them into Miller's, where Dave Matthews tended bar before hitting the big time not so long ago. It's cave-dark inside, and they're overdressed in their gray and black silk dresses. Most of the other early afternoon drinkers are decked out in T-shirts and tattoos. A gold ring flashes at the bartender's eyebrow, catching the dim light over the bar. Noreen and Ruth take seats at the counter, and Noreen orders a beer.

"I think Nonie would've gone for bourbon," Ruth says and orders one on the rocks. "If you're sneaking out of your mother's funeral reception, you have to make it worthwhile. That's what she would've said."

"Cheers to that."

Despite all the food at the reception and her own prodding to get her mother to eat something, Noreen realizes the only thing she's eaten for hours is that one carrot stick she swiped from her brother's plate. She palms a handful of peanuts and pretzels from a dish at the bar and pops a nut into her mouth. Her mother surveys the room.

"Not quite as gloomy as my living room," she says. "But not exactly a laugh riot either. I guess afternoon drinking tends toward the morose."

Noreen laughs. Her mother's right about the atmosphere at the bar, but something between them changes in this place, lightens. "Are there any funny stories about Grammy? I feel like you tell funny stories in a bar at a time like this."

"Your grandmother was not a funny woman," Ruth says, which makes Noreen laugh anyway. The drinks arrive, and Ruth takes a slow sip. "I remember talking to her not long after Nonie died. I said, 'She must have felt so alone, to do something like that.'" Ruth's eyes fix on something along the wall behind the bar. "For my mother, though, everything was either one way or the other. 'Your sister,' she told me, 'just wanted to hurt me the worst possible way.'"

"You know what she said to me at the funeral?" Noreen says over the rim of her beer. She takes a sip, swallows. "'Don't you turn out the same, little Miss Head in the Clouds.'"

Ruth's mouth drops open as if she'd been slapped. "I wish you'd told me. That was a crappy thing to say."

"Grammy said some crappy things." Noreen twiddles the corner of the napkin her beer rests on. "Made her worry sound like a weapon."

"She did, didn't she?" Ruth meets her eyes, and for one moment they seem to share Nonie as an equal loss.

Ruth lifts her glass for another sip but sets it down instead, shakes her head. "The way our mother saw it, Nonie lived and died spiteful, but Nonie didn't have a spiteful bone in her body. She was miserable is all."

"Except when she was delightful," Noreen says.

"Yes, that's exactly it," Ruth says. "And when she was delightful, there was no one better on earth."

Her mother's feet dangle from the barstool, reminding Noreen of the child she must once have been and of how strong she must have had to be, trying to pick up her mother's slack with Nonie, which she must have done. An image rushes back to her of Ruth kneeling at her feet the morning after Nonie died, breaking the news. That message carved away so much of Noreen's child-heart that, until this moment, she hadn't fully grasped that her mother was speaking of her own loss, too. She's ashamed it took her so long to recognize this.

"We could tell funny Nonie stories," Ruth says. She stirs the bourbon with an index finger, and the ice clacks against the sides of the glass. "There are plenty of those."

"Talk about Nonie then."

So they do. The baby powder incident, when Nonie was three. How she used the drawers of her dresser as steps to climb to the top. How she dumped an entire container of baby powder on her head. How Grammy screeched when she opened the door to check on her, seeing only a heap of white powder with two blinking eyes. How Nonie "rescued" a bird she found while out climbing trees. How she fashioned a pallet for it from pine needles and an old shoebox from the basement. How she carried the bird carefully into the house, nestled it onto the mahogany dinner table. How she tended its wounds until Grammy came in, screeching yet again. "That's not what dining room tables are for!" Nonie blinked back at her, just like with the baby powder. "There's no telling what that girl is thinking!" Grammy had said, not just then but other times, so many other times.

"Mother was always forgetting that Nonie was a child," Ruth says. "Brynne and I were much older then, and we did predictable things. Brynne ran track. I played tennis. We won trophies, made honor roll. Neither of us colored outside any kind of lines. By the time Nonie came along, it's like Mother forgot what children were like, and she'd had no experience with a child who went her own way like Nonie did. A girl who didn't want to join Girl Scouts or glee clubs or give herself over to anything she hadn't created for herself."

"A girl like me."

Her mother studies her for a moment, then smiles in a way that makes her face look sadder. "Yes, like you, and my mother didn't understand such a child. Blamed her for needing what she needed. I never forgave her for that."

The bartender offers more with a gesture of his head. Ruth covers her glass. "It's funny," she says. "Nonie never quite left that world in a way, never finished being a child."

Noreen sips the last of her beer while her mother's ice cubes puddle into the last of her bourbon. The thrum of nearby conversation spikes now and then with a shout or a table slap, and the sunlight outside hardly penetrates the dingy plate-glass window.

Ruth moves as if to descend from the bar, then stops herself, faces Noreen with a tenuous expression. "Noreen, are you happy?"

The closeness between them loosens, disintegrates. "As happy as anyone, I guess."

"How happy do you guess other people are?" Ruth asks. "Because aside from right now, I'm happy most of the time."

Noreen grabs the bill from the counter and thumbs some cash on top of it. It really is impossible for her mother to talk with her about Nonie without translating their mutual affection into some kind of secret message of doom.

"I'm sorry, Noreen. My words must have been clumsy. I just want you to be happy," she says. "You deserve to be happy."

Noreen's facial muscles tighten, so it's hard to smile, but she forces herself. "Thanks," she says because she knows her mother doesn't mean to drag out old worries and wrap her in them like a dirty blanket. She can't seem to keep those old worries at bay, no matter how hard she tries.

Sliding down from her stool, Ruth stumbles a little and laughs at herself. Noreen holds the door open for her. Most of their visit had been perfect. She stands in the doorway for an extra beat, pulls in a breath of fresh spring air, and lets it out slowly. Then she links arms with her mother, and they walk that way all the way back to the house on Lexington Avenue.

It looks as busy as when they left. Chains of parked cars line both sides of the street. "Thank you," Ruth says to Noreen, giving her hand a final pat before they step back through the mudroom door. "I needed that."

Inside, only a few people have left. A lot of food is gone. Brynne gathers abandoned cups and plates from around the living room and dining room. She's the only one to look up when Ruth and Noreen walk back in. Her expression registers somewhere between annoyance and confusion. No one else seems to have missed them.

*Two Months
After.*

THE TEACHER CONFERENCE is set for a Wednesday afternoon. The other children drain out of the classroom and leave
Noreen alone. While they wait for her mother, Miss Simpkins
marks in her grade book at her desk, and of course Noreen reads
a book. That's what the trouble's about. Ever since she could,
she's read lots of books. Her mother brings home an armload
each week from her job at the central library. She'll read encyclo-
pedia entries or books about butterflies. Even dictionaries when
nothing else is available. So why is anybody surprised to find out
that in third grade she spends most of her day reading?

Whenever she looks up from her book this afternoon, she
notices how the sunlight brightens dust specks in the air. How
one strand of Miss Simpkins' hair escapes its ponytail and dangles
in her eye. How she curls it behind her ear, over and over.

Noreen's mother arrives straight from her half day of work,
wearing her gray skirt and a cowl neck sweater the color of an
Easter egg. Miss Simpkins closes her grade book and greets her
from her desk, then escorts both of them to the craft table at the
back of the room.

Her mother's usual splash of Shalimar mixes with the odor of
crayons, the burnt-dust heat of the classroom, and soap flakes
from the dispenser at the craft sink behind the little table. Eight
small metal chairs circle it, and stacks of orange and black construction paper spread across its top along with bottles of paste,
mounds of pencils and scissors, and stencils of jagged grins and

different-shaped eyes and noses.

Noreen plops into one of the chairs, and Miss Simpkins settles easily onto another. Her mother lowers herself less smoothly. Noreen feels embarrassed for her, caught not knowing how to do such a simple thing. She studies Miss Simpkins' reactions as her mother struggles to keep her legs from banging the tabletop and her purse from spilling from her lap to the floor. She's felt protective of her mother ever since that day in the grocery store, though, true to her promise, her mother hasn't done anything like it in the weeks since.

"That time of year again," Miss Simpkins says, indicating the lineup of paper jack-o'-lantern supplies.

"Oh, yes," Ruth answers. "Busy days." She rubs her hands together. It is cold outside, but so hot in this room she couldn't need to warm herself. Her mother must be nervous, like she is. Noreen prefers to be on the good side of teachers, and parents must prefer that, too. Miss Simpkins awards golden eggs to one boy and one girl each week in class based on their behavior the week before. Egg winners get to wash down the chalkboard at the end of the day or take Herman the class hermit crab home for the weekend. Noreen never gets the golden egg. After a meeting like this, she's afraid she never will.

Miss Simpkins swivels in her seat to face Ruth. "Mrs. Jamison, let's talk about our concerns for your daughter."

"You mean the reading?" her mother says. She flits a look between the teacher and Noreen. "I don't know that I'd use the word 'concern,' exactly. I've always considered Noreen's reading a gift of some kind. Don't you?"

"Certainly she reads well above grade level," Miss Simpkins says. "If that's what you mean." Miss Simpkins' manner minces any possible goodness out of the words.

"Sure, that, but also her passion for it. I'm a librarian, as you might know, and I'm always pleased when young people take such a keen interest in books." She smiles at Noreen, showing her she's on her side, but she looks uncomfortable and not quite herself in the too-small chair.

"Except when that interest overshadows everything else."

"Everything? Is it that bad?" Ruth adjusts her purse in her lap again.

"I'm afraid so, Mrs. Jamison."

Noreen misses Mrs. Ebersole from last year's class who only worried that she was shy. Until Claudia moved in and changed everything. Claudia has a different teacher this year, and no one in Noreen's new class bothered spending time with her the first several weeks while her cast kept her on the bench during recess. The cast came off only a couple of weeks ago, and Noreen isn't finished getting back to normal yet. Outside, her classmates still ignore her, partly because she has to be so careful of her healing arm, but mostly because friend groups are set with no room to spare for her. They ignore her inside, too, because her arm isn't strong enough for schoolwork yet, so a helper teacher keeps her separate at their own little table, writing things down for her and helping her cut things out for crafts. What else could she do all this time but read?

Miss Simpkins seems to be waiting for her to add something about these *concerns*, but Noreen isn't concerned, so she doesn't know what to say and settles on the obvious. "I like books."

"Reading the way Noreen does," Miss Simpkins says, "builds a wall between her and the other children. How can they get to know her if she's always too busy for them? How can they ask her to play kickball or come to a birthday party?"

"I don't *like* kickball," Noreen says.

"Mind you, she shouldn't really be back to sports yet," Ruth says. "But I did notice that, about the birthday parties." Her mother makes a sad face toward Noreen. "When I was your age, I was invited to birthday parties all the time. I might not even know the child very well, but Grammy insisted I go anytime I was invited. It's good practice. Socializing. Using your manners." She nods with each example. "Imagine if I didn't know how to talk to people? Even though my job involves a lot of shushing, I still have to know how to talk." Ruth laughs, egging Noreen on to join her, but she doesn't. It turns out all this time she's really been on Miss Simpkins' side.

"I know how to talk to people. I'm talking to people right now," Noreen says.

Miss Simpkins says that sometimes big changes at home show up in funny ways in the classroom and asks if there have been any big changes in the family recently.

"Such a good question," Ruth answers, hemming, while Noreen digs her fingernails into her palm. "Actually, we did have a death in the family." She doesn't mention that it was her sister or how it happened, but she does mention that Nonie and Noreen were close.

Miss Simpkins leans across the table. Her eyes look so watery she might start crying at any moment. She takes hold of Noreen's fingers. "Oh, my little dear," she says. "I'm so very sorry to hear about that."

Miss Simpkins' hands are ice cold, and Noreen wiggles her fingers free as soon as she can. She's sick of people apologizing. No matter how sorry they are, Nonie is still dead. None of the rest matters. So what if other kids don't play with her? What good are they, always wanting to do things she doesn't want to do? Maybe some of those things are things she used to like doing with Nonie, like playing on the playground or hunting for caterpillars, but she never liked doing them with anyone else anyway. And so what if all she wants to do is read? When she's reading, she doesn't think about things she might have said to keep Nonie from doing what she did or about the dull ache in her stomach that won't go away or how the whole world seems smaller and stupider without Nonie in it.

"I don't want you to think of this meeting as a punishment," Miss Simpkins says. "Think of it as an opportunity to get to know your classmates better instead. To make friends to play with."

It was the same last year, everybody wanting her to be different from how she is. What got everyone off her back was spending time with Claudia. Which she still does and hopes she can get some credit for it. "I don't need to play all the time. I have a best friend. I play with her."

This is news to Miss Simpkins. "I'm so glad to hear that, Noreen."

"She was in my class last year, but she has Mrs. Rowan this year."

"Isn't that nice. And maybe we can help you make a few new friends this year. Wouldn't that be nice, too?"

Noreen shrugs.

"Let's try this. From now on we'll make books off limits, except during language arts. No reading at recess. No reading when you finish your lessons. No reading when you're in the lunchroom."

Each new prohibition hits like a jab, and Noreen grimaces.

"She reads in the lunchroom, too?" Ruth says. "Isn't it loud in there?"

"Quite loud."

"She does love to read."

"Indeed." Miss Simpkins straightens the stacks of construction paper and evens the edges of the piles of stencils.

Maybe her mother couldn't change Miss Simpkins' mind if she tried, but she doesn't try. Noreen feels as if heavy bags of sand press down on her shoulders. School days drag long enough already.

"After a week or so without hiding behind any books," Miss Simpkins says, "I bet Noreen will have a whole classroom of new friends."

Miss Simpkins and her mother seem convinced that Noreen would be happier if children lined up to play with her on the playground or knocked on her door at home with their pogo sticks and roller skates. Something must be wrong with her that she doesn't care about any of that. She likes reading for hours straight and studying butterfly wings in her backyard or tossing stones into the pond and watching the splashes sparkle in the sun.

The grownups seem to notice her disappointment. Her mother starts to reach toward her, then falters and lets her hand resettle in her lap. Miss Simpkins taps a pearly pink painted fingernail against her lip and announces a new plan. "Talk of your friend gave me another idea, Noreen. Something more we can do."

She doesn't trust Miss Simpkins' enthusiasm, but her mother seems to. Her forehead unpleats, and she half-smiles toward the teacher.

"I can't make any promises," Miss Simpkins says. "It would have to be all right with her family, too, but I could try switching your friend into our classroom. If the other kids see her playing with you, Noreen, surely they'll follow her example. And like I said, I don't want this meeting to feel like a punishment. I want you to be happier in the classroom."

Why do people always think they know what makes you happy better than you do? Walking out to their car, Noreen holds her mother's hand and kicks pebbles along the way. The squat brick school building looks lonesome with all the buses gone and no one else in sight. A breeze whips brown and orange leaves around the nearly empty parking lot. With her free hand, Noreen gathers her coat more tightly.

Helen Reddy sings out of the 8-track once her mother starts the car. Ruth cuts the volume and cranks the heat. The scent of Shalimar rises up around them again.

"I thought reading was a good thing," Noreen says.

"Of course it is," her mother says. She pats Noreen's knee. As if that could help.

"I don't want to play with the other kids. They're boring."

"Every kid is boring?" Ruth says, playful but earnest. She buckles her seat belt, waits for Noreen to do the same. "How could you know if you haven't tried playing with any of them?" She frames her arm on the seat behind Noreen, turns to look behind them, and eases the car out of its space. "At least Claudia's not boring, right? If Miss Simpkins can bring her into your class?"

Over the summer, when Noreen found out she and Claudia were assigned different teachers this year, she'd been relieved. Once last year Claudia called her over to the coat closet in a sweet voice but then pulled her hair where the teacher couldn't see. Twice she refused to play on the same kickball team. Even now whenever Noreen gets upset with her, Claudia clucks and tells her she can't take a joke. She doesn't know how to say any of this to her mother, or she's afraid if she does, it will be one of those times her mother hears her say one thing, then understands it as something else entirely, like there's a secret code about ways to be in the world that Noreen hasn't deciphered.

"I know somebody else who didn't think she needed so many friends at school," Ruth says in her storybook voice.

Noreen isn't in the mood but doesn't want her mother to badger her about her attitude, so she asks, "Who?"

"Aunt Nonie." They pull into traffic. "I was in high school by the time she started kindergarten, and it was my job to meet her at the bus and walk her home each day. Even when she was little, she had all those frizzy, beautiful curls like yours, and somehow she could never keep them tidy."

Despite herself, Noreen is curious. She loves any story about Nonie. Her mother must have figured this out. Whenever she wants Noreen to do something, out comes a Nonie story to explain why she should. It doesn't seem fair to use Nonie that way, as a trick or warning, but still, picturing Nonie as a tiny kid with her hair floating around her head like bubbles in a bathtub makes her feel good.

"And you know how her attention flew all over the place, just like her hair."

Noreen laughs. She remembers that about Nonie. The way she skidded from one idea to the next.

"She always sat way in the back of the school bus. It took forever for everybody ahead of her to file out. The whole time, the other kids would call her Bride of Frankenstein or ask if she'd stuck her fingers in a socket that day. I was sure Nonie would pop out of the bus angry or sad or shouting something back, but she never did. She'd just hurry over to me with a new drawing she'd done on the ride home or a sequin she found on the bus floor, and she'd smile. A big smile, wide and peaceful, like this." She demonstrates for Noreen, exaggerating enough to coax another quick laugh out of her. "She said it didn't bother her at all."

The afternoon sun casts everything in soft golden light. Ahead of them a pickup truck puts on its turn signal, slows, stops. They stop behind it.

"Different things bother different people," Noreen says. Like how her reading bothers everyone but her.

"Kids calling names though. Don't you think that would bother you?" her mother says.

"Maybe?"

"Of course it would." They pull past the pickup. Almost home now. "It feels better to have people around you who like you. I think it's going to work out for you in Miss Simpkins' class, with or without Claudia. Even if it feels different for a little while first." She turns to smile at Noreen. All the smiles today, during the meeting and now, so full of pity. "Pretty soon those birthday party invitations will start rolling in."

❦

Long enough after the conference for Noreen to forget about the possibility, she arrives at her classroom to find Claudia unpacking into a desk in the back corner. Miss Simpkins grins at her as if she expects a drastic display of joy, so Noreen smiles back,

162

but her stomach feels squishy.

Last school year when Claudia was mean to her, Noreen's mother said she was probably still adjusting to being new, so Noreen gave her extra chances and tried to be nice about it. Claudia's usually better when they're playing at one of their houses, just the two of them, which they do once every week, taking turns riding home on each other's buses. Today is her turn to have Claudia over. She must be finished adjusting by now, so maybe having her in the same class will help with whatever it is Miss Simpkins wants to fix about Noreen. If she's broken, of course she wants to be fixed.

At reading circle time, Noreen's favorite part of the day, Miss Simpkins calls the class to the UVA orange-and-blue braided rug at the back of the room, catty-corner to the craft table where stacks of brown, yellow, orange, and red construction paper wait in tidy pre-hand-turkey arrays. Miss Simpkins sits in a chair in front of the carpet holding a new book in her hand while the class drops into crisscross position at her feet.

The first book she read out loud to them this year was *Cricket in Times Square*, and they finished *Brighty of the Grand Canyon* at the end of last week. Today they'll begin *Little House in the Big Woods*. Miss Simpkins starts off with a few words about Laura Ingalls Wilder and pioneer days, but she doesn't tell them anything they don't know from the TV show.

After Miss Simpkins reads for a few minutes—looking up now and then to hush Hilary Butler or to stop Andy Perwitz from pulling Annabeth's hair—she replaces the bookmark and lowers the book into her lap. "I'd like to start something new with our reading circle and ask students to help read a few pages aloud with me each day."

Before this, Miss Simpkins only asked them to read out loud from their language arts book. Its pages are mostly white space with pictures that use too much purple and blue. The very few words on each page are all short and easy. Noreen likes reading those stories out loud more than she likes reading them to herself, but either way they're boring. From the little Miss Simpkins has read so far, Noreen can tell the *Little House* book will be as interesting to read in your head as it will be to read out loud. She hadn't been sure from the TV show. She'll have to ask her mother to bring the *Little House* books home from the library for her.

"Who would like to read for us first?" Miss Simpkins asks.

Noreen shoots her arm up in the air. Beside her, Claudia scowls. "It's babyish to read out loud," she says so only Noreen can hear. Noreen loves to read out loud, but she doesn't want to be babyish, so she lets her hand drop back into her lap. Miss Simpkins never picks her anyway.

The other kids don't seem worried about seeming babyish. Hands poke up all around them. Eventually Miss Simpkins points right in their direction. Secretly relieved, Noreen lays a hand across her chest and mouths, "Me?"

But Miss Simpkins shakes her head. "Claudia, could you please read for us?"

Claudia, who wasn't even raising her hand.

Grumbling, Claudia tiptoes her way through all the children between her and the teacher. Without looking at Miss Simpkins, she takes the book. Miss Simpkins points to a spot on the page to show her where to begin. Her words come out choppily. Miss Simpkins helps her with the longer ones. Claudia seethes the whole time, like she's spitting each word from her mouth.

Recess comes right after reading circle, and Noreen and Claudia pull on their coats and file to the playground together. Mostly bare trees edge the field beyond the playground, with the purple hills of the Blue Ridge in the distance. They both choose jump ropes from the equipment box and start jumping, competing for who can go longest without stepping on the rope. Last year, Claudia always won.

"Why don't you like that book?" Noreen asks her,

concentrating on her feet. She hasn't gotten any practice for ages because of her cast.

"What do you mean? I like it fine." Claudia stops jumping. On purpose, so it doesn't count that Noreen hasn't stepped on her rope yet.

"Why did you read it that way then? It sounded like you hated it."

Claudia glares at Noreen, then grabs both handles of her jump rope in one hand and thrashes them to the ground. "I'm going to the swings." When she moves to join her, Claudia adds, "With-out *you.*"

Stunned, Noreen holds the handles of her stilled jump rope, trying to keep tears from slipping from her eyes.

"Why would you say that to her?" She hadn't seen Miss Simp-kins standing nearby, so her voice and the sharpness of it startle Noreen.

"What did I say?" She only remembers what Claudia had said, but maybe Miss Simpkins hadn't heard that part.

"Couldn't you tell that was hard for her?" Miss Simpkins' face is all stern lines, her arms folded at her chest.

"What was hard?"

"Gracious, child," Miss Simpkins says. "You have to realize, it's a lot more unusual for a little girl to read as well as you can than it is for a little girl to have trouble like Claudia. You embar-rassed her."

The word *unusual* sticks in Noreen's mind. It has lovely sounds, soft and rolling, but she knows perfectly well what it means. She doesn't want to be unusual any more than she wants to embarrass her friend. She wants to ask Miss Simpkins some-thing—about being unusual or about how to un-embarrass Claudia—but before she can put words to her question, Miss Simpkins has raced to the other end of the playground to fuss at some children who are straying farther from the edge of the schoolyard than they're supposed to.

What if, here on Claudia's first day of class, Noreen ruins their friendship for good? How long would it take for Miss Simpkins to drum up a new plan to fix her?

At the end of recess, Noreen rushes to line up next to Claudia. "I'm sorry," she says, but Claudia pretends not to hear and steps into the classroom ahead of her without looking around again.

Last thing before Noreen crosses the threshold, a swirl of motion in the courtyard between their classroom and the school library catches her eye. She hesitates in the doorway, double-checking. She could have sworn she saw Nonie's hair flowing behind her, as if she were disappearing around the corner toward the library entrance.

Nonie loved when Noreen read to her and would listen to as many books as Noreen could gather into her arms. To her aunt, she was fine exactly the way she was.

Of course she isn't here at the school. Not really. Nonie isn't anywhere anymore, but Noreen cranes around as far as she can, hoping at least to figure out what she saw, until Miss Simpkins shouts her name from inside.

⁂

Later, Claudia follows her onto her bus as planned. She plops into the seat beside Noreen and balances her book bag on her knees before turning toward her and saying, "If I stop being your friend, you won't have any friends at all."

Miss Simpkins must have explained why she moved her into class with Noreen. She must have told Claudia how unusual she is. The thought makes Noreen's face burn.

"It wasn't my idea," she says.

"What wasn't?"

"Moving you into class with me. It was Miss Simpkins' idea."

"You don't want me there?" Claudia says.

How is it possible for her to go from being mean to hurt so fast? "I just thought you didn't want to be there is all," Noreen says.

Claudia looks into her lap and fidgets with her fingers. "I didn't really know anybody in my other class," she says. "I think it was my idea."

Noreen feels funny for both of them. She doesn't know what to say, so she cups her hands over her ears like she does in the cafeteria sometimes, hinging one hand open a little at a time to dull the rumble of chatter around her so it sounds the same as when you put a seashell on your ear. She shows Claudia how to do it. At her first listen, Claudia's surprise softens the last tension between them. They make seashell sounds together until Jean Tipton, several rows ahead of them, distracts Claudia.

Jean Tipton has greasy hair, or at least that's what Claudia says, and her mother bags groceries at the Kroger. "She bagged our groceries last week," Claudia tells Noreen, a sound of disgust in her voice. The kind of sound that means Noreen's supposed to understand what's wrong with someone's mother bagging groceries, so she can't admit she doesn't know. Instead she wonders if Jean Tipton's mother was the woman who bent over her own mother's skinned knees and bandaged her up like a hurt child a couple months ago. She cringes thinking about someone she almost knows seeing her mother that way.

Claudia rolls bits of paper and gets them soggy in her mouth, then spits them through a leftover cafeteria straw she pulled from her book bag. She aims for Jean Tipton's head. When she tears the next paper scrap, she hands it to Noreen to roll into a ball for her. Each time Jean turns around to see who's shooting spitballs at her, Claudia smiles and waves. When Jean gathers her books to get off the bus, she looks like she's crying.

At the house, Noreen's mother sets out a snack of sliced cheese and apples. They eat quickly, then dash outside to play in the yard. They still have to take it a little slow because of Noreen's arm, but they run short races, kick balls, see who can throw pebbles farthest across the pond even though Noreen's throwing arm is still pretty weak. Claudia never wants to read books, which is okay, but sometimes Noreen wants to pick what they do even if it isn't reading.

Today Claudia says, "Let's wade in the pond."

"It's too cold," Noreen says. It's warm for November, but that's not the same as being warm enough for wading.

Noreen follows Claudia down to the water's edge. Along the mostly wooded banks, only the pines and cedars are still green. Most other trees are leafless except for ones with shriveled brown leaves clinging in place or a few with their last tired-looking red and yellow leaves speckling otherwise bare branches.

"Right here," Claudia says. "You first."

"I said it's too cold."

"Come on, Noreen. I'll get in after you. It's like initiation. For a secret club."

Mark and his best friend, Donny, scratched nicks in their thumbs over the summer and pressed them together. That has to hurt a little to count. If this is like being blood brothers, it's probably okay.

She looks back and forth between the dark water and her friend. Claudia smiles at her and nods, urging her on. Finally, Noreen sits down on the bank and works at her shoelaces. When her coat and shoes and socks are in a pile beside her and she's barefoot on the ground—even the dirt feels icy on the bottoms of her feet—Claudia says, "That's not all."

"What?"

"Pants, too."

"No way!" Noreen says. She sneaks a glance up to the house. If anyone happens to look out the sunroom window, they would see them here, but no one seems to be looking.

"I'll call my mom and go home then." Claudia pivots toward the house.

Noreen swallows hard. It always feels like she's one step away from losing Claudia as a friend because things happen between them like what happened on the playground today and on the bus and right now. She doesn't want to go back to having no friends or find out what Miss Simpkins might do next to try to make her more like everybody else. Everything would be so much easier if she were allowed to be herself.

"Don't go." Noreen's hands shake as she takes hold of her waistband. "I'll do it."

Claudia faces her again. "Okay then," she says. "Go ahead."

Her hands shake so much it's hard to pull down her pants.

"Panties, too."

She steadies her hands and looks straight ahead. Standing by the pond in the cool air with her bare feet sucking cold from the ground, chill bumps rise up all over her body. She doesn't know what to do next.

Claudia has a funny look on her face, something between happy and angry. Then she swivels her head around. "Oh, crap!" she says. "It's Mark! Mark and Donny are coming! Get in the water!"

Noreen splashes in and plunges into a crouch to shield herself in the shallow water. It's so cold it feels sharp and prickles against her skin. She squeals with the shock of it. Icy mud suctions her feet in place. When she looks back at the shore, Claudia is doubled over laughing.

"They're not really here," she gasps, hardly able to speak. "I'm sorry. It's just so funny."

It's not funny to Noreen. She squelches back out of the water as fast as she can, her whole body shaking and streaming with water, burned red from the cold. Claudia is sitting on Noreen's pants and underwear, and she won't budge. She rocks back and forth on top of them, still laughing. Whenever she glances up at Noreen standing in front of her, hiding herself with her hands and waiting to put her clothes back on, she laughs harder.

Finally, Noreen gives up and sits down on the bare ground beside her, hugging her shivering legs and trying not to cry. She wants to say, "Your turn," and make Claudia do the same thing because she said she would. Somehow she knows Claudia won't though, that there's not really a secret club, and, beyond a sense of fairness, she has no interest in making Claudia do what she's just done.

Eventually, Claudia moves off her clothes.

"Oh, there you go," she says. "You don't have to whine about it anymore."

❦

After her bath that night, while Noreen stands combing her wet hair, her mother lifts her pants from the bathroom floor to put them in the laundry basket. "How did you get mud on the inside of your pants?"

"Me and Claudia were sitting down by the pond for a while. Maybe that's how."

"Claudia and I," Ruth corrects. "And that's how you got mud on the *inside* of your pants?"

Noreen shrugs. "It was a secret club thing. You wouldn't understand." She trots away, leaving her mother holding the filthy pants. She can't tell her what really happened or what it's really like to be Claudia's friend. Not when she and Miss Simpkins are so worried about Noreen. Not today, Claudia's first day in her class.

She could've told Nonie. Nonie would've made a mud pie for them to squash with their rain boots or piled paper shreds in a bowl to burn. Something to use up the feelings choking inside her. Her mother would only look sorry for her and make her feel like no matter how hard she tries, it's never hard enough.

Nineteen Years After.

NOREEN, GEORGE, AND Evie leave the house at 7 a.m. so they can drop George at Charlottesville's little airport in plenty of time to make his 9:30 flight for his conference in Chicago. Evie sleeps in the car, then waves at airplanes lifting behind the terminal as if her father could be in every one. Bluish ridges line the horizon beyond the airstrip, and Noreen wonders if they're the opposite slopes of the mountains they see from home.

Balancing Evie on her hip, she stands with one leg out of the car and waves along with her. As each plane buoys into the air, an answering relief buoys inside Noreen. She's still amazed George didn't manage to sabotage this little getaway of hers, though why would he? Why does she think he would? But she remembers feeling cautious when she brought it up, then cringing when her suggestion came out more like a request for permission. "When you're gone, let's let Evie stay with my mom so Lizbeth and I can have a reunion weekend."

"Why should you get vacation while I'm off presenting a paper?" What George loves most about his job is the research, the teaching next, and writing and presenting papers not at all, which helped explain his poor-sport-reflex complaint about her having fun when he wouldn't be, but didn't excuse it. As if Noreen's life at home with Evie is one unstoppable spree of fun and his is the only work that matters. His expression had flickered between jealous and bashful though, with a tint of shame that softened her toward him, offered a hint of hope for what she wanted.

"I haven't seen her in ages, George. I've hardly been any-where."

She stuck to her main point to avoid revealing her secret gnawing regret about delaying her certification and to keep from reiterating old arguments about a second car that waged away in her mind anyway. How at first he'd promised they'd buy a second car when he made tenure when his raise will bring enough money for it, free and clear of oversized bank loans and Grady Putnam's string-loaded gifts. How the closer he gets to tenure though, the more extenuations seem to arise, like when he recently resur-rected the news story about that woman's disappearance off Route 29 three years ago as a reason to rethink getting a second car at all. "She was young and pretty, like you. They said the guy had a type, that he was trawling the roads." When Noreen looked skeptical, George reminded her that the man had never been caught. "It's dangerous to think it couldn't happen to you" is how he'd closed that argument, his eyebrows bunched in reproof at her seeming disregard for her own safety. Only afterward did she think of what she could've said, that she should have a right to choose her own risks, the same way he does, but in the moment, she hadn't been able to articulate what he was taking away from her when he let his worry dictate what she could do.

Occasionally he'll work a morning or afternoon from home so Noreen and Evie can use the car to join a weekday story hour at the local library or playdate at the quirky coffee shop in Harri-sonburg with its indoor climbing structures and trove of kids' toys. The balance of the time, though, it's just Noreen and Evie and the rolling hills, the wide sky, the lonely trees, while George gets the car, his life and work beyond them, plus the hours of solitude his commute provides. So George agreed about Evie staying with her mother and Hugh for the weekend, and withheld his usual arguments about spending time there—that at Hugh's age, more than a dozen years older than Ruth, he might not have enough energy to keep up with Evie; that no matter what grandparents say, no one wants new responsibilities clouding their sunset years; that Evie's a sensitive girl and often sleeps badly away from home, and who will have to deal with the over-tired little girl afterward but Noreen herself because George will be away, and what kind of a break is that?

He offered no resistance this time, maybe because Noreen hasn't had any time on her own in she can't remember how long. So he would go to his conference. Lizbeth would send her husband to visit his parents. Then the two of them would lounge in a beach hotel all weekend. Lizbeth made the reservations and gave Noreen directions. They would meet there.

That was the plan. It feels dishonest the way things worked out, but it wasn't intentional.

When Lizbeth had to cancel at the last minute because of a stomach virus, at first Noreen was devastated. The luxury of un-hurried Lizbeth-time had sounded like a perfect release from her daily routines of taking care of everyone but herself, but the sur-prise prospect of spending hours and hours with only herself to think of made her quickly dismiss any thought of canceling. Can-celing so late they would've had to pay for their room anyway.

What makes it feel dishonest is that she hadn't mentioned to George that Lizbeth wasn't coming. After Lizbeth's call the night before, George asked what had prompted all Noreen's sympa-thetic *oh no*'s, and she pretended they'd been talking about something at Lizbeth's work. If Noreen admitted wanting to spend a weekend alone, he'd only question why and try to talk her out of it. There'd be time to explain later, after she got back, when she was sure the benefits of having had time to herself would manifest themselves in a dozen different ways that would be good for all of them.

At her mother's house, Evie reaches for Ruth right away. Noreen can see how Evie's affection charms her mother. Chil-dren want you in such an unquestioning, absorbing way. Hugh looks happy just to see Ruth happy, and Noreen loves how friendly and easy he is with her. Maybe George will be like that when he's older; his fitfulness will season out of him over time. People say you mellow.

Excitement swells as Noreen pulls away from her mother's curb. She hadn't expected that. For weeks, she's ached for the time with Lizbeth, the breather from fixer-upper maintenance and endless parenting to-do lists, but she expected a pang, maybe even tears, when she released Evie into her mother's hands and said goodbye.

Waving from her Gram's shoulder, Evie calls, "Bye-bye, Momma!" over and over, then slowly disappears in the rearview mirror. Instead of a bite of regret, Noreen feels her neck muscles unclench, her forehead unwrinkle. In some lost hallway of her mind, she remembers feeling the same release from being with George, back when she'd craved safety and stillness.

"I'd keep you in a box if I could," he'd said once, after she'd bought him a bakery cake for his birthday early in their relationship. The cake had come in a white box with a bright blue ribbon. His favorite flavors (marzipan and chocolate), iced in his favorite colors (green and blue). When he'd said that, about keeping her in a box, he'd meant that she was like a present to him the way the cake had been a present—with everything the way he liked. He was saying that she was everything he liked. Not that he wanted to trap her. Store her away. Box her in.

Yet there is such a thing as too much safety, too much stillness. She turns up the radio and drives faster.

After Charlottesville, Route 64 unrolls in miles of tree-lined highway, slowly ironing the foothills into tidewater. A snarl of interstates interrupts at Richmond, then a burst of exits at Williamsburg, and finally, three hours after dropping Evie off, she reaches the cluster of spur routes close to the beach. With one eye on the hand-scrawled directions spread across the steering wheel, the other on the road, Noreen navigates the last miles to the hotel Lizbeth booked for them.

She leaves the car in the half-round drive marked for reception. She's never checked into a hotel on her own before, but she strides toward the front desk as if she's perfectly used to registration desks, to going places by herself. She pretends she's nobody's mother, nobody's wife.

The sand, the froth of ocean breaking and breaking, show through the windows behind the desk. Virginia Beach in the off-season is quiet and uncrowded. She can feel something inside herself expanding to fill the open space.

Through the sliding glass door to the balcony, the beach stretches as far as she can see, smudging into the horizon. There are two queen-sized beds, which she'll have all to herself. Noreen sinks into one of them and lolls backwards. She could lie here all weekend if she wants. Pop the TV on. Order room service. Open the balcony door and let in the hush of the ocean. How long has it been since she's had anything all to herself?

Still, she'd rather have Lizbeth with her. Over a year she's been married, and Noreen has only met her husband, Diego, a couple of times. Rare occasions when she finagled the car from George during the week to meet Lizbeth for lunch in Charlottesville, their halfway point, dropping Evie with her mother. Or rarer occasions when she met Lizbeth all the way in Richmond, leaving George with Evie on a Saturday. Evie's bouts with strep or tummy bugs nixed a few plans, and George always frets about her taking road trips alone with Evie, as if that highway stalker were hot on her heels at all times, their sturdy Volvo a breakdown risk, and a three-hour drive some Odyssean journey. Noreen is sorry to lose a shot at new adventures with her old friend, at reversing some of the seriousness that has crept into her life.

Serious George. The tenure track breathes heavy down his neck. He treats every research project or committee assignment like each one will make or break his career. He loves Evie, but her energy often wears him out. He doesn't exactly complain, but

Noreen senses when nonsense songs and toddler fingers clutching at his pants legs have breached some interior boundary. His eyes squint, his shoulders hunch ever so slightly, as if he's bracing to endure physical injury. The worst thing would be for Evie to notice, so Noreen limits how long she leaves her with her dad and swoops in when he's had too much, regardless of how hard a day she might've had, trundling Evie off to another room, a new distraction, a space where she's allowed to be as noisy and goofy as she needs to be. On her more exhausted or mind-numbed days, Noreen exaggerates her silliness with Evie, a trick to stave off her own frustration. So far, that's worked for them.

This weekend won't be like that. She wants to wind herself backwards, to before other people needed so much from her. No one to satisfy but herself.

A noise in the hallway—a child's voice, needing something—jerks her back to sitting. But it can't be Evie. She's not here. Noreen laughs at herself for forgetting for that blink of time. She can count on the fingers of one hand the number of nights she's been without Evie since she was born, the number of nights she's been without George, for that matter, since they got together. But she leans toward the phone and dials out on her phone card. She tells her mother she made it safely and asks if Evie's doing all right. Noreen hears her laughter in the background and Hugh's raspy, happy voice saying something in a sing-song rhythm. Trot trot to Boston, maybe. Pat-a-cake.

Out on the balcony, Noreen basks in the surprisingly warm October air while afternoon light falls in golden shafts across the water. Ocean wind ruffles her hair. In an old movie, this would be the moment for a cigarette. But Noreen never smoked.

Nonie did. Clouds of cigarette smoke halo her in Noreen's every childhood memory of her, her lips pinching with each inhale, face relaxing with each exhale. If Nonie were alive today, would she still smoke? If she were here in place of Lizbeth, would she tamp her cigarette against the railing, inhale with eyes closed, exhale to the view of the sea? Would all that hair of hers be gray? Would she look at Noreen with the same pure love as when Noreen was eight, uncomplicated, and absolutely in Nonie's thrall? Or would their connection have loosened over the years? Soured from disappointments and conflicts they never had to bridge since Nonie left when she did?

I didn't leave you, little angel.

"No, you didn't leave. You killed what I loved most in the world."

Seawater sucks and thrashes several stories below. Beautiful and dangerous. Noreen turns her back on it and slides the balcony door closed behind her.

*Weeks
Before.*

AUNT NONIE LEANS over the pass-through to the living room and peers down at the card table where Noreen works the same fish and ocean puzzle for the third time. She's babysitting while Noreen's mom back-to-school shops with her brother. Out the kitchen window behind Nonie, crepe myrtles blow bright pink blossoms into the wind, and lightning-bright goldfinches dart from feeder to feeder in the backyard. The colors and sunshine make Noreen want to run outside, even though she can't run anywhere with her arm the way it is, but it all seems too bright for Nonie. She actually shields her eyes with one hand, and when she catches sight of Noreen's cast, she winces. Like it hurts her to look at it, not just hurts her *eyes* but her *feelings*, too.

Noreen drags her clumsy left hand through fragments of goldfish and watery swaths of blues and blue greens. She hates how stupid her left hand is, and she's sick of puzzles. Summer's a lousy time for a cast—the way it keeps her from doing things and also itches, especially when she's outside and her arm sweats and bakes inside the plaster. She's been stuck inside for three weeks, and already she's done enough puzzles and colored in enough messy left-handed pictures to last a thousand summers of boredom, all while Mark and his friends swim and run through sprinklers and climb trees. And Claudia's spent most of the summer with her grandmother in North Carolina. The few times she's been home long enough to come over, she's gotten bored and whined about being cooped up. Noreen speeds through books so fast it's hard for her mother to swap them out quickly enough to keep up. She brings books home three times a week now instead of once, and Noreen's read through this latest batch two or three times over. She's sick of having to think up new things to do. Of doing the same nothing things over and over.

If it weren't one of Nonie's cloud days, it would be fun to have her here. Even the puzzle could be fun if Nonie helped instead of stared. Today clouds seem to hover around Nonie, so thick and heavy Noreen can almost reach out and touch them. She thinks Nonie even smells different on cloud days. Moves slower. Her voice sounds muffled and far away.

What good is Nonie, standing there, mouth half open, eyes glazy and slow? Isn't it her job to think up something to do? Though all her mother said before walking out the door was, "Make sure Noreen doesn't jostle the cast. She has to play gently or she'll hurt that arm again." In Noreen's dreams, doctors are always telling her the cast has to stay on for six more months, or it's disintegrating like a wet tissue and leaving her arm bare, looking scalded and bloody with bone still spearing through the skin.

Normal days, Aunt Nonie is really good at playing. Her laugh is the best of anyone's. Rumbly and sweet, bursting through her lips in short, happy coughs. Laughing-Nonie thinks up good games to play and tickle-chases her and makes her laugh so hard she nearly pees her pants. But cloud-Nonie only stares off at some invisible nothing on the ground. Noreen wants to kick at that patch of floor or lie down and writhe in it, make her see *something* at least.

If they're going to do anything together, it's up to Noreen to think of it, same as the whole rest of summer. At least when school starts in a few weeks, everyone will rush up and ask what happened and when the cast will come off and if they can sign it. It'll cancel out some of the boring parts of having a cast, and she's sure it'll make everyone want to talk to her, even though last year she was so shy Mrs. Ebersole called her mom for a conference. She said Noreen's voice was so quiet no one could tell when she was talking.

Nonie always hears her talking. Sometimes on a cloud day, if Noreen talks the exactly right amount, the sad look clears away from Nonie's face and the laughing comes back.

"At school," Noreen says, "they'll have to get me a helper, to write things down for me. Just like last year? When this new kid showed up in our class? He had a helper."

"Did he now?" Nonie's eyes fix on something behind Noreen again. When she turns to find out what it is, all she sees is carpet.

"Yeah, that kid with the helper? He almost drowned last summer, and something went wrong with his brain. His helper taught him his sounds all over again."

Nonie's eyes focus, and her face looks scared, and she says, "Oh God." So this was the wrong story to tell for getting rid of clouds. Nonie puts her spoon down on the counter, walks over to the kitchen sink, and pours the rest of her coffee down the drain. From the side, Noreen sees how Nonie's shoulders droop, like her skin is too heavy for her body. She hates thinking of bones hidden under everyone's skin, but she thinks of Nonie's bones. Her skull, her shoulder blades, her finger bones, and she feels a little queasy. She drops a handful of puzzle pieces, letting them scatter into the ones she's sorted by color, edges, and corners.

On days Noreen feels the way she thinks Nonie feels right now, her mother scolds her. "Don't be a pill. Feeling sorry for yourself makes things worse." But her mother isn't here, and Nonie's too old for scolding, so Noreen has to fix this herself. She pops out of her seat at the card table and backwards-walks to the sofa, keeping Nonie in her sights.

"Let's do something."

Nonie follows her, a good sign, and lowers herself to the floor in front of where Noreen's bare toes wiggle over the sofa's fuzzy brown edge. Her mother calls her a pill only when she's feeling a way she'd rather not feel, so Nonie must not want to feel the way she's feeling either. Noreen flops onto her back so her head is level with Nonie's, and she twiddles a strand of Nonie's hair between her fingers. Wild frizzy ringlets, so much like her own.

An idea comes to Noreen, and she bounds from the sofa. Landing on the floor, she almost tilts backwards. She forgets how the cast unbalances her. Then she plops a throw pillow at the head of the couch, like a bed pillow, and pulls her aunt to her feet next to the sofa. "Now, lie down."

Nonie follows her instruction and sinks into the cushions, lets her eyes close. Next Noreen yanks the curtains closed with her left hand and flicks off the living room light. "There. It's nighttime. Night, night, Nonie." Not that it's dark with the sun still shining behind, around, and under the curtains, but it's less light. Better for imagining.

"Night night, little angel."

Huddled in the hallway, waiting, giggling, Noreen listens to Nonie's slow even breaths. Then she charges back into the room, thrusting open the half of the curtains she can work with one hand. "Ta-da! Morning!" She dances into place beside the sofa and leans over Nonie. "Well, good morning, Aunt Nonie," she says in a funny, fake voice. "I am the Sunshine, and it is morning now."

"Good morning, Sunshine," Nonie says.

"It is a new day," she continues in the sunshine announcer voice. "And today is a very good day."

"Is it?" Nonie asks. Her face comes a little bit back to itself. The gaping blank look shrinks away.

"It is, and now it's time to get up. Sit up and stretch." The sunshine voice slips back to her regular voice, but Nonie's already sitting up and stretching, pretending to yawn.

"What a good sleep," Nonie says. "Wow. What a nice sunshine you are."

"Why, thank you." Noreen carries on for a while as the

Sunshine, until Nonie's back in the kitchen, dumping out the remaining pot of lukewarm coffee and starting a fresh one. Standing straighter, moving a tiny bit faster than before.

The smell of coffee brewing fills the kitchen. Noreen fetches an armload of books, steadying them as best she can with her left hand, and climbs into Nonie's lap at the kitchen table while she waits for the coffee. The only sounds are the plink plink plink of the pot filling, birds calling to each other outside, pages turning in Noreen's lap, and her own voice reading all the words.

For a few minutes, it's enough. Until Nonie refills her mug and goes back to staring at an empty space on the floor.

Noreen pretends not to mind. What good would it do to mind when her best tricks already stopped working? She puts the books away in her room, returns to the card table where the many broken pieces of fish and water wait to be put together again, and wishes one last time for a day when someone else would think of something fun to do with her.

Outside, the real sunshine shifts patches of tree shadows around the yard, and it occurs to Noreen for the first time how heavy shadows must be. How hard to move around. How tired the sun must get from all that work.

Concluded.

A WALL OF floor-to-ceiling windows separates the heated indoor swimming pool from the beach. Noreen steps out of her cover-up and hangs it over a white latticework chair. The air is moist and chlorine-thick. A mother and her two young children splash in the shallow end. Another woman, about Noreen's age, lies back on a chaise lounge with a book, droplets of water still glistening in the short bristle of her almost crewcut. Noreen passes her on her way to the ladder, and they nod, sharing a half-smile.

Noreen feels giddy with anonymity. How easy it will be, for just this weekend, to seek pleasure where she finds it, even if pleasure seeking now means something laughably different from what it meant before she was married. The whims and needs of others rule her life these days, so her barest wish is to follow her own. To choose what she does next. Eat wherever and whenever she wants. Stay up late. Sleep until noon if she likes.

Lap after lap, the exertion invigorates her. Whenever she comes up for air, she glimpses the ocean through the bank of windows. When she's tired, she climbs the ladder again, wrings excess water from her hair, wipes her face. The woman who had been reading now soaks in the hot tub at the far end of the pool near the door. Noreen's muscles are tight from her long drive and the swimming. The hot tub would feel indulgent—an easy pleasure.

The water scalds as she lowers into it. Again, she and the other woman exchange friendly nods. The woman is slender and broad shouldered with a tuft of white hair above her left ear.

"This is so decadent," Noreen says, letting her arms and legs drift into the jetted streams. Muscles she didn't know were sore loosen in the heat.

"Nothing wrong with a little decadence," the woman says. Her hands float to the surface, flashing red nail polish. "Business or pleasure?"

"Definitely pleasure," Noreen says. "I just decided everything I do this weekend will be entirely for pleasure."

The woman's laugh is hardly louder than the hot tub's bubbling. "Cheers to that."

Noreen closes her eyes and rests her head against the edge of the tub. "It's like sitting in a cloud."

"A very hot cloud," the woman says, and they trade names. Hers is Greta. "What do you do?"

Noreen opens her eyes again and sits straighter. An answer is half out of her mouth—how the original plan was for her to stay home until Evie starts preschool, which she's pretty sure she'd love if she had that second car, but she's been rethinking the timing around finishing her teacher certification for the freedom it would buy her. She swallows it back. Thoughts that don't belong to this weekend. Besides, the woman's being polite, not asking for a confession. "I'd rather be mysterious. I don't get a lot of time to myself. I want to be just Noreen for now. Nothing else."

"Well, Just Noreen, I like a little mystery myself." Greta leans into the railing at the steps and rises from the tub, lifting a towel from a nearby chair to wipe water from her face. "If you're hungry later, the restaurant next door has a nice atmosphere. They play good music, serve pretty drinks. Maybe I'll see you there."

After the hot tub and a shower in her room, Noreen takes a long walk on the beach, dangling her sandals from one hand. The churning of the surf lulls her thoughts. She's happy to be alone and to be here. The sun bleeds into night. The colors dance in the water, then gutter away. The warmth of day fades with twilight, reminding Noreen it's not summer anymore. Her lightweight sweater is hardly enough. When the chill becomes too much, she slides her feet back into her shoes and quickens her pace along the boardwalk.

Next door to the hotel, lights blaze in the window of one of the few nearby restaurants open for the off-season. At another time, Noreen might have felt self-conscious entering a restaurant alone, but this weekend she's embodying her younger, braver self and channeling a little of what she remembers of Nonie's best days. Fearless is too bold a word, but she does feel a little fearless anyway. She nods at the hostess, chooses a seat at the bar, taps a fingernail along the counter edge in time with the Django Reinhardt tune thrumming from unseen speakers.

Behind her, through yet another wall of windows, vast midnight blue swallows surf and sky together, the glitter of distant lights against the water the only signal that a whole ocean stretches out there in the darkness. Dim lights over the bar feel bright in comparison. Noreen's eyes have to adjust. She orders a cosmopolitan because the color of it reminds her of the sunset. Still chilly from outside, she balls her hands into fists in her lap to warm them and waits for her drink. In a mirror behind the bar, she sees how the ocean breeze has tossed her hair. The frizz and fluff remind her of Nonie's wild hair and make her feel like she's living up to her intentions for the weekend.

"You came." The woman from the pool leaves her own stool farther down the bar and slips onto one beside her. Noreen hadn't seen her there when she arrived. She reaches the back of a hand to Noreen's cheek. "Getting cold out there, huh?" she says. "Were you walking?"

The surprise of a stranger's touch disarms her. "I was watching the sunset. Then suddenly it was cold."

"It seems like it's always supposed to be summer at the beach," Greta says, her eyes lively in the dull light. "I'm so glad you came. Eating out alone can be a drag."

"I haven't eaten out alone for quite some time," Noreen says.

Out of politeness, she doesn't admit that she'd been looking forward to it. "I guess there aren't too many restaurants open along here this time of year."

"You have to know where to look." Greta raises a finger in the air to get the bartender's attention. "I'll have what she's having."

Noreen is aware of her own long fingers grasping the stem of her cocktail glass, of her loose curls twirling at the sides of her face, relaxing again after the steady ocean wind. Aware of the tightrope sensation she gets when she lets go of what she thinks she's supposed to do. Aware, too, that Greta seems to be watching her.

They sip their cosmopolitans. When the bartender asks if they want another round, Greta places a hand on Noreen's wrist as a gesture for her to wait. "Let's see the cocktail menu," she says half to the bartender and half to Noreen. He leaves to get them, and Greta says, "Let's order something we'd never get."

The cocktail menu has all sorts of standards—martinis and old-fashioneds—but Greta skims the list for the bar's house recipes. "How about this one? Skid-Row-Tini?" She lists the ingredients: Jägermeister, tequila, vodka. "Or Monkey Mash," she says, with rum and bananas and chocolate liqueur. Whenever Greta laughs, she leans closer, and her fingers brush lightly against Noreen's wrist. If Lizbeth hadn't canceled, something like this feeling would have hovered between the two of them—easy comfort, intimacy. It seems strange to share those feelings with someone Noreen doesn't know, but it feels good, too. Greta's quiet confidences and soft gestures tingle in Noreen's stomach.

Their next drinks arrive garnished with fruit slices and paper umbrellas. "People say you are what you drink," Greta says and holds her glass up for a toast.

"What people say that?" Noreen asks and clinks Greta's glass with her own.

Greta laughs. "I do, I guess. I just made it up."

They share sips because they each got something different, and they order food. Shrimp quesadillas, artichoke dip, a plate of mini crab cakes. Eventually, the roster of appetizers amounts to a meal. The drinks infuse Noreen with calm and thrill, feelings that should be at odds with each other but aren't. When Greta reaches a hand toward her hair and says, "Such pretty curls," her eyes searching Noreen's, Noreen is dazed by an answering feeling, something like dropping from a high wire, plummeting and never landing.

The bill is paid. Outside in the ocean-fresh, autumn-cool air, Greta drops her shoes on the boardwalk and sprints toward the ocean. Noreen follows. They play chicken with the water's edge, daring each other to rush closer and closer to the surf until it finally laps their toes. They leap away at the sudden licks of cold water and switch between chasing the receding tide and each other. As free as children. The crisp air spurs them to keep in motion. Moonlight lilts on the water, rising and falling and shattering with the waves.

Noreen wades ankle-deep into the ocean, and Greta rushes up behind her, planting her own feet outside Noreen's. Greta's breath warms her neck. Her hands clasp Noreen's hips, drawing her backward until they fall together onto the wet sand. Noreen can hardly hear over the ocean crashing and her heart thundering.

Greta rolls over, above her. Sand, damp and cold, presses into her back. "You're so beautiful." Words George used to say. Hearing them again calls up a yearning she hadn't known was there. Seawater races closer and closer, nipping at their feet, their shins. They ignore it. Greta frames Noreen's face with her hands and kisses her slowly. How long has it been since George kissed her this way? Clutched his fingers in her curls this way. Smoothed his hands along the curves of her body. Her body surges with wanting, ebbs with uncertainty.

"Not here," Noreen says. When was the last time touch felt this good? The last time she let herself unwind instead of reeling herself in, tighter and tighter? She doesn't want to analyze what's happening or wonder if it's what she wants; it's so clear she wants something.

In Greta's room with the balcony doors thrown open to the ocean, they peel out of their clothes. Greta's skin is smooth and lustrous in the moonlight. They run hands along each other's bodies, exploring, caressing, tasting. Noreen loses herself in the pleasure of it, doesn't stop to wonder how she knows what to ask for or what to offer in return.

The sun rises outside their window, first a crimson line on the horizon, then light slowly overspreads the entire sky, washing the room in gold and white. Greta lies beside her, nude and swathed in the white sheet.

The desire and abandon Noreen remembers from the night before have unhooked themselves from her. Noreen's engagement ring and wedding band weigh heavy on her hand. Greta closed the balcony doors at some point in the night and cranked up the heat, so now the room is as warm as an incubator.

What if Evie had needed her? What if George had called?

Greta rolls toward her, reaching for Noreen in her half-sleep. Noreen sits up, not exactly pulling away. Here she is, in another place where someone wanted something from her, and she gave it. This time she wanted something, too, but somehow she feels left with more wanting than she started with.

"What is it?" Greta stretches and opens her eyes slowly against the sun.

A phrase or two escapes before Noreen knows what she means to say. "I've never done that before."

"At all?" Greta rises on an elbow, surprised.

"With a woman."

"Well, you did fine," Greta says. "If that's what you're worried about. You were good."

"Thanks," Noreen says. She places a hand on Greta's cheek, then lets it slide away. "You, too."

The last time Noreen and George made love, she lay on her back waiting for it to end. She had blamed becoming a mom for sapping that appetite away from her. She had no idea she had any desire left.

"Does this mean I'm gay?"

Greta sits up now, too, her back to Noreen. She snatches her clothes from the floor and begins yanking them back on. "I'm no therapist."

"No, I know. I didn't mean to put that on you." Noreen hadn't meant to say it out loud, but in the light of morning, with a head clear of alcohol, she's not sure what to make of anything that happened here. She had never imagined cheating on George. Or sleeping with a woman.

"Look, it was sex, you know? It was fun. It doesn't have to mean more than you want it to. Plenty of people are bi." Greta's smile pairs disappointment and pity. She goes into the bathroom and closes the door.

What feels most true to Noreen is that she's lonely. Lonely enough for the who and the what—or whatever terms there may be—not to matter. This makes Noreen gather her knees to her chest, as if protecting against a chill that isn't there. She feels naked in these bright white sheets and daylight. She whisks her clothes back on and lets herself out of the room before Greta comes out of the bathroom. She walks barefoot down the carpeted hallway, her shoes forgotten somewhere along the boardwalk. At least she kept track of her purse.

The number 8 is posted between the two elevators at the end of the hall, so Noreen knows to push the down button to get back to her own floor. She pretends she's used to assignations with strangers, that she feels perfectly collected standing barefoot in a sandy hallway with mussed hair wearing yesterday's clothes. She puts her mind on breakfast and the wildlife refuge nearby she plans to explore later, alone. Tonight she'll order supper from room service and eat it while watching old movies in her room.

The elevator doors open. The opposite wall is a mirror. Noreen looks at the floor instead, then faces the doors to wait for her stop.

Four Months Before.

THE USUAL MOTLEY of students, faculty, and town characters slump along the bar at the Virginian, slurring drunken lines of poetry. Cigarette smoke mixes with smells of spilled beer and steaks cooking and swirls with the fresh scent of early spring whenever the front door opens and shifts the air around inside. Nonie, Cooper, and Becky occupy their usual of the high wood-paneled booths that parallel the bar in the narrow place.

Becky rarely drinks, and Cooper stretches his single beer across an entire evening, so Nonie keeps to herself how much she likes to drink, how much she likes the musky, smoke-filled air of the Virginian, the glances from men at the bar. She's got a martini in hand at the moment, a drink she chose because she thinks cocktails make her look sexy. Tweezing bobby pins out of place one by one, she shakes the enormity of her hair free from its workday bun so her curls fall and bounce at her shoulders. The second before plucking the first pin, she made eye contact with a man at the bar who's been watching her all evening—tall, lanky, with a thick moustache and a belted leather jacket.

Nonie manages to sip her drink with Becky and Cooper slowly so she'll have a few swallows left by the time they're both ready to go. "Oh, I can wait until you finish that," Becky said the first time it happened, but Nonie assured her she planned to stay a while, that she liked a few minutes alone here and there, especially after a long work week. True or not, the statement is entirely misleading, because after Cooper and Becky clear out, Nonie's hardly ever alone for more than five minutes. Tonight, the mustache man arrives at Nonie's booth with a second martini for her before Cooper or Becky could even have reached their cars.

"For you?" he says and extends the hand with the cocktail.

"Me?" Nonie pretends surprise. "How sweet!" When he gestures for permission to sit down across from her, she nods.

He goes by Bix, he says, and squeezes her hand. His skin is rough and warm. He lingers in the handshake a few extra beats. His eyebrows are nearly as bushy as his moustache, and he has muddy brown eyes and chapped lips. "What's a pretty girl like you doing alone on a Friday night?"

Nonie laughs as though he's said something original. "I've only been alone for about thirty seconds," she teases. "Remember?"

Now it's Bix's turn to laugh. They drink their drinks, and another round, and the room pulses with the noise of Friday night, getting later and later. They whisper privately to each other across the table and laugh as if they know each other. Their hands fumble together. No matter where they go from here, she won't have to leave alone.

"My place?" He wraps her into her coat and slings his arm around her waist. As they walk toward the door, he lets his hand drift down and squeezes her ass before they've hit the sidewalk.

Nonie's head buzzes with the alcohol and the human touch. The air outside is crisp for spring. You can feel the memory of snow sweeping up beneath the breeze. Stars hang like splintered ice in the sky. Bix pulls Nonie close, so they walk hip to hip to his car, a battered brown Plymouth Cricket.

His squat vinyl-sided house sits in a row of similar houses in a subdivision off Barracks Road that, before now, she didn't know existed. A dog barks. The street is dark but for porch lights and distantly spaced streetlights that splash yellow swaths across dark pavement. Bix opens the car door and hurries toward his house, gesturing for her to wait and slipping inside before she reaches the front stoop.

Soon a young woman emerges, folding money into a purse, telling Bix, "She went to sleep about eight, like normal. Ate dinner like normal, never said a word about her tummy ache from school."

"Well, thanks, Angie," Bix says. Now he loops his arm with Nonie's and ushers her into the house around the departing babysitter.

Angie says a few more things, seeming unfazed to see him at the end of an evening with a strange woman in tow, and not hurrying, despite Bix's obvious impatience for her to leave.

"You have a child?" Nonie asks as soon as the sitter has made it down the porch steps. They usually don't have children.

Bix nods. An inflatable pink Easter bunny perches on the coffee table, listing drunkenly to one side. Bix latches the door behind them and pulls her toward him. "Kid sleeps like a rock." They clutch together. His hands run up and down her arms, then inside her coat. "Divorce," he says, and a slant of streetlight from outside glimmers in his eyes, "it's a bitch."

His mustache pricks against her nose as his tongue searches for hers, probing past her lips and teeth. His hands are hot against the base of her back, circling and pressing her closer, still right in front of the door. He peels her coat to the floor. His breath comes in short bursts. His erection presses into her hip through his jeans.

It seems strange, right in the middle of the living room, in sight of a sad, crooked little Easter rabbit with a child sleeping somewhere nearby. She closes her eyes, lets the next wave of martini wipe her brain clean of worry, of memories of other men and other moments like this one. Her university job makes her feel at all times like an actor in a play, forever forgetting her lines, her role, but she knows what to do here, now.

Bix reaches up inside her clothes. He kisses her face, her jaw, her neck below her ear. He skims a hand along her ribs, slipping it underneath the fabric of her bra, his fingers finding her nipples, one at a time. His short breaths come with moans now, like a dog in pain. His other hand finds Nonie's knee beneath the hem of her skirt, then her thigh. He works around the top of her pantyhose, fingers the edge of her underwear.

His next moan is loud, and he leans Nonie into the front door and unzips his fly right there. She's never done it standing up, and she whispers, "Yes," into his ear, and they bump together against the door. The knob thuds and squeaks as it heaves back and forth in its socket, and the movement speeds up, and they're both making noises, different noises, primal moans and gasps.

A throat-clearing finally registers above their own sounds, and they turn to face the hallway across from the front door, and there stands a girl, Noreen's age, in a seafoam-colored flannel nightie hanging a few inches above her ankles. She holds a ratty blanket that might once have been pink. "Daddy?" Her eyes are wide with terror as her father spins toward her, his dick hanging out of his pants, purpled and bulging, while Nonie grabs at her clothes in their odd disarray. The girl vomits, convulsively, over and over, and she's crying.

At least Nonie doesn't have to say anything, doesn't even have to make an excuse. She grabs her coat from the floor, swings toward the door for privacy, straightens her pantyhose and underwear, reclasps her bra. Her face flushes with sex and embarrassment and drink and humiliation. Somehow, it is both inevitable and mortally wrong to be yourself. Nonie can never find the balance. She lets herself out the door, closing it tightly behind her.

Her car is still in its parking space at the university a few miles away. For now, she's stranded, here where she doesn't belong, in this place of families and babysitters. She's a slut, a sex freak, a loser. She's been called all these things. It's never the sex she regrets but the feeling afterward that nothing fills her up, only leaves her emptier than before.

It will be a long walk back to her car, and she's not familiar with this neighborhood, so she isn't sure which way to go. There are streetlights, but long stretches of darkness, too. Nonie scuffs into curbs now and then. She makes wrong turns. She's still wearing her clothes from work, clothes she bought to look more professional, more serious. Her modest-heeled pumps are terrible for walking, pinching her heels and her toes, raising blisters. Her legs are cold.

Boarded-up buildings flank one side of the street, an empty lot the other. She thinks it's a rat that scuttles across the road in front of her. She doesn't know where she is anymore. She's aware of the breadth of the universe stretching out above and beyond her. Of how very minuscule she is.

"You're better than this, Nonie," her father had said last summer, grimacing over the burrito she'd just served him, considering it and her job equally worthless.

Back then, she was used to catching flak at every family gathering. Brynne and her mother tsking about how no one would take her seriously if she didn't take herself seriously—and by *take herself seriously,* they meant she should get a more "suitable" job, and by *no one,* they meant men, and that she'd never marry and would die alone. Ruth took a different tack, more earnest—everything about Ruth is earnest—promising that people at a more traditional job would share more of Nonie's interests, more of her intelligence. Though none of them knew her El Mercado friends, who were savvy and clever in their own ways. Marco wrote beautiful songs, and Sueann read philosophy, from Kant to Ram Dass. Lenny spent more time stoned than the rest of them, which is saying a lot, but, back when she was part of them, his kindness was impossible to miss.

As impossible to miss as the look on her dad's face. Eating out during a workday was a treat he rarely allowed himself, but there he was at El Mercado to speak to her, choking down a perfectly tasty burrito because, for him, it was flavored with his disgust for her. She felt herself shrink, as if she aged backwards, until she was standing before him at four years old and afraid of the dark, her work apron still tied sturdily about her and a pad and pencil at her hip. He wasn't there for the food or a quick visit with his youngest daughter. His attitude made it clear that Nonie gave him no reason to smile, only heartburn and that now-permanent crease in the center of his forehead. And he didn't hide it. Didn't ask how she was, if she was getting along okay. Her father off-gassed shame of having her for a daughter.

Facing him alone, Nonie couldn't protect herself against the burn of his judgment. So, this time, when he slid a scrap of paper toward her with a contact at the university he'd scrounged up on her behalf, a called-in favor that cost him another kind of disgrace, she curled it into her palm, pressed it into a pocket, then also remembered it later. Made the call. Quit her job and left her friends behind and a place that made sense to her, a job that made sense, yet when her father looks at her, even now, months into the job she took to please him, still his face furrows with remnants of embarrassment and worry about when she'll fuck up next and where she'll call him from when she does. Hospital or prison cell.

From somewhere down a side street, Nonie hears a squeak like a screen door. And right there, on a dark, lonesome road, in the middle of rats and abandoned buildings, that first shiver begins. Not from cold. The tiniest sensation under the toenail of her big toes, as if her toenails are falling asleep.

The shivers march up her feet, her ankles, then begin to retrace each spot on her body that man had been touching. And she thinks now how he's unattractive. His breath reeked of sour cheese. As long as she doesn't have to be alone, she'll do almost anything, and enjoy it. Her need is bottomless. And she shivers with it, in the middle of this dark, lonely place, so overcome that finally she collapses onto the asphalt, folds herself in half, so her knees cradle her head. Her hands tether in her hair.

A car swerves to keep from hitting her, blares its horn, then peals away with a rush of tires against pavement. A second car screeches to a stop beside her, as Nonie thuds her head against her knees, hands tight around her shins, hoping to squeeze the feeling away.

The car door slams. Hazard lights flash pink and dark, pink and dark. Footsteps scrape across the pavement. "You lucky I saw you," comes a gruff voice, the driver of the car. "Invisible as the night itself." She moves closer to Nonie's shape, a lump in the middle of the road.

The street is dark, but for the flashing hazards and twin head-light beams slicing the air between Nonie and the woman, so Nonie can't see her face. "Girl, you looking rough, you know that?" A hand lands on Nonie's head, pats her hair. "Hush now, I'm right here."

Nonie rocks back and forth a while longer. Another car swerves by but doesn't honk this time. The woman half-drags, half-coaxes Nonie to the side of the road, then sits down on the pavement beside her, lights up a cigarette. "I ain't in no hurry," she says. The orange dot of her cigarette draws close to where the woman's face must be. "You take your time. Get it all outta your system." She takes a drag, exhales the smoke. "Got us a pretty night for stars, when you get yourself ready to look," she says. "Cold as a baboon's ass, but pretty."

The woman's words hardly register at first, as if she's calling down from the Milky Way, unreachable as stars. She keeps pat-ting Nonie's head, saying, "Shh. That's it now, baby," and slowly the nighttime sounds come back—cars whooshing by on a busy road nearby but out of sight, wind bristling newly budding trees in the empty lot behind them, the first peeper frogs of the season chirping into the darkness by some unseen creek.

The woman waits with Nonie until the shivers have spent themselves, then she offers her a cigarette. "If I ever seen a body need a smoke, it was you." They smoke together in the dark, and the woman points out constellations with her cigarette hand. "Don't know too many, but I grew up in Nelson County, used to be a country girl, if you can believe that." She lets out a low laugh that growls its way into a cough. "They was some angry gods once upon a time," the woman tells her when her voice steadies, and she lays out the story of a beautiful maiden and a monster set to eat her up, all captured in the dark globe of the night sky. The name Cassiopeia lodges in Nonie's head, the first word she deciphers, and such a pretty-sounding one, and she follows the stubby orange light of the woman's cigarette as she points toward Andromeda. Soon Nonie's able to see the stars again and all their hopeful, mystical gleaming—a maiden saved.

Eventually, they crush their cigarettes into the dirt at the edge of the road. The frosty air bites into them. The woman heaves forward to stand. "Well now, sugar, I know you need a ride somewhere. Why don't you hop on in and show me the way."

Eight Years After.

HUGE SNOWFLAKES FALL like lazy confetti from the night sky. The reason the car skidded into the ditch and lodged in the bank. Noreen, Claudia, and the stranger who picked them up wait on the shoulder while other cars sluice by, splashing them with slush. Lights from the police car flash behind them into the woods in the median while the stranger brushes shards of glass from his hair and clothes.

First Claudia and Noreen were talking music with the driver, a scrawny 40-something man with a sliver of a mustache whose car stank of cigarettes and general staleness. He listed the string of Grateful Dead shows he'd been to while they tried to explain the Violent Femmes, Noreen's favorite band and the concert they were hitchhiking to Richmond to see. Mostly he looked at the road, but in the last second he swiveled around to look at them in the backseat. Some point he was making about Jerry Garcia and the definitive greatness of Dead shows over any other live concert. When he looked forward again, something happened in the lane ahead. Either he'd caught sight of an ice slick or else he'd drifted out of the lane. Either way, he overcorrected, and the tires lost purchase. The car fishtailed and spun in a circle, slamming them into the bank at the median. An overhanging tree branch smashed the windshield as they crashed to a stop, and for a moment it seemed like the whole world was about to end. Instead, they all climbed out unharmed. Standing there on the roadside a few minutes later, it still feels surreal.

A police officer unloads himself from the flashing car and lumbers over. Police officers always seem to walk bow-legged. Noreen blames the heavy load of weapons strung to their waists. That bow-leggedness gives the officer's approach the flavor of a bad Western. "There ain't room in this town for the both of us," Noreen whispers to Claudia, but Claudia rarely gets her jokes and stares at her angry-eyed. This was Noreen's idea, so, to Claudia, it's also her fault. Plus, probably she's scared. Noreen is scared, too, and colder by the second.

When the officer asks Noreen what number to call, she has to think. The crash rattled her, and she can't remember any number right away. When she does, it's her mom's, the only phone number she's ever had, but she thinks her father should have to clean up this mess. He moved out a couple months ago—his idea to walk out instead of work things out. She overheard enough arguments to gather that much. He deserves the trouble more than her mother who worries enough without any extra excuse.

"What number?" the officer says again, impatient in the manner of a sitcom father. To him, theirs was a pratfall, a foiled prank, not a real offense. Punky-rock short skirts and extra black eyeliner or no, he'd never question the unearned slack the easy privilege of their lives affords them. He strikes a different tone with the driver. "Picking up two young girls on the highway at night? Old enough to be their father. Old enough to know better, that's for damn sure."

With Claudia's parents, there's an off chance they'd ask the cops to lock them up for the night to teach them a lesson, or they'd both come pick them up, and her mother would stare darts while her father would cuss in his eerily quiet angry voice. So it has to be one of her parents.

Finally, she gives the officer her home number. Her mother won't see this the way the cop does, as a moment's foolishness. No, for Ruth Jamison, this will register as a near-death experience and one more way her daughter's life got written in her sister's tea leaves long before Noreen was born.

Falling snow layers onto the gravel on the shoulder and in the grasses just beyond. The officer radios for someone at the station to call Ruth. Most of the other cruisers are dispatched for similar weather incidents across town, and they're only five miles down Route 64, so it would be faster for Ruth to come out here and pick them up herself.

"People think Jeeps can't skid," the officer grumbles, casting another hateful glance at the driver. "Worst thing that ever happened to traffic, my opinion."

It's cold, and Claudia and Noreen are dressed for the concert they will now most definitely miss. Since middle school, whenever a plan hasn't involved a couple of older boys, Claudia's seen no point in it, but this afternoon, when Noreen said let's hitchhike to Richmond, she didn't fuss. Right now, Claudia folds her arms tightly across her chest, bouncing on the balls of her feet at the brim of a gravelly ditch, trying to stay warm. She doesn't complain, but she won't look at Noreen either. They're both wearing miniskirts and T-shirts and little leather jackets. Snow litters their hair.

"I'm sorry, Claudia." Noreen has followed Claudia's bum ideas since grade school, at first from desperation, then from habit, and lately from a growing sense of pity for her friend, so she hates apologizing. But she is sorry.

Claudia shrugs it off. "Doesn't matter. It's an adventure, right?"

Ever since Noreen's father moved out, Claudia's been nicer. At the moment, Noreen only refers to him as Ted. As in, Ted says he's coming by to pick up some of his stuff from the basement. Can I come over so I won't have to see him? Or, Ted wants to take me to a movie or something. Can we make plans so I can tell him I'm busy without having to lie? Claudia says yes and sure and whatever you need, as if she'd been doing that all along and Noreen hadn't noticed. Surely that's why Claudia said yes tonight, and why Noreen guessed she would. Milking her pity for all it's worth. She smooths her miniskirt for the thousandth time.

"I'm sorry," she says again, touching Claudia's elbow. "Really."

The officer places flares and cones to divert traffic from where smashed glass glints in the slick road, but cars continue to stream past. Some slow, others fishtail, but not as drastically as their car had.

"Might as well wait in the car," the officer says and opens the back door for them. They slide across the vinyl bench seat. A mesh cage separates them from the front. "You'll be safer in here." The officer leans over the open door and pokes his head inside. "Mind you, you were nowhere close to safe earlier. Hitching a ride in the middle of a winter storm. Spinning out might've saved your asses, forgive my French, but don't let me hear of either one of you ever flagging down another strange man for rides again. You hear me?"

They both nod, then he shuts their door. It's less cold in the car. They scoot closer together for warmth.

Before they see her, they hear Noreen's mother outside, questioning the police officer. Her voice is muffled but loud. The officer's words are clear. "Yes, ma'am," he says. "They're okay. Yes, ma'am, of course I told them they shouldn't've been doing that. On a night like tonight"—the door opens, and he faces them again—"or any other night. Isn't that right?"

As soon as Noreen straightens out of the car, her mother grabs her hand, as if she were a naughty child about to wander into traffic. Noreen snatches it back and loops a wide circle to their car, veering close enough to the highway to scare her mother but not close enough to scare herself. Again, she and Claudia nestle into the back seat together. Noreen slams her door shut, but the sound is lost to the noise of wet traffic whizzing past.

In the car, her mother slices glares her way through the

rearview mirror. "Noreen, I don't know where to begin."

"We're okay, Mom." Her voice hardly travels to the front seat it's so quiet. Being okay is, and is not, the most important thing.

Noreen isn't sure her mother heard until she starts listing all the worst things that could've happened. If the car had caught fire. If the driver had been going ten miles an hour faster. Even five miles. "If he hadn't wrecked at all, for the love of God, but had taken you wherever he felt like. If he'd been the perfectly wrong man and you'd never seen the light of day again. Do you understand what kind of world we live in, girls? How dangerous it is? How big a risk you took tonight?"

It's never just right now for Noreen's mom. It's down a dark hallway from now, at the bottom of the pit of worst-case scenarios from now, on the brink of a future of misguided and harrowing near misses from now. By the time they reach Claudia's front door, they have hypothetically died a thousand different deaths.

Mrs. Mays leans out the door, hand on the knob, as soon as the car pulls up. Noreen's mother describes what happened quickly, simply and in a calm, even voice. Claudia's mother's jaw drops lower with every syllable.

"Claudia Mays, you get in here right now. And say goodbye to your little friend. You'll be grounded so long you'll be old ladies before you see each other again."

Their last half-mile toward home, the snow falls thicker and harder. Their headlights shine weak cones of light into the white blur. The wipers squeak back and forth, and the heat, still on high, pumps loudly through the vents, the only noises in the car.

They pull up in front of the house, and her mother cuts the engine. Light from inside catches the snow as it feathers through the air and powders the grass, glowing like fallen moonlight. Ruth drops her hands from the steering wheel but makes no move to get out. "It's really coming down now."

The hush of the stopped car, the shine of the snow, and the

silhouette of her mother's head change the moment from fraught to tentatively intimate.

"It's pretty," Noreen says.

"They're saying nine to twelve inches." The seat crunches as her mother rounds toward Noreen, tense again. "What if you couldn't get home again?"

"Turns out I couldn't get very far *away* from home." It's an effort at a joke, but it fails. Her mother's face still grim, every muscle starched into place.

"When I was a kid, there was this great sledding hill out behind the elementary school." Ruth looks forward again. "We'd get a good snow, and everybody would bundle up and grab whatever sled or garbage can lid they had and show up in flocks. Nonie loved it. She'd drag me out there. Her cheeks would pink up and her eyes would shine in the cold. The same kind of shine that came later, when she got her panics, but with the sledding there was happiness in it, a good kind of excitement, you know what I mean?"

"Sure."

"I don't know if you do. I'm not sure you know the difference. Or if Nonie did."

Cold air seeps in around them. Noreen hugs her arms to her chest, casts glances at the house, wondering when this part will be over and they can go inside. She's still not used to how their house looks the same after so much has changed. Her mother keeps talking.

"Nonie always wanted to go down the steepest, longest hill. The one I never wanted to go down. Not when I was as small as she was. Not years later when she dragged me back up there as her chaperone. This one time, though, she made me swear I'd jump onto my sled exactly when she jumped onto hers. She counted us down."

A car creeps down their street. Snow thickens on the pavement.

"She counted down and leapt onto her sled, but I stayed at the top of the hill. I couldn't do it." Her mother shoots another look through the rear-view, one Noreen doesn't know how to read. "She trucked back up the hill later, the sled dragging behind her, snow crusting her hair, eyes brighter than ever. 'That was amazing!'" Ruth says, mimicking Nonie's voice the way she always does. "'But what happened to you?'"

Noreen's teeth threaten to chatter. She clenches to still them. She doesn't want her mother to know that she's cold or that she was as scared as her mother thinks she should've been. It'll only make things worse.

"I had to admit I couldn't do it," Ruth says. "Here I was nine years older, and she was this tiny little girl. Hand on her hip, little knit cap fighting her curls. 'It's just a hill,' she said." Her mother shakes her head and knocks a gloved hand against the steering wheel. Gloves Noreen gave her for Christmas. "It's funny because for a long time I saw it the way Nonie did. That some weakness in me kept me up at the top of that hill, made me into a person who avoids trouble, chooses the quieter path. I mean, look at me. I'm a divorced librarian. You don't get much quieter than that." Ruth chuckles and gathers her purse to her side, finally readying to leave the car. "But now I know it's not that simple." Another look back at Noreen. This time she holds the gaze. "Eventually I realized that some hills, once you start down them, you never come back up."

After that, her mother turns away a final time, opens her car door, steps onto the carpet of snow, and leaves a trail of footprints up the sidewalk to the house. Somehow Noreen knows her mother has said her last words about the entire incident, and she wishes she could be grounded and cussed at like Claudia or get extra chores or something to earn back her mother's confidence. Instead, she gets this grim reminder of her mother's worst fears. She's the object of most of them.

The last warmth drains from the car. Her clothes are still

damp from standing on the roadside in the snow before the police car came and before her mother picked them up with the heat blasting and her catalog of potential disasters they'd nearly, theoretically, brought upon themselves.

In the end, though, nothing much had happened. They made it all of five miles before the car lost traction and skittered across the highway, scaring the breath out of them, but everyone got out and walked away. One stupid thing she did, not a one-way ticket down some cursed, metaphoric hill.

It only ever occurs to Noreen too late to remind her mother that she isn't Nonie. The cold air shimmers around her, and wind sweeps up through unsealed nooks of car doors while snow, falling harder than ever, blurs light from her distant house, gathers night darker, closer around her. Her body, with its chattering teeth and shivering bones and its own memories of Nonie and disaster and her own fears, and the car, hardly an hour earlier, that had hurtled her sense of gravity away from her. She squeezes her eyes shut and rocks herself as much as the cramped back seat allows. Waiting for the feeling that grips her to let go.

Not what happened to Nonie. It can't be the same, because they're not the same person. This thing that happens to her, she can handle it, even if Nonie couldn't, and she'll always be able to handle it because she isn't Nonie. What she did tonight was stupid, and it freaked her out a little, and her mother probably won't sleep tonight, thrashing in her bed, afraid of what's becoming of her. But nothing's becoming of her. She's fine. She's going to be fine.

Her hand trembles when she reaches for the door handle, so she takes a strong breath before shoving it open, then trudges up the snowy walkway toward the house she's always known, but different now in every way. Her father gone. Mark, in college, hasn't come home once since the split. Nonie long, long, long gone. Her mother inside somewhere storing up all the losses. Noreen winding up the sidewalk to join her.

Nineteen Years After.

NOREEN KNEELS ON the guest room floor and slithers the portable crib out of its carrying sack. George's father and his new fiancée, Marcella, timed the Thanksgiving meal to coincide with Evie's nap, less than an hour from now. Prepping the space provides Noreen's first perfect excuse to duck out of a visit that's sure to feel as interminable as every one before it.

She thinks of visits here as *The Grady Putnam Show*. George's father has a tiresome, performative personality, seeming to narrate his own life, and yours, too, announcing everything to an unseen audience as if he expects a laugh track or rounds of applause. Holidays, and the accompanying free-flowing alcohol, amplify the effects. And here they are with him, the third Thanksgiving in a row.

The flattened heap of deconstructed crib hulks at her knees. A mystery of turquoise netting and folded hinges. A relic leftover from a long-ago baby shower her aunt Brynne had thrown for her at Grammy's house only a few months before Grammy's first stroke. Noreen marvels at how rarely they used the crib, how rarely they'd traveled, even before Evie graduated to sleeping in a big bed. George had dragged the crib from the attic last night while Noreen was packing, blathering about what Evie might do in the middle of the night, waking up in a house she doesn't recognize. What if she fell down the stairs? His father doesn't have gates up anywhere. What if she managed to unlatch the front door and wandered into the busy street? His father doesn't have safety guards for his doorknobs.

Noreen found it difficult to concentrate on his arguments while she dialed her mind backwards to land on the last night they'd spent away from home together. Could it have been all the way back to the previous Christmas? Other than that, George had traveled for occasional conferences. If he drove rather than flew, Noreen would be left behind carless with Evie, and often she'd invite her mother to keep her company. After those visits, though, George complained about where Ruth moved the spatula or how she'd stacked the frying pan or why the towels weren't folded the regular way, so Noreen slowly forgot how pleasant it had been to wake up late in her own house with the smell of breakfast wafting up the steps and a fresh load of laundry, folded and ready to be put away, before she even got out of bed.

From downstairs, Marcella's voice pitches impossibly high to chatter nonsense at Evie. How are children meant to learn to speak properly if you coo at them like puppies? So far, the only upside to adding Marcella into the family mix is Grady's resulting switch to near radio silence with George. No more weekends complicated by last-minute errands or emergencies in Roanoke. No more late nights with George thrashing sleepless beside her on those rare times he'd found the courage to tell his father no. Calls from Grady have become so scarce, though, Noreen's waiting for George to register the snub. Now that Grady has his lady love, his son has become all but irrelevant, except to complete the expected holiday tableau.

If they'd had Thanksgiving with her family this year, they would've had three unprecedentedly uninterrupted days with her brother and his wife. Such sprees of off-call time during holidays are extraordinary, but somehow Grady's invitation trumped her family's. Who knows how much one Thanksgiving with Mark and Betty could do to heal the post-parental-divorce rift that had forked Mark, who was away at college, more toward their dad, and Noreen, who'd witnessed the last angsty years of the marriage by herself, toward their mother. Rejecting the chance to be together certainly won't help though.

Yet, here she is, in Roanoke, wrestling with Evie's outmoded travel crib.

A sleeping bag would be more fun for Evie, but George is right about Grady's house being entirely unsuited to children, with hand-blown glass vases on every surface, uncovered electrical sockets, hardwood steps with nothing blocking a toddler's way, and she wore out her energy for arguing with the latest round-and-round that landed them here yet again.

So why did she relent? She hates this guest room, its dull blond walls, Marcella's addition of glass bowls of potpourri scenting the air with a spice-and-floral combination that mocks rather than mimics the natural world, the tight space, the feeling of floating on the orbit of this family, never sure she wants to move any closer than a thousand miles away.

Marcella's squeal of laughter signals some latest cute thing Evie's up to downstairs. She can picture the flip of Marcella's fake platinum hair as she rounds to face everyone else, to share a reaction to Evie saying, "Potty, peez." *A whole sentence, oh my! Who's da big girlie-wirlie?* Or simply holding her arms to be lifted into George's lap. *The wittle wady knows what she wants, doesn't she?* Insipid.

The first Thanksgiving with Marcella. That's why Noreen said yes. How would it look for Grady if his only child didn't turn up for their first Thanksgiving as a family? Rhetoric George had whined at her, surely lifting the script from Grady himself, and she fears the same argument will work as well next year since Marcella technically won't join the family until their wedding in three months.

There's no telling when Mark and Betty will get another Thanksgiving, or any other holiday, off call. At least she got George to agree to leave tomorrow after lunch, when they'll drive to join her family to finish out the last day and a half of

Thanksgiving weekend. Better than nothing.

She runs her fingers along the collapsed posts, searching for buttons or joints or whatever magic pieces turn the mass of fabric and plastic into a proper sleeping place until, finally, the crib seems to exhale and secures its position. The sheet stays in place instead of flying off or bunching the mattress in half. Noreen roots through her suitcase for Evie's special blanket and Esmé the Elephant, her favorite soft toy. She arranges them in the crib, then scoots the suitcases out of the middle of the floor, tucking them next to the antique dresser with its marble surface and mirror splotched and smoky with age. She catches sight of her own face there, surprised to see it so drawn. She's lost a little weight recently. She's lacked appetite ever since her beach trip. Not guilt so much as a new throb at the back of her mind, some untended business she's half-forgotten, like a list unfurled from a pocket after it's gone through the wash, words smeared away but a shred of paper proving there was something to remember.

Another volley of coos from Marcella reminds Noreen that she can't hide out here all day, no matter how much she'd prefer to stretch out on the bed with a book. Her reading appetite persists at least. Each day she craves Evie's bedtime when she can crawl into the extra twin bed and read by lamplight until Evie falls asleep. Most days she reads until she's so drowsy the best she can do is snuggle into the extra bed there and click off the lamp, leaving George to himself.

"Here she comes," calls George's father, narrating Noreen's descent into the living room, where Evie perches in Marcella's lap, humming a song to herself. Marcella's ever-present spike heels prop up her legs, stiff as rods. From the rigid caution of her hands and the discomfort on her face, you might guess she was holding a bag of raw eggs rather than a happy child.

"I was just telling everyone how much Marcella reminds me of you," George's father says.

Noreen takes a seat on a wing chair beside the sofa. Grady

sits in his wheelchair at the opposite end with Marcella, and George sits closest to Noreen, paging absently through a book he must've picked up from the coffee table.

"Just as pretty," George's father says, tweaking Marcella's knee, accidentally tickling her so her leg shoots forward out of reflex and Evie jostles, almost falling. Marcella's hands close around Evie's chest, and she extends her toward Noreen in the manner of passing potatoes around a dinner table.

George flicks a look at Noreen, abstracted but seeming aware of his father's veer into familiar, peculiar territory. "What am I supposed to say when he compares me to his fiancée?" she'd asked him before. George had had no answer and says nothing now.

Noreen gives a weak, toothless smile. A soft acknowledgment of what Grady must consider a compliment as well as an effort to ease any oddness for Marcella.

"Who knew we'd get to spend holidays with such lovely ladies, hey, George?" He winks at George, who follows Noreen's lead with a sealed-lip smile. The air feels stagnant, thick with the same potpourri as upstairs.

It's Thanksgiving, so Noreen counts gratitudes in her mind while trying not to let her exhaustion show. First, there's Evie, in her lap, thumbing the board book she'd drawn from her purse. They have their house and its views. She pictures mountains, sky, trees from their south-facing windows, all cast in late-afternoon's dusty pink glow. Then there's George, meeting her eyes again. Something in his gaze still reaches her, if not as forcefully as in their early days. Waves of energy she can almost see connect them across their separate spaces. Most days she's happy for that, too.

A steady breath in, then out. Every family compromises on holidays. It's not George's fault she can't stand his father. The man wears them both out, even if George doesn't always admit it. He could learn to handle him better, be more proactive, respond to some of the bombshells his father drops into conversation, but it has to be harder for him than it is for her to sit in his own father's house, wishing he didn't have to be here.

Vise-like pressure grips the base of her skull. A migraine threatening. Evie tugs at her and asks her to read the book in her hands. "I'll read to you at naptime. Just a few more minutes." Tugs and asks for the potty. "Again? Are you sure?" She's sure. Back again, she tugs for a snack. Noreen rifles her purse for a granola bar and a juice box and cups her hand under Evie's mouth to catch crumbs.

George flips pages in the book he isn't actually reading. Marcella brings a tray bearing bowls of nuts and celebratory martinis in long-stemmed cocktail glasses, glinting in the sunlight that pours through the window behind the sofa. The light show transfixes Evie, who pauses her tugging. The migraine tightens its hold. Any second Evie might reach out to touch the floating lights, knock into the fragile glassware.

Noreen would like to make it through one visit here without breakage. Since Marcella's arrival on the scene, she's become first responder for broken things, which she faces with hurt feelings and nervous twitchy looks toward Grady, then high-pitched reassurances that it's no trouble at all while she tidies each mess. Noreen's on constant lookout, and George, distracted by the visit's tax on his own energies and his new drive to vie with Marcella for his father's attention, leaves Evie's care entirely to her.

At naptime after a quick round of storybooks, Noreen's relieved to coax Evie into the crib with her blanket and toy. Evie rubs a fist into her eye, already letting go of the wakeful world. Leaning over her, Noreen laughs at herself. How can she be glad to shuffle Evie off to naptime when she'd choose to be with her over the rest of them if she could? The bed pillows call to her again, but George would never let her hear the end of it if she relented to her migraine and surrendered herself to this bed for the rest of the day. Instead, she kisses her fingers and blows toward Evie, who smiles back sleepily and rolls away from her.

The dining table is draped in gold linen with a complicated centerpiece of pinecones and white candles. More scents that practically smother aromas of freshly reheated deli-ordered food, presented tidily in fancy china serving ware. Each dish incorporates some kind of twist on tradition. Garlic and chive mashed potatoes. Cranberry apple stuffing. Bourbon pecan sweet potatoes. Talk merges from pass-the-turkey requests to superficial chatter about how they're spending their time these days.

George laments tenure track expectations. A thinly veiled plea for his father to appreciate how hard he works, how important he is. Instead, Grady chews and nods, then says, "I had a shot at teaching law back in the day, but I could never be satisfied with academia. It's too insular. The law is about the real world. When you get tired of all that research and those busybody students, you can always go back for a law degree. Or a business degree, hey, George? See what the real world is all about." A rough laugh, then the next shovel of food.

"What about you, Noreen? How do you manage so much alone time with Evie?" Marcella says. Both her prior marriages were childless, which seemed to suit her and her exes alike, so overtones of awe and pity color her questions about childcare.

Generally, Noreen likes to deal plainly with people, but she doesn't even consider admitting to Marcella how much more she'd enjoy time with Evie if she had a car of her own to shuttle them place to place, bring some variety into their days. Imagine the tired argument George would wage if Noreen broached such a topic at his father's house. "He'd think I don't take care of you," he might say, as if she were a pet from the pound. Or, "You're the one who won't take his money, and now you're complaining about it?"

No use would come of speaking of it here, but Noreen wishes she could crack whatever code seems to lock George away from seeing her side. If he could understand how much energy it takes to keep Evie stimulated, just the two of them all day, or how her thoughts turn viscous and slow after endless hours interacting with a toddler and no one else. If he could understand all that and not blame her for it.

Instead, he comes home each night, still hectic from his day, and she resents how entitled to distraction he feels, along with the extra work it makes for her to compensate for it with Evie, moderating greetings between them like a talk show host in case George, on his own, might forget to say hello to his own daughter. It's exhausting and frustrating, and when she advocates for something different—a new car, or at least a car sharing plan— George resists with his stale arguments about highway stalker villains or how much easier it would be to let Grady kick in extra cash than bog themselves down with car loans.

So she doesn't say any of that, and it's a relief, if a stinging one, when George answers Marcella for her. "Oh, Noreen's quite the reader," he says. "She's always got her nose in a book. I think that helps keep her going really." He side-eyes her with a mischievous grin, and she wonders if he's brought up her reading as a jab for how often she falls asleep reading in Evie's room. "I didn't get married to sleep by myself every night," he said once, though when she pretended she hadn't heard and asked him to repeat himself, he shrugged it off.

"I've been reading this book you would absolutely love," Grady says, though he's never asked her what she likes to read. "It's by this Nobel Prize winning physicist."

"About physics, then?"

"Not exactly. He covers quite a lot of territory, actually, which is what makes it so interesting. Why pharmaceutical companies want us to believe that HIV causes AIDS, why there's not really any ozone hole. I mean, he's a genius of a man, so it's really something to hear him argue against prevailing ideas of the day. Tossing them aside like toenail clippings." Grady laughs in his hearty, egging-everyone-on-to-join-him way.

"Experts in those other fields would disagree with him, I expect," Noreen says, irresistibly drawn into countering his nonsense.

"That's not the point though. You have to read it. You'll see. It's about crafting the argument, not getting stuck in right or wrong."

Noreen nods and sips from her glass, the last of her martini, so strong her eyes smart. She casts her gaze to the corner of the room farthest from Grady.

"He has a go at astrology, too. Not my tastes exactly, but so refreshing to hear a reasoned argument for it."

"I read my horoscope every day," Marcella chimes in. "It's eerie how often it gets things right."

"I mostly read fiction," Noreen says.

"But this book, you'll love it. I swear." He cranes a look through to the living room. "Marcella, it's right there on the coffee table. Would you grab it for Noreen?"

Marcella scoots her chair away from the table and dashes for the coffee table. "This one?"

"No, no, no, the other one." Noreen hates how he talks to Marcella, always irritable. Her migraine spreads, clamping more and more of her head.

When Marcella brings her the book, right in the middle of their meal, she wants to hurl it straight at Grady or wave it away with her hands, but, to keep the peace, she nods yet again, with another pressed-lip smile and tucks it under her seat. Where she intends to leave it. Let them think she forgot it. Even if the writer didn't sound like a quack intellectual, she wouldn't want to read something Grady so heavily praised, leaving her no room for her own opinion.

The food is tasty but rich, and Noreen mostly picks at it. Marcella looks at her plate and frowns. "I think they do so such a good job at Connelly's. Did you not like the food?"

"It tastes perfect," Noreen says. "I'm just not quite as hungry as I thought I was."

"Eats like a bird," Grady says. "That's how gals keep their figures." A comment Noreen can't help but think he aims at Marcella, who lays aside her next forkful of food to busy herself with the napkin in her lap. "What are you there, Noreen, a 2? a 4?"

The numbers ring meaningless in her ears, until she realizes he must be talking sizes.

"I always say even at a 6 you get thickness. Haunches and whatnot."

Noreen kneads her forehead. The pressure of the headache, of stifling every genuine thought, becomes too much. She shakes her head and steels herself to lock eyes with Grady. "That's disgusting."

"What?" He lifts his hands in the air, twists in his seat to look elsewhere for potential offense. "It's just an observation."

She scrapes her chair backward, folds her napkin, and sets it beside her plate. "I'm going to lie down with Evie."

"Reading again," George says. It comes out in a tone of complaint. If he's annoyed with her for leaving the table early or for talking back to his father, she doesn't care. He should've said something himself, should've stopped any of the string of nonsense Grady went on about this afternoon, or at any other visit. She's annoyed with Grady for being Grady, with Marcella for being nice and accommodating and frustratingly empty. And with herself for sitting there pretending as long as she has, today and other days, that any of this banter could be humane or enlightening. And for capitulating to yet another Thanksgiving, or meal of any kind, here in this suffocating home with this tiring, tyrant of a man.

"Take the book at least," Grady says. His tone suggests taking the book could smooth over everything she's just ruffled, but she has no interest in smoothing anything.

"No," she says and spins out of the room.

Upstairs she slips quietly into the dark guest room, kicks off her shoes, and peels the covers back. The fake rose and clove scents of the room slowly fall away as she lets her eyes close at last.

❧

She wakes to pressure, shaking. Or Evie crying? The heavy curtains would block the sun, but by now the sun has set. The only light comes through the slit where the door is cracked. The smell of whiskey. Her eyes make out the shape of her husband, leaning over the bed toward her. "George?"

"Get up," he says. Evie sniffles in the background, the first whimpers of her nap ending.

"Are you drunk?"

"Get up. You're embarrassing me, up here so long."

It's George shaking her, grasping her wrist and pulling her arm like a cord. Now that she's more awake, the cloying scent of the room joins the whiskey on George's breath, and her headache pulses again. "What are you doing?"

"You can't walk out on Thanksgiving. You have to come back down."

She shimmies backward through the sheets, away from George and toward the headboard. Her wrist throbs where he'd held it. A red mark the shape of his thumb lingers there, certain to bruise.

"Momma?" Evie says groggily. "What happen?"

"It's okay, love," Noreen says, swooping her arm out of George's reach as he lunges for another yank. He must not realize how much he's had to drink or how hard his grasp was. "Sorry we woke you, Evie."

George plops to seated beside her. "You've already made us cut the visit in half to see your brother. How hard is it for you to grin and bear it for the measly time we're actually here?"

"Cut it in half? Why are we here at all? To fill out your dad's Thanksgiving table and boost his ego all day? Pretending everything he says is clever instead of offensive?"

George fumbles his fingers toward her lips, still rougher than he must realize. "Shhh. They'll hear you."

"They'll hear *you*," she says, throwing back the covers and sliding out the opposite side of the bed to keep more distance between them. The bed is so close to the wall she has to sidle along it toward Evie before she can hoist her into her arms. The luscious sleepy smell of her cancels out the stink of the room, and the warmth of her in her arms eases some of her anger. She nuzzles Evie's forehead, and Evie clings tight to her, uneasy. "And you're scaring your daughter," Noreen whispers. There's no hope that Evie won't hear, but at least she can't see the stern glance Noreen shoots over her head at George.

"I'm not scary," he says. "Don't say that."

Noreen fiddles with Evie's dress and tights, then finger-combs her own nap-tousled hair.

"You left me alone," George says. "I needed you."

She double-takes toward him. His drunken clumsiness stilled now, he looks like a heap of sorrow on the edge of the bed. He cups his head in his hands and stares at the floor.

"You might've said that first." She shades her tone toward sympathy. He's never quite himself at his father's house. Needier, more changeable. Trying to get what he needs from his dad, then trying to siphon it from her when he fails. Who will teach him to be a better man if she doesn't try? She jostles Evie against one hip, plants her free hand on his shoulder. "I'm sorry you felt alone."

He lays a hand on top of hers.

"You're everything, Noreen," he says. "Everything. Promise me you won't leave me."

"I had a migraine, George. It's going to be okay."

"Promise." Light slants from the hallway through the cracked door and streaks across his face, showing the tight purse of his forehead, the fear in his eyes. "He doesn't even know I'm here.

You leave the room, and he goes silent, like he's by himself."

"He's a difficult man. It's not your fault."

"You love me, right? You still love me?"

"Yes, I love you, George," she says, though the words taste like nothing in her mouth. "Of course I love you."

He drops his head against her shoulder, and she leans into him to keep them upright, to comfort him. It takes all her strength.

Nine Years After.

NOREEN'S UNIVERSITY BOY wears pressed khakis and a navy fleece pullover with a bright orange polo underneath—as UVA as Wahoowa and belting out "The Good Old Song" at football games. His thick brown hair is carefully arranged around his cowlick. His name is Chaz, of all things, and he's telling her about his family's summer snorkeling trip to Belize while they follow in the footsteps of Claudia and her university boy, Emerson.

Ever since their sophomore year in high school, Claudia has been doing her homework in Clemons Library, pretending to be a college student like everyone there, and it works. By now, fall of their senior year, the arrangement is ritual. Tonight, yet again, Claudia has snagged double dates for them. The four of them walk along the railroad tracks near the university, not far from her grandparents' house, a shortcut between parties.

Claudia's giggles jingle in the chilly November air. Now and then, she tips her head when she laughs, letting her hair cascade down her back. According to her, boys like this. "They like to see your neck," she says, and Claudia would know. *Cosmo* quizzes and sex tips are her personal bible, and she carries at least three condoms in her purse at all times, zippered into the cosmetic pocket beside her lipstick.

"I don't care what they like," Noreen sometimes says, but Claudia mistakes her lack of interest for envy.

Most of the time, Noreen feels like she's outgrown Claudia,

but she can't bring herself to cut ties. It would be cruel to strand Claudia in best-friendlessness halfway through their last year of high school. Besides, sometimes she acts exactly like a friend should, exactly when Noreen needs it. The little bit of comfort she gave when her aunt died when they were small. How she called to check on her every night for months during her parents' separation and divorce. How she let Noreen talk her into hitch-hiking that one time. Claudia isn't perfect, but she's available and durable. They're each other's habit by now.

The air is cool and turning sharp. She wishes Claudia hadn't talked her out of bringing a coat. "You don't want to have to figure out where to put it once we get there, and you definitely don't want to waste time tracking it down when they're ready to leave," she had said. By *ready to leave* she meant *ready to take us back to their apartments for a quick fuck*, and Claudia never wants to interrupt that momentum. At that point in most of these evenings, Noreen ducks out and finds her own way home. Usually she can catch a university bus and ride to within a couple blocks of her house. Weekend nights the drivers rarely check for student IDs.

"You don't drink, then?" Chaz asks her. At their first party, there were three kegs, grain alcohol Jell-O shots, and too many people crammed into a small apartment.

"Let's just say beer and Jell-O shots aren't my thing."

"Choosy." Chaz gives a flirty smile.

"Yeah, I don't take what I don't want." Maybe she sounded too harsh because the flirty smile shrinks away. Claudia always warns her about tone of voice.

"If it's just that you're not twenty-one yet, you don't have to worry," Chaz says. "Nobody cards at parties." Claudia loves selling them as wide-eyed first-years, and the boys seem to love playing teacher.

"It's not that, it's just boring. Drinking like it's a sport."

Chaz sputters a laugh. "You've just been drinking with the wrong people."

Yeah, people exactly like you, she doesn't say.

A few small clouds skid across the night sky, edged with silver where they meet the glow of lights from downtown. Noreen thinks of watching cloud shapes with her aunt a zillion years ago and itches to feel that connected to someone again. Itches for it, but avoids it, too. Connection seems to travel too close to loneliness. Like with losing Nonie. Her dad leaving. Getting stuck on a Friday night with a couple of college boys who see nothing about her or Claudia beyond their imminent fuckability.

"There's this one frat," she says, more from compulsion than friendliness. "They play the same mix tape every night." It's a frat Claudia's dates keep dragging them to. Luckily, tonight's boys seem mostly into parties away from the frats along Rugby Row, so she might be spared a trip there this time. Typical of the boys Claudia finds, though, Chaz is more interested in how she looks than in what she has to say. He only gazes at her in reply. She prefers being *seen* to being looked at.

"The exact same songs," Noreen says. "You've got your 'Free Bird,' then your 'Driver 8,' 'Blister in the Sun,' 'White Wedding.'"

"Sounds awesome," Chaz says.

Noreen can picture him head bobbing to Billy Idol along with the usual crowd of drunk dudes. "Then the tape starts over again, and the next time you go there, as soon as you hear one of those songs, you know what comes next. The whole party is like that. The same thing after the same thing. With some asshole swinging in front of me, saying, 'Dude! You don't have a beer!'"

"Noreen," Claudia calls in a singsong voice. "Are you killing every last joy again?"

Everybody laughs.

"Sorry."

But it is boring. Last weekend they wound up at that repetitive frat just days after the Berlin Wall fell. Everything impossible suddenly felt possible, but walking into that frat with the stereo wailing "Sweet Child O' Mine," suddenly it was any other day, when exactly nothing was possible.

"It'll be different tonight," Chaz says. "We'll give you some fun lessons." He nudges her with his elbow and gives a look Noreen finds as boring as the parties. That *I know how to take care of you* look, the *I'm different from other guys* look. A total bullshit look from a guy named Chaz, sporting the most obvious preppy uniform available—khakis and a polo with the collar flipped up, Docksiders like he's still on some boat in Belize.

Streetlights catch the trees' remaining leaves, and they blaze red and dark orange or smudge into a murky brown. A train whistle blasts in the distance. The music of going places. "Maybe it's just because I've lived here all my life," she says. "Maybe somewhere else a party would feel different." She feels like she's always explaining herself. Next year maybe she won't have to. She refuses even to apply to UVA, so no matter where she ends up, at least it won't be here.

Claudia throws a cautionary look over her shoulder to remind Noreen how tonight they're UVA students, not high school kids, not Charlottesville townies. The train whistles again, closer, and Noreen feels the ground's first quaking. Sometimes when she's alone, she likes to come down to the tracks and watch trains go by. When she has time, she'll walk or run along them from one end of town to the other.

"Just down the road," Noreen points the way, "there's a bridge over the tracks, and if you stand right, it's like the train is flowing out of you."

"Girl, you definitely need those fun lessons," Claudia says, not turning around.

"You've never tried it, have you?" Noreen speeds up ahead of everyone and walks backwards beside the track, facing them now. "Fun is a matter of perspective."

Her pace quickens, and her voice gets louder. The train gets closer. Puffing its way from the center of town, it moves slowly now, destined to speed up as soon as its engine crosses under the nearby overpass and into a long stretch before the next town.

"Fun isn't something people all do the same way, and you can't make something fun just by saying it is," she says.

The train is fifty yards away. Forty. Thirty. A giddy laugh bellies up inside her. When the train is close enough to rattle the rails, she laughs harder. "Watch this!"

The train is a few engine lengths away, and Noreen leaps across the tracks right in front of it. The whistle blasts again. Maybe it would have anyway. On the other side, Noreen folds over herself, laughing too hard to keep upright. The train's wind whooshes her hair, and she leans into it. "That's what fun is!" she calls out, but she can't even hear her own voice over the clacking of the train.

The farther the train goes, the faster it goes. Clackety-clacks and tossed pebbles and fallen leaves churn around her along with the smell of grease and dirt. She sits on a rock beside the tracks, kicks at an empty bottle of Mad Dog 20/20 and a tattered page ripped out of some porn magazine.

It's a cargo train. She loses count after the thirty-seventh car. Her laughter works its way from thrilled to thready. Shapes itself into tiny icy pellets that needle through her veins. The shivers, like that thing that happened to Nonie. That knocked her out of herself, buckled her to the ground. Washed her face with a look of death. Noreen keeps her seat. No one knows what's happening as long as she holds her body tight and concentrates. It's like Nonie, but not like her at the same time, like everything about Noreen.

She closes her eyes, feels the train shuddering past, the chill of its wind, as if each sensation whirls up from inside her. She waits for the rush to dissipate.

Sometimes her mother checks on her in a particular way. A telltale expression on her face or a strange time to ask if she's okay. Noreen can tell when she's worried Nonie will steal her away one day. Their distinctive samenesses like one long seduction—their eyes, their hair, their tendency to get lost in thought. Why wouldn't Noreen get the attacks, too? The intrinsic despair? When her mother calls her Nonie by mistake, her face freeze-frames, hoping Noreen hasn't noticed or at least that she won't take a deeper meaning from the slip, but Noreen always notices, and that deeper meaning has hung between them like a wraith since Nonie died. *Will you become her?*

Will she?

Noreen grips her arms to her sides and balls into herself on the back of the cold rock. She breathes fast breaths between her teeth in the rhythm of the *Friday the 13th* movie soundtrack. *Chee-chee. Ha-ha. Chee-chee. Ha-ha.* Holding herself tighter and tighter. *Chee-chee. Ha-ha.* She has to wait it out. Hopes it'll end before the train does. Before Claudia and the preppy boys freak at the sight of her and bother her with their questions and fears.

The sound of the train changes, the cars speeding up as the first ones reach the outskirts of town. The frenzy inside her funnels away, and she feels the train's breeze and hears its sounds right side out again. A separate cool wind rattles dead leaves behind her. Near where a path parts the kudzu and scrabbles through to a street where the next party apparently is.

Everyone else waits on the other side of the train. They couldn't know for sure she made it across the tracks okay. The train wasn't going very fast, and she's walked along these tracks as long as she can remember, but, if she's being honest, she couldn't have known for sure she'd make it across either. She doesn't know what drives her to do some of the things she does, but jumping in front of that train really was fun. Much more fun than drinking crap beer out of stadium cups and watching preppy college boys play beer pong. No one seems to understand how everything about this town stands too still for her sometimes. She can't help it.

The last car clacks past, and Chaz, Emerson, and Claudia rush across the tracks toward her. Chaz's eyes bulge, and his cowlick pokes up from the middle of his windswept hair as if it could show surprise. Not Claudia, though. Her arms bulb into fists at her side, and her face pinches with rage. "What the hell were you thinking? How could you do something like that? Are you crazy?"

Crazy. Even her own grandparents mutter the word below their breath when they talk about Nonie. As if one itty-bitty word or a diagnosis or two could explain anything at all. As if it disqualified you from sympathy.

"I'm just bored." She's tired, too. The shivers drain her. She casts her head backward to look up at the sky, sure to show the length of her neck, and lets out a yearning bellow. "So fucking bored!" That display is enough to startle Claudia into silence. "I showed my neck, Claudia," Noreen fake whispers. "Do you think they'll like me now?"

"What is wrong with you?" Claudia backs away from her.

"What? You don't think they'll like us if they know our tricks?" she taunts. "Or if they know we're still in …"

"Shut up, Noreen! *Shut up!*" Claudia panics, checking side to side to see what the boys are doing and hearing. They've chosen a patch of ground beyond the tracks where they can loiter and wait out whatever's going on. They pose casually, as if they would have been standing there anyway.

"…*high school!*" Noreen finishes and starts laughing again. "I'm outta here."

"Yeah, well, don't come back!" Claudia yells as Noreen scuffs down the tracks, the opposite direction from the train. To the boys, she says, "Just ignore her."

"Is your friend okay?" Emerson asks.

Noreen turns around to scream at them, "I'm fine!" Gravel scrapes under her feet. "God! I hate this town!"

The last thing she hears is Chaz asking, "Are you two really still in high school?"

What she wants is to leave them behind as fast as she can. Tonight's boring boys and Claudia, each fuck like a pearl on the

Add-a-Bead necklace of her life. So obsessed with collecting the next one, she doesn't even notice how dull the boys are. How they suck at conversation. How they're not even nice about sex. Or good at it. The couple of times Noreen went along with it all, the boys rushed through and got embarrassed afterward. There must be plenty of boys who aren't like that, but she doesn't expect to run across any of them by hiding out in Clemons Library pretending to be somebody she's not.

She knows she pissed Claudia off, and she'll have to pay for that later. If it goes true to pattern, Claudia will make a big play of ignoring her for at least half of next week, refusing to give her a ride to school or to acknowledge her in the halls. Probably Noreen deserves it this time, but, come Wednesday or so, finally too lonely to resist, Claudia will rush up to her at her locker first thing in the morning and start chatting like nothing happened, and Noreen will feel sorry for her and go along with it.

For now, Noreen speeds to a jog. Her shoes scrape against the dust and stones with a rhythm something like a train's. Next year, wherever she lands for college, she promises herself she'll find at least one person who thinks of fun as something more than doing the same thing over and over, someone she doesn't feel sorry for, and maybe she won't need to scare herself half to death anymore.

And she'll be anywhere but here.

Two Months Before.

NONIE HASN'T BEEN back to El Mercado since she quit almost a year ago. The suggestion had bubbled out of her mouth from nowhere when she and Becky and Cooper had decided to abandon their brown-bag break room lunches and go out for a change. She remembers a vague notion she had that it was time her friends learned more about who she really is, but the maraca music and smoky atmosphere that used to make her feel a part of the place now seem as false and distant as her own image reflected in El Mercado's plate-glass front window, showing her in the same kind of clothes Cooper and Becky wear, preppy as models from the latest L.L.Bean catalog. More in keeping with the waves of students and tourists who chug yards of beer across the pedestrian mall at the ever-popular Hardware Store Restaurant.

She doesn't recognize the two waitresses smoking at the bar in the back, but Marco, her old boss, is the same as ever. He perks up at the sight of her and sashays across the restaurant to greet her and her friends. "Nonie? I can hardly believe my eyes."

Seeing him brings back the slipping feeling that comes with spending time here, a cozy feeling that distracts you as a pinch of your soul oozes out to help create the ambience of the place. She settles on *nostalgia* to describe the blend of hungers and nausea that swell inside her at the sight of him.

"Nonie," he says again, making her name fill the whole chamber of his mouth. His breath has the same onions-and-cumin quality of the restaurant. He braces her by the elbow in a semi-hug. "Any friend of Nonie's," he says and grips Cooper's and Becky's hands in turn.

He escorts them to one of the booths, the seats upholstered in vinyl and the backs in brightly colored Mexican-style blankets. Cooper and Becky slip into one side, and all three fold their blazers into a single heap between the wall and Nonie on her side of the table.

"Happy homecoming," Marco says. His hand lingers on Nonie's shoulder after she sits down. His finger hooks a loose curl at the nape of her neck before he snags laminated menus from between the tray of hot sauces and the napkin holder that stand in the center of the table. He leaves them to browse. The only other customers are an old man at a table across the room by himself, a pair at another table that appears to be mother and daughter, and a group of university students splitting a pitcher of beer and a huge plate of nachos by the door.

Soon Marco returns with a pitcher and three salt-rimmed glasses. "Margaritas, on the house." Lingering beside her while Nonie pours them all a drink, Marco says in a quiet voice meant for her, "Can't stay away, huh?"

Her face warms. Does he not realize how long it's been since she's been here? True, everything but the wait staff looks the same, down to the duct-taped rip on the seat beside her. For him, all that time might have stood still, but for her, it didn't, and she's not used to the intensity of his attention anymore. Her university boss says, "Excuse me, Nonie, do you have a moment?" when she pokes her head around Nonie's cubicle, and she only does this when she's making completely work-related observations or requests. No one looks at her there the way Marco looks at her now.

His next comment is loud enough for everyone at the table to hear. "So what do you do in that new job of yours?"

"We work in the Development Office," Becky says, her words eclipsing Nonie's answer of, "New? I've been there almost a year."

Cooper adds, "We solicit funding for the university."

Marco looks skeptical, so Nonie rephrases. "We hit up millionaire alumni for cash."

"Like the pimps of higher ed?" he says.

She flinches at his wording, but instead of offending Cooper and Becky, his joke casts Marco's typical strange magic spell. When he includes you, somehow it just feels good. She'd forgotten about that, and about his easy laugh, twinkling eyes, the way he can look at her, like right now, and see through the weekday-Nonie veneer of neatly fastened hair and perfectly pressed office wardrobe to the Saturday-Nonie with shabby sandals exposing paint-chipped toenails and tousled curls tumbling around her face. She'd forgotten, too, what, besides her family's disapproval, had convinced her three years was long enough after college to wait tables.

Marco laughs again about something Cooper says and leaves them to their drinks. Nonie watches him walk away, so familiar to her, from his casual swagger to the swivel wave he offers customers he's checking on but doesn't know. She sips her first margarita and listens to Cooper and Becky, but their voices sound far away now. Will she ever know them the way she knows this place?

Halfway through the meal, and Nonie's second margarita, the group relaxes a little. Nonie notices for the first time how Becky's eyes stay wide almost all the time, as if she's in a constant state of surprise, and Cooper, despite his baby face, has a man's jawline and strong, square hands. Noticing these things makes Nonie like them more, the same way the scrunched-up left ear of a puppy she'd had as a girl had made him seem cuter rather than deformed.

When they're together at the Virginian, Nonie sticks to one drink, saving her excesses for after Becky and Cooper leave, but here, with a free pitcher on the table, Nonie helps herself. Each time before she pours, she offers Cooper and Becky refills with the polite flourishes she learned waiting tables. Becky hasn't touched hers beyond a first sporting sip, but Cooper took one refill. Now the pitcher's nearing the bottom. No one seems to notice.

When Cooper starts checking his watch, and Becky starts saying *um* a lot, and they both keep mentioning the office, Nonie begins to think they don't like her, that they never will. She's sure if she chooses the right topic of conversation, they'll get back into rhythm together, and she'll remember the things about them that had started to make her feel so fond of them. But nothing works.

"We should be getting back," Cooper says for about the fifth time. That's when Nonie remembers that she's the one who drove them here. That's why Becky and Cooper can't do more than talk about leaving.

"I don't think I'm fit for work," Nonie says. She covers her mouth over a spastic laugh. Suddenly everything around her is hilarious. Cooper's man jaw on a baby's face, for example, makes him look as though he's been assembled incorrectly from some sort of build-a-man kit. Meanwhile, Becky's eyes are so wide it looks like her eyeballs could tip right out of their sockets if she leaned forward too quickly. Nonie manages to pull her keys out of her purse. In a moment, she's settled enough to say, "You can drive my car. I'll find another way home."

Cooper accepts her keys, but they dangle from his hand uncertainly. "Just leave you here?"

"Remember? They know me here," she says. "I'll be fine. This was fun." She tries to make it true by saying so, but looking at them now, she isn't sure. They were all having fun earlier though. She's almost sure of that.

"You're really not coming back to work?" Becky says. Clearly someone who never skipped a class, in high school or college. To her, ditching half a workday must seem like high treason.

"Yeah, go on. Don't worry about me."

Alone in the booth, Nonie sips the dregs of her fourth margarita. She doesn't know how long she kept Cooper and Becky here for lunch. She checks her wrist for a watch but isn't wearing one. It has to be well past one, though. No wonder they were so impatient. Their boss, Ms. Strom, won't approve of such a long break.

Nonie pulls herself up to the bar. "Marco, I'm in sorry shape." She asks him to call her boss for her and rests her head against the edge of the bar while she reels off the number. He asks her to repeat it several times. She's not sure if that's because pressing her face against the bar muffles her words or because her words are slurring.

"Tell Ms. Strom I got sick, a fever or something, and my friends stayed to make sure I was okay. I don't want Cooper and Becky to get in trouble," because now all Nonie can think is how nice it was of them to come to lunch with her, to try to get to know her better.

Marco's voice is clear and uncharacteristically formal on the phone. "This is Marco Vasquez. Nonie O'Malley asked me to call… Well, I'm afraid she isn't well. Her friends stayed with her to get her settled. Cooper and Becky, I think it was… Yes, Nonie was concerned about them returning late to work but wasn't well enough to call you herself… She's come down with a sudden high fever…"

But were they really trying to get to know her? They sat together on the other side of the booth, shoulder to shoulder, sometimes sharing their own private laughs. Nonie might as well have been somewhere else. All that talk about how they needed to get back to work—they'd rather work than spend an afternoon with her. They didn't want to know her after all.

Nonie braces her head against the bar to stop the room from spinning. She doesn't want to stare at stale gray cubicle walls and write letters charming money from rich people anymore. Suddenly, so many things about waiting tables seem more honest to her. So many things about Marco's simple life—selling burritos most of the day, hanging out at his apartment by the train tracks late into the night with his guitar and a savory stash of his closet grow-light weed—seem spawned of purer impulses than the ones that drive her department at the university, with all their tastefully embossed stationery and matching forty-pound ecru business envelopes and so many catered black-tie events. When she waited tables here, she never asked for money outright the way she does every day at work now. If she had asked for tips from customers, taking their money afterward would have felt crude and trashy.

After the phone call, Marco says, "Don't worry, Nonie. I remember how to take care of you."

His face blurs at the edges, and the way that makes him look like Humphrey Bogart starts Nonie laughing again. Fits of laughter happen to her sometimes, overtaking her the same way the trembling does, making Nonie feel as though she's riding inside her own body like a passenger. She closes her eyes, trying to make it stop.

When she opens her eyes again, at first she can't place the cluttered room where she finds herself, stretched out on an old, frayed brown sofa that smells like beer and cigar smoke, a desk close enough to reach out and touch with her hand. The distant reek of disinfectant suggests that the narrow door off the end of the room leads to a bathroom. Her head and stomach swirl. Pieces of paper litter the floor.

She picks one up. A dinner check. She looks around again and can't believe she hadn't known the place immediately—El Mercado's back room—except for how that happens sometimes when you wake up, especially when you wake up somewhere you didn't mean to fall asleep or black out or whatever she did. Even the heap of coats piled on the edge of the sofa behind her are familiar. The back of the sofa—the closest thing to a lost and found here—is buried in forgotten coats, including her own blazer, which she notices folded neatly at the top of the stack.

Nonie's head hurts. She checks her wrist again for a watch, remembers she's not wearing one. There's no window, so she can't tell if it's still light outside. The music from the restaurant is louder than it was at lunchtime, which means it's probably closing in on the dinner rush. Nonie waits to see if the pain in her head will subside—it doesn't, it never does—then she balances herself to standing and eases her way to the bathroom. She flicks on the light and examines her face in the small rectangle of mirror that hangs over the sink. Her eyes are red, and sleep pulled strands of her hair from its workday bun and left the rest of it smooshed and matted at the side of her head.

Cold water to her face does nothing to relieve her headache. She uses the toilet, fights off feelings of dizziness and nausea, splashes herself with more cold water, fiddles with her hair. She still feels the remnants of a buzz.

Marco straddles one arm of the sofa when Nonie comes out again. Seeing him startles her but also brings back that familiar slipping feeling. Smoke spirals off something in his hand. He offers her a toke. "I figured you'd be in here feeling lousy. Little Mary Jane'll take the edge off."

Even doctors say it helps with nausea. Didn't she read that somewhere? Maybe it'll help a headache, too. Nonie drops to the sofa beside him, then pushes drooping hair out of her face, rubs her forehead, and takes the joint. They pass it back and forth a while without talking. It doesn't make the headache go away, but the pain shifts to the background. Everything feels soft.

"Yeah, that's it." Marco links their hands to pull her closer. "Feeling better now."

It's not the first time a day at El Mercado wound up this way, Nonie in the back getting high with her boss. Not the first time he nestled himself onto the cushion beside her. Stretched one arm behind her. Told her, "God, you're beautiful. You know that?" Held her face in his hands.

It's not the first time, and Nonie starts to remember how she meant for at least one of those other times to be the last. Maybe it wasn't so much her father's disgust and her mother's constant nagging that made her walk away from here. Maybe there were some things about this simple life that hadn't suited her any better than her new office clothes, which, piece by piece, Marco peels away and tosses into a pile on the floor at their feet. Next Nonie braces herself against the sofa and lets him touch her, push himself inside her, right there on that filthy brown sofa, with the lost-and-found coat zippers catching in her hair, scratching against her face.

"Feeling real good now," Marco moans, clamping his fingers around her wrists to steady himself, his skin there taut and crisp from years of kitchen work. Nonie's never been sure how old he is. Spent, he collapses on top of her, reeking of sweat and pot.

Nonie's head still hurts, and her mouth tastes rancid. She doesn't want to be here, wants never to have been here. And she wants a shower, and a second chance with her friends back at the university tomorrow, because she knows now that she embarrassed them acting the way she did, or embarrassed herself, or both. They won't look at her the same after this.

"It's so good to see you," Marco says. "I been missing you."

Nonie jerks away from him and pulls her clothes back on. She hates when her fits of shudders happen in front of people, but one comes on now, starting with that feeling in her toes. She tries to hide the tremors from Marco, but these are bad, and her teeth chatter.

Marco looks worried. He grabs one of the forgotten coats from the back of the sofa—not hers, hers has fallen to the floor—and stands to wrap her in it, circling his hands around her along with the coat. She wants to throw him off herself with superhuman power or shrink to the size of an eyelash and drift away on the air.

But she has to wait it out. She has to grit her teeth against the clatter of her body and the revulsion in the pit of her stomach, deep down where a tiny part of herself screams and screams that she's not worth a penny in this world, not a penny.

*Nineteen Years
After.*

NOREEN AND GEORGE watch over Evie and the Christmas tree from their blue velvet sofa. In the daylight, the living room windows across from them open onto their ancient overgrown boxwood hedge, then past it to the winding dirt road, and beyond that to wide sky and blue-tinged mountains rimming the horizon. Now darkness cloaks everything beyond, and the windows only reflect green and red flashes of Christmas tree lights.

They chopped the tree from their own yard. Underneath, Evie handles one wrapped package after another. Brynne's Christmas gifts arrived the first of December, two weeks ago now. Noreen's cousin Henry, Brynne's oldest, married last year and apparently hasn't said a word about children yet, and Luke, promoted in the fall to assistant vice president of the loan department at a new branch in Newport News where he hardly knows a soul yet (according to the note that accompanied Evie's gifts), has no current prospects for family making, so Noreen figures Brynne transfers her urges to spoil as-yet-unborn grandchildren onto her almost three-year-old great-niece instead.

The lavish gift giving began toward the end of Noreen's pregnancy with the Peter Rabbit blanket they wrapped Evie in to bring her home from the hospital. A frilly affection attaches to her gifts under the tree, silver boxes with opalescent white dots and wide ribbons of pink satin. Their shining perfection makes it seem that Noreen should have expected them, should have known her aunt would shower her and Evie, mostly Evie, with such attention.

It's interesting how age changes people. Brynne never seemed the type to go gaga for a baby, yet now her attachment to Evie is simply a fact. Of course she demonstrates it in her signature way—her packages impeccably wrapped, the outfits she sends bearing tiny tags of designers someone other than Noreen might recognize. Noreen writes faithful thank-you notes, filling them with newsy details of their life out here in the boondocks, of what Evie can do now that she couldn't do on the last gift-giving occasion. Brynne often writes back in leaning, loopy script, sweet letters that suggest a long-standing fondness between them that hadn't seemed to exist before. Beyond their one dancing binge the day Nonie died, she and Brynne have remained mostly aloof with each other, ashamed in some way, maybe, for enjoying themselves during a tragedy they weren't yet aware was taking place.

A beer bottle dangles from George's fingers. His other hand spreads across the back of the sofa behind her, not quite touching her. When she unpacked their Christmas decorations this year, she came across a plastic sprig of mistletoe she bought the first year they were married. She'd hung it just inside the front door of their Blacksburg house all the years they were there, and she'd hung it in this house the last two years. But when the tissue paper fell away from it in her hands a week ago, she tucked it quietly back into its storage nest and made sure it went back up into the attic with all the ornament packing materials and unused strings of lights.

In the wackily lit semidarkness, she searches George's face for the features that had attracted her in the first place. His sharply angled jaw had once stood for his certainty. The coiled tufts of hair frizzing at the edge of his forehead and along his neck suggested his boyishness. Now the blinking lights cast his face in a shifting garish glow. His jaw is fuller, his hair beginning to recede. His certainty can verge on pomposity. His playfulness can veer into selfishness.

Noreen leans forward to disengage one of Brynne's packages from Evie's hands. She has learned to make substitutions. When Evie wants what she can't have, she'll insert something else into her grasp to distract her. It has to be something desirable. Right now it's a snowman snow globe from her own childhood. The heft of it interests Evie enough to steal her attention from the pretty wrapping that Noreen hopes will survive until Christmas morning.

Resting against the cushions beside George again, she calculates a hypothetical roster of substitutions she'll have to make to get them through the last week and a half to the holiday. Evie's getting old enough to be wise to some of her tactics, so she has to work harder to stay one step ahead.

George tilts his beer up for a swig and brushes Noreen's shoulder. She twitches at his unexpected touch. Her marriage demands its own substitutions. Taking what she can get in place of what she wants. She hopes George didn't notice her flinch.

In a few weeks, 1999 will yield to 2000. She remembers a puffy cloud day with Nonie years ago when they imagined where they would be at just this moment. Did Nonie already know then that she wouldn't be here? Noreen remembers something about horses, about riding them anywhere she wanted. Climbing onto Nonie's back, fake galloping around the yard. Back then, she was small and innocent. The future still something that could be crafted from imaginary horses and sunny afternoons. That child wouldn't recognize the woman she's become—the sum of everyone else's desires, unsure of her own.

"I've been thinking," Noreen says. Evie drops the snow globe. Noreen lifts it gently back into her hands. "Wouldn't it be fun to invite Lizbeth and Diego to spend the night for New Year's? We could have our own mini-party to ring in the new millennium." Hosting Lizbeth and her husband would be a small thing, but it's something Noreen knows she wants. Her new millennium resolution is to ask for things she's sure of.

"I don't know." George sets his beer bottle onto the hardwood floor beside the sofa.

"It's been ages since we had them for a visit." The last time Lizbeth and her now-husband Diego had come to their house—they were only engaged back then—George had managed to punch a hole in a window he was trying to open, so he and Noreen had spent half the visit in the emergency room, waiting for the doctor to tweeze tiny shards of broken glass from his hand and stitch him up while Lizbeth and Diego babysat for one-year-old, teething Evie.

"True, but you did just see her."

She doesn't correct him. Setting out for her beach trip, she'd assumed she'd come clean with George about Lizbeth's absence after she was home again, when she was sure her unplanned time alone would have refreshed her in ways he would notice and appreciate. Improved energy, maybe, better humor, brighter skin. Something. No doubt the weekend had changed her, but not as she'd expected, and she never figured out how to tell him about the special solitary weekend that had turned out to be not as solitary as she'd imagined. Luckily, his questions afterward were generic enough that she could answer without lying. How was the weather? Did you have a good time?

"Would they even want to travel with Lizbeth so pregnant?" George says. "Isn't she due soon?"

"Still two months to go, actually." Lizbeth's whole reason for planning the October trip had been to tell Noreen about the baby in person, but then she'd had some spotting and was afraid she was about to miscarry, which is why she canceled, inventing the stomach virus as her excuse. It took a few weeks after that for Lizbeth to regain her confidence in the pregnancy, and that's when she finally broke the news to Noreen about it, over the phone.

"We could invite them," Noreen says, "and let them decide.

It's not that big a trip."

If Lizbeth does come for New Year's, Noreen will have to tell her something to keep her from tipping George off about their weekend that wasn't. Lizbeth knew Noreen went without her, but she has no idea Noreen kept that a secret from George, and no one knows about Greta. Noreen stores memories of that weekend somewhere private inside her—a collage of flesh and ocean and moonlight. She hasn't been able to drum up full-fledged guilt about it anymore than she wants to repeat it. Most of the time, she doesn't feel a need to explain it, either, not even to herself, yet excuses whisper themselves to her of their own power sometimes—that she'd been living in the moment, and that moment ended. That this was why she'd married George to begin with, as ballast against loose winds inside her. Getting Lizbeth to help keep her secret would require more articulate explanations and invite questions she'd rather not answer about herself. She'll have to trust Lizbeth to reserve judgment and respect that she doesn't have the energy right now to pick apart the life she's made or to try to make a new one.

"I had a different idea," George says, and his face takes on the bashful, boyish quality she likes, that pinch of insecurity. "I hope you won't think it's stupid, but I thought we could plan a romantic night for just the two us."

He seems shy and uncertain of her, the way he was when they first started dating. A pang strikes her, that she's done this to him. Humbled him by icing him out. She twitches at his touch, sleeps in Evie's room. What has she done lately to draw them closer? An appetite stirs in her that she thought she'd buried with that mistletoe. Or long before.

"We can have a nice dinner." George scoots closer, hugs his arm around her shoulder. This time, she lets her body sink into his. Such closeness has been rare for months. More than months? If you believe women's magazine covers at the grocery checkout, it's perfectly normal for sex lives to hit the skids after children come along. That could explain everything.

The warmth of George's arm against her neck, the light tickle of his touch. How nice, how uncomplicated it would be if she could want him again. If she could believe that her life with him could hold the comfort she's been aching for.

"You can sleep in our bed." George's breath is damp in her ear. The daybed in Evie's room was originally intended for bad nights of teething, fevers, nightmares, but Evie sleeps better with someone in the room with her. Noreen sleeps better there, too.

"I'll make everything special," he says.

The snow globe clunks to the floor again. George stifles Noreen's forward motion to pick it up. He raises her chin gently so she'll look into his eyes. "Please?"

And Noreen says yes, because of the guilt around the hidden mistletoe, because this flicker could always turn back into a flame. She's been so tired lately and hasn't paid him enough attention, and that means she hasn't gotten enough attention either. That alone might account for why she's not always attracted to him anymore and why Greta's allure mesmerized her. Maybe all these things are what make her so tired anyway.

New Year's Eve by themselves could be exactly what they need. Maybe that really is what she wants.

Seventeen Years
After.

NOREEN IS SO tired she sleeps through George's morning routine and well past when he leaves for work. When she finally wakes, she wanders barefoot through the bedrooms, checking everything. A late-pregnancy habit. She admires the soft green paint in the baby's room, rubs her tight belly.

"It won't be long now, Evie," she says. Her name is Eva, but when Noreen talks to her, she always ends up calling her Evie. For the last couple of months, she's been conversing with her, getting Eva ready for the world, herself ready for Eva, and enjoying the figment of her company.

Out the window—reaching branches of nearby trees and their new bright green leaves and the cascade of ridges beyond. Under the window—a daybed with throw pillows and a stuffed elephant and a teddy bear. Noreen taps the butterfly mobile over the crib, and it wobbles and lets out a single note. A pattern of tiny sheep and hearts repeats across the crib sheet. Lizbeth sent a soft toy rabbit and a brightly colored polka-dotted rattle, and they wait for Eva inside the crib, too. She pulls out the top dresser drawer and realigns the stacks of diapers, opens the next drawer and fingers the onesies. Everything in order.

Next stop is the yellow room, hers and George's. She doesn't linger, just confirms that it remains the way she left it, the white chenille bedspread tidily smoothed and the curtains open to the same view as the baby's. The third bedroom is a study, and she spends the least amount of time here. George keeps it messy.

Right now, sloppy piles of papers and books crowd his desk and make her insides swim. The fourth bedroom isn't finished yet, and she keeps that door closed. It still needs painting. The hardwood floors need staining. The rest of the farmhouse has come a long way, and she trusts, though doesn't quite believe, that they'll scrounge up time to conquer the last improvements after Eva is born.

Downstairs she pads into the kitchen and sets a pan of milk to warm for cream of wheat. Morning sickness finally eased after her eighth month, but a lot of good that did. The one late-pregnancy craving she can't shake is basically baby food.

Her side crimps on the walk back toward the refrigerator to put the milk away, and the carton slips out of her hand. Milk splashes everywhere. It's so hard to bend over now, to move in her usual ways, that she understands the urge to cry over spilt milk. The mop is in the pantry, beyond the refrigerator, but first she has to grip the counter edge until her side finally uncrimps. If she hadn't called George home from work to drive her into her midwife's office for two false alarms already, she might think this was labor starting.

Their house sits on a knoll, so nearly every room looks out onto the Blue Ridge. While she waits for the stitch in her side to let go, she focuses on the pale waves of ridges outside the kitchen window, trying to remember which is Church, which is Hogback, which is Knob. Then she sloshes water into the bucket, squeegees the mop a few times, sops up the milk, wrings the mop, rinses.

The milk in the pan is burnt and smoking by the time she remembers it. Stupid, stupid, stupid. Now tears do well up in her eyes. She's so tired, so damn tired of all this time alone. What if labor really is starting, with her stranded here alone? Their nearest neighbors are a five-minute walk in either direction, and she hardly knows them. On one side, a couple older than her parents, on the other, a very religious family with three children under four years old. Noreen can relate to the notion of a loving power out there somewhere, but the woman next door can't talk about her turnip yield without bringing Jesus into it.

Farther down the road, a mile maybe, there's a Mennonite family who brought fresh-baked bread to welcome her and George shortly after they moved in. If Noreen could drag herself that far, she's sure they'd want to help, but they're one of many local Mennonite families who ignore modern conveniences. Even if it could get her there fast enough, she can't imagine laboring in the back of their horse-drawn buggy. So here she is, pacing the rooms of her house, splattering milk across the floor, burning it on the stovetop, without a soul to talk to.

You can always talk to me.

Nonie, or the idea of her, shows up at the uncanniest times. Noreen would love to talk to her now. Pull up a chair, have a cup of coffee together. Or herbal tea or a glass of milk—Nonie might insist on something healthful for her. Eva's three days past her due date, and Noreen aches all over. Any diversion that would pull her outside herself is welcome, even a phantasmic one.

"What do you want to talk about?" she says to the empty room while she fills the burnt pan with suds. Her stomach rumbles. To speed up her breakfast, she could skip scrubbing for now and use a clean pan instead, but lately she dreads delaying any task. She pictures stacks of unwashed dishes, piles of dirty laundry, and loose packages of hardware for minor household improvements strewn into an obstacle course around the house and blocking her path to Eva's room when she arrives home from the hospital with her.

We could talk about how you'll leave here when the time comes.

"That's easy." Noreen scrapes the burnt milk from the bottom of the pan. "We've got a bag packed and ready." Three onesies and a pair of footed pajamas for Eva, the hat with elephants on it, a package of newborn-sized diapers, a nightgown and change of clothes for herself, the necessary toiletries, a plush blanket edged in satin and embroidered with Peter Rabbit from Brynne for the hospital bassinet.

Another twinge takes her, this one more forceful than the last. *Not when it's time to leave for the baby. When it's time to leave for good.* Why must Nonie always say morbid things?

"I'm not leaving for good. I'm staying for good," Noreen says. "That's the whole point of this place and all the work we've put into it." Through the window over the sink, she glimpses a cardinal in a tree. The flash of scarlet flames against the softer browns and greens of early spring. The yard slopes out of view, toward a rocky creek she can't see from here but imagines as an eventual natural playground for Eva. Through the partly open window, she can smell spring earth, the promise of change. The brown skin of burnt milk gives way to her scrubbing, finally, and she swirls it all down the garbage disposal.

When she whirls back toward the stove with the pan, the lights flicker, and the floor tilts. She loses her footing and lands on her behind, confused and out of breath. The pan clatters away from her. If only George were here, making her breakfast. She would be sitting at the table, not spilling milk and mopping it up. Not falling on her ass. Her back is always sore these days, and she's always tired. If George were here, he might have poured her coffee already, and he could talk to her about the students he advises, or tell her how beautiful she looks even though she feels bloated and wrecked.

You know he wouldn't do any of those things.

Nine-months' pregnant bodies require so much work. The most reply she can muster is a cringe. She flattens her palm on the tile floor next to her, then leans into the closest chair with her other hand, hoisting herself to her knees, then one leg up, the next leg up. Finally standing again, she breaks a banana from a bunch in the brown ceramic bowl on the counter, a housewarming gift from her brother, and rips into it. She'll start her breakfast over again afterward, but she needs something on her stomach right away.

Nonie's right though. If George were here, he wouldn't make her breakfast, and he wouldn't make small talk to distract her. It would never occur to him to ask her about the deer herd she watches every day in the yard, her best company out here. She even has a favorite, the particularly dainty one she calls Priscilla. He doesn't notice things like that, doesn't chat that way.

He does other things. Digs fence posts. Spreads mulch in their garden beds. Moves shrubbery and perennials around the yard. Paints the shed. If she asks him to rub her shoulders or pour her some ice water, he's likely to duck out of it in favor of one more project in the yard. "After the baby, it'll be a long time before we're up for tackling yard projects again. Let me see how much I can get done before then." His fixation with the yard annoys her, but she tries not to begrudge him the work. It's for both of them, the three of them, really. His version of nesting, she supposes.

Her second effort at cream of wheat succeeds. While she's eating it, another cramp digs in. She has to clutch the table edge to get through it. She notes the time on the microwave clock. Breathes through her teeth. Tries to remember what relaxed shoulders feel like.

The next one comes seven minutes later. The next, seven and half minutes after that. The third, seven minutes again, and she finally calls George. His extension rings and rings and goes to voicemail. "Heads-up, honey. I think today's really the day."

Eva Marie Putnam. Eva is George's grandmother's name, and Marie is Ruth's middle name. Noreen can't wait to see what she looks like, this little person who's been living inside her for so long. The symbiosis fascinates her, and she enjoys the constant company, as if someone is thinking her thoughts and dreaming her dreams with her from the inside. It'll be strange, in a way, for Eva to live apart from her, her first breath her first act of separation.

Every morning Noreen reminds George to keep an ear out for the phone at work because every day for the past few weeks could have been *the* day. Oversleeping means she hadn't been able to remind him today, but you would think he would remember on his own. She punches the numbers again. It rings, rings, goes to voicemail. She calls her mother instead.

"It might be time."

"Should I head over?"

"Not quite yet. I'll call you when she's here though." George wants just the two of them at the birth, though he seemed to agree to Ruth's offer to come stay for a week or two to help them get adjusted afterward. When Noreen and George talked over birth plans with the midwife, the midwife reminded them it was Noreen's choice about who's in the room during labor, nobody else's. The birthing plan is all about supporting the mom. The problem is that George hangs back when her mother's around, and she doesn't want him hanging back the first time he holds his own daughter. If that means only the two of them get to be in the birthing room, then that is her choice, too.

If he'd only answer his goddamn phone.

A contraction takes hold while she's talking to her mother. Not even seven minutes this time. She manages monosyllabic answers to keep her mother from noticing, then asking where George is. It's easier to end the phone call after that, even though she was hoping to talk to her mother until the return call from George beeped through on call waiting. She would call Lizbeth, but now she's afraid she'd get a contraction at the moment of saying hello, and she doesn't want to scare her.

Only nonsense on TV. News anchors making omelets, boyfriends shouting at cheating girlfriends, an ad for dog food that amplifies the sound of the dog's chewing. The sound flips Noreen's breakfast inside her. She turns it off. Dials George again.

"George, for God's sake, they're less than seven minutes apart now. Things are happening fast. Please, please, please call me back! I need you!"

Her mother lives a little over an hour away. Noreen doesn't have the Jesus neighbor's phone number or the older couple's. She doesn't think the Mennonites even have a phone. Could she jog down the road in either direction and knock for help? What if none of them are home?

She puts water on for herbal tea. A relaxing blend her midwife recommended. The teakettle squeals and keeps squealing through the next contraction. The tea is too hot to drink. She paces the kitchen. Looks outside. Dials George again. Slams the phone instead of leaving a message.

In one of a zillion pregnancy books, she read that the volume of your blood doubles when you're pregnant. All that extra blood swells, swells, swells in her veins and throbs in her head. She doesn't want to call an ambulance. It's not an emergency yet, is it? But they're way out here in the sticks. Will help get here in time if she waits?

She tries George again. Waits for the beep. "Fuck! Fuck! Fuck!" she screams.

She gives herself tasks. Wipes the kitchen counter. Puts away breakfast dishes. Folds the last load of clean towels. Sets the bag for the hospital by the door. Breathing through each interrupting pain as best she can.

At the crunch of gravel in the drive, she rushes to the front door. The second George's feet land on the ground, she bursts into tears. "Where were you?"

"What? At work. I came as soon as I got the message." He ambles up the sidewalk, up the front steps.

"It's been two hours, George! I left so many messages. Why didn't you at least call to tell me you got them? I didn't know where you were." He eases his briefcase from the back seat.

Why isn't he hurrying?

"I told you. I was at work. I came as soon as I could. I didn't want to waste time calling you back. Wasn't it better for me to get here two minutes sooner?" He stands in front of her unruffled, smelling faintly of spices, his oxford shirt prim and pressed, his pants pleated perfectly. Why does he get to be so calm?

Noreen can only imagine what she looks like, tears slopping down her unwashed face. Wearing the same maternity sweatshirt for the third day in a row, flecked with dried cream of wheat.

"Your contractions are only seven minutes apart anyway, Noreen. I don't understand why you're panicking."

"Six minutes now."

"Still, plenty of time." George sets his briefcase beside her packed bag at the door, hangs his coat on the rack as if he thinks he's in for the night. "They said to wait until they're about four minutes apart, right?"

"How was I supposed to know you'd make it home in time?"

"I said I'd be here, didn't I?" Tidy and formal in his business clothes. Rigid as the walls beside him. "Why wouldn't you believe me?" His face all hurt feelings and no compassion.

"I thought you'd be in your office or at least checking your messages. I've been calling for ages."

"Jesus, Noreen, do I have to keep reminding you I'm nobody at JMU yet? Least senior hire in my department. We had a meeting. I can't ask for special favors. Not before tenure."

"Who would fault you for listening out for your pregnant wife?"

"Do you think I'm lying? Are you accusing me of something?"

She hadn't been. The idea hadn't crossed her mind.

"Because I'm here, and you're fine. I don't understand what the fuss is about."

"I'm afraid, George. I was afraid." What makes him turn her fear into suspicion? In her mind, she parses the image of him now—his face self-pitying and distant—with the image of him the moment they met. When he seemed to emanate calm, and muscles at the base of her neck eased in response. She must have needed soothing for eons by then.

A contraction sears her, this one not five minutes after the last. Tighter and harder and tighter and harder. It sucks the breath from her, plunges her into a deep pit, and she claws and claws her way up, reaches and reaches but can't get out. She feels there's no bottom beneath her, that she'll be falling forever. Until George reaches out at last. He takes her hand. He is soft again beside her.

"Breathe," he says. "Remember to breathe."

So she does.

Later, with Eva swaddled in the Peter Rabbit blanket in the bassinet beside the hospital bed, brightness drains from the day outside, leaving only a dim yellow light over the sink and limning the edges of the doorway. Eva's breathing lulls Noreen into quiet. Sweet short puffs. Now and then a snuffle. Everyone told her she wouldn't believe what it felt like to hold her baby in her arms for the first time. Her mother, Brynne, strangers at the grocery store. They were right. The baby shook up the insides of her meaning and left her with a new one.

One of the nurses explained how the chair in the corner unfolded into a series of foam cubes that worked as a bed, and George asked Noreen if she wanted him to stay the night in the room with her. If he'd offered instead of asked, she would've been grateful for his company, but she doesn't want to decide for him. The way his father has over the years, asking things of him he shouldn't owe.

"Go home. At least one of us can sleep tonight," she'd said, then asked him to bring Eva to her so she could nurse once more before he left. He helped position Eva in her arms, and she cradled the baby against her chest. Eva's fresh new skin flush with her own. Her little head snug against the palm of Noreen's hand.

What more could Noreen need tonight anyway?

When Eva finished, Noreen checked her diaper—still clean—and reswaddled her. George placed her gently back in the bassinet. "I'll get everything ready," he said, leaning to kiss Noreen's forehead.

She imagines he's still awake at home, these many hours later, puttering room to room in search of projects to justify his presence there instead of here. There will be no projects to find. She's been making things ready for weeks. Before he'd walked away from her bedside, though, she'd squeezed his hand and kissed him because at least he had wanted to help and because they made this beautiful baby and because every cell of her exhausted body tingled with love. Still does, and she isn't sorry she sent him home. She and Eva will spend the first night of her life alone together.

Lying against the bed pillows, Noreen rolls her head toward the bassinet and watches Eva's breath lift and lower her tiny chest. Whenever she wakes up to nurse, Noreen pushes the button for help. She tore when she pushed Eva into the world, so getting up and down strains the stitches and scares her a little. Besides, the nurses told her to buzz any time she got out of bed during the night.

When they come to her, the nurses bring Eva to the bed, show her how to hold her like a football, how to make sure her little lips latch onto the nipple rather than suctioning the skin beside it. They prepare her to expect the first post-birth, sticky, spinachy poops and help her clean them when they come. They check Eva's vitals and hers and encourage her to go to the restroom, drink water, walk a few extra steps here and there.

For much of the night, Noreen is too happy and wired to rest, even though she's never been so tired before. Her eyes close sometimes, and sleep comes in small spurts, interrupted when Eva peeps or when a nurse's cold hands brush her wrist, checking her pulse. She can't stay asleep. Can't keep from gazing at Eva, amazed each time by the sight of her. Perfect, new, untried by the world. Even her cry, a tiny, struggling demand, fills Noreen with pride and affection.

Sometime in the deepest realm of night, Noreen wakes up, quivering. It starts as a small pulse from deep inside, then her knees are jouncing, causing her stitches to stretch and smart, her teeth to chatter. The bed rattles. Far more dramatic than her usual shivers.

This hurts worse than labor and lasts longer than a contraction. Did Nonie hurt, too? Can you die from this alone?

And why wasn't George listening for his phone today? Was a department meeting really that important? Why wouldn't he have found a way to stay within earshot, with their baby past due and Noreen stuck alone at home without a car? That goddamn non-existent car. The quaking complicates pushing the buzzer for the nurse. It takes several tries.

Why now, in the most placid moment of her life, would her panics finally jump the threshold into Nonie territory? With Eva sleeping beautifully beside her, content after a recent nursing, her breath huffing in and out exactly the way it's supposed to?

What if, after downplaying it and hiding it for so many years, Nonie's panic steals her from her baby once and for all? What if she never gets to sit by Eva's bedside reading books or soothing fevers or playing make believe with an army of stuffed animal friends?

By the time a nurse appears at her bedside, Noreen is too terrified to speak. This one has long brown hair pulled into a tight ponytail and royal blue scrubs with polar bears all over them. "Getting some shakes?" she says. Noreen nods. "Nothing to be scared of."

"No?" Noreen says, able to form only a single word.

"It's just adrenaline. Doesn't happen to everybody, but it's totally normal. I'll be right back with something to help."

Excretions of every bodily fluid, the muck of babies, the muck of mothers is everyday business for the nurse. What's a little shivering to her? To Noreen it feels like an omen, until the nurse returns with heated blankets and the warmth seeps into her.

The nurse lays a hand on top of the blanket over Noreen's forearm. "It takes all kinds of hormones to squirt these little folks out into the world." She flicks her head toward Eva.

"Nobody warned me," Noreen says.

"Nobody ever does," the nurse says, chuckling. "I don't know why they don't talk about it in birthing classes. It scares people so, but it's natural as air."

"Will it happen again?"

The nurse shrugs. "Maybe? Not likely as bad. You might feel some contractions with the nursing for a while, too." The nurse straightens and thumbs the papers on a clipboard hanging at the end of the bed. "Now let me go ahead and take this next round of vitals a little early, give you some extra time to sleep before the next check."

In the morning George arrives at breakfast time, freshly showered. He kisses her forehead. Eva snuggles against her chest, and he kisses the back of her head, too. He produces from his coat pocket a silver rattle from Tiffany's that his father had given him months ago to have ready for this moment. Noreen can't look at it without thinking of silver spoons and the strange bought-and-sold forces that strain between George and his father, forces she has no intention of allowing into this next generation.

George sets the rattle among a nest of burp cloths, as uninterested in it as she is, and shrugs his coat onto the back of the chair. Then he regards her meal tray with skepticism and adds a paper bag to it. Inside, her favorite muffin from the bakery in town, still warm. He lowers himself to sit on the bed beside her, rests one hand on her blanketed knee.

"How was the night?" His voice the husky whisper meant for her alone.

The night was a spectrum of sensations, barely sleeping, fragmented with her terrifying adrenaline rush, interruptions from Eva's squeals, and regular visits from the nursing staff. Everything hurts.

He peels the paper away from the base of the muffin for her, pokes a straw into the orange juice untouched on her breakfast tray, then brushes unkempt hair from her face. Tiny gestures, but honest. People step away from phones for zillions of reasons. He couldn't have meant to scare her, and he did manage to make it home in time. Sometimes she thinks losing Nonie so young set her up for expecting to lose everyone else. She takes his hand in hers, and it feels solid and warm.

When he lifts Eva from her chest and into his arms, his face beams like starshine.

"The night was perfect," she says. "Everything is perfect."

Eight Months Before.

NONIE DROVE FROM her apartment as early as she could drag herself from bed, but it's clear everyone's been waiting. The Christmas tree stands in its usual place in the den, a few branches are all Nonie can see from the front door, its lights winking faintly against daylight.

"Finally," her mother calls, her voice shrill, at the same time her father growls a sarcastic, "So glad you could join us." Neither parent rises from their seats on the sofa. At least Ruth meets her at the door, but even she levels Nonie with a sharp glance before pulling her in for a hug. "I was worried," she says privately into her ear.

"You're always worried."

"Prove me wrong sometime."

"I proved you wrong *this* time. I'm fine. Just late." But she returns the hug with affectionate force because at least Ruth loves her, even when she doubts her.

All this in their parents' foyer, with Uncle Percy howling in stilled laughter from the framed photo by the door, a ghost from another generation, repeating his perpetual warning, *This joy, everything that is joy, turns to dust one day.*

She is fine, though, and she is here, no matter how heavy Ruth's brow. No matter how cutting her parents' greetings from the next room. Only Noreen charges toward her, purely happy to see her. She clutches Nonie's legs, and Nonie pretends to lose her balance. "Whoa!" she says, rocking to and fro as if the carpet turned to ocean under her feet. Noreen belly laughs and sticks out her arms, mimicking her, both of them fake surfing across the entryway and down the two steps into the den.

Under the tree, Luke rips plastic wrap from his Millennium Falcon box, and Mark spins brand-new lime green skateboard wheels to listen to the ball bearings whiz in his ear. From the farthest corner of the room, Henry pounds out a primitive "Rudolph the Red-Nosed Reindeer" on the piano.

"We had to let them get started," Brynne says with a nod toward the kids' mounds of mostly unwrapped gifts. She tends to sound constipated and like she blames you for the condition. "We saved the ones from you."

Used to things starting without her, Nonie swallows back the sting. She should've gotten here earlier. She'd set the alarm clock by her bed, but it hadn't woken her because she'd fallen asleep on the sofa instead after toasting the holiday with the real eggnog Doug brought for them to share. A family recipe his mother made and sealed into Mason jars for all four of her children. His family celebrated on Christmas Eve, and he got home near midnight. When he knocked, she could've told him she was busy, that she had to get up early, but there he was at her doorstep, her only real friend, and she could tell he was sad. He didn't have to explain all over again how his family tiptoes around him as if he were one of the landmines he still has nightmares about. She hugged him at her doorway, and they drank the whole jar and sang every holiday song they knew between them until neighbors started thwacking the walls and threatening to call police.

At least her angel ornament survived its post at the top of the tree after the tree-trimming gathering two weeks earlier, though now it's tucked behind a blown glass ball swirling with holiday colors. Hidden but not removed, which warms a spot inside her. Handmade in first grade from baked flour paste, its thumbprint of a head has been reglued to the flying angel body a dozen times by now. Its blue robes have bled to a watery turquoise, and the black-dot eyes have smeared.

The year Nonie made it, she brought it home from school the same day they planned to decorate their tree. Her father's hefting boxes of decorations from the basement reminded her, and she scampered to her bedroom to dig through the little blue-and-white satchel she carried her schoolbooks in to find the angel, then presented it to her family with a shy flourish. Her mother met eyes with her father and said, "How nice," with a hint of sarcasm Nonie didn't understand at the time, but in retrospect she recognizes that the tone carried the most tolerance her mother could muster after years of child-made crafts. So much younger than her sisters, Nonie extended the period that her mother's dream aesthetic must remain unattainable. A Christmas tree fit to grace the cover of *Better Homes and Gardens* would not be hers yet again that year, and for many years afterward. She was too young then to understand how a mother could yearn for a house free and clear of children's artifacts, so her mother's lack-luster reply and her father's corroborating laugh only reminded her that there was a code about how she was supposed to act, at school, at home, everywhere she went, and no one would help her crack it.

Now, when the grandchildren bring their annual holiday crafts from school, Grammy piles them in a bowl on a small table beside the front door. "A place of honor," she says as the chil-dren hand over their latest goods. For the most part, they accept her pronouncement and treat the bowl as something special, never suspecting their grandmother is simply shunting their gifts aside. Out of all the kids, Nonie imagines Noreen senses some-thing lesser in the arrangement and would benefit from some proof that children belong here, too, so she unhooks her angel gently and moves it a notch higher than the glass ornament.

"I made that one, Noreen," she says. "When I was younger than you are now. Long before you were my little angel instead."

Noreen tiptoes under the tree with her hands behind her

back, craning for a good look. Christmas lights seem to glint in her wild nest of blond hair, and the exhaustion and excitement of the day flush her cheeks red. "It's perfect," she says and gazes at Nonie with so much admiration Nonie stops feeling like a walking disaster. She belongs to the family again.

Treeside, Noreen brings Nonie up to date, cataloging each gift. The "Don't Get Mad, Get Even" iron-on T-shirt Mark picked out for her, the Easy Bake oven, *Black Beauty* from Grammy (because Grammy doesn't know she already read it), and a cabled pink cardigan Brynne knitted herself, probably too eager to have an excuse to make something for a girl-child to notice that Noreen doesn't wear girly clothes. She prefers plain shirts and printed T-shirts with jeans and corduroys. Primary colors. The only girly accessories Noreen gets excited about are hair ribbons and barrettes, which is why Nonie braided slim ribbons into rainbows of color onto hair clips for one of her Christmas gifts. She digs through the remaining packages under the tree until she finds it and hands it to Noreen.

The last of the presents swap back and forth. Socks and ties and winter scarves. Brynne presents a platter of homemade cinnamon rolls fresh from the oven and offers them around. Nonie watches their mother's eyes widen with appreciation. Delicious aroma drifts off the perfectly shaped rolls, drizzled with white sugar icing in deft zigzags. If Nonie had tried to make them, the dough wouldn't have risen, or she would've mistaken chili powder for cinnamon, or the icing would've been too thin and wet. Her failures would've made everyone laugh, and her efforts would've been wasted. That's the way family works for her. The code, still unbroken.

Morning merges slowly into afternoon. The children disperse to various parts of the house with new toys. Luke zooms his Millennium Falcon through every room. Noreen perches at the dining table, biting her lip as she and Ruth piece the new oven together. "Oh, we don't need more sweets!" Brynne says, scrubbing the cinnamon roll pan at the kitchen sink, visible across the countertop that divides the two rooms. Nonie's happy that Ruth ignores her, and she falls into place beside her and Noreen for a while, helping to measure thimble-sized amounts of flour and baking powder.

Before slipping back into the living room to pick her way through the careful pile Grammy made of her new things, Noreen carts a tiny cake pan from her oven and slides it onto a trivet for cooling. Without warning, the kitchen empties, but for Nonie and her mother. Nonie twitches a look to either side, unbelieving. The house seems too full for anyone to be left alone together, and she works hard especially to keep from being alone with her mother. So close, her mother's Shalimar is unmistakable. The scent would repel her altogether if Ruth hadn't chosen it as her own. Funny how people's associations of the exact same thing can be so different.

"You're looking well." The surprise in her mother's voice scrapes inside Nonie, suggesting she stumbled upon Nonie's wellness while searching for evidence of the opposite. "That doctor must be helping."

Roughly a dozen sessions in with Dr. Yang, Nonie's still getting used to her and to what she's learning there. That she's not, in fact, a falling-apart failure of a person, just someone with an illness. Panic disorder. Complicated by manic depression. That, like any illnesses, hers can be treated, and, eventually, if she's patient, her life can work like anyone else's.

Almost like.

Dr. Yang omits the *almost*, but Nonie hears it anyway. She hears it when Dr. Yang rips a prescription for her from one of her little white pads. Or when Nonie shakes a pill into her palm from one of the new bottles. Or when she wakes up with ears ringing after one of her new extra-vivid nightmares. She hears it now, too, in her mother's wearied effort at checking up on her.

"I'm not sure if she's helping," Nonie says.

Her mother turns toward the sink and rinses and slots dirty dishes into the dishwasher. With her back to Nonie, she says, "Percy was too stubborn for doctors."

She rarely speaks about Percy, so Nonie holds still to keep from disturbing her. Her mother's shoulders pitch backward like frozen birds' wings. It strikes Nonie how painful that must be, to hold so much inside that it turns your whole body rigid. She almost reaches her hand to her mother's back to gentle the muscles there, but her mother would flinch and ruin the moment.

"He wouldn't listen to them. I hope you will." She faces Nonie now, twisting the dishrag in her hand, lips so tight together they remind Nonie of a rubber band about to snap. Her mother's left eye twitches, and a perfect swoop of hair sags over her forehead.

"I'll do my best," Nonie says, though she's always done her best and it's hardly mattered. In every family photo, there's Nonie, in front, hair frizzed in all directions and her clothes ragtag and hippie, as her mother says, while her mother's hair takes the latest style. Her clothes, too. Her sisters the same. Despite what her mother says, Nonie does care what she looks like. She wears what appeals to her, what feels right—and it is right, until she catches sight of herself in a reflection with friends from her new job or in a family photo. Photos of just herself and Noreen are different. Side by side, their matching outrageous hair reminds Nonie more of seafoam than Medusa snakes. Their daydreamy faces seem curious and awestruck instead of aloof or distracted. Their laughter sounds like a celebration of seagulls, never like a horror movie sound effect. Why does it have to be so hard to be herself? To find a place where she fits?

"I wish you really would do your best." Her mother's voice, heavy with skepticism, as if Nonie never did her best at anything. As if her own brother never had either. As if with all her stiff muscles and tight-lipped remonstrances, her mother is the only one who has tried at all while everyone else has simply failed.

"Just because it's easy for you," Nonie says, her compassion for her mother curdling in her mouth, "doesn't mean it is for me."

"What's easy?"

"Life. Living. Doing the right things."

"I don't know what you're talking about." Her mother slaps the dishrag into the emptied sink and leans against the counter.

"That's because it's so easy, you don't realize you're doing it."

"Nonsense."

"It's not nonsense. Your brother wasn't stubborn, he was ill. Like I am." With as little as he's spoken of, maybe it's just a guess, but Nonie never risked comparing herself to Percy before.

"Then he should've listened to his doctors. I listen to doctors when I'm ill."

"What exactly did his doctors say to him? Do you even know?"

Her mother's face reddens, and her hands clap together in front of her, a kind of prayer made with a fist. "I'll tell you what they didn't say." Her voice wobbles and pitches louder. "They didn't say, 'Go drive your fancy little car off a bridge,' now did they?"

Again Nonie's heart twists toward her mother, her pain and anger wound too tightly together to allow either a chance to unravel. This time she follows her instinct to touch her mother and rests one hand on her wrist. Her mother draws away, joins her hands together at her waist.

"You don't have any idea what it's like to be me, Nonie. Nothing about my life is easy." She clears her throat, and her usual cool, level tone returns. "Nothing is easy, but I do what's expected. I make myself keep going. I don't let myself fall apart, like Percy did, like you do, for other people to come along and pick up the pieces and put you back together." She swings back toward the sink and scrubs at it with quick strokes of the rag. Her body a tight fist again.

"People don't fall apart, Grammy." Noreen's voice startles them both. How long has she been standing there? Her tiny cake out of its pan and in her hands, she shakes her head at them with a teasing expression, like she's used to teaching grownups how the world works.

"They better not."

By which her mother means, of course, that Nonie better not. That if she did fall apart, whatever that might mean, she'd be doing it on purpose, to spite her mother, and not because she needs things she can't understand and doesn't know how to ask for. Not because the medicine is better, but not perfect, and still leaves Nonie feeling like she's scrabbling across a sheet of ice a lot of the time. *It'll take time to get used to*, Dr. Yang tells her, and her voice is so full of confident kindness Nonie wants to believe. So she pours out the next pill, the next glass of water, and tries again.

Nonie's mother scissors briskly from the room, her slacks making a zipping sound in her wake. As sensitive to the moods of a room as Nonie is, Noreen tiptoes closer to offer a bite of her little cake. Crouching to her height, Nonie takes the first one, Noreen the next. Then Noreen lays her hand against Nonie's face, smoothing it along her jaw, her cheeks.

"What is it, Noreen?"

"Just like I thought," she says. "All in one piece." Her face wears the same expression as when she jokes around to cheer Nonie up, but she looks a little afraid, too.

"All in one piece," Nonie says and plops to a seat on the floor, tugging Noreen's hand so she settles into her lap, warm and nearly limp with tiredness. Her close presence does seem to patch Nonie's broken pieces together. She rocks backward against the kitchen cabinets and rests her chin on Noreen's head. They both close their eyes and rest that way for a little while.

Nineteen Years After.

MARCELLA'S PARENTS SPLURGED for a holiday Bahamas cruise for her and George's father, eliminating any visiting obligations on George's side, and Betty and Mark traded shifts and called in favors so they could spend a few days through Christmas Eve with Betty's family in Maryland, then Christmas plus two more days in Charlottesville, which brings all of them to crowd Ruth and Hugh's living room for a long, lazy morning around the Christmas tree. Adults palm steaming mugs of coffee and nibble corners of pumpkin bread Ruth made the day before while Evie plows wide-eyed through stacks of glittery gifts.

A week earlier, Noreen's mother had called when she found out Mark and Betty could join them after all. "They vacationed in Nantucket this summer with Betty's family, and your father joined them there for a few days. I think Mark feels guilty. He's very sensitive about keeping things even between me and your father."

By that metric, Noreen is entirely out of whack, because she keeps even with her father's afterthought efforts to be with her, rather than splicing her own availability down the middle, an availability already compromised by demanding in-laws. When Evie was born, her father sent flowers, a card, a package of onesies, and matching bibs. He's been a devoted special-occasion check-sender since, writes weekly emails, but he calls no more than once a month. She doesn't confide in him but keeps him apprised of big happenings, of Evie's milestones. Often when they're together, Noreen catches herself searching his face for similarities with her own or Evie's, finding none. Her brother's loyalty confounds her, how he contents himself with the fragment of relationship their father offers, immune from wishing for more. Then he sits here in their mother's house looking cozy and satisfied, too. As if he belongs everywhere. Noreen can't stop inserting herself between her brother and Evie, threatened somehow by his easy friendship with her, or else wishing for a piece of it for herself.

Evie doesn't notice, and for the first half of the morning, she's the star of show. Noreen helps her rip paper and ribbons, then displays each unwrapped present for the group to see. Rompers with ice-cream cones, with ballerinas, with dinosaurs. Stuffed bears and mermaid rag dolls. Books about dogs and gorillas and little girls. Last year the ribbons and glossy papers seemed to be the whole point of the day for Evie. This year she understands presents better, but brightly colored wrappings and empty boxes still delight her most. Sometimes she mistakes Noreen's gifts for her own and tears those open, too. Which is what happens with a slim jeweler's box. If Betty hadn't gasped at the sight of what was inside, Noreen would have missed it altogether. Across the room she catches George's eager eye, watching her as if she's a jack-in-the-box about to pop.

In a bed of black velvet lies a white gold chain with a peapod pendant, tinted green, and three pink pearls inside. "One for each of us," George says, eliciting Betty's appreciative, *Aww*, because, for Betty, the shiny necklace tells a story of an affectionate husband and doting father. For Noreen it's one more expense delaying that second car. One more reflection of George's father's equation of price tags with value. Veneer in place of meaning. She doesn't understand his family's language of objects. Gifts that seem aimed to buy something in return.

From across the room, she tries to read George's eyes. Does he mistake her for one of those prissy TV ad women who swoon for diamonds every holiday season? Or could he be trying to buy his way into that little pea pod? Rather than loving his way there?

Here, with her family, he wears perfectly pressed oxford shirts under handsome cashmere pullovers. A light, spicy cologne wafts off him. He wears freshly polished loafers and sits on the periphery of every group, flicking open the newspaper, light glinting off his gold watch. He's never comfortable or casual. If she didn't know him better, she'd use the word *calculated* to describe the image he projects of himself. Knowing him, though, she understands that *trained* is a more accurate word. He's been groomed to suit the world his father dominates, to earn worth with power, to prove affection with expensive gifts, very much to confuse veneer for meaning.

In his eyes she finds apprehension, though, rather than bombast, as if nothing between them is guaranteed, and she recognizes how much she must mean to him, how hard he must have been trying for months to regain ease between them, how he can't help but love in the language he knows. She recalls the press of his hand into hers when he pleaded to make New Year's Eve a night just for them.

Meanwhile, what has she done to meet him halfway?

A flash of Greta's smile in her mind's side-eye coincides with a stray ribbon from Evie's tossing hand swatting into her nose. Noreen's the one who cheated, who lost faith. At least he's trying. Even if he communicates differently from how she does, from how she wishes he would, she knows he loves her, and love is what matters. Isn't it? Translate this necklace into his best effort then. She lifts the box toward him and mouths a thank you, then watches relief flow through him and release the set of his shoulders. Evie grabs for the gift paper, ivy trailing across a silver background, and Noreen has to steady the box to keep it from spilling over.

Next, another gasp spins the room's attention toward Ruth. In her hands, a single tiny sock. She leaps across mounds of tissue paper and open boxes to throw her arms around Betty.

"We just started the second trimester," Betty says. "I didn't want to mention anything sooner." Betty sits on the floor in the V between Mark's knees, and he bends to kiss her head. No wonder they bartered for holiday time off.

In the quick hush before a general whoop rises up, and before Hugh wades through gift debris toward the kitchen to open a bottle of champagne originally meant for supper, Noreen peeks again at George for his reaction. What would make him look afraid?

Motion sets in around them again, and she gets it, or thinks she does, his fear of how this family will keep getting larger and his own family will keep moving on, his soon-to-be new stepmother outmoding him, while he slips into the background of both families, invisible as wallpaper.

Just stand up and join in, she wants to shout over to him. But that sideline feeling is too familiar. Isn't it, in fact, the similarity that draws them together? Their ability to exist just beyond the reach of belonging, on the outside of it looking in, unable to break through? The way she felt when she was small and her brother and cousins ruckused around her like agitated wasps, so if she ever actually drew their attention, she was afraid of it. Only with Nonie nearby, coaxing her closer, did she feel she mattered again, separate from the mayhem and part of something larger and lovelier. After Nonie was gone, there was no one left to make her feel that way. Who will make her feel it again if George can't? And who can make George feel it if she can't?

By the time her brother stoops onto the floor beside her, taking Evie's hands in his, singing a soft, silly version of "Twist and Shout," something has chilled inside her. Mark pumps Evie's little arms like pistons to the beat, and her laughter bubbles out of her while Noreen imagines future holidays with more and more children scampering around, chasing each other, whispering secrets, shouting—the grand kinetic machinery of family whirring and whirring—and it frightens her. If her whole little family splinters apart and spirals out of reach, who will put them back together? She bites her lower lip, tousles Evie's hair, and leaves her to dance with Mark while she seeks the perimeter, where George sits with perfect posture on a chair borrowed from the dining room. Behind him, she lays her hands on his tense shoulders and squeezes. Maybe this is as connected as she'll ever feel. Maybe you have to love through your losses and lonelinesses and trust that it will be enough.

George covers one of her hands with his, and she tries to let the warmth in it flow up her arm and into her heart. It's the three of them against the world. Didn't Nonie used to say something like that? *Without you here, I'd think this was someone else's family.*

❧

New Year's Eve, Noreen dices and minces and bakes, making George's favorites—roasted-herbed vegetables, pot roast, lemon pound cake from his grandmother's recipe. She sets the table with dishes she inherited from Nonie. She even sets Evie's place with one of the delicate plates, bordered with blush-colored roses.

Thanks to George, the stereo belts out Prince's "Party Like It's 1999" for the twenty-somethingth time. Noreen has to cut the volume when the phone rings.

"Happy almost New Year," her mother says and scoffs about the latest apocalyptic Y2K theories. "Superstition as far as I can tell. The idea that computers everywhere will shut down at the stroke of midnight, halting things like grocery store deliveries across the entire country? Absurd."

Noreen mumbles in agreement. She eyes the lineup of serving dishes and flicks on the oven light to peek at the roast and vegetables.

"Can you imagine it, Noreen? Thousands of eighteen-wheelers stranded on roadsides all over the country, food rotting in back, because they lost access to a computer manifest? Like suddenly no one has a brain anymore. Even if some of this Y2K ridiculousness does happen, people will figure out some way to carry on."

"At the store yesterday all the paper towels were gone," Noreen says. "I guess Y2K's supposed to cause catastrophic spilling, too."

"Exactly!" Ruth laughs. "It's definitely not what I pictured when I wondered about the year 2000 as a kid. I was thinking more like jet packs and world peace."

"Or time travel," Noreen says. "A colony on Mars." Though somewhere in the back of her mind, a wild horse stamps its feet.

"Maybe next millennium, right?"

Noreen straightens silverware on the table, readjusts the centerpiece she made from clippings from the yard, a display of pinecones edged with holly leaves and berries.

"The reason I called, Noreen." Ruth's voice shifts now from playful to careful. Her mother's most routine transition. "The newspaper fell back behind Hugh's lounge chair in the living room earlier, and when I went to pick it up tonight, I spied a shred of wrapping paper left over from Christmas." The paper was pretty, a pattern of ivy splayed across silver foil. Did Noreen remember?

She remembers the paper, though she'd forgotten the present entirely. That elegant white gold chain and the peapod pendant with three pink pearls nestled inside.

"When I pulled at the strip of paper," Ruth says, "a whole box slid out. If it hadn't been for that shiny paper, I doubt I would've seen it at all."

Noreen hopes George hasn't noticed its absence. Despite her mixed feelings about it, she hadn't meant to leave it behind and certainly hadn't meant to forget it altogether. She spent Christmas morning kneeling on the floor playing with empty boxes with Evie and the afternoon drinking herbal tea with Betty and answering her pregnancy questions. Betty's medical background made her questions especially specific and scatological. Anytime she started with, "Can I ask you something personal?" it usually meant, "Can I ask you something that involves your vagina and bodily fluids?" Her directness made them both laugh.

She forgot the present, along with her long-festering wish that George would tune his gift giving toward ritual and thoughtfulness over cost. Model his choices after the candy bars Nonie used to buy for a dime or a quarter, then hide in her giant, leather-fringed pocketbook. If Nonie walked through the door this second from the other side of time, she would be carrying that same fringy purse, and there would be a candy bar in it, just for Noreen. That's what a gift is supposed to be like. Perfect, even if it's the wrong flavor.

No matter, it would've been kinder if Noreen had remembered, if at least she'd brought the necklace home. "I'll have to pick that up next time I visit."

Her mother offered to mail it, then segued into a quick run-down of her evening plans with Hugh—a ten o'clock toast and early to bed; both are early risers—followed by requisite pleas for tidbits about Evie's day: Did she play outside at all? Does she still love that wooden scooter with the giraffe neck? Then goodbyes.

While Noreen cooks, George busies himself upstairs in their bedroom. She doesn't know what he's planning, but obviously, for him, the peak of the evening will have little to do with the meal she's preparing, which makes her nervous and curious at the same time. Since her beach trip back in October, George has initiated sex a couple of times, but Noreen invented peeps from Evie that she had to check on so she could climb into bed there instead. In the couple of weeks since they started planning their New Year's night, she's tried at least to flirt again. On the phone with Lizbeth a few days earlier, she'd mentioned that fact glibly, a veteran mom sharing notes with a rookie.

"Jesus, Nor, tell me this parenting gig's not *that* grim," Lizbeth had snorted into the phone. They might go months without chatting, but as soon as they're on the line together, it's like no time has passed. "I figured Diego and I had a decade or so before we'd need any prompting to hop into bed together."

"Kids are tiring," Noreen said. "They're worth every ounce of energy, but they wear you out."

"Sex revs you up. A perfect cure."

"Maybe it'll work that way for you." Noreen tried to sound wise and unbothered, but she had no fellow toddler moms to talk such things over with. Occasional Saturday play dates didn't lend themselves to real heart-to-hearts, with children in earshot and often tugging on mothers' sleeves or wielding dangerous objects they had to be parted from.

"Or maybe love shouldn't be so hard?"

She'd hoped her call with Lizbeth would make her feel more normal, less edgy, like it usually did, but this call left her with a tingle of dread.

Fussing over the meat, Noreen brushes off leftover fragments of that dread. Decides to believe lust and passion must have been building up between them all this time, like steam rising, seeking release.

❦

After dessert, and after Noreen carefully cleans and dries the fragile dishes, George points to the clock and motions his head toward Evie.

"She can go to bed any time now." He gives Noreen his meant-to-be-sexy but accidentally sad-child look.

Though she'd rather it wasn't true, part of her still wishes Lizbeth and Diego were here to celebrate with them after all, or that she could slip off to the extra bed in Evie's room like any other night. She's been more tired than usual with the demands of the holidays—shopping, wrapping, cooking, organizing. She'd thought staying home with Evie versus working outside the home would make for a more restful lifestyle, a break from the hectic pace of the typical working world. Matching energy and wits with a toddler, day in, day out, takes far more work than she'd guessed.

The eve of a new millennium feels symbolic though. A time to change your life or make a new one. Rekindling passion suits the moment. Noreen recalls her earliest times with George—the way her body seemed to swell with an ocean that always surged toward him. Early in their marriage, friction dissolved in sex, as if their bodies could synchronize like watches. Maybe no love stays as fresh as its first days, but Noreen wants to believe one night of especially good sex could break the tension between them, make them new again.

So she bathes Evie about half an hour early. Her purple ducky floats in the soapy water and Noreen sings her favorite songs— "Twinkle, Twinkle, Little Star" and the one about the rhododendron. In the background, George putters and pokes his head into the bathroom. "Just checking progress!" Now and again he tweaks Evie's nose or calls her his buttercup, more playful than usual, but Noreen can tell he's mostly courting her time and attention, and she likes that.

If she puts Evie to bed too early, she'll never fall asleep, and Noreen won't be sleeping in the room with her tonight, so she reads extra books, sings extra lullabies. George's anxious face at Evie's doorway begins to make her feel rushed. In a good way. She feels wanted.

Was that all that mattered at the beach? An at-home mom, peddling in successful missions to the potty and the finding of lost toys, forgets what sexy feels like. So each bed-readying step for Evie is also a step toward feeling desirable again, toward feeling desire for her husband.

As soon as she closes Evie's bedroom door, George meets her in the hallway and presents her with a slim, gift-wrapped box. "I know my Christmas present missed the mark," he says. "I meant for it to make you feel special." She feels caught between breaths. Here he is thinking he hasn't seen the necklace because she set it aside out of disdain. How much worse would he feel if he knew she'd forgotten about it altogether?

"This is a different kind of present," he says, "to make you feel a different kind of special. I hope this one hits its mark." He uses his made-for-Noreen voice, which means he isn't angry with her for missing his point with the necklace, just sad. And he's trying again. Maybe he wants the new millennium to be different as much as she does.

George slinks off to the upstairs hall bathroom, still fresh with the scent of Evie's baby shampoo, to change into whatever he's gotten himself for the occasion, and leaves Noreen the privacy of the master bedroom to change into what he brought her.

The negligee in the small box is stiff lace strung together in such a way that the bristly panels of fabric easily push aside to unveil flesh beneath it. She works her way out of her own clothes and pulls the scanty garment into place. George must have bought it thinking about the effect of seeing her in it. He probably only looked at it, didn't test its texture, so how would he know about its abrasiveness against her skin? If it's the thought that counts, how can she blame him for drawing this illusion of desire for them to play out together? Isn't that what she wants, too? Desire? At least she won't need to wear it for long.

A plate of chocolate-covered strawberries waits on her bedside table. Behind them, two bottles of champagne chill in an ice bucket next to the pair of champagne flutes they bought for themselves when they moved here. Expensive things. George things. But at least these are things she likes, too.

George swirls into the room, showing off his new silky blue bathrobe and pulls her against him so she can feel the sheen of it along her mostly bare skin. The same as those sheets he used to have. The ones she found twisted in the trash can behind their old apartment.

George folds back their bedspread to reveal a scattering of red rose petals, and the motion releases their mild perfume. She lets the scent flood out unpleasant memories and accepts a bubbling glass of champagne along with George's toast to his beautiful wife. He lets his eyes rove along every inch of her and turns her this way and that, beaming with pleasure, prolonging and prolonging the ultimate moment when, pulsing with her own urgency, Noreen finally pulls him on top of her, shoving the folds of his robe out of the way.

It's been so long since they've been intimate, even in conversation, they finish quickly. Noreen rolls over afterward, languorous and refreshed. (Lizbeth was so right that sex cured fatigue. How had she forgotten that?) And she is relieved, too, that she could muster such an appetite for him again. He hands her a refilled champagne glass. They toast each other one more time.

His eyes smolder for her over his glass. Have they always done that? She's glad his passion matters to her again. She sips more champagne, eats one of the strawberries. When she stands to change back into something more comfortable, though, George stops her. His bashful look returns.

"I was thinking of that as round one." What he wants—in fact, since his boyhood daydreams, what he's always wanted—is to climax at the stroke of midnight, the turn of the new millennium.

She laughs, thinking of cloud watching with Nonie so long ago and romping around the yard on her back like riding a horse. Some magic dream of a future full of adventure and fun, as different from her real life as from George's fantasy.

"I can see we had very different childhoods," she says. "I'll do my best, Romeo."

Huddled in their mutual post-sex heat, Noreen falls asleep right away. Lately, sleep has been more escape than rest. Tonight it feels luscious.

As the clock ticks toward midnight, George nudges her awake. "Hang in there, Noreen. Hang in there for me." It feels like part of a dream. "Please, Noreen," comes his softest voice. "You don't know how hard it's been, knowing you were down the hallway all those nights, out of reach. I've been lying here, alone and wanting you."

She fights to keep her eyelids open. Wanting her all that time and never once knocking on the door?

George's face is more boyish than ever, vulnerable and open. Those nights in Evie's room, she had rested peacefully, not wanting him at all. Her heart breaks for him at the disparity. She sits up, cradles his head on her chest. "Shh," she says. "It's all right."

His words come muffled now. "I try to be a good man."

"Hush now, George. You are a good man." With his head warm across her chest, it's easy to believe in all the things about him that are good.

At midnight, his features meld his own brand of repentance with desire, and she finds herself letting him start again. To make him feel better, to keep him from feeling ashamed of what he wants. He gives a fleeting look of humility, then pins her wrists and thrusts with hungry force.

The room around her swims in gray. She had done things with Greta she'd never tried before, but there had been no coaxing, no pleading, only gentle invitation. What is this love that comes from sorrow and regret? Setting aside what she wants, time and again. Has all that they ever shared come about this same way—the slow swerve of her own desires toward his?

George's motions are rough and wild as the grandfather clock in the downstairs hallway tolls the first stroke of midnight. Above her, he ogles where her negligee slides away, moans his gratitude and spreads his fingers across her breasts, thrusting harder, faster. Her mind flashes to that silk sheet night, years ago, when he'd lurched toward her, but tripping in his vomit kept him from— from doing what? Why hadn't she questioned that before? And at Thanksgiving, the way he practically throttled her awake. The bruise that lingered on her arm for a couple of weeks afterward. The way he made her feel guilty for being upset when he'd been so slow to answer the phone after she'd gone into labor. Even how he treats her arguments for access to a car like pleas for permission. So many moments she'd accepted unequal footing and given way to him. For what?

When she'd grabbed onto that boxcar ladder with Lizbeth and felt herself swooped into motion, the moon was so bright it almost hypnotized her, the ground flew past underneath her, and she felt like the world spun faster and faster. At the gas station that night, George seemed to walk out of a magic spell. Her life hurtling forward, forward, forward, and he would reel it back under control. Free her from all that speed and fear.

This is freedom?

The clock chimes on and on. George grunts above her, biting his lip, his eyes half-closed and upturned, away from her, and she feels her skin chafe and burn. The stroke of midnight matches his climax, exactly as he'd hoped. Finished, he rolls to his side, heaving with satisfaction, mumbling his pleasure.

A stir of leaves outside brushes the window closest to the bed. The breeze beats a rhythm against the house. Noreen peels away from George, slithers toward the edge of the mattress. His zeal left her seared and sore. He spoons against her, pulling her back into the arch of his body. His fingers softly clasp her breast.

So this is how Nonie felt. Lost to the world. A passenger riding in her own body.

"We did it." George's breath fogs her neck, and he kisses her there. "Aren't you glad it was just the two of us tonight?"

How much of this marriage could be measured in things she's left unsaid? This new year, this whole fucking millennium stretches in front of her. Is this what it will be like? A thousand more years of this?

*Days
Before.*

WHENEVER THE PACE is slow, Nonie sits at the El Mercado bar with a cigarette, keeping an eye on the door for customers who might wander in. Most other restaurants in town are closed on Mondays, but they're light days anyway. Nights are busier any day of the week, but today she's only working lunch. From her seat, she looks out beyond the glass restaurant door where heat wiggles up off the pedestrian mall. Four years ago, city planners herringboned that brick walkway out front, replacing Main Street with promises of urban revitalization, new business, throngs of people. Instead, most of the time wind blows hot dust down the promenade, and scraggly trees, harnessed to protective stakes, struggle toward the sky. Everything looks warped and lonely.

Nonie hardly recognizes her sister when she swings through the door, glancing side to side, surely looking for whomever she plans to meet because she couldn't know to look for Nonie. She finally admitted to her family that she got demoted from her development office job, relegated to touring spoiled high schoolers around grounds, but she never got around to telling them when she quit the university altogether.

Fake smiling while guiding prospective students around UVA hurt her jaws by the end of every workday, and spieling superlatives about a university she hadn't attended, and that clearly disliked her, left her feeling wrung out and stupid. She quit after one of the prospective students waited for everyone else to leave at the end of a tour and cornered her in a portico, jammed his hand up her skirt, then laughed while he strolled off into the sunshine like nothing had happened. After that, she didn't feel like she owed anyone an explanation, not her coworkers, not her family, so she hadn't bothered.

At least Marco welcomed her back to El Mercado with a big bear hug, saying, *I knew you'd come back, I knew you'd come back*, like pieces falling back together instead of falling apart.

Shifting back to waitress pay is the hardest part. That and how she can't keep track of things. Her thoughts sputter like so many gnats caught in her mind, and the sight of her sister in the doorway kicks her mother into her head. *Why is it so hard for you to grow up? Losing that good job your father got for you.* "Dad got me a contact. I got the job myself." *And lost it, too.* Her father. *Moving down the ladder instead of up.* "Do you want me to feel bad?" *I want you to work harder.*

Everything is hard. She presses her knuckles into her temples. In seconds Ruth will see her and spout with questions. *You seemed all right in college. Last week. Last month. Last time I saw you… Has something happened?*

Everything happens. Noreen fell from that swing, as if she'd fallen out of Nonie's arms or she'd thrown her onto the ground herself. And every day at the end of her shift, Marco finds her, rests his hand at the small of her back, claiming her, and everything is a cycle she can't get out of.

The door swoops open again, and Ted joins Ruth with a quick kiss. Nonie watches her sister tiptoe to meet his lips, the way she had with high school dates on the front porch, Nonie waiting up late and peeking through her bedroom curtains to see. Something about tiptoes, so hopeful and fond, swells inside her and squeezes aside stagnant debris for a moment—happiness for her sister, to have found such solid ground for her feet to land on, while the ground shifts ceaselessly under her own. Quakes or gives way like quicksand. Ever ready to swallow her.

She grinds her knuckles across her forehead, takes a long drag off her cigarette, then blows it out hard. Psssshhhhh. *Think of a tight, tight balloon deflating.* Dr. Yang.

Nonie smooths her work apron, grabs two menus, and marches over to seat Ted and Ruth, chatting over their surprise to see her here. Ruth blames a dentist appointment and an unexpectedly free afternoon for their decision to eat here, an impromptu lunch. Nonie wonders instead if someone ratted her out. A family friend or former high school chum whose table she'd waited on or passed by unwittingly. They'd never come here for a meal when she worked here before.

"It's temporary, let's not dwell," Nonie says in a playful falsetto that surprises her. Her thoughts have been monotone for days. More and more she sees herself as if from the opposite end of a long hallway, herself witnessing herself, moving herself around like a puppet, following steps she remembers about what's expected and proper, but feeling attached to nothing.

Mexican guitar music plays on the restaurant stereo, a piece-of-crap machine with small speakers Marco strung over the bar. Quick strumming music filters in and out of earshot, competing with plates clanking in the kitchen, feet scraping the floor, the sunshine, the very bright sunshine Nonie has to squint against, her eyes and ears both, the light is so bright and loud.

Tortilla chips and guacamole. Burritos and iced tea. Ruth orders a coffee, then curls her nose at it when she thinks Nonie isn't watching. Leaves it to cool in her mug. Nonie pulls the puppet string to smile when she pages a bill onto their table, lifts away dirty dishes, but Ruth stops her, a cold hand to her wrist, threatening to topple plate and mug together. Nonie lets go of the dishes. "What is it?"

"What can we do?" Ruth says. Her eyes glue onto Nonie's features, probe her eyes. Ruth, too earnest for this world.

"What do you think needs doing?" Nonie's voice is petulant but weak, scaling, as it has to, the height of her throat and a lifetime's backlog of things left unsaid.

"I could cut your hair for you? Wash it out in your sink?"

Nonie jerks her hand away. "You think I'm *dirty*?"

"I think you need caring." Ruth keeps her hand exactly where Nonie left it, palm up, open.

Outside, a homeless man settles onto a bench. Nonie has seen him every day since she returned, has watched a local police officer reason him off the bench, scoot him down the street and away, day after day. A different officer each time, thinking he's solved a problem rather than agitated a resting man. The man's patience astounds her. His unsmiling cooperation when he agrees to leave, his sense of belonging each time he comes back. His bench. His view of the naked avenue, the stretch of sky above. She wishes she felt that connected to anything.

She shouldn't be surprised when Ruth knocks on her apartment door the next afternoon, Ted lingering at the doorway beside her as if he's come by accident rather than on his wife's insistence, her hand clutching his elbow as if he might yet run away. Ted doesn't want to know other people's business, finds Ruth's deep investments in people as charming as it is bothersome. Nonie knows this from how he sits deeper into a chair whenever Ruth lists worries about Noreen: She reads too much, she's too withdrawn, her one friend is too controlling. His replies run the gamut from cajoling—*They're just kids being kids*—to warning—*Let's not start this again*—though even then his tone remains gentle, his temper cool, and he smiles his usual bland, agreeable smile. The one he spreads across his face as he steps over Nonie's threshold now.

Once inside, Ruth covers her nose with a slant of her hand and dashes to the kitchen window, trying to jiggle it open. Underneath, dishes cluster in leaning piles in the sink, spilling over onto the surrounding counter. Pots clutter the stovetop. Nonie hadn't noticed a smell until her sister's reaction. Now she follows after her, each step like slogging through mud, and unlocks and slides open the one kitchen window that isn't painted shut.

"Ted, why don't you look through the papers there on the kitchen table?" Ruth says, and he unburies the only chair from layers of junk mail coupon fliers, quick to parse from the useless pages any actual mail.

"That's a nice breeze now, isn't it?" Ruth says. Sweat beads across her lip. Nonie has no air conditioning, and it's a hot August afternoon. The air in the room hangs moist, dank. "How about we open a few more?" Ruth meets Nonie's eyes as she crosses the apartment to the trio of windows in her living room. Towels tacked to woodwork for curtains. Ruth untacks them. Grunts at the windows until they give way. "Here's a fan," she says, finding one leaning against the wall behind Nonie's sagging old sofa, unplugged, forgotten. "Help me out?" She boosts the fan onto the sill and waits while Nonie closes the window onto it, cinching it in place. At Ruth's gesture, Nonie plugs it in. Ruth clicks it on, and the fan rattles to life. The sound of a small airplane fills the room. Wet air sifts around. The newly made stacks of bills flutter. Ted hides a smirk with his bland smile, readjusts piles so the conjured winds don't disperse them.

"We'll just get cleaning in this kitchen then." Ruth narrates each step, and Nonie follows behind her, arms dangling dumbly at her sides. First, Ruth empties the dirty piles from the drying rack, then bleaches the rack itself. "You must have a basin somewhere?" She digs in the cupboard below the sink. Flinches when two surprised cockroaches skitter across the floor. Then she roots around behind cleansers and crusty tins of Drano until she finds what she needs.

Soon enough the scent of cheap dish soap eats away the sour-milkiness of the place. Ted draws a calculator from his shirt pocket, a pencil from Ruth's purse, tallies overdue bill amounts in the margins of grocery store advertising circulars. Ruth scrubs plates, pots, pans. Nonie dries. Not thinking. Only keeping up the rhythm.

Ted's voice competes with the fan's throttle while Nonie pictures herself, Ruth, and even Brynne squaring off with a fan in the front window of their parents' house, countless years ago, saying "Ahhhh" and letting the blades chop sound into bits. It takes Ted a few tries to get her to hear his words. "Late notices." "Overdue rent." "Overdraft charges."

"Here's what to do," he says. Even the way he sits is practical. Shoulders braced, leaning forward from the edge of the chair that's too small for his large frame. He's the only one not sweating. "Explain that you're reorganizing your finances after a job change. Ask to pay a little extra for a couple months, rather than square up all at once."

"A little extra for a couple months," Nonie echoes. She holds her hand out in front of her, testing if she can still see it. She feels like a hologram, fading in and out of view.

Ted holds up an overdue rent notice and taps it with his pencil. "Start with this one. Call that number there. First thing Monday."

"First thing Monday."

"Nonie?" Ruth says.

It feels like a century passes in the time it takes to turn her head toward her sister.

"Are you okay?" Ruth's words smear like paint on glass. Nonie slides to the floor. Her knees thunk into the hard wood. Her sister's feet rush out of view. The water faucet in the kitchen, turning on, turning off. Ted easing her to sitting, replacing him in the chair. Ruth wrapping Nonie's fingers around a cool glass of water.

"It's so hot in here, Nonie. I think you're dehydrated. Drink this, and let's get you in front of that fan. Do you think we can do that?" Ruth says. "Ted, please. Let's just pack her up and bring her to our house. Get her back on her feet."

Nonie says, "Ahhhhh," into the blades, and all she hears is,

"Ah-ahh-ahh-ahh-ahh," until Ruth and Ted swarm into view.

"We have an idea for you, Nonie," Ruth says. Something about moving into the empty room in her parents' basement. That way Nonie could come and go through the back door. Mother and Dad wouldn't have to know where she was all the time, but she could catch up on her debts. Get a new start.

"A new start." The phrase smells like springtime. "A new start sounds good." Her voice high and thin. A helium balloon escaping into the sky. "So what do I need?"

"You mean right now? But I bet you can work out timing with your landlord, isn't that right, Ted? You don't have to leave this minute."

Nonie skims over to the kitchen counter, groping the countertop for her keys. "I can't stay here just waiting to go."

"You'll have to talk to Mother and Dad though. Set things up with them."

The look on Ruth's face. Nonie must be doing something wrong. She's always doing things wrong. She pockets her keys. Swipes hair from her eyes. Tightens the elastic holding her ponytail in place. Her hair is sore where it meets her head, the ponytail days old by now. She straightens her T-shirt. "What is it? What did I do? Do I look funny?"

"No, love," Ruth says. She calls Noreen "love." "No, you look fine. Why don't you pack a few things, then, an overnight bag? I could call over there for you while you take a shower?"

See how she did that. Snuck in about a shower. "Phone's cut off."

Ruth nods. Face like a baby doll's. Ideas blanked out of it.

"What do I need right now?" Nonie says.

"How about a hairbrush? A toothbrush?" Ruth flits glances between her and Ted, silently signaling things Nonie can't decode. A hairbrush and a toothbrush. That much she understands.

"I'll throw together a wash and bring you some clothes later. How about that?"

Clothes are everywhere, dropped from hangers onto her closet floor, strewn across her bed, hanging off the back of the sofa. She hadn't bothered to notice before. Like a laundry basket exploded. *Poof.* Nonie makes the noise, a soft burst between her lips, and Ruth and Ted's faces crimp. Nonie smiles, pats Ruth's shoulder. "There, there." And as she walks toward her bathroom for the hairbrush and toothbrush, *poof* again, and a dry, quiet laugh.

Ted snugs Ruth under his arm when Nonie comes out again, as if protecting her or holding her back from something. Hairbrush and toothbrush, one in each hand, and her car keys dangling from one pinky.

Ruth opens the door for her. "I could take you over there?"

Nonie lifts the toothbrush hand, jingles her keys. "I got it." Then she puts one foot in front of the other, in front of the other, down the hallway. A window at the opposite end lets in a blaze of sun that sparkles in swirling dust particles.

At the staircase, Nonie hears Ruth quietly close her door. Thrumming down the steps toward her is Doug from upstairs.

"I was just coming to check on you," he says.

He looks sad, so Nonie puppets herself to lean into him, wrap her arms around him the way she knows she would want to if she were more herself. The hairbrush and toothbrush meet each other at the nape of his neck. He smells of hamburgers and onions from his job at the diner off the Route 250 bypass. She holds him tight, and he braces his arm across her back.

"What is it, Nonie? What's happening?"

"A new start." She rests back onto her own feet again.

"What kind of new start?"

"A new start at my old house." She holds up the hairbrush and toothbrush, as if they could explain anything.

Doug stands almost a foot taller than Nonie, and he straightens to his full height, casting a doubtful look down at her. "You leaving me?"

"Not you. Just leaving."

"You'll come back and see me?"

She tiptoes, like Ruth, and plants a kiss on his cheek. The rest of the steps drum under her feet. The heavy front door at the bottom of the hot stairwell spills her out into hotter air. The blacktop of the city street sucks the sun's heat and sends it back up again. The sun burns the sky colorless.

At a stoplight, Nonie's eyes roam to the seat next to her where her toothbrush and hairbrush lay side by side in the cracked black vinyl seat. *Poof.* The sound puffs from between her lips yet again, plus the same dry laugh, but no joy to go along with it. For days, she hasn't felt anything.

Dr. Yang would ask about her medicines. She'd warned Nonie that if she ever wanted to stop taking them, not to do it alone, that she should let her help. The same way guys she dropped acid and shroomed with in college used to talk—how they wanted to show her the way, like they were giving her something good. But she'd never liked how those things made her feel, as if thousands of tiny pins were darting about inside her brain or under her skin. As if the ceiling were swirling into the walls, walls into ceiling, wind tasting like candy, trees coming alive.

She doesn't like Dr. Yang's medicine any better. It made her tired and nauseous and dizzy. It made her dreams too loud and busy, and she'd wake up not knowing where she was. Dr. Yang would've said something about changing the dosage and maybe trying something new, but Nonie skipped her last five appointments, so she hasn't said anything at all.

Nonie's decrepit black Peugeot traps the heat, and its stiff, old windows require too much strength to unroll all the way. She doesn't want to bother. She doesn't want to do anything but let herself sink into the seat beneath her, but she follows the roads and makes all the right turns until she's sitting in front of her parents' house.

Both their cars are in the driveway. She sits, listening to the ticking of her engine cooling. The inside of the car gets hotter and hotter, the air thicker and thicker. Nonie doesn't want to get out and walk up the sidewalk to the front porch. She doesn't want to knock on their door and ask to come in. She looks at the toothbrush and hairbrush again. Back at the apartment, Ruth was wearing her careful face. Nonie doesn't like being a burden, doesn't like knowing she's a burden.

If she lets herself get much hotter, her face will turn as pink as a playground ball. Her parents will assume heat stroke before she gets the chance to explain herself. She doesn't want to explain. Doesn't want any of this to happen, but now that it is happening, she wants it to go fast. So she clasps the toothbrush and hairbrush in one hand and scoops herself out of the car.

Nonie knocks on the door for a long time. Then she goes around to the back of the house. Her father is watering tomato plants while her mother kneels in the flower garden, pinching and twisting weeds from the ground beneath waving heads of sunflowers. Nonie plops into a patio lawn chair that squawks under her weight, and both her parents turn to look in her direction.

"Nonie?" Her mother stands and brushes earth from her gardening gloves.

It wouldn't hurt right now to be wanted. The whole series of actions that got her this far fogs in her memory. She remembers tidying herself and asking Ruth if she looked okay. The way she kept trading looks with Ted. Something she said about their parents' house, and now she's here. She made it. In her hands she still holds the hairbrush and toothbrush. She'll need those. She did something right.

"Everything is too much," Nonie says.

"Prices, you mean? Groceries?" her dad says. "You need some money?" The hose drizzles to a stop. "We have money." He pats his pockets, lands on his wallet.

"I thought I'd stay here for a while." She squeezes both hands against her head, which means she's pressing the toothbrush and hairbrush into the sides of her head, too. She tries to squeeze tightly enough to slow the rapid movements inside, to make it feel less like she's holding a tiny ocean in there.

Nonie's mother eyes the toothbrush and hairbrush. "What? Did you lose another job? Why would you want to stay here?"

"For a few days?" her father asks. "A few weeks? What about your apartment?"

"I don't know. For a long time? I need to save up for a new start," Nonie says. That was what Ruth had said. It had been Nonie's favorite part.

"What does that doctor of yours say about this?" Her mother pulls her gardening gloves from her hands one finger at a time. "Does she think it would be a good idea for you to stay here instead of on your own?"

Nonie presses her head more tightly. "I don't know, Mother. I don't know what the doctor says."

"Well, I'd really like to know because I think it can be dangerous for grown women to move back in with their parents."

"I'll be quiet, Mother. I'll stay out of your way. In that room down in the basement. You won't know I'm here. I promise. I just need to rest. My head is killing me. Please can I stay?"

Surprise and suspense hover in the air between her parents. Nonie squeezes her head yet tighter, squints her eyes closed.

"The basement," her mother says. "Okay."

"Everything is too much," Nonie says again. The sunshine is too much. It hurts Nonie's eyes. The heat is too much. But she's also cold. "I need to go inside."

"Go on then." Her mother points at the door, her soiled gloves wagging in the air. "Go inside. Do what you want with that room in the basement. But hear this: This is temporary. You need a plan. For something better."

Nonie drags open their screen door. It makes a whole different sound from Mrs. Mackey's. It doesn't remind her of anything. She almost doesn't hear her mother saying, "Did you hear me,

Noreen Faith? Did you hear what I said?"

Inside, Nonie isn't sure if she said yes or if she answered at all. What she wants is to lie down. The basement is cool and dank. The room she'll be staying in has a forsaken one-wheeled bicycle in it, a mattress leaning up against one wall, and a few cardboard boxes filled with odds and ends, a broken record player, decks of cards, board games, books.

Nonie drags the boxes across the lime green shag carpet and into the open space that separates her new room from the stairway. The floor here is concrete with a drain near the base of the stairs. Beyond the stairs are the washer and dryer and a laundry sink. Above is a messy network of cobwebs, rafters, and exposed pipes. Bright orange coils of extension cord hang from a nail in one of the beams. When she ducks under them to walk by, her head bumps into them, and they sway like nooses.

She lugs the boxes out to the ranks of steel shelves, brimming with other items her parents never threw out—hidden evidence of the three children who grew up here. Jutting out among piles of forgotten things is the red wagon they had all pulled around the neighborhood, rusty around the edges. Then there are wooden sleds with red metal runners, most of the paint peeling down to a dull bullet gray. Under the lid of a beat-up cardboard box, Nonie finds a purple velvet bedspread that belonged to her in high school.

Back in her new, windowless room, Nonie tips the mattress from the wall and onto the floor, spreads the velvet blanket, and sinks across it. Then she does what she has wanted to do all day. Maybe longer. She closes her eyes and doesn't think of anything.

Five Months After.

IT'S A BLEARY WINTER day, but not as cold as her mother must have guessed when she shrugged Noreen into her bulky winter coat before school this morning. The walk home from the bus stop feels extra long because she's so hot, but it's easier to wear the coat than carry it along with her book bag and lunchbox and the folder of graded papers her mother has to sign.

Noreen skips up the three brick steps to their porch and creaks the front door open, eager to yank off her coat and hang it on the rack. A hush seems to breathe out of the house at her. Her mother usually at least calls out a hello.

Mark is at basketball practice, her father still at work. Everything is quiet except for a soft noise from the den. Her mother never watches TV during the day, but that's where Noreen finds her, staring at the screen in amazement, shoulders sloped forward, tears streaming unchecked down her face. When she turns to see Noreen at the door, she gives a weak smile and pats the sofa beside her. "Come here, Noreen. You've got to see this."

The sight of her mother, overpowered and sloppy, reminds Noreen of the promise she made that day in the grocery store. Maybe today is the day she'll break it.

"They made it home." Ruth forces her spine straight, wipes tears from her eyes. "The hostages." She pats the space beside her again. "Come see."

At school Miss Simpkins already announced how the hostages were free. That was days ago. On TV, the newsman's voice sounds different from usual, excited instead of businessy. Next, there's film of people getting off an airplane. Everybody wears overcoats like the one Noreen's father wears to work. It's a crowd of dull colors and people's backs.

"They're safe," Ruth says. "They've been free for a few days, with doctors checking them out and things like that, but now they're more than free. They're home." She grips Noreen's wrist for emphasis, eases her closer to the sofa.

"Then why are you crying?"

"It's really big news," Ruth says. "I'm happy. The whole country is happy."

Noreen drops into the seat beside her mother, feels the warmth of being next to her. "You don't look happy."

"Sometimes joy looks a lot like sadness," Ruth says, but Noreen doesn't think it does. Her mother tucks Noreen's tag back into her shirt, then motions for her to wait. Her footsteps hurry up the stairs, then silence, then her feet clomp back down. At the sofa again, Ruth lays a notebook in her lap. "Do you know what this is?"

Noreen hates obvious questions. "A notebook."

"I keep a diary in it," Ruth says. "You know, like the one Aunt Brynne got you for Christmas, with the lock on it."

"I know what a diary is." The one Brynne gave her had a goofy Pink Panther across the front of it. Like Noreen wouldn't be turning nine in a few months. Like they hadn't danced together in the sunroom before everyone found out about Nonie. Like Brynne didn't know her at all. She crammed that Pink Panther diary under her bed Christmas night with an old Nerf football she stole from Mark one time when she was mad.

"This is a special kind of diary." Ruth rubs her palm across the cover. "For me, anyway. I write letters to Nonie in it."

"You do what?" Every time Noreen thinks this will be the day she doesn't hurt from missing Nonie so much, something happens to flare the pain. A breeze with the scent of her shampoo on it. Someone in a crowd with hair like hers coming into view, but always eventually not being her. A dream so vivid she wakes up forgetting Nonie's gone.

"I write letters to my sister because I miss her. Sometimes it feels like she's just very far away. Like if I mailed these, she might even get to read them. Do you know what I mean?"

Noreen nods. She always feels like Nonie is about to walk through the door with today's surprise candy bar nestled in her big purse. It hurts to think and talk about her. The way it hurts to pull off a scab but feels better after. No matter that people in her family, like Grammy and Grampy or Brynne, try to change the subject or tell her to think of something else anytime Nonie comes up. If her mother wants to talk about Nonie, Noreen will let her take as long as she likes.

"Those hostages, they were really far away. Iran is thousands of miles from here. Halfway around the world," Ruth says. "I've never been that far from home." A toilet paper commercial jingle sings in the background. Ruth twists a strand of Noreen's frizzy hair away from her eyes, and the curl holds its shape. "I bet some of their families kept notebooks like this, with letters they couldn't send. Saying all sorts of things that needed to be said."

Yet another image of the plane and the crowd around it fills the TV screen. A few people walk down the steps out of the plane, waving. Ruth gestures toward the image. "I don't mean to do it"—she lets out a slow breath—"but I keep thinking that if I look hard enough, I'll see Nonie. She'll hobble down those stairs in her platform espadrilles, home safe, with all the rest." She laughs a little, and her eyes blur with more tears. Noreen pats her knee, but Ruth clasps her hand, stops her. "We're going to be okay, you and I, even when things get difficult. We'll always come home safe, okay?"

Noreen can't tell if her mother wants an answer or not, but she's so serious. Obviously she expects something.

The new president's face flashes onto the screen. He looks

like a giant marionette puppet, with hair sculpted from wood and red dots for cheeks. Ruth grasps Noreen's hand so tightly her fingers crush together.

"Promise me," her mother says, "that even if things get scary and awful, you'll remember you're strong enough to make the next day better. Can you promise me that?"

Was that what happened to Nonie, then? She forgot she was strong enough? What Noreen overhears about her aunt's death confuses her. Something about an electric cord, a rafter in her grandparents' basement. A certain sound of wind, any rhythmic swing, sends icy splinters through her whole body. It had to be bigger than forgetting. Bigger than anything promises could fix.

"Promise me," Ruth says again.

The tips of Noreen's fingers are turning red. If she promises, her mother will let go. "Okay. I promise I'll remember."

A reporter on TV says the number *444*, the word *captivity*. He talks about the doctors who examined the hostages.

"Can we watch something else now?"

Her mother laughs. "This is all that's on." She points to yet another clip of the hostages walking down the steps from the plane. "It's on every channel."

First Moments.

THE TREE AGAINST the window beats a familiar rhythm. Like cord against pipe. Noreen lies brick still beside her husband. Pain flares between her legs. All the pain in her life traces back to ways people didn't mean to hurt her.

What if he did mean to hurt you though?

That swinging sound. It feels like it's just outside the window or in the hallway beyond the bedroom door. Heavy and dull.

Nothing is left for us here.

That scraping outside, or down the hall, pulls at her. She holds her breath and slides out from under her husband's enclosing arm. He snorts once in his sleep, rolls over to face the opposite wall. Noreen tiptoes toward the window, hot pain spreading, and eases back the curtain. Thick darkness hugs the house. Stars are icy pinpoints in the sky. You can see the cold in the air. The scraping noise is so close. Noreen wants to think Nonie's out there with the noise, holding out a hand for her.

I can take you away from all this.

Pooled on the floor on her side of the bed are the clothes she was wearing before George gave her the negligee that now scratches against her flesh. Hardly enough fabric to make a napkin. Not even pretty. She sheds it and steps back into her jeans, sweater, and fuzzy socks, then slips out of the room and closes the door behind her soundlessly. She can't hear the scraping anymore, but she feels Nonie's nearness all the same, her breath at her neck.

Evie's nightlight glows a cool blue in the corner of her room. She still looks so tiny in her big girl bed. Her body a lump at the top of it. Noreen leans toward her cherub cheek. The perfect spot for kisses, she always tells Evie, and she kisses her there now.

Ever since Nonie died, Noreen has been afraid the same black hole that sucked her aunt away would come for her one day, too, send her skidding down its spiral into a world beyond escaping. Here in the middle of the night at the dawn of a new era, she feels its full force.

Queasy, she swirls Evie's princess toothpaste in her mouth to gargle out the flavor of her husband. In the mirror, dark circles shadow her eyes, her face looks haggard and spent. Other times she's seen her aunt looking back from her own reflection, but this time she sees there's been no difference between them all along. Was it drawn on her cells from the start to mistrust the world? To choose the wrong people? To shut herself down from what opened her up? For fear that opening up was the problem.

Is it? If she opens herself up, will she fulfill the enduring prophecy of other people's worries and follow Nonie?

But she's not Nonie.

I never wanted you to be another me.

Noreen bends to splash cold water on her face and instead feels warm summer earth beneath her, a bristle of Nonie's arm hair beside her.

What do you think you'll be doing in the year 2000?

On the floor in a pile are George's clothes from the day and the empty plastic wrapping from his new robe. She reaches toward his pants, lifts them, hears the muted jangle of keys, and a thrill bubbles through her. Until now, she hadn't fully realized how strictly he controls these keys, how each time she uses their car she has to ask for them, having to bargain to use it at all unless she's buying groceries or getting it serviced. Now she clutches them cold in her hand. A blizzard of thoughts whirls in her mind, gathers strength, leads her toward exactly what she wants. A millennium-worthy resolution.

She rushes back into Evie's room and switches on the lamp beside her bed. Evie moans and rubs tiny fists into her eyes. "Momma? Is it morning time?"

Noreen puts a finger to her lips. Then she winks and drags the pillowcase free, jams some of Evie's outfits inside, adds Esmé the elephant and her blue bunny and a few other stuffed toys from the mounds surrounding the bed. Then she shimmies a heavy sweatshirt over Evie's pajamas, snugs her feet into her ladybug slippers, and coaxes her out of bed.

"Shh." She pantomimes a horse's trot and gestures for Evie to follow her. Evie loves to play games and picks up on rules quickly. They tiptoe-trot down the hallway, lit only from the bathroom's open door and Evie's bedside lamp. They giggle, covering their mouths to muffle the sound.

Halfway down the stairway, Noreen feels George's presence at the top of the steps behind them. "Baby?" he calls after her, her least favorite endearment. Does he notice the makeshift pillowcase sack? He can't know she has the car keys because she clenches them inside her fist, out of sight and silenced. Does he think she's taking Evie on a once-in-a-lifetime New Year's adventure? Maybe he imagines them lolloping around in the dark, lying back in the cold grass to watch for shooting stars. The making of what could become Evie's first childhood memory, the very first thing she did in the year 2000.

Let him think so.

At the bottom of the steps, Noreen helps Evie into her winter coat. She keeps giggling and telling her daddy to shhh. Noreen makes goofy faces and hushes him too. George seems content to play along, untroubled, as he watches them clamber out the front door. Noreen closes it behind her and stands in the dark, breathing in the cold, fresh air of the new year, keys still clasped in her fist.

A burst of energy surges up in her as she buckles Evie into

her car seat, flicking looks back at the house, hoping George won't step outside after them to see what she's doing.

How did it take her this long to realize that the things that make you feel alive aren't the ones that kill you?

Her hands tremble, and it takes three tries to thread Evie's buckle correctly. Then she hops in front and slowly, slowly backs the car down their gravel drive. She keeps the lights off until half a mile down the The Road Out of Here, where she knows George can't see them anymore.

Five miles down, the headlights finally flash against mica chips embedded in the paved road. Behind them, only a splash of red from her taillights. Nothing else but darkness.

Acknowledgments

ENORMOUS THANKS TO Flexible Press for believing in *Without You Here* and for their mission to connect literature with social improvement. This book was inspired in part by a friend who delayed leaving an abusive marriage for fear that her mental health history would cost her the custody of her children in a divorce. Despite advancements in treating and understanding mental illness, stigma persists and adds agonies of its own. Rendering the characters in this book with depth, complexity, and fullness was crucial to me. Any shortcomings in that endeavor are my own. In the end, love was the most defining influence that shaped Nonie and Noreen's relationship, which is what I hope readers take away from their story.

I would like to acknowledge the generosity of specialists and friends who rounded out my research about panic disorder, mental health emergencies, broken arms, and more. Specifically, I would like to thank anxiety treatment specialist Dr. Rafael Triana, PhD, LCSW, psychoanalyst, assistant professor of psychiatric and neurobehavioral sciences, University of Virginia; Dr. Devon Lowdon; Dee and Mattie Weikle; and Mary Beck. Some of the resources I consulted include *Panic Diaries*, Jackie Orr, 2006; *Monkey Mind*, Daniel Smith, 2012; *My Age of Anxiety: Fear, Hope, Dread and the Search for Peace of Mind*, Scott Stossel, 2014; and hosts of YouTube videos, personal vlogs, and Australian government-sponsored documentaries on anxiety and panic disorders.

Many thanks to early readers, some of whom read more than one version as I wrote my way toward a structure that could hold the story: Priscilla Cutler Bourgoine, Ellen Prentiss Campbell, Amani Elkassabany, Kim Fitzhugh, Susan Guerrant, Teresa Burns Gunther, Cindy House, Carolyn McGrath, Betty Joyce

Nash, Margaretta Noonan, Carter Sickels, Hurley Winkler, and my family (so many drafts, dear family). Bonus thanks to Priscilla Cutler Bourgoine for her expertise in helping to compose a companion Q&A for book clubs, with an eye toward serving readers who might be treating or experiencing some of the mental health crossroads this novel explores. A special shout-out to Clara and Jillian Hesler for their work producing the spreadsheet and sample timeline. Thanks also to Jane Alison for her craft book *Spiral, Meander, Explode* that celebrates unique plot shapes.

Special thanks also to the Virginia Center for the Creative Arts, Ragdale Foundation, Vermont Studio Center, the Writers' Colony at Dairy Hollow, and their communities, for time, space, fellowship, and nurture during different stages of this work, and to the support and community of Bread Loaf and Sewanee Writers' Conferences, Charlottesville Women Writers, Juniper Summer Writing Institute, all the good folks at the *Los Angeles Review*, Mosely Writers, WriterHouse, and the Writer's Hotel. And affectionate thanks to my booster club of other writers and artists, especially my Armadill-hers (Sue Baller-Shepard, Teresa Burns Gunther, and Charmaine Wilkerson); Derek Furr, who read the original short story ("Little Angel") eons ago, saying, "I want more of this story..."; Shelly Cato; Sharon Harrigan; Jocelyn Johnson; Ayesu Lartey; Louise Marburg; Celeste Mohammed; Pam Petro; Eric Sasson; and another shout-out to Priscilla. And to cherished friends Karen Adametz, Rebecca Beers Cook, Elizabeth Clark, Nagini Paravastu Dalal, Steve and Luisa Dowd, Kathryn Easton, Hugh Geiger, Yana Goddard, Jennifer and Mary Jane Lee, Anne Lindberg, Lindsay Lowdon, Maggie Bassen McGary, Tina Panella, Pascale Perrot, and Stacy Warner Price.

For my mother, who's been with me from the first story, and deep love and gratitude to CJ Grooms, my child from another mother, and to Clara and Jillian Hesler, for their unflagging faith in me and my work. For Jeffrey, with love and thanks for all the things, always and forever.

About the Author

JODY HOBBS HESLER lives, writes, and teaches in the foothills of the Blue Ridge Mountains. She is the author of the story collection *What Makes You Think You're Supposed to Feel Better* from Cornerstone Press, and her words also appear in *Necessary Fiction*, *Gargoyle*, *Valparaiso Fiction Review*, *Atticus Review*, *Writer's Digest*, *Electric Literature*, CRAFT, *Arts & Letters*, and many other journals. She teaches at WriterHouse in Charlottesville, Virginia; writes and copy edits for *Virginia Wine & Country Life* and *Charlottesville Family Magazine*; and serves as assistant fiction editor for the *Los Angeles Review*.

Book Club Q&A

1. Nonie and Noreen both struggle with their mental health. Has mental illness—yours, a family member's, a friend's, or otherwise—impacted your life? Was there a character or relationship in the book that spoke directly to your experience?

2. Martha, the family matriarch, has suffered unfathomable losses in her lifetime. How does that shape how she parents (and grandparents)? And how does that shape your impression of her cruelty?

3. What impact did Martha's long deceased brother, Percy, have on the rest of the story? Do you feel compassion toward Martha? If not, why not?

4. Relationships with Nonie require hard work. Which characters show acceptance and welcome? Which respond by excluding or avoiding? Have you been on the receiving end of these kinds of connection and disconnection? If so, how do they feel, and how are they different?

5. Describe the different patterns of relationships among Nonie and her siblings. How do you explain Ruth's relationship with Nonie versus Brynne's? Which of the three siblings do you identify with most and why? What are some examples of how family both helped and harmed Nonie?

6. How do you explain Martha and Jack's different approaches and reactions to Nonie when she returns home?

7. Neighbors complain about and sometimes call the

police on Doug. How is Nonie able to develop a friendship with him when others tend to disregard him? What do you think drew them to each other?

8. When Doug encounters Nonie on the stairway as she's moving out, how is he able to zero in on the gravity of her predicament?

9. How do Nonie and Noreen make their lives harder for themselves sometimes? How did it make you feel when they did? How did Nonie and Noreen's self-perception impact and impel their choices?

10. How do you account for the lingering impact Nonie has on Noreen's life, even though she was only eight when Nonie died? Have you ever experienced a connection that was brief but enduring?

11. Noreen thinks of George as a calming influence on some of her extreme behaviors. Do you agree with her? Can you trace moments when Noreen mistakes George's control for concern or when she excuses troublesome behavior without questioning it? Have you ever been in a relationship with someone who made you doubt your own judgments?

12. How does Noreen's experience with her aunt affect risks she takes throughout her life? What role does it play in her eventual decision to change her life?

13. What did you think about the ending? Were you surprised? If so, could you trace Noreen's motivation to that moment after the fact? If you weren't surprised, what tipped you off?